Safekeeping

ROXIE NOIR

Convict

Safekeeping was originally published as *Slow Burn*. The title has been changed, but the text is the same.

Please be aware that this book contains: depictions of religious abuse, depictions of religion (specifically American fundamentalist Christianity) being used to control, coerce, and gaslight people, depictions of stalking, depictions of gun violence, and homophobia.

A NOTE ON CHANGES

SAFEKEEPING WAS ORIGINALLY PUBLISHED, in 2017, as *Slow Burn*. When the title changed in 2022, the rest of the text (except a few typos) remained the same.

More recently, in the spring of 2024, I took out a handful of references to the *Harry Potter* books and replaced them with references to *His Dark Materials* by Phillip Pullman. This doesn't change the plot of *Safekeeping* at all; both sets of books were widely loathed, feared, and banned by far-right conservative Christians in the United States.

I made the switch because, to put it in a way that will not get me sued, I don't agree with J.K. Rowling's hateful views on or actions toward transgender people. I doubt anyone went out and bought *Harry Potter* because of this book, but I hated knowing it was in here. (It also took me a while to figure out what to do about the references—whether I could just replace them with something else, or if removing them would require bigger rewrites. In the end, a very smart friend suggested the Pullman books.)

To summarize: in this house we love trans people and

repudiate J.K. Rowling, so please enjoy this book about a hot bodyguard.

CHAPTER ONE

RUBY

MY HAIR STICKS to my neck as I scoop the sticky, bubbling, pink-orange goop into the funnel, making sure to leave half an inch of air between the jam and the top of the jar. I tap the funnel gently on the side of the jar, dislodging any leftover peach chunks, and as I lift the funnel from the jar, my sister Pearl takes it and wipes the top rim with a damp paper towel.

She hands it to Joy, who drops a seal onto the jar, then puts it on the kitchen counter, next to thirty other identical jars.

We do it all in silence, like we're a well-oiled machine.

"Even through Jim's campaigns and his work in Washington, it's always been my top priority that I remain at home, raising our children and running the household," my mother says in her soft, quiet voice.

The reporter taking notes makes a noise of agreement.

"Right now we're making peach jam from the very last of the peaches in the family orchard," she goes on. "So many homemaking skills are becoming lost due to the moral decay in today's society. Girls are growing up not knowing the simple, basic homemaking tasks that made this country great in the first place. These are the valuable, much-needed arts that become lost when women are forced into the workplace and out of the home."

I'm facing the window, but I can hear the reporter tapping his pen against his notepad. I've lost track of which newspaper he's from, but it's something fairly small and local, which means he won't be pushing back too hard against my mother's outrageous claims.

"Mrs. Burgess, there are many women who would say that they prefer to work outside the home," he says.

I don't have to look at her to know she's smiling a soft, pitying smile at him.

"Of course there are," she says, in her most sympathetic, understanding voice. "But when I go out with my husband to his speeches and rallies, and I talk to the strong, hard-working women of South Carolina, what I hear over and over again is that so many of them have a desire to return to traditional life and values, to be keepers of the home. I'm sure some women enjoy doing a man's work in a man's world, but modern society has robbed wives and mothers of the chance to truly make a difference in the lives of their husbands and children by serving them at home."

I blob more peach jam into a jar. Pearl wipes it. Joy plops the lid on. All three of us have heard our mother's canned responses so many times that we know them by heart and could quote them verbatim.

"Yes," the reporter is saying. "But aren't there women out there whose desire isn't to stay at home, but to..."

This one's got more backbone than I expected, I think, scooping again. Usually they only pretend to argue for a sentence or two, then roll over and accept everything she says about how a woman's true purpose in life is to serve her husband's needs and focus the rest of her energies on her children.

None of them have the nerve to ask about me, of course. That's a surefire way to ensure that you never get another interview with Senator Jim Burgess, any member of his staff, or any member of his family, ever again.

As my mother is quietly, sweetly, and kindly answering another question, the kitchen door opens and my father's aide Mason steps through. He's wearing khakis and a long-sleeve Oxford shirt despite the September heat.

"Miss Burgess, the Senator would like to see you," he says.

The three Misses Burgess in the room turn, as does Mrs. Burgess, but he's looking at me. I raise my eyebrows. Mason nods.

"Excuse me," I say to everyone in the room, wipe my hands on a kitchen towel, and follow Mason. He holds the door for me and I step into the hallway, which is about fifteen degrees cooler.

It's an incredible relief. It doesn't matter that it's over eighty degrees outside or that the air conditioning in our antebellum house doesn't work very well, I'm wearing a high-necked shirt with long sleeves, a denim skirt that goes below my knees, and pantyhose.

That's something I miss about being married: Lucas didn't require me to wear pantyhose at all times.

I follow Mason across the house and up two flights of steps in silence, because there's no point in asking him why my father wishes to speak with me. Either Mason doesn't know, or he knows better than to discuss it with me.

Besides, there's no way it's anything *good*. I think the last *good* conversation I had with my father was a year after my wedding, back when my marriage was only uncomfortable and unsatisfying, not a complete wreck.

My father's home office has a huge, wooden double door. It's original to this house, and he'll tell anyone visiting the story of how his great-great-great-great grandmother used this house as a field hospital during the Civil War and hung bloody sheets over all her beautiful, hand-carved door frames so the Yankees wouldn't loot them.

It might be true. I have no idea. I just know that my father's a politician through and through, and at age twenty-six, I finally know better than to believe everything he says.

Mason pushes the door open and nods me through to the Senator, who's sitting at his immense desk in his shirt-sleeves, busily writing something.

"Thank you, Mason," he says without looking up. "Ruby, you may sit."

I do, silently, crossing one leg over the other, and wait for him to finish whatever he's writing. Probably yet another letter to a donor, thanking them for their important work in stemming the tide of moral decay in modern America, blah blah blah. Finally he places it in his inbox and looks at me.

"I'm afraid that your situation has generated a great deal of unwarranted attention," he begins.

I swallow and say nothing. There's no point in arguing with him.

"And while this family has weathered the storm of your disgrace, and will continue to weather that storm as a strong, stable unit, I'm afraid a new problem has presented itself and it must be dealt with accordingly."

My stomach twists and my pulse speeds up as I wonder what, exactly, he's found out about me now.

"What's the problem, father?" I ask, keeping my face as perfectly neutral as I can.

Without answering, he reaches into a desk drawer and produces a small bundle of letters, letting them plop on his desk.

"You've received a substantial amount of mail from a single correspondent," he says. "Of course, I took the liberty of reviewing your letters, given your situation—"

My blood boils, but I force myself not to show it.

Keep sweet, I tell myself. *Keep sweet. Keep sweet.*

"—And I'm afraid that what began as misguided interest has escalated into some very disturbing accusations and threats against your safety."

I blink. I was expecting yet another lecture on my behavior and attitude.

"What kind of threats?" I ask, doing my best to channel my mother and keep my voice soft, quiet, and meek.

He frowns.

"I won't be discussing that with you," he says. "They're completely unsuitable for a woman to read, but they're very upsetting. After extensive discussions with my security team, we've decided that you'll be receiving your own detail for the time being."

He pauses. I pause, and for a long moment, my father and I just look at each other.

"You're giving me a bodyguard?" I ask, finally.

Now my stomach is clenched into a knot, fury raging inside me.

I'd bet almost anything that the letters aren't real.

I may not be a politician, but I'm not stupid. Either those envelopes are empty, or my father wrote them himself as an excuse to hire someone. Voters tend to not look kindly on fathers who hire someone to scrutinize their adults daughters' every move, but if it's in the name of safety? Then it's fine.

My bodyguard's real job isn't going to be guarding me. It's going to be watching me, twenty-four/seven, and reporting every single thing I do back to my father.

"Yes," my father says. "Since I'm your guardian once more, it falls to me to protect you from harm, and these—" he taps the bundle of letters, "—constitute potential harm. Despite your life choices, you're still my daughter, and it's my duty to ensure your safety."

Not *I love you and I'm worried*, but *your safety is my duty*. I swallow, my mouth dry, cold fury pumping through my veins. I hate this so much my hands are nearly shaking.

"Thank you, father," I say.

"His name is Gabriel Kane," my father says. "He's a Secret Service agent on leave and he'll be arriving tomorrow."

And he'll be on you constantly, following your every move, I think.

It's moderately interesting that they chose a man for my bodyguard, but not that surprising. On one hand, my father would prefer that I literally never be alone in a room with a man who isn't related to me, but on the other, his opinion of women is so low that I doubt he'd trust one to guard me.

Besides, I'm already damaged goods. It isn't like my father has to defend my innocence or something. Everyone knows *that's* long gone.

"I expect that you'll show him proper hospitality," my father goes on, leaning back in his massive leather chair. He's flanked on either side by tall windows, the heavy curtains pulled back to reveal the rooftops of Huntsburg and the thick, lush forest beyond. "And I also expect that you'll continue to uphold the standards of the Burgess name, as befits my eldest daughter."

His stare could cut through iron right now, but like he

just admitted: I'm his daughter. His stare isn't doing a damn thing to me.

I think he means *don't have sex with your bodyguard*, because my father seems to think that any woman, if allowed the slightest bit of freedom, will simply lie back and open her legs to any man who happens by.

As if I'm going to be interested in whatever ex-military meathead he's hired to keep tabs on me. Thugs who report on my behavior to my father aren't exactly my type.

But I don't say any of that. I smile sweetly at him, hands clasped atop my knee, and answer, "Of course, father."

Before he can respond, there's a knock on the door, and then Mason's face pokes through.

"Senator," he says. "The photographer from the Sun-Herald has arrived, and Mrs. Burgess asked me to fetch you."

My father nods, then stands. Mason's face disappears, and my father pulls on his sport jacket, slicking his salt-and-pepper hair back with one hand. I glance one more time at the bundle of letters that he's left lying on the desk.

"We'll be meeting here at eleven sharp," he tells me, and we both exit his office, the heavy door shutting behind him.

My father and Mason both walk down the stairs, and I walk in the opposite direction, along the upstairs hallway until they're gone.

Then I stop. For a long moment I stand in the hallway, motionless and quiet, listening to their voices echoing from further and further away.

When they're gone, I go back to my father's office. I don't give myself time to think about how furious he would be if he found me here, I just push the heavy door open quietly and shut it behind me.

If I get caught in here, I'll have hell to pay. He can't kick me out onto the street until the election is over, because it would look absolutely awful to the voters, but he could make my life pretty unpleasant because I have no money, no job, and nowhere else to go.

But I have to know. I have to read those letters, see whether I'm actually in danger or whether my father's invented the whole thing so he has a reason to hire someone to watch me.

Hands shaking, I pull a letter from the bundle near the top, then one other from further down. There are enough that he won't notice a few missing — or at least, I have to hope he won't.

I pull up my shirt and cram the two envelopes into the top of my pantyhose, which keeps them flat against my belly, and put the bundle of letters back on his desk, exactly where he left it.

Then I tiptoe back to the heavy door, slip through it, and turn back down the hall, away from the staircase, the paper stiff against my skin.

I'm smiling as I open my bedroom door, take the letters out, and stash them in a secret spot.

I was raised to be meek, subservient, sweet, and trusting. My father was the absolute authority in my life until the day I got married, and then that authority was transferred to my husband.

But I didn't turn out meek, or sweet, or any of those things. I got divorced, even though it left me with nothing.

And if my father thinks he can control me again, he's got another think coming.

CHAPTER TWO

GABRIEL

I OPEN the waist-high beverage fridge and crouch slowly, my head hammering and my stomach sloshing. The guy behind the counter of this liquor store, a skinny kid with a scraggly goatee who looks barely twenty-one, watches me with a mixture of suspicion and concern, like I'm either going to rob him or pass out on the floor.

The second one's much more likely. I don't rob stores to begin with, but after last night, passing out on this grimy tile floor sounds like a fucking relief, not that I have time. I've got to be in the Senator's office at ten on the dot or I'll have blown the very last chance I've got.

Then I'd be well and truly fucked.

I reach in, pushing aside a red bottle of Gatorade. The movement wobbles me a little off-balance, and I go down on one knee. Then I go down on the other, because kneeling in front of this fridge is better than crouching in front of it.

I pause, closing my eyes, letting the blessedly cool air wash over me. I've taken four Advil already this morning, and even though I somehow kept them down, they haven't done a goddamn thing. I still feel like someone's filled my skull with rocks and shaken it.

Probably shouldn't have gotten stumble-drunk wasted at the Best Western motel bar last night, you dipshit, I think.

And hell, I knew that as I was doing it. I didn't even have a good time drinking shitty whiskey until I was porch-crawling sloshed, I just knew that it was my last chance to do it before I spent a couple of months babysitting a stuck-up princess of a Senator's daughter and living on the estate of a man so famously prudish he probably showers in long johns.

Just get through it, Kane, I tell myself. *You've gotten through shit before.*

Slowly, I reach my arm out and start going through the fridge. I move aside bottles of Coke, Diet Coke, and Sprite. I move aside orange and red bottles of Gatorade, then the green Gatorade, getting more and more frantic.

Where the fuck is it? They have to fucking have it.

Don't tell me they're sold out or some shit.

I start pulling bottles out and putting them on the floor. Soon there's a line of them next to me on the dirty off-white tiles, and even though the kid behind the counter is clearly getting agitated, I ignore him.

He can fucking try whatever he wants, because even hungover as *shit* I can kick his skinny ass from here to Georgia. I just need my fucking blue Gatorade and then I'll fucking get out of here.

I'm about to give up, the fridge almost empty, when I finally see them. Bright electric blue, a color no fruit has ever been or ever will be, huddled together like the final two survivors in the very back of the bottom shelf.

I grab them both, open one and chug a third of it. I don't give a damn that I haven't paid for it, because even thinking about any other color of Gatorade just makes me more nauseous.

Blue Gatorade. It's the one true hangover cure.

Damned if I know why, but it is. I chug another third of the bottle, still kneeling on the dirty tile floor, then finally put everything else back and stand. Already I feel a tiny bit better, like maybe I've got a chance of rescuing this stupid fucking day from being the shitshow it's looking like right now.

Bottles in one arm, I grab a couple energy bars from the shelf behind me. I think about getting just a little something to take the edge off, hair of the dog and all that, but the thought turns my stomach so I head to the register instead.

There's a short line: a man paying for something in a paper bag, and a blonde woman with a toddler holding one hand, a pint bottle of vodka in the other, wearing a frumpy jean skirt and a sweater that's a couple sizes too big.

And yet, I still fucking stare. I've got no goddamn idea what it is about her, but for a moment I stop in my tracks, eyes glued to her denim-tented ass, the lumps of her sweater over where her waist ought to be. Call it a sixth sense for smoking-hot women — god knows I've seen more than enough of them that by now I can just tell, even if they're wearing a cardboard box.

Even if I've more or less taken a vow of celibacy for the next couple of months.

"Beebee!" the toddler shouts excitedly. "Guess what I am now!"

He didn't call her Mom, I think, and the woman turns to watch him, his arms held out stiffly as he starts spinning. There's a display of Fireball whiskey behind him, and it makes me a little nervous, but he's still a couple of feet away.

I was right about the woman. A space suit can't hide that kind of hot—curves to make a man curse his own mother, paired with sharp cheekbones, wicked green eyes, and plush lips just *begging* to be bitten.

"A bat?" she says, nervously tapping the vodka bottle against her leg, and even though she's crazy hot, a bad feeling starts to gather in the pit of my stomach. A woman with a toddler—hers or not—buying a single bottle of vodka at eight in the morning?

No women for a couple of months, remember? It doesn't matter whether she's a hot alcoholic or not.

"Wrong!" the kid says, laughing.

"A bumblebee," she guesses again.

"NO!" the kid shouts, nearly in hysterics.

"Are you an airplane?"

The kid just squeals, spinning faster.

"Beebee!" he yelps. "I'm a—"

And he careens into a corner of the whiskey display, clipping a bottle and toppling it from the shelf.

I don't think, I just drop the energy bar I'm holding, leap forward, and catch the bottle before it falls. My stomach lurches with the sudden movement, but I put the whiskey back on the shelf, gritting my teeth and swallowing hard.

Don't save a bottle of whiskey just to puke on the floor. Keep it the fuck together, Kane.

When I finally turn, all four people—three adults and the kid—exhale in unison, all looking at me.

But I'm looking at the woman again, because it's like she reflects all the light in this shitty liquor store, somehow fucking gorgeous despite her clothes, the setting, the vodka, everything. There may as well not be anyone else here.

And she's got this almost-ethereal thing going on, like the

dinginess of this shitty liquor store isn't touching her. Despite myself I think: *if I could get that ugly sweater off, underneath she'd be all curves and dimples and fluttering eyelashes.*

Meek in the streets and a freak in the sheets. Like she'd rake her nails down my back and leave me with scars I'd be proud of later.

A shiver travels my spine. Like fingernails, only I'm in this shitty store and staring at a girl I don't know, who might be this kid's mom. No wedding ring, though.

What's my fucking problem? I turned down both those girls last night, no big deal, and that was a sure thing if I'd wanted it.

"Isaac," she says.

The kid looks at me, his wide eyes nervous.

"Sorry," he whispers.

"It's all right," I tell him.

"Thank you for catching that bottle," she says to me.

We make eye contact. Another thrill goes through me, hangover notwithstanding.

"No problem," I say.

The man at the counter turns back and continues counting out change, and I walk back to the line, standing next to the blonde woman.

"Rough day ahead?" I ask her, giving her my best charming, cocky smile.

I'm not hitting on her, because I'm fucking celibate, but I can't help turning on the charm around a beautiful woman. It's second nature.

She tilts her head slightly and gives me a slow, considering look, her green eyes studying my face intently. I suddenly feel like there are lasers going through my skull.

I'm too fucking hungover for this.

"Not rougher than your night was," she finally says, a smile teasing at the corner of her eyes.

"My *night* was pretty good," I tell her, raising one eyebrow. "It's this morning that's the rough part, but I'll get over it."

The guy at the counter finally takes his paper-bag-wrapped booze and leaves. The blonde puts her vodka on the counter and pulls out her wallet, glancing down at the kid next to her.

"Celebrating?" she finally asks me as she pays.

"Last night of freedom," I say.

She takes her change and glances at me again, her green eyes cool.

"Well, I hope your wedding isn't until tonight," she says, giving me a quick up-and-down. "Looks like you could use some more recovery time."

I just laugh.

"It's a new job, not a wedding," I tell her. "And it's going to be a full-time months-long fucking nightmare, so I had a last hurrah. But I'm single as hell, sweetheart."

Her back straightens, and I can tell I got to her, just a little. I don't know why, but I like it.

She takes her change from the cashier and sticks the vodka in her purse, then glances at me again, eyes flashing for just a split second.

"Good luck with that," she says, slinging her purse over her shoulder. "And thanks for catching that whiskey. Isaac, come on."

And with that, she walks out the door and back onto the street, the toddler running, skipping, and jumping after her. For a moment I think about leaving the Gatorade and snacks there, following her, and at least getting her number, but I don't.

It's been one damn week, I tell myself. *At least give yourself a chance before you fuck everything in this town, too.*

Women are why you're here in the first place, in this shitty town with this shitty job.

Well, more specifically, one woman.

And no, she wasn't worth it. Not even close.

AT TEN-FIFTY-FIVE, I'm in the waiting room to my father's office. When the house was built I think it was some sort of sitting room, where the ladies would go and sew after dinner while the men drank and smoked cigars and enjoyed themselves, but now it's where Mason sits, his spine ramrod-straight, as he taps away on a keyboard and tries not to act uncomfortable about being alone in a room with a woman.

Though alone is a strong word. The door to the hallway is open, meaning that any of my family members could walk in at any second, not to mention that my father and my new bodyguard are right next door. But it's not very hard to make Mason uncomfortable if you've got breasts, no matter how well-hidden.

Even his girlfriend Lilah, who's quiet and demure and almost painfully sweet, seems to make him a little nervous every time he remembers she's female.

So it's really easy for me, the family harlot, to make the poor kid sweat. If I'm being honest, I kind of enjoy it. I couldn't be less interested in him, but it's nice to know that

I've got some kind of power over someone here, no matter how small and insignificant.

The intercom on his desk beeps at five after eleven. Mason clears his throat.

"Yes, Senator?" he asks, his voice a little higher-pitched than normal.

I force myself not to smile.

"Please send my daughter in," the voice says.

"Yes, sir," he responds, and stands. He straightens the cuffs on his Oxford shirt, not making eye contact with me, steps out from behind his desk, and holds the door into my father's office open.

"Thank you," I say, and repress the urge to wink at him, just to see what he'd do.

"You're welcome," he squeaks, and then the door shuts behind me.

And I stop dead in my tracks.

The hungover whiskey-catcher from this morning is sitting in one of the leather chairs opposite my father's desk.

He's wearing a suit and tie, looking confident and cocky as *fuck*, like this is his house and the two of us just happen to be in it.

It's a good look on him. If I'm being totally honest, hungover wasn't a *bad* look on him, because even though he was practically gray this morning he still had those intense blue eyes, the dimple in his chin, the superhero-comic jawline, and muscles.

Lord help me, the muscles. Even in a suit, *the muscles*.

I look away first, glancing at my father. I don't think Gabriel knew who I was this morning, but what if he did? What if he's just spent the past hour telling my father that he saw his eldest daughter buying vodka at eight in the morning while caring for a toddler?

I'd never see the light of day again, that's what. At best, I'd be in the basement until the election was over and he could quietly toss me out onto the street. At worst, he'd send me to one of our church's re-education camps for *wayward* women.

Neither of us says a word.

"Mr. Kane, this is my eldest daughter Ruby," my father says, holding out one hand in my direction, addressing Gabriel first. "Ruby, this is Gabriel Kane, your new security detail."

Gabriel stands. I fold my hands in front of myself, smile as sweetly as I can, and walk toward him. We shake hands and I break eye contact first, looking demurely at the floor as his big, rough hand envelops mine.

It's the hand of someone who knows how to use them, who does things with his hands. For all my father's talk of a *return to traditional values*, his talk of men who are men and women who are women, all the men I know have soft hands and gentle handshakes.

But not Gabriel. When I shake his hand, there's a weird twinge, deep down inside me.

"Pleased to meet you, Miss Burgess," he says politely. There's a hint of a twang there, and I wonder where he's from.

"Thank you so much for coming all this way, Mr. Kane," I say softly. "And please, it's Ruby."

"Likewise, I'm Gabriel," he says.

We sit. I keep my back straight, knees clenched together so tightly it would take heavy machinery to pry them apart.

Please don't tell my father, I think, over and over again. I'm thinking it so loud that I'm not even listening to what they're saying, just politely watching the conversation, a sweet, innocent smile on my face.

That, at least—smiling sweetly while everything inside me is going straight to hell—I've mastered. I've had plenty of practice, after all.

Gradually, my heart stops pounding. They're talking about security detail stuff: entrances and exits to the property, my schedule, how he'll interface with other security at my father's campaign events. Gabriel's not telling my father *oh, by the way I saw her buying hard liquor this morning with a toddler in tow*. At least, not yet he isn't.

We'll see how this all shakes out.

The worst part is, I knew it was stupid and I did it anyway. I was helping my younger sister Grace run some errands in town, and she asked if I'd go return a book to the library for her. She had her baby, Emma, with her, so I offered to take Isaac with me to keep him out of her hair.

Grabbing the vodka was an impulse. My father's got a campaign rally the day after tomorrow, my attendance is mandatory, and in the past few months I've discovered that they're considerably easier to get through with a little liquid help.

But my biggest fear was that Isaac, who's almost two and mostly talks about his favorite kind of bear and whether there are sharks in any given body of water, would somehow tell his parents all about our side trip with crystal-clear recollection.

Grace wouldn't be happy about it. We'd get into a huge fight, that's for sure. If her husband Tim found out, *he* might go to my father, but Grace wouldn't. Even though she's the perfect daughter, the happily-married stay-at-home mother with two children at age twenty-four, she wouldn't tell my father.

Gabriel's a wild card, though. Just because he hasn't yet doesn't mean he won't. He might still think that his job is actually security and not surveillance, because my father's a smart man and won't come right out and say *I've hired you to keep close tabs on my daughter and chaperone her everywhere.*

The voters wouldn't like that. They're traditional and conservative, but not that traditional.

"You'll be living in the carriage house," my father is telling Gabriel, whose expression hasn't changed. "I've taken the liberty of having some aides unload your car and unpack your suitcases, so please, make yourself at home. It's not a large dwelling, but I think you'll find it adequate."

His face stays perfectly blank, even through the revelation that my father's employees have gone through his things. I'm impressed.

"Thank you, sir," he says. "That's very kind."

My father stands, signaling that the meeting is drawing to a close. Gabriel and I stand as well, and he buttons a button on his suit jacket. I glance over. Even though the air conditioning is on, I can see a bead of sweat trickle into his collar.

And *then* I imagine things: that single droplet, running down the skin of his shoulder and his back, coursing over the thick muscles, making its way downward. I imagine him without his suit and tie on, shirtless, sweaty, outside in the yard lifting something heavy —

"Ruby will give you a quick tour of the main house, and you two can become acquainted," my father says.

I swallow and force myself to stop thinking about Gabriel shirtless. I have *no* idea what's gotten into me, because as strange as it sounds, I've never done that before.

"That sounds wonderful, sir," Gabriel says.

"Of course, father," I chime in, the sweet smile still frozen on my face.

"Excellent," he says, and shakes Gabriel's hand again. "Looking forward to working with you, and God bless."

We turn and leave. Gabriel holds the heavy door for me, and I duck my head as I walk through, the perfect sweet, innocent, meek daughter. When it shuts behind us we're alone in the hall for a split second, but then there's a noise from the other end and one of my younger brothers, Zeke, walks in.

I introduce them. Zeke is only eighteen, gangly and lanky, and though he's the tallest man in the family at nearly six feet, Gabriel's still got a couple of inches on him.

I also *like* Zeke. He's the only other one who's ever stood up to my parents, and though it's only been about inconsequential stuff so far being allowed to wear shorts outside when it's hot, quitting piano lessons because he hated them —it makes me feel like I've got some kind of ally, even if it's my dumb little brother.

He walks off, and then we're alone again, in the hallway outside my father's office, and Gabriel looks down at me, half a knowing smile on his face.

"All right, I'll make you a deal," he starts.

"You should be sure to keep your voice down in the house," I say, looking up at him with my sweetest, most innocent face. "Sound travels in strange ways because it's so old, so it's easy to disturb others unintentionally."

I wait to see if he's picked up on what I'm saying. After a moment, his eyes narrow. He nods.

"Of course," he says, his voice quiet and just a little gravelly. "My apologies."

"Come on," I say, my smile frozen in place as relief trickles through me. "I'll give you the tour."

———

THE TOUR COMES with a history of both the house and the Burgess family, who have owned it since it was built back before the Civil War. Back then, this was the townhouse, where the family only spent a few months of the year—most of the time, they were out on their plantation, several miles away.

They sold the plantation during the depression. The building is still there, but it's now a corporate retreat center, surrounded by a massive soybean farm.

"It must be nice to have roots that go back so far," Gabriel says as we walk down a massive staircase, into the entry hall. It's not quite like *Gone With the Wind*, since this is only the townhouse and not the plantation, but it's still impressive.

"Yes," I agree. "It's really wonderful to feel so strongly a part of my home, with all its history, culture, and my family."

It's a rehearsed response.

"This is the main entry way," I say, gesturing at the massive front doors. "It was built to impress guests, so right now, we mostly use it when my father is hosting events in the home. The family and staff use the kitchen and side doors much more frequently, since they're a little less onerous."

The front doors are each at least ten feet tall, and getting them open is a *task*.

"Of course," Gabriel says.

I show him the rooms on the ground floor. They've all been modernized, though this floor is still fairly formal: living room, dining room, sunroom. Even the kitchen and family room are conspicuously clean, thanks to my mother. She runs a tight ship.

I introduce Gabriel to everyone else who's here: my mother, my brothers Daniel and Paul, my sisters Pearl and

Joy. Everyone is perfectly polite, stiffly courteous, ready with polished and canned answers to nearly anything he could say.

He compliments my mother on her beautiful home. He asks my siblings what grade they're in, whether they play sports, that sort of thing.

Finally, we head outside. The heat hits us like a warm, wet blanket as we cross the carefully-manicured lawn, and I take a deep breath of the humidity, my heart hammering again, because now's the time.

"Sound carries much less easily out here," I say. "So you don't need to worry about disturbing anyone."

I slow my pace. He matches me and looks over, his hands in his pockets. Another bead of sweat trickles down his neck and I force myself not to think about where it might be heading.

"All right," Gabriel begins. "Now that we're out of earshot, I propose a deal."

CHAPTER FOUR

GABRIEL

RUBY'S facial expression doesn't change, even though she looks up at me. Aside from the moment she saw me, sitting in her father's office, it's barely changed at all: a lovely, warm, nice-girl smile that looks like it belongs on the front of a book about raising perfect daughters.

It's beautiful. She's beautiful. But it's also a little strange.

"What's that?" she asks.

"We start over," I say. "Both of us forget about this morning. The first time we ever met was in your father's office an hour ago."

Ruby exhales softly. It sounds like she's relieved, but the girl is nearly impossible to read behind her façade.

"I think that would be for the best," she says evenly. "My father frowns on drinking, either by his family or his staff. He's a teetotaler himself. I'm sure some people would consider this job a months-long, full-time nightmare."

She glances at me quickly, and for a moment, there's something teasing and wicked in Ruby's eyes, but then it's gone and she's all sweetness and light again.

"I'm sure some people would consider it that," I agree. "But I'm thrilled and honored to be part of the Senator's service detail, and I look forward to the unique challenges that this position will offer."

I think I'm teasing her, just a little, though it's so slight I can barely tell myself.

"Good," Ruby says, and she's smiling. I open the door.

We're to the front door of the carriage house. The Senator said it was small, but it's two stories, bigger than any apartment I've ever lived in before.

"Can I offer you a drink?" I ask. I have no idea whether there's anything in here besides water, but this environment is so painfully, rigidly polite that I feel rude otherwise.

"No, thank you, I should be getting back," she says, and tucks one strand of blonde hair behind an ear. "Besides, it might look improper if I were alone with you in your lodgings."

I have to clench my teeth together before I tell her she's welcome to come by any time and do more than *look* improper. Since this morning, she's changed out of her ugly sweater and into a t-shirt that doesn't do her any favors either, but it doesn't change the fact that when I look at her, I can practically hear her shouting my name.

"That wouldn't do at all," I answer her, turning the knob. "We'll have to be sure to guard against impropriety."

"Certainly."

"If you ever have a suitable chaperone, feel free to stop by," I say. "Maybe we'll have tea and scones and discuss suitable topics."

Ruby glances at the main house, and I swear there's a hint of a smile—a *real* one, not the sweet, innocent one—around her perfect lips.

"Then you'd better learn something about cross-stitch, knitting, or flower-arranging pretty fast," she says, and for just a moment there's an edge in her voice. "We ladies prefer not to trouble ourselves with weightier matters."

Then the sweet smile is back.

"Please, make yourself at home," she says. "And thank you again."

"My pleasure," I say, and open the door as she walks away.

After two steps, she turns, my hand still on the knob.

"By the way, they're going to ask you to say grace tonight at dinner, since you're a guest," she says. "You might want to brush up, just in case it's been a while."

"It has," I say. "Thank you for advising."

"Of course," she says, and walks away again.

I close the door behind me and try not to watch the way her body moves underneath her clothes as she crosses the lawn, her hips rolling from side to side.

Fucking quit it, I tell myself, and pull the curtains closed on the window. *Of all the women in South Carolina, you had to find the last one you should go sticking your dick in.*

It's just a couple of months, Kane. I don't care if she ties you down and hops on your dick, you push her off.

I walk into the main room of the carriage house, which is half-kitchen, half dining room, find a glass, fill it, and take a long drink of water.

Get through it. That's all you do, and then you can go back to your real life.

Just get the fuck through it.

———

I SPEND a while in the kitchen, on my phone, trying to figure out how to say grace. My memories of it are fuzzy at best, and mostly from my grandparents' house back in Wisconsin while we still lived there, when I was really little.

The problem is that I have no real idea what exactly the tenets of the Senator's faith are. I know he's regarded as a near-insane extremist by most of the people in Washington, D.C., and he's got some pretty backwards ideas about... well, everything, but beyond that I don't know what the man believes.

But *in God* is a pretty solid bet, as is *in Jesus*, so I settle on a simple pre-meal prayer that doesn't get fancy, memorize it quickly, and then check out the rest of my new apartment.

It's nice. Nicer than anywhere I've ever lived before, but it's not hard to beat Marine barracks or the apartments where I lived in D.C. They weren't bad, but Secret Service is a pretty demanding job, so I wasn't home enough to pay for more than the bare minimum.

But the carriage house has been redone recently, Ruby said. It's got three bedrooms, a state-of-the-art kitchen, and redone bathrooms. The Burgesses are very old money, rich back when my ancestors were still peasants in Ireland and Germany, probably eating dirt and gruel.

And they put all my clothes away, even though I wish they hadn't. It gives me the damn creeps to think of someone going through my stuff, judging it, then brushing it off and hanging it. I was furious and, okay, slightly drunk when I was packing, so most of my things were just crammed into suitcases.

Then I think of another reason I didn't want someone else unpacking for me. I tossed half a box of condoms into a suitcase after ten minutes of deliberation. Because yeah, I took a vow of celibacy, no women while I'm on this job. Sure.

But I've also been Gabriel Goddamn Kane for almost thirty years, and that means I don't exactly trust myself. No matter how fucking gung-ho I am about my newfound monk status, it's good to have protection around just in case.

I'm not gonna fuck anyone. But if I do, I'm not gonna catch anything or get her pregnant.

I start going through drawers, hoping that maybe they got caught in some shirts or something, but no luck until I open my bedside table, and *there* they are. Neatly arranged and everything.

Well, fuck. I'm not in the Senator's family. I'm not working seven days a week. He's got no say over whether I go out, meet a girl, and have some fun, right?

Yeah, right. I've heard the shit people whisper about Burgess.

I slam the drawer shut, nervousness prickling up my spine. It's day one and I've already run into his daughter while I was hungover as fuck, thought endlessly about running my hands up under her ugly denim skirt until she moans, and now his staff knows I've brought a shitload of condoms with me.

For a guy who's supposed to be redeeming himself from a scandal, I'm doing a pretty piss-poor job of it.

AT DINNER, they seat me across from Mrs. Burgess, next to the Senator, and catty-corner from Ruby. Her brother Zeke is on my other side, and even though there's a part of me that would much rather have Ruby next to me, it's for the best.

Besides, I'd be shocked if her father allowed her to sit a mere six inches from a man who wasn't her husband. I might touch her thigh by accident, and next thing you know, there's sin *everywhere*.

"Your speech at High Country Bible College is *next* Wednesday, dear," Mrs. Burgess is saying as she serves the Senator creamed spinach. "I think this Wednesday you've got committee in the morning, and then you're flying back here from Washington in the afternoon to address the League of Concerned Ladies down in Charleston at their Annual Supper that evening."

She sets down the creamed spinach, then takes a plate piled with pork roast, giving him two pieces. The man hasn't served himself a single bite of food. I'm beginning to wonder if Mrs. Burgess is going to feed him, as well.

The Senator frowns.

"Are you sure?" he asks, watching her put food on his plate. When she finishes, he doesn't even thank her, just starts eating.

"Well, no, and if you think that's this Wednesday I'm sure you're right," Mrs. Burgess says, and takes a small, dainty bite of food.

"This is a wonderful meal, Mrs. Burgess," I say, because I know my damn manners.

"Thank you, Gabriel," she says. "How was your drive down from Washington yesterday?"

I make polite chit chat about nothing with Ruby's mother. The whole time, Ruby's words echo through my head: *we ladies prefer not to trouble ourselves with weightier matters.* I still don't know if she was being serious or sarcastic, but every time I glance over at her, I *think* I see that spark in her eyes.

I don't know what to make of it. I don't know what to

make of any of this. It's one of the strangest dinners I've ever had, and I've had some strange fucking dinners.

But every so often, I catch Ruby looking at me, across the table.

The next couple of months are going to be sheer torture, one way or another, but I'd be lying if I said I weren't looking forward to it, at least a little.

CHAPTER FIVE

RUBY

I SIGH, sitting back on my heels in front of the kitchen table, examining the tableau I've set out one more time. Technically, it looks fine — a small pyramid of jam jars, a bunch of flowers in a mason jar, all on a checkered napkin on a rustic wooden table — but when I do this, it always looks like a collection of items I've shoved together instead of a picture.

The heavy camera thuds softly against my chest as I lean forward, chin on the table, and try to figure out what looks wrong. For once, I'm alone in the informal dining room, and I can let my guard down for thirty seconds.

I can sigh. Roll my eyes. Be annoyed that I'm so crappy at things that my mom and sisters make look so easy.

Stop *keeping sweet* for a couple of minutes, because keeping a perfect, angelic smile on your face all the time, acting like the Most Blessed Girl In The World, no matter what you really think? It's exhausting.

Chin still resting on the table, I reach out and nudge a snapdragon, then scoot the mason jar full of flowers—grown in our garden, by my mother, of course—closer to the three jam jars, stacked in a pyramid.

It doesn't help, but I'm out of ideas, so I raise the camera and start taking pictures. Ever since my parents took me in again, I've been helping my mother with her homemaking blog. It's a huge part of her and my father's image as the perfect old-fashioned, traditional, woman-at-home, man-at-work couple.

The blog also brings in a fair amount of money, from advertisements, as well as campaign donations, despite my mother's talk of women ideally having no income of their own. Actually, all her daughters are part of my father's career and campaign in some way. We work, we just don't get paid.

I'm pretty sure that makes my parents hypocrites, but there's nothing I can do about it.

I snap a few more pictures, and the door to the kitchen opens and someone walks in. Someone's always walking in, no matter where I am, so I just ignore it until the footsteps stop about five feet away from me.

I take one last picture and look over. It's Gabriel.

I'm not exactly surprised, because he *is* my bodyguard, but my heart does skip a beat. Since he got in yesterday he's been spending most of his time getting up to speed on his duties here, meeting with my the rest of my father's security team, that sort of thing.

While I'm stuck in the house, at least, I'm not in that much danger. It's traveling with my father for his campaign that's the weak spot.

"Sorry to disturb you," he says. "But I was hoping we could go over your new security procedures for the events this weekend."

I rock back onto my feet, and Gabriel steps forward, offering me his hand, but I'm already standing. I fight the urge to take it anyway, just to feel his strong, rough fingers against mine.

Just the thought sends a slight tingle across my skin, and I wonder just what the hell is wrong with me.

"Of course," I say, a smile on my face automatically. "I'm finished here. Have a seat."

I move the jam tableau out of the way, definitely ruining it, and we both sit at the table, around the corner from each other. Gabriel's not wearing a suit today, just slacks and a long-sleeved button-down shirt. My father doesn't let his staff make many concessions to the heat, but at least he allows the men to remove their suit jackets when it's above eighty degrees.

But *that* means I can just barely see the outline of the hard muscles in his shoulders, the way his wide shoulders fill out his shirt, his biceps bunching under his sleeves as he rests his hands on the table. My mouth goes dry, and I lower my eyes, trying not to look, even though I feel like there's something strange and new vibrating through me.

"I generally find that operations go much more smoothly if the target — sorry, that's you — is briefed on all the measures and procedures ahead of time," he begins, placing a manila folder on the table.

"I see."

"Stop me if you have any questions, of course," he goes on. "Now, the event on Saturday is going to be indoors, and you'll be sitting on stage behind the speakers. I'm sure I don't need to tell you that security is much easier at an indoor event, so I'll likely be right off stage, keeping an eye on things without needing to intervene too much..."

Gabriel goes on about security. He's got layouts and floor plans of the places we'll be: the indoor speeches and ceremony on Saturday, then Sunday's after-church outdoor rally, and he points out where I'll be, where he'll be, what the escape routes are, where any "dangerous elements" could be lurking.

In other words, he's treating me like an adult. Like I've got some element of control over my own life, instead of like I'm a slightly shameful prop to be moved from one place to another while I smile and look pretty.

After the past couple of months, it's a huge relief just to be told what's going to happen. It's a consideration I rarely get.

"Now, we're not really expecting anything to happen," he says, folding his hands on the table and leaning forward slightly. "As upsetting as those letters were, I don't think the man who sent them has any sort of solid plan, nor do I think he has the military training to actually carry anything out."

I look at Gabriel for a moment, then look away, through the window, then at the flowers on the table.

"I haven't read them," I say.

It's not true. I read the two that I took, and they were creepy, but not terrifying—one was just describing a television appearance I did in detail, and another went on for a full two pages about my pretty, pretty hair.

Honestly, I was more concerned with trying to figure out whether it was my father's handwriting, disguised, or not. It could be someone else on his staff, though I'm not sure who he'd trust enough to ask for that sort of favor.

Gabriel exhales, tapping one finger against the wooden table. I remember to smile at him.

"You probably should," he says. "They're pretty upsetting, and they say some pretty ugly things, but in my opinion it's always best that the target understands their stalker as best they can. That way you'll be more able to assess situations for yourself."

I must have stolen the wrong letters, I think. The ones I read were creepy, but not really *upsetting*.

"I haven't read them because I'm not permitted," I explain. "My father says they're much too graphic and upsetting for ladies."

Gabriel swallows, then lowers his voice.

"Does this room have the same echo problem as the rest of the house?" he asks.

"Not if there's no one else in it."

He leans forward slightly, and now he's close enough that I can smell him: the faint scent of Old Spice, combined with an earthy smell, cedar or something. It makes something sinewy and hot constrict around my stomach.

"I get the feeling you're not as easily upset as the Senator thinks," Gabriel says, his voice low and gravelly.

I scrunch my toes in my shoes, but my smile doesn't waver.

"Why would you think that?"

Gabriel half-smiles, a cocky little smirk that I haven't seen him make before. My toes scrunch harder.

"You just don't seem the type," he says. "I've met a lot of delicate flowers, and you're not one of them. In this kind of job you learn to read people pretty quickly. Get a sense of what they can handle. And I think these letters would piss you off, but I don't think you'd fall to pieces or anything."

"Well," I say softly. "That's not up to me to decide, is it?"

I almost tell him that I've got a few, but I bite my tongue. Just because he's nice to look at and he's making one overture of kindness right now doesn't mean he won't be in my father's pocket this time next week.

"It should be," he says.

"You should tell my father that."

"I need to keep this job."

"Then I guess I won't be reading these letters."

We lock eyes, and my smile fades. His gaze is a deep blue, the color of the ocean miles away from the shore where all you can see is water and horizon. I can tell he's got a thousand million questions about what's going on here, what he's gotten himself into, but I can't answer any of them right now.

"Gabriel," I start, glancing at my hands on the table.

"Yes?"

I look him dead in the eyes again. I don't smile.

"You should forget everything you've just said to me," I say, my voice low and quiet. "As far as you know, I'm the most fragile, delicate flower in the world. I'll fall apart if my stalker so much as looks as me the wrong way. Just trust me."

Gabriel opens his mouth, but the dining room door opens again and we both sit up straight instantly.

My youngest brother Paul, Joy's twin, pokes his head through. He's going through a surly stage right now.

"Kyle's here," he says. "Mother says walk him through the garden, it's important."

He disappears.

I glance at Gabriel again. Half a second later, I remember to smile, which is the opposite of how Kyle makes me feel.

"Please excuse me," I say. "But thank you for the overview. It was very thoughtful of you."

"Of course," Gabriel says, rising as well.

I leave the dining room without looking back at him, no matter how much I want to.

———

KYLE'S WAITING RIGHT outside the back door, a bouquet of daisies at his side. When he sees me, he smiles nervously, his wet lips stretching just a little too far over his teeth, and holds them out.

"These reminded me of you," he says.

I take them, a smile plastered on my face.

"Thank you," I say. "They're lovely."

Last Valentine's Day, I know Kyle and I both sat through the same sermon, given by the Reverend Russell Dawson of the Word of God Apostolic Covenant Church, on whether flowers were too sinful to be given as a token of affection between unmarried couples.

The answer: yes, mostly, because they represent *the female parts*. Only a few flowers—daisies, for one—are innocent enough to be given as a token of unwed affection.

"I was nearby and thought you might appreciate the company on a quiet Friday afternoon," Kyle starts, folding his hands behind himself and rocking forward on his toes.

"I always appreciate your company," I lie, keeping my voice soft.

Kyle just nods and swallows, his Adam's apple bobbing.

"I had a very eventful week," he says. "Since *Raising Up Godly Sons* was released last week, the Reverend has been continually dogged in the press. It's enough to wear down a lesser man, but God has given him the strength to battle on..."

This is a one-way conversation, so I don't really bother listening. All that's required of me right now is to nod and say *mhm* every so often, and as long as I keep smiling, Kyle will never know the difference.

There's a good reason that the Reverend's book, *Raising*

Up Godly Sons, has been released to serious criticism and scorn, at least from anyone who isn't somewhere to the right of the Westboro Baptist Church, politically speaking.

The Reverend's own son, Lucas, is my ex-husband.

And he's anything but godly, at least according to the Church's definition.

CHAPTER SIX

GABRIEL

I STAND at the huge window in the Senator's office, hands in my pockets, looking down at the flower garden as Ruby and Kyle slowly walk along the brick paths. They keep at least a foot apart, her hands clasped in front of her, his hands behind him.

Even from here I can tell the conversation is one-sided. Ruby's just been smiling and nodding along for as long as I've been watching, and while I haven't been waiting for the Senator all that long yet, if they were having a real conversation she'd have said something by now.

I want to go down there and give Kyle a piece of my mind, let him know that maybe, every once in awhile, you ask the other person in a conversation a question. That it's a back and forth, not a lecture, and maybe he'd get more than that empty, fake smile from her if he gave even a half-assed try.

But just the thought tightens my stomach, the shadow of something ugly and black snaking through me, because I'm lying to myself.

I don't want to go give that dumb asshole advice on

talking to girls. I want to go down there, send him packing, and walk Ruby through the garden myself. I want her *real* smile. I want to see the way her pretty eyes flash when I say something she likes.

I want—

The door opens, and I turn. The Senator walks through, trailing Mason behind him, the poor boy hurriedly taking notes.

"Write Mrs. Witherson on letterhead and express deep sorrow over the loss of her nephew," he instructs Mason. "For good measure, have some flowers sent to the funeral. After Murphy's gaffe last week, we can really consolidate our hold on the rural vote out in hill country, so go in with both barrels blazing. Next week is all stump speeches and kissing babies. Hi, Gabriel, thanks for waiting."

"Not a problem, sir," I answer.

Mason heads back next door, and the Senator walks over to me, jacket unbuttoned, hands in his pockets. For a fifty-five year old man, he's still physically imposing, tall and broad, still in good shape. I could take him in a fight, but I could take most people in a fight, so that doesn't count.

No, it's the way he carries himself, coupled with his reputation, that makes him a presence in any room he's in. Whenever you talk to him, there's an unspoken expectation that you, too, want nothing more than to please the Senator and remain in his good graces.

And that's the problem: most people do. He's been in the Senate for nearly twenty years, and despite being on the fringe politically, he's accrued plenty of power. He comes from money. He belongs to a church that believes a man is the absolute head of his household, that his authority over his wife and children should be total.

From everything I've seen, it is. Or at least it's very, *very* close.

We stand at the window, looking down at Ruby and Kyle in the garden.

"You don't have children, correct?" he asks.

"No, sir."

He nods once, brusquely.

"I didn't truly know worry until the day Ruby was born," he says. "It's a cliché, son, but it's a cliché because it's true. They really do change everything."

"I have no doubt, sir."

I feel a little like he's giving *me* a stump speech.

"Gabriel, I would do anything to protect my daughter. I would walk through a burning building. I would swim across the ocean. I would run through a war zone."

"Of course."

"That's why I hired you, obviously. I can't be by her side twenty-four-seven, and even if I could, I'm getting old. Even if I'd give up my life in an instant, I'm not trained in protection. Sometimes the best thing a man can do is step aside and let a professional do his job."

"Thank you, sir."

I don't think it matters what I say.

"So far I've entrusted Ruby's physical wellbeing to you," he says. "But now that you've been here for another day, I need to alert you to a danger I believe is far greater than any stalker could possibly be."

He turns to me, his face dark and serious.

"I have grave concerns about Ruby's spiritual well being. Are you a religious man, Gabriel?"

I clear my throat. The answer is *no*, but that's definitely the wrong answer right now.

"I'm not as devout as I should be," I say.

He walks, hands in pockets, to a huge gold cross that's hanging on one wall, lit from behind. It's not a crucifix—there's no Jesus on it—just a cross.

"This household is at war," he says solemnly. "We are all fighting against Satan for Ruby's soul, and every day, I fear we're losing."

I have absolutely no answer for this. I went to church growing up, but we were never at war with Satan for anything. We had potlucks, held clothing drives for the homeless, sang hymns, that kind of thing.

"She has abandoned her husband," he goes on. "Women are like children, Gabriel. They need to be kept in hand, led gently. A woman without a husband, particularly at her age, is a dangerous thing indeed. I'm sure that Satan sees her as a tear in the fabric of this family, and he plans on slipping into our midst, using Ruby as a vessel."

I clench my hands behind my back, my fingernails digging into my palms.

Children? Kept in hand?

The Senator's a fucking lunatic, but I need this job. Dear God do I need this job.

"That's why I'm asking you to guard her spiritually as well as physically," he says, finally turning to me, the cross on the wall now behind him. It's very dramatic. He's a very good politician, that's for damn sure. "I'm afraid that my daughter is lost, confused, open to sin. She needs my strong, steady hand to guide her back to the light, and I cannot guide her away from the darkness if I don't know what darkness she's facing."

"I see," I say.

I do *not* see.

"Part of your duties here are to join in our spiritual warfare," he goes on, spreading his hands in front of himself.

"If you see Ruby stumble along the path to righteousness, tell me, so I may guide her back. If she is led astray by sin, tell me, and I will help her sin no more."

Finally, it clicks.

If I were, for example, to catch Ruby buying vodka at eight o'clock in the morning, that's stumbling on the path to righteousness.

He's not just asking me to keep her safe. He's asking me to report back to him on everything she does.

"Understood, sir," I say.

"And you think you can do that for me, son?"

I swallow.

"Of course, sir."

It's right there, on the tip of my tongue: *she was in the liquor store yesterday*.

I don't even have to tell him I was hung over. I could tell him about Ruby, do my job, curry some favor with one of the most powerful men in Washington, D.C. When this gig is over, he pulls some strings and I get reinstated with the Secret Service.

But I don't. Something stops me. I barely know Ruby, but I can't bring myself to do it.

The Senator reaches out and claps me on the shoulder.

"God bless, son," he says. "We'll have you back at your position in no time."

I try to smile.

"Thank you, sir. I'm honored to be working for you."

The Senator smiles at me, a huge, fake, politician smile.

"Glad to have you on board, and thanks for your help. I'll see you bright and early tomorrow."

I know when I'm being dismissed, so I shake his hand and leave. As I close the door behind myself, I realize the hairs on my neck are standing up.

Spiritual warfare against Satan, I think, heading down the stairs. *All I really remember from church is 'love thy neighbor.'*

As I walk to my carriage house, I catch a glimpse of Ruby and Kyle, still walking. He's still lecturing, but Ruby catches my eye for just a moment and I swear there's a flash of something there before she looks away.

Then I head into my apartment, pull off my sweaty shirt, and think for a while about loving *that* particular neighbor.

CHAPTER SEVEN

RUBY

I POUND on the door for the third time, the heavy wood shaking on its hinges.

"We are leaving in forty-five minutes," I call.

From inside the room there's the sound of a blanket hitting the floor, then a long, dramatic groan. Feet shuffle to the door, and it's pulled open to reveal the surly face of my little sister Pearl.

"It's *early*," is all she says.

I can read the rest of it on her face, too, even though vocalizing her complaints was trained out of her years ago: it's early, she hates going to our father's rallies, she hates campaign events, she'd rather stay home.

Pearl's sixteen, and I love her but she's been going through a bitchy phase for months now, grouching and sniping at anyone who crosses her path.

But she's a rule-follower, through and through, and she'll probably grow up like Grace: marry the man my parents choose for her and have two kids by the time she's twenty-four.

Even I started down that path, though I made sure early on that kids weren't in the equation.

"Yes, and we're still leaving in forty-five minutes," I say.

Pearl makes a face. I lean into the doorway and peek at the other bed, which still has my youngest sister's motionless form sprawled in the middle.

"Get ready," I say, and walk away from the door. "And make sure Joy does, too."

We've had this conversation before, about a thousand times. Pearl and Joy are ten and twelve years younger than me, so I half-raised them both.

I head back to my room to finish getting myself ready. Having a bedroom all to myself, even though it's about the size of a closet, is one of the few concessions my parents made to my adulthood—they nearly made me share a room with Pearl and Joy when I moved back home.

It was the only thing I fought them on. After all, they didn't have to take me back. I'm still half-convinced that they only did because my father is campaigning for re-election, and putting your own daughter on the street doesn't play well with voters.

In my room, I put on my shoes—black ballet flats, because heels are designed to accentuate a woman's bosom and buttocks, therefore tempting men—and then I kneel on the floor by my dresser, open the bottom drawer, and reach in.

All the way in the back, jammed into a corner, is the bottle of vodka from the day before yesterday next to a flask shaped like a makeup compact, as long as no one looks too closely. Sitting on my floor, I very *very* carefully fill the flask, then put the vodka back.

It might be dumb to bring this, but on the other hand, I've discovered how much easier is it to smile nicely, nod ycur head, and keep sweet when you've braced yourself with a swig of vodka.

So really, it's a toss-up: do I get in trouble for having an attitude, or do I get in trouble for drinking?

I put the flask in the bottom of my purse, hide it as well as I can, and head downstairs.

———

GABRIEL'S WAITING NEXT to the campaign bus, wearing a suit, as the whole Burgess family comes outside. Besides the eight Burgess children—me, Grace, James Jr., Daniel, Zeke, Pearl, Joy, and Paul—there's Grace's husband and her two children, James Jr.'s pregnant wife, the girl Daniel's courting, my father's aide Mason and his girlfriend Lilah, not to mention the rest of my father's campaign staff.

Bless his heart, Gabriel doesn't even raise his eyebrows. On the bus, he sits in the row behind me, next to another security guy. I sit with Grace and her kids, while her husband sits in the front of the bus with the rest of the men.

"Kyle came to the house again yesterday?" Grace asks, bouncing Emma, her four-month old. Emma just looks at me, her tiny face completely unamused.

"He did," I say evenly, although I don't want to talk about Kyle.

"He brought flowers?"

"Yes," I confirm, because when you have seven siblings there are no secrets.

"He's a very appropriate young man," she says.

I give my younger sister a sharp look.

"Is he?"

She frowns at me, still bouncing Emma. In the row

behind us, I hear Gabriel say something to the guy next to him, and it sends a slight prickle down the back of my neck.

Kyle gives me zero prickles. Well, that's not true. Is revulsion a prickle?

"Ruby," she says admonishingly. "You know he's reformed."

"Yeah, that's worked out well for me in the past."

"You didn't give it a chance in the past."

"I gave it years of chances."

Grace glances over at me, and I can tell she's getting mad. It's nine in the morning, and I've already angered the closest thing I've got to an ally on this bus. It's gonna be a hell of a day.

"Marriage vows aren't *until I get tired of you* or *unless you mess up big time*," she says, her voice tightly controlled. "They're *'til death do us part*."

"Spare me the lecture," I snap.

"If you weren't prepared to commit to Lucas you shouldn't have gotten married," she says in her haughtiest voice.

I take a deep, deep breath and look away, all the muscles in my back knotting with tension. I didn't really have a choice in the matter of marrying Lucas. Besides, I'd spent my entire life learning to obey my father's every word. It didn't occur to me to say no.

"I was *nineteen* when we got engaged," I point out, keeping my voice steady and quiet.

"That's more than old enough," she goes on, still lecturing. "And now, you're lucky anyone is interested. Really, Ruby, what are your options?"

I turn my head away as the bus rolls out of the driveway. I can't believe we've barely left and I'm already fighting with my sister over Kyle of all people.

The only reason Kyle brings me flowers and then talks at me for an hour is that we're both damaged goods, and everyone knows it. He's the son of the President of Calvary Bible College, an extremely conservative Christian school near Huntsburg.

Last year he got arrested for visiting a prostitute. It was a huge scandal, and it also came out that he had a pornography addiction, not to mention a problem with texting students at Calvary College inappropriate pictures.

His father nearly disowned him, but Kyle went on an apology tour, going on Christian talk shows and to Christian churches, giving interviews in the Christian press, talking about his recovery from his problems and how his faith helped him heal. He pleaded guilty to the charges and got probation plus community service.

Conveniently, he got to count the lectures at churches and schools about the insidious danger of pornography as his service.

I, of course, am divorced. Basically the same thing as frequenting prostitutes, sending out pictures of my genitals to people who don't want them, and masturbating to pictures of cartoon characters having sex, right?

"I'm only telling you this because you're my sister and I love you," Grace says softly. "Someone has to talk reason into you."

The worst part is that it's true. She *is* telling me because she thinks she's helping, and that might be the thing that makes me feel most trapped of all.

"I know," I say, and lean my head back, closing my eyes. We don't talk for the next two hours.

———

WHEN WE GET to Greentown Community College, there's a small crowd of protesters already gathered. They're waving rainbow signs that say things like IT'S OKAY TO BE GAY, wearing flowers in their hair, the girls in tank tops and the guys in shorts.

I think they're having a lot more fun than I am.

On the bus, I stand in the aisle and wait for everyone in front of me to disembark. Grace hands me Emma, who's half-asleep, so I hold her while my sister gathers all her things together in one place.

She definitely has more baby stuff than she does baby.

"Hey there, cutie," says Gabriel's voice.

Emma stares, and I turn my head.

"What are you looking at?" he asks, keeping his voice soft. "What do you think you're looking at?"

Then he reaches out and taps Emma on the nose very lightly.

After a second, she gives him a giant toothless grin, and I laugh.

"She likes you," I say.

"Kids usually do," says Gabriel. "I have no idea why."

He holds a manila folder up in front of his face. Emma's smile drops, but after a moment, Gabriel lowers the folder and she grins again, even bigger this time.

"Boo!" Gabriel says, and does it again.

I try to act normal, but I think my ovaries might actually explode, because it's just about the cutest thing I've ever seen. They play peek-a-boo until Grace takes Emma back, I grab her diaper bag, and we finally start moving for the front of the bus.

"You remember everything we talked about, right?" he says. "Lines of sight, exit routes?"

"I think so," I say, even though I'm scrambling to remember, and then we're getting off the bus.

Gabriel stands between me and the protesters, though he only gives them a cursory glance before glancing around at the trees, the tops of the buildings, the other knots of people milling around.

"Then you remember that the most important thing is to stay alert," he goes on. "Don't let yourself get distracted. If someone tries something, it's likely that there will be some sort of distraction first, just to make sure as little attention as possible is on you."

I still haven't told him that I'm nearly positive my father wrote those letters. I don't think he'd believe me—why would he?—and he'd still have to do his job anyway.

"Right," I say.

Two of the protesting women, both in shorts and tight-fitting tank tops, have stopped waving signs and shouting. They're just staring at Gabriel, whispering to each other.

He glances at them for a second, then looks away, but they keep gawking until we walk through the auditorium doors. Gabriel acts like nothing happened, even though I know he saw them.

"You remember the exits?" he asks.

I look around, trying to picture the floor plans in my head.

"Right there, obviously," I say, pointing behind me. "Same place, on the other side of the stage, halfway down the auditorium, back of the auditorium."

"And?"

I narrow my eyes, looking at him. He smiles.

"One more."

"...underneath the stage at the back?"

"I had a feeling you were a quick study," he says. "Nice work."

He holds out one fist, and I bump it with my own, smiling back at him.

"*Ruby,*" my mother's voice says, and I jump about a foot, wiping the smile off my face.

She gives me a sharp look, then settles her glance on Gabriel, features melting into her usual sweet smile.

"Your brother needs help sorting out name tags," she says. "Could you be a dear?"

"Of course," I say, returning her empty, sweet smile, even though my stomach is in a knot.

I didn't do anything, I remind myself, over and over again.

The next hour goes by in an exhausting blur. There are children everywhere, one of the speakers cancelled last minute so we have to redo the schedule, not to mention set up the table in the foyer of books, CDs, pamphlets, and homeschooling materials that my mother sells.

The women do all this. The men stand around talking, except Gabriel, who does whatever I'm doing.

Finally, ten minutes before the event is scheduled to begin, my father calls a prayer circle. I hold hands with Grace and Daniel while my father calls on Jesus to bless this endeavor, open the hearts of his supporters, turn the wickedness away from the hearts of his detractors, continue to defend against Satan, et cetera.

To be honest, I kind of tune out after a minute. When it's over I get pulled away again to re-tape a red, white, and blue ribbon to the back of a chair, Gabriel hovering in the background.

As I'm taping, my mother swishes around a stage curtain, practically dragging Joy behind her.

"Ow," Joy mutters, because she knows better than to shout.

"You will *not* disrespect me like that," my mother snaps, pulling on Joy's arm a little harder. Joy's only an inch or two shorter than my mom—she's fourteen—but there's still fear in her eyes.

"Sorry, ma'am," Joy whispers.

My mother grabs Joy by the chin, squeezing my sister's face tightly. I wince in sympathy, even though I don't do anything. I know how much that hurts. I've had my chin grabbed a lot.

"Now go out there with a pleasant, pleasing countenance," she says.

Joy nods.

"Keep sweet," my mother says, lets Joy go, then walks away without even looking at us again.

Joy glances our way, eyes shining, then scurries off. Gabriel looks at me, and I make my face as neutral as possible, like nothing just happened.

But inside, I'm furious. I'm mortified. I think I might throw up, and it's half because I hate that he just saw that and half because I hate that I didn't do a single thing.

I remember the vodka in my purse. If I can't do anything, maybe at least I can care less.

"Excuse me," I tell him. "I need to go to the ladies' room."

I grab my purse and walk off.

CHAPTER EIGHT

GABRIEL

I'M STANDING in the hallway, waiting for Ruby, when a portly middle-aged man hustles my way.

"We need Ruby," he informs me.

"She's using the facilities," I tell him, gesturing at the door to the hallway where the bathrooms are. I didn't follow her in there because it seemed rude, and I doubt there's much danger there.

"She's been gone quite a while," the man says, glancing at an expensive watch. He's the Senator's Chief of Staff, and I'm fairly sure his name is Beau. "Could you go check?"

I open my mouth to protest, but he holds up one hand.

"Son, just do it," he says, with the air of someone who thinks he always knows what's best, and quick anger flares inside me.

I remind myself that I'm at work. This is my job.

I go do it.

She's not in the hallway, so I steel myself and push open the door to the ladies' room just a crack, eyes shut.

"Ruby?" I call.

My voice echoes off empty tile. No one answers. There's not even a sound.

I open my eyes.

"Ruby?" I call again, pushing the door wider. The bathroom's completely empty, just four metal stalls, a few sinks, and a hand dryer that looks older than me.

I go into alert mode, whip out my phone, and call the Senator's chief of security. In the Secret Service we had earbuds and radios, always in communication, but things down here are a little more basic.

"Ray," he answers as I push open each stall door, just to make sure.

"Ruby's out of pocket," I say. "She went to the ladies' room and now she's gone. I'm following up. Have someone circle the building and check the exits."

Adrenaline is leaking through my veins, sharpening everything into crystal-clear focus as plans and orders spin through my head. We need to secure the exits, make sure someone's on the parking lot. The Senator's biggest fear was kidnapping, and my stomach tightens.

She probably stepped outside for some air, I remind myself. Ninety-nine times out of a hundred, if the target disappears, they've just forgotten that they had security watching them in the first place and wandered off.

That doesn't change my job, though. Ray sighs into the phone.

"All right," he says, not sounding all that concerned. "We'll do that."

I hang up and jog down the hallway, in the opposite direction I came from. It turns, and there's a door to the outside, probably where she went.

I open it and look around. Bright sunshine, incredible heat, and the smell of fresh-cut grass, but no Ruby. I shut it and keep jogging down the hallway, which turns again, toward the back of the stage. Now I'm looking at the tall black curtain, light seeping underneath it, surrounded by a forest of other curtains.

She's not here. If she were back with the group, Ray would have just told me. There aren't many other places she can *be*, so she must have gone outside, maybe walked around the building when she couldn't get back in that door.

Or worse, someone's—

A curtain moves, at the very edge of my vision, but in two steps I'm there and I push it open, sending ripples through the whole setup backstage.

Ruby stares back at me, a flask halfway to her barely-parted lips, frozen.

Thank God.

I swallow. The spikes of adrenaline recede, the cool buzz of relief taking over. She's here, she's fine, she isn't being kidnapped and held for ransom or worse.

"You can't do that," I tell her, my voice low, my hand still holding the curtain up.

She gives me that sweet, sunny smile, locking eyes with me as she lifts the flask to her lips and takes a swig.

"Trust me, it's for the best," she says, an edge to her voice.

"I meant you can't walk off without telling me," I say.

I step forward and let the curtain go, blocking our view of the backstage area. Suddenly it's almost pitch-black, just the two of us, the pale oval of her face and the gleam of the flask all that's really visible.

"Apparently I can," she says, like it's a challenge.

I open my mouth to answer, but my phone buzzes. It's Ray.

"I just found her," I tell him before he can say anything.

"Phew," he says. "We've been looking all over the place for that girl."

Ruby's staring at me, eyes wide, silently screwing the cap back onto her flask, and I think of my last meeting with the Senator.

This is exactly what he meant, I think. *I could score so many points with him right now.*

I pause. Ruby blinks, her green eyes nervous and brave and challenging all at once, even in the dark.

"She just stepped out for a moment and forgot to tell me," I say. "I found her backstage."

Her jaw flexes, and her eyes feel like they might bore a hole straight through my skull. I stare right back into those green depths, serious and beautiful.

Her father asked me to spy on her, and he's my boss, one of the most powerful men in Washington.

Her gaze doesn't waver for a second, and really, there's no fucking choice here.

"She said she wanted a quiet moment alone to... pray," I tell Ray. "For... strength."

That gets an honest-to-God smile out of Ruby, her green eyes lighting up in the darkness. I grin back at her.

"Oh, well, of course. She's just got to tell someone first instead of runnin' off like that," Ray admonishes me. He's perfectly audible to Ruby, too, and she rolls her eyes for a split second.

"We're heading back now. Sorry for the scare."

"That girl's always been a handful," he says, and hangs up.

I slide my phone back into my pocket. Ruby holds up the flask, offering it to me.

"Got anything to pray for?" she asks softly, her eyes teasing in the dark.

"I don't pray on the job," I say.

We're keeping our voices low, telling secrets in the dark.

"You only pray before the job?"

"I thought we agreed that never happened," I say, smiling slowly.

"Is it as bad as you thought, or is it worse?"

"Parts are better, actually."

I don't say *this is the part that's better*.

We lock eyes for a moment, and then she looks away, toward the curtain separating us from the rest of backstage.

"Thanks for lying," she says. "I'll try to behave on your watch."

I nearly tell her that she doesn't have to, that she can misbehave all she wants with me, but I bite my tongue. This isn't what I'm here for.

"That's a tall order," I tell her. "Everything you do is my watch."

"Then I guess I'll try to behave all the time."

I take half a step closer to her, lower my voice even further. I've only been around the Burgesses two and a half days, but I already feel like I'm constantly being monitored.

"I don't care if you need some liquid courage before you go on stage," I tell her. "I was worried because I thought you'd been kidnapped."

Her mouths twitches into a half-smile, and she flicks me a quick glance like she knows something I don't.

"Right," she murmurs, then clears her throat.

"Someone's stalking you, Ruby. I've seen the letters."

She tilts her head slightly, though she doesn't move away from me.

"I haven't," she says.

I swallow. I hate saying this out loud, but I want her to take my protection seriously.

"He said he would take you," I start, trying to soft pedal this as much as I can. "Tie you up in the trunk of his car, drive you to the woods, strap you to a tree, and cut your clothes off with a knife."

I stop and close my eyes. Reading it was hard, saying it out loud, to *her*, is close to impossible.

"He said he'd cut you, and then... do things."

Ruby's green eyes nearly glow in the dark, and for the first time, she looks shocked, appalled, and uncertain. For a moment she looks away from me, her face even paler in the dark.

"What things?" she whispers.

I take a deep breath and straighten my jacket, unconsciously feeling for my gun in its holster.

"He said he would..."

And then I have to imagine it, Ruby tied to a tree and bleeding, this pervert with his dick out. I shake my head.

"I can't. I'm sorry. I can't."

She just nods.

"I think I get it," she murmurs, then looks back at me. "Thanks for telling me."

"I'm sorry I couldn't."

"I understand," she says, and then we're both quiet for a moment. I know people are waiting for us, and I know that with every second we don't leave this pocket of backstage curtains we risk someone finding us here, but I like it being here, caught in the glow of Ruby's eyes, the only sound the thump of my own heartbeat.

"We should go before we get caught," she finally says.

"Caught doing what?" I ask, even though I know what she means.

"We're alone together."

Still, neither of us moves. I feel rooted to the spot,

unwilling to give up this sixty seconds of intimacy, this glimpse of the real Ruby. There's a totally different girl behind the innocent smiles and the obedience and the faux-meekness, and I like talking to her.

"Are you saying I can't be trusted?" I tease.

"I'm saying this could look improper," she murmurs, looking up at me. "And appearances are everything around here."

"You like that word, improper."

"I don't *like* it. I've just heard it a lot."

"Have you?"

"Endlessly, and I'd like to avoid hearing it again."

I feel like I'm walking along a cliff, right on the edge of *dangerous*, because I'm alone with the Senator's daughter and there's something about the shape of her mouth, the curve of her waist, the gleam in her eye that makes me want to crush my mouth against hers and push her against this wall.

Which is just about the worst possible thing I could do.

Somewhere, a door opens. Ruby takes a quick step back from me, her face tightening, and I push aside the curtain, letting the light in. As we step out, she turns to me, footsteps approaching.

"Can I give you a piece of advice?" she asks.

"Anything."

Ruby smiles her sweet, innocent, fake smile, and it's like the girl who was with me behind the curtain is erased.

"Keep sweet," she says, and walks for the door.

CHAPTER NINE

RUBY

"WHERE *WERE* YOU?" my mother hisses as I re-appear, flanked by Gabriel on one side and Ray on the other.

Thanks to the vodka, I smile sweetly and apologetically at her.

"Sorry, mother," I say. "I didn't mean to worry everyone."

Her face softens, and my father walks up to her, head held high without speaking. He doesn't even have to ask her to adjust his tie, she just knows it's what he wants.

Five years ago—hell, even two years ago—I'd have watched this and thought *this is what I should be working toward.* But now, watching my mother just understand what my father's demanding of her just sends a shiver down my spine.

Then it's time. The lights go down over the audience. The lights on the stage go up. Over the loudspeaker, a faceless voice tells everyone to please look for the nearest exit in case of an emergency, and then we're all herded onto stage, where I'll be sitting for at least an hour in an uncomfortable metal folding chair.

As the oldest, I sit next to my mother, though Grace gets to sit closest to the edge of the stage since she's holding a baby and might have to go at any moment. I, on the other hand, don't have to do anything. My job is to sit here and look pretty, just another piece of my father's perfect family.

The broken piece, sure. The piece that everyone thinks should be grateful to be allowed on stage at all.

Years and years of keeping sweet have made me pretty good at sitting quietly and smiling gently, but the years haven't really made it easier. My face still feels like it might crack into a thousand pieces.

Everyone's seated. There's a row of American flags behind us, enough red, white, and blue to outfit an entire parade, as if one flag simply wouldn't do.

A speaker walks out. I think it's the president of the college, but again, it's not my job to pay attention, so I don't. He starts talking about what a wonderful man my father is, his lovely family, his hard line on morals, all the good he's done for South Carolina. There's polite applause. Someone else gets up there and praises my father more.

I'm not listening. Not even a little. Over on the side of the stage, barely visible, Gabriel's standing, hands folded in front of himself, watching attentively.

It's distracting. No matter how much I try not to think about him, about how good he looks in a suit, about the calm, self-assured way he carries himself, about the way he smiles at me sometimes when he thinks no one is looking.

My mind's not here. It's back between the curtains, just the two of us alone. Gabriel, on the phone, telling Ray I was *praying for strength.*

He didn't have to. I'm positive my father would *love* proof that I'm the problem he thinks I am.

But he did. And he smiled at me and it felt like it was a

hundred and fifty degrees backstage, close enough that I could smell his shaving cream from that morning. Nearly close enough to feel his body heat.

And his eyes. I swear I can feel it when he looks at me, like fingertips tracing over bare skin, my heart pounding like it's trying to escape my chest. Whenever I'm near him I have the insane desire to touch him, run my hands along the muscles in his arms, sit on his lap and let him kiss my neck…

A molten knot of desire starts to unfurl inside me, and suddenly I snap back to reality, because I am *on stage behind my father,* sitting next to my mother, and fantasizing about my bodyguard.

I look down at the floor of the stage, fold my hands in my lap, and cross my legs. It doesn't help, but it's probably better than nothing. I feel a little lost and adrift, out of my element with the sheer intensity of everything.

I knew I had a silly, girlish crush on Gabriel. Of course I do. He's handsome, sexy, has that *voice*, and isn't related to me, but this feels more intense than some crush.

My father drones on. I look out at the audience, trying to calm my nerves, but I glance over at Gabriel instead. He's looking straight at me.

And suddenly I realize what this is.

This is *lust*.

I almost gasp out loud. I feel like an idiot. A total, complete, childish idiot, because I'm twenty-six and just had the crashing realization of what lust feels like.

It feels like being completely and utterly unable to stop thinking about your bodyguard with his shirt off. I feels like thinking about his hands on your skin every time you close your eyes, like thinking of straddling his lap while you kiss him, tongue in his mouth—

"Ruby, are you alright?" my mother murmurs.

I freeze, and for a split second, I wonder if she can somehow hear my thoughts. Then I smile sweeter and turn my head slightly.

"I'm fine," I say.

"You're bright red."

"I shouldn't have worn this cardigan on stage is all," I whisper.

She nods once and turns her head forward again. I settle back against the uncomfortable chair and pretend my palms aren't sweating, refocusing my attention on my father.

I've thought I was in lust before. When I was fifteen, I went to an all-girls, very Christian sleepaway camp. We were heavily supervised, of course, and there were to be no boys whatsoever on the premises.

But there was an all-boys camp about two miles away, and like Ray told Gabriel: I've always been a handful. Another girl had a cousin at the boys' camp, and apparently he was being sent there in the hopes that it would reform him, because she somehow arranged for her, me, and another friend to meet him and some friends outside his camp.

His name was Douglas, and I kissed him. I kissed him several times, and once, we even used tongue. I didn't even really like him—I met him that night and never saw him again—but as a teenage girl who may as well have lived under a rock, kissing a boy was one of the most thrilling things I ever did.

And of course, within a couple of days I was completely miserable about it. Totally consumed by guilt. I'd heard endless lectures on the demons who cause lust. I'd been raised with the notion that my very first kiss would happen at the altar, on my wedding day.

Now my stupid, thoughtless teenage actions had robbed

my future husband, whoever he may be, of that special moment with me. I cried. A *lot*. I prayed for the lust in my heart to be taken from me, for me to no longer feel that horrible, sinful feeling. I felt awful about it for years, and I never told a single person.

Not even Lucas, my ex-husband, though for the record we did kiss once before our wedding day, because we wanted our *actual* first kiss to be private. It made us feel very rebellious.

But that wasn't lust. None of that was. I never even came close to feeling that for Lucas, no matter how hard I tried.

This is it. The real thing, like devils dancing gleefully in my belly. Except this time, I don't feel bad about it. I tried to live the way my parents wanted, and look where it got me.

The auditorium bursts into applause, and I start clapping automatically, the smile still on my face. To be honest, I'm kind of thrilled with my dumb realization. I'm sort of amazed that I *can* lust after someone.

I can't do anything about it, of course. Gabriel works for my father, and despite lying to Ray, he could start reporting on me at any time. Getting anywhere close to him would be dangerous for me and dangerous for him.

This won't go anywhere, because it can't. But I've still got my little secret, and I'm defying them in this small, personal way, by lusting after someone and not even feeling bad about it.

For no reason, I glance over at Gabriel. His eyes flick to mine, and I look away.

No, I tell myself. *Not a chance.*

CHAPTER TEN

FOR DAYS after our moment between the curtains, I don't really see Ruby.

I mean, I *see* her. I spend most of my days in the same room as her, but she's almost always surrounded by other people. If we talk, we make small, unimportant talk, her façade firmly in place.

She tells me that she thinks the weather is lovely and I agree.

I tell her that the cookies she's made are absolutely delicious and she thanks me.

It's all formal, completely appropriate, above-board. The only hints of that other Ruby are the looks she gives me sometimes. When she's sitting on a sofa, knees together, studying her bible and absent-mindedly running her hair through her fingers and glances up suddenly, her fingers slowing as she looks me in the eye, lets her gaze run down my body, glances at me again and goes back to reading.

When she's in the kitchen, kneading bread dough, one of her sisters nearby and I ask if I can help. She shows me how to knead it properly, and I roll up my sleeves to the elbow, forearms bare.

I knead. She watches my hands, her face a mask, and then just before she thanks me she looks at me through her eyelashes and I swear it leaves a burn, it's so heated. I wash my hands and roll my sleeves back down.

It's like that with us. I follow her around, as if someone might jump out of the pantry and take her away, trying not to think about what's under her modest clothing.

And then I go back to the carriage house every night and jerk off thinking about it. I wonder if I should go back to the Best Western where I spent my first night in town, get drunk at the bar, and pick up some other woman, but I don't, because there's no way it would help.

———

THE BURGESS HOUSEHOLD goes to bed early. Most of the lights are usually out by ten o'clock with just a few bedrooms still lit. I'm sure there's some grand moral reasoning behind it, but I haven't bothered to find out.

The truth is, I kind of like it. I stay up later myself, and it's good to have an hour or two of my day when I don't feel like I'm being watched, like whatever I do might get reported back to my boss. I've even hidden the condoms under the bed, because I know he's got a key to the carriage house where I live.

It's still warm at night, even though the trees are just barely starting to turn yellow and orange around the edges, so I've taken to sitting outside, on the tiny piece of grass that could pass as a patio, and drinking a glass of iced tea.

I wish it was whiskey, and I wish I had someone to talk to—or better yet, keep me company some *other* way—but I tell myself that it's good for me not to drink, and good for me to spend some time alone like this. Introspection and all that bullshit.

Next thing I know I'll be doing yoga, I think, swiping one finger down the condensation on my glass.

Well, not here. I've never asked the Senator's opinion on the practice but if he doesn't think it proceeds directly from Satan himself, I'll eat my hat.

I'm about to stand, the back of the house and my own apartment completely dark, when something moves around the side of the big house.

Instantly, every muscle in my body goes rigid, and I hold perfectly still. It could be an intruder who somehow got past the gate, or it could be a cat. All I saw was a split second of motion, and then nothing.

Quietly, I stand, careful not to scrape my chair back. I go to the side of the carriage house and press my back against it, peering around the corner, the flow chart of what to do if it's someone, if they're dangerous, if they're trying to break in and hurt Ruby running through my brain.

For a long moment there's nothing, and I move slowly around the front of the carriage house, using the dark and the bushes as cover. Even so, I don't see anything else, and I start to relax. More than likely, the movement was an animal, a tree branch, maybe just a weird shadow.

It didn't move like a tree branch or a weird shadow, but I've been wrong before.

Then there's something else, another movement. I reach for my sidearm but it's not there, because I'm not wearing it, because I was off-duty and enjoying iced tea on my patio.

Shit.

There's a window open at the side of the house, and I realize: that was the motion I saw a moment ago, the window opening. I crouch and move behind more bushes, thinking that I can get in the side door, pull the alarm, and cut the intruder off at the—

A leg sticks out of the window, and I stop dead. The leg is wearing skinny jeans and I think it's wearing Converse, and no one who lives in that house wears either of those things.

Another leg joins the first, and now I'm virtually certain it's either a woman or a man with great legs and an even greater ass. She drops to the ground, and I don't even have to see her face for me to be about ninety percent sure I know which woman it is.

She turns, her back to the wall, and scans the yard. Of course it's Ruby, though she doesn't see me, her eyes probably not acclimated to the dark just yet.

I scan *her*. I haven't seen her in pants before, let alone pants that hug her curves that way. They're not skin-tight, but they show off about a thousand percent more of her body than I've seen before, not to mention her more-form-fitting-than usual t-shirt.

It's like seeing anyone else in lingerie. My mouth goes dry and I stare at her, hiding in the bushes like a total fucking creep, thinking about grabbing her ass in those jeans and grinding her against me.

Fuck. I'm hard. All the effort I put into not walking around the Burgess household with a huge erection, and all it takes is Ruby in pants.

Her back still pressed against the wall, she reaches out one arm and awkwardly pushes the window down until it's only about an inch open, probably so she can get back in. There's a flower bed right up against the house—Mrs. Burgess's prize rosebushes, naturally—and Ruby walks through them until she stops, looks up, examines a rosebush, and then walks away from the house at a right angle, in my general direction.

I frown, then keep watching as she circles in a wide arc, glancing up at the house every so often, looking nervous. It takes me a minute, but I finally realize that she's avoiding the motion sensors on the floodlights, so she doesn't trip them and risk waking someone up.

Meaning she's done this before. Meaning she's done this plenty of times before.

Finally she reaches the hedges along the edge of the yard and disappears into them, staying low between the bushes and the stone wall that separates their property from their neighbors'. I follow her, nearly silent, until she comes to the wrought iron fence at the front of her parents' property. The guard shack is fifty feet away, and though there are no guards there right now—the gate is closed, and Huntsburg isn't nearly a big or dangerous enough town to justify a 24/7 guard in there—I know there are security cameras up the wazoo on that thing.

I'm crouching on the ground, watching her feet and legs.

I could stop her. I could tell her to go back inside, stop sneaking out.

Hell, if I stopped her now we'd be alone together again, in this dark, secluded spot between the hedge and the wall. That's the real reason I'm thinking about it.

But I don't. I'm curious. And if I follow her, I might have the chance to talk to her alone, somewhere outside this house, away from her family.

Ruby grabs one of the wrought iron bars in the fence with both hands. I can't see her head from where am, but I can see what she's doing, and she wrenches it up, then down, and suddenly the piece comes away in her hands.

Holy *shit*, that's a security concern. If she can get out it means someone else could get in; and if she knows about it then it's nearly certain that someone else does as well...

She's leaving. I let her go, let her put the bar back in place. I let her walk for a count of fifty, and she walks far enough away that she's not likely to see me before I approach the fence.

I grab the same bar, hold my breath, and pull. After a moment of resistance it comes away in my hands with a scraping noise, and I freeze, but nothing happens. Ruby's form, walking away from me down the sidewalk, doesn't even turn.

It's a tighter squeeze for me than it was for her, but I get through the fence, replace the bar, start following her down the sidewalk about two blocks behind. I try to stick to the shadows, and though Ruby is alert, she's not trained in spotting a follower so she doesn't see me.

We walk for about twenty minutes. A mile or so. The Burgess mansion is right on the edge of Huntsburg's quaint downtown area, which also dates to back before the Civil War: uneven brick sidewalks, two-story brick storefronts, the occasional newer building, made of concrete or stone. The streets are lined with magnolias and oaks, making the wrought-iron street lamps cast splotchy orange light that moves as the breeze shakes the branches.

It's warm, the town itself is charming as hell, and it *should* be cozy. But instead with every shadow that moves and every car that drives along this two-lane street, I'm on high alert, ready for someone to jump out at Ruby, try to take her away.

I speed up so I'm only about a block behind her, but I'm torn. I want to protect her, but I want to let her be, let her have this tiny amount of freedom that I know she deserves.

Finally, she reaches the center of downtown, the only

part where people are still walking around and the store-fronts are still lit. Ruby makes straight for a storefront with big glass windows that says FINNEGAN'S PUB on its sign, big gold letters against a green background.

I stop, still a block away, my chest tightening, because I've realized something.

Ruby's at a bar, alone, dressed normally, late at night. It's a weekday, sure, but her options for going out are probably pretty limited.

She's on a date.

Of course she is. She has to be.

And even though it's none of my business whatsoever, I hate it. I stand on the corner of Beauregard and Main, arms crossed in front of me, staring at the door of the bar, and just hate it.

I want to go in there, find whoever she's meeting, and get in his face until he leaves. Then I want to sit down at his seat while Ruby smiles at me, that look sparkling in her green eyes, and tells me how glad she is I'm there.

Except that's fucking stupid. That's some middle-school level bullshit, not least because I'm pretty sure Ruby's had more than enough of men telling her what to do in her life. She deserves being on this date with someone she chose. Hopefully someone she likes.

I pace around the block, trying to calm myself down. I don't want to leave her there, alone, because she's still in danger, but the danger of a pub filled with people is less than the danger of an empty street at night.

I come back. I stand on the corner and look through the window, but I can't see her, so I walk past the front of the pub slowly, looking in.

No Ruby.

Are you fucking kidding me?

She's not at the bar, she's not at a table, she's not in any of the high-backed booths. Now I'm stopped in front of the windows, staring in blatantly like a total fucking creep, but I don't care because Ruby's gone. Taken.

Exactly the kind of thing I was hired to prevent.

I pull the front door open so hard that the bells on it smack against the frame, and half the people inside look up. It's a weeknight, so it's pretty quiet inside, the place all classy low lighting and fake candles on every table.

The bartender nods and I nod back, already scanning for Ruby.

She could have left of her own accord, you know, I think. That's probably more likely than a kidnapping.

I pace through the restaurant, the old wooden floor creaking beneath my feet. By now I'm praying that I find Ruby tucked away in a booth, sitting on someone else's lap. Just as long as I find her.

Then, finally, at last: a blonde head in the booth against the far wall. I can't see whoever she's facing, just her.

The knot in my chest unwinds all at once, and I take a deep breath. I deserve a fucking drink.

—————

CHAPTER ELEVEN

I FLIP the page and pull one foot onto the bench seat with me. It took me forever to sneak *The Golden Compass* into my house under my father's nose, and I wanted to read it somewhere with no distractions, no one calling or shouting for me, no threat that one of my parents or siblings might walk in suddenly and bust me.

Was sneaking out risky? Sure. I'm always afraid that my father's security has changed the camera setup or where the motion sensors are pointing, and I'll get busted.

But Thursdays are half-off Jack Daniels at Finnegan's Pub, it's always quiet, and I can sit in the back and have an hour or two actually, totally, and completely to myself.

I take another sip of whiskey. I flip another page.

Someone steps up to my booth and stops, both hands resting lightly on the table.

I look up at him and my heart plummets. Instantly, I know that this is all over: drinking, reading, getting to be alone.

"Buy you a drink?" Gabriel asks.

I lose my grip on my thick paperback, and it flops shut, making me lose my place, but I just shove it aside.

"Who else is here?" I say, my voice thick and slow.

Gabriel frowns.

"It's just me."

I lean out of the booth and look around. No one looks back, so at least the rest of my father's security team isn't here.

"What are you doing here?" I say, my heart still in my throat, beating so hard it feels like a war drum.

"Funny, that's what I was going to ask you," he says, a half-smile settling onto his face. "Is that a yes on the drink, or…?"

He taps his knuckles against the table, and I just shake my head *no*.

"Do you mind if I get one?" Gabriel says, jerking his thumb over his shoulder. "And can I trust you to not run away while I—"

"I can take care of you," says a waitress who's just appeared by his elbow.

She pulls a pad from her apron and smiles up at him through her thick eyelashes, a dimple forming in one cheek. The Jack Daniels sloshes around in my stomach unpleasantly, and I look away.

"Oh, thank you," Gabriel says. "I'll have what she's having."

"Of course," she says, smiles again, and walks away. Gabriel slides into the booth opposite me, his big hands on the table.

My palms are still sweating, my nerves still jangling, but nothing terrible has happened. Not yet.

"*I* had to order at the bar," I say.

He glances in her direction. I wish he wouldn't.

"She probably didn't see you come in," he says, shrugging and smiling at me.

"I'm sure," I say, taking another sip for fortitude.

"Are you trying to imply something, Ruby?"

"Just that only one of us got instant service from a cute waitress."

A frown flickers across his face again, and he glances in her direction.

Quit looking at her, I think.

"I did enter in a rush," he says.

"You think that's it?" I ask, drawing shapes in the condensation that's pooled around my glass. "It's not that you're—"

I stop for a second.

Tall, ripped, handsome, sexy, and masculine-ly alluring in ways I don't quite have words for?

"—A man?" I finish.

"I must look like I tip well."

"Sure," I say, and I let it drop, because I think we both know why she practically sprinted to take his drink order.

I make a triangle in the condensation water on the table, tap my finger in it once, and look up at Gabriel.

"Did you find me or follow me?" I ask.

He smiles.

"Followed you," he says. "Until now I've been behaving myself as part of my new employment situation."

I lean back in the booth, my back against hardwood, finally starting to relax a little.

"And what about this constitutes not behaving yourself?" I ask, tilting my head a little to one side. I know I've got nothing on the waitress, but around Gabriel I can't help but flirt. Only a little.

"Just the drink," he says, lacing his fingers behind his

head and leaning back in the booth as well, blue eyes dancing. With his arms like that I can see the lines of his muscles highlighted by the low light of the electric candle, and I have to look away before I start thinking about what I want him to *do* with those arms.

"I haven't had one in a little over a week, you know," he goes on.

"You're not getting up to something else after this?"

I don't know why I'm prodding. It's not like I *want* him to say *oh, and I'm going to go have sex with the waitress and also the other waitress and probably a few more very attractive ladies while I'm at it, see you at tomorrow's flower-arranging session.*

Gabriel laughs.

"What else is there to get up to in Huntsburg on a Thursday night?" he asks. "If I had my car maybe we could go to IHOP or Wal-Mart and really raise some heck, but I followed you here on foot."

The waitress comes back and sets Gabriel's whiskey in front of him. It's significantly fuller than mine was.

"Can I get you anything else, hon?" she asks, touching his shoulder.

I swear it feels like something pops inside me, and I look away. I've never touched him, aside from a handshake.

"No, thank you," he says.

"Just holler if you need something," she says, smiles, and walks away. I glare after her, feeling like the ugly girl in middle school.

Or, at least, how I think the ugly girl in middle school probably felt. I was homeschooled.

"You sure you're not up to something else?" I ask. I don't even mean to say it, because it's childish and I know it's childish, but it just comes out.

I think he finally picks up on what I'm asking, and glances after her again as he takes a sip of his drink.

"Ruby," he says, settling his elbows on the table and leaning forward a little. "We both sneaked off your compound and now we're drinking together. We'd both be in a metric fuckton of trouble if we got busted, so we can speak candidly, right?"

"I think you just did."

"Are you trying to find out if I'm going to fuck the waitress?"

I look down at the table, and I can feel myself blush so hard it's like my face is in front of a furnace.

"No," I say. "Nothing like that at all, I was just asking if there were any parties or—"

"I'm not," he says, lifting his glass to his lips again.

"I wasn't asking that."

Yes, I was.

"Then whether or not you were asking, I'm still not gonna fuck her," he says, putting his glass down. There's a teasing smile tugging at his mouth, and I suddenly realize that he's enjoying getting a rise out of me.

I swallow and try to stop blushing. It's like plugging a broken dam with one finger: ineffective.

"I think you could," I say.

"I think I could too."

Heat slithers inside me, and I pull my other foot onto the seat. There's something about his quietly cocky confidence that I like, I mean really *like*, but I hate that I like it.

"But I'm celibate for as long as I'm working for your father," Gabriel goes on.

I raise one eyebrow.

"Is that in your contract?" I ask. I know it's a strange,

invasive thing to put in someone's employment contract, but my father's a strange, invasive employer.

"No," Gabriel says. He doesn't elaborate.

"Is that the only reason you're not going to..."

I try to say *fuck her* and fail, my face heating up again. I can't even say the word *fuck* out loud in front of him. God, I'm a wreck.

"...take her home tonight?" I finish.

"No," he says again. "I've got to take you back home, for one thing. For another thing, she's not my type."

"What *is* your type?"

I'm flirting with him. Oh no. *Oh no.*

Gabriel just smiles, his elbows on the table again.

"Harder to get," he says.

"Well, I'm also celibate," I say, trying to joke because obviously I'm not having sex with anyone. "Maybe we can have a support group."

"I think your parents would really hate that idea," Gabriel says, grinning. "The two of us bemoaning the hardship of not getting laid."

I take another sip of whiskey, my glass getting close to empty, and I nearly say *it wasn't much of a hardship until you showed up*, but I keep my mouth shut.

"My parents already hate a lot of things, including my presence in their house," I say. "Though I think I could kill my mother if I told her that I missed, uh, you know... marital intimacy."

Cool, I'm blushing again.

"Do you?"

And I'm blushing *even harder*, so I drain my whiskey glass, the ice cubes falling against my upper lip. I put the glass back on the table with a clunk and look at it for a long second, because that question is a little off. I mean, it's nosy and far too familiar and probably borderline rude, but it also makes me realize something.

I lean my chin on one hand, propping it up on the table.

"You don't know why I'm divorced, do you?" I ask.

"I guess it's not the usual reasons."

"Not exactly."

Gabriel twists his glass in one hand, his face darkening.

"He hurt you?" he asks, not looking at me, his voice nearly a growl.

I'm a little surprised.

"Not at all. Nothing like that," I say quickly.

His shoulders relax, and he looks at me.

"Lucas is gay," I say.

He leans back in the booth, folding his arms over his chest, and looks at me for a moment. I try not to watch the muscles in his forearms and look at his face instead.

"And people are upset that you divorced a gay guy?" he asks, puzzled. "Finding out your spouse is gay seems... like a pretty good reason for a divorce."

I tilt my glass up to my mouth, even though it's already empty, and get the very last drops out. Even though it feels like everyone knows this story already, I've never actually told it to anyone before. The gossip mill has done all the work for me, but Gabriel's not part of the gossip mill.

That means I have to start from the beginning, and I don't even know where the beginning *is*.

"I didn't *find out* that he was gay," I tell him, looking at my glass between my hands. "It wasn't a secret. It's never been a secret."

Gabriel nods at my empty glass.

"You want another one of those?" he asks. "Don't worry, I'll walk you home."

He winks, and I smile, despite myself.

"You mean you'll do your job?" I tease.

"Technically, I'm off-duty right now," he says, grabbing my glass and standing. "I'm seeing you home out of the goodness of my heart."

"And because there's nothing else to do around here."

Gabriel grins, then walks to the bar across the room. I try not to stare, but I can't help but watch the way his t-shirt is a tiny bit too tight around his shoulders. The way the muscles in his forearms move as he sets the glass on the bar and orders another one.

The way his jeans hug his butt *just* right.

Then I look away and try to figure out where to start. I don't really want to tell him the whole story, because it makes me sound like a naïve moron, but there's no way around it. I *was* a naïve moron. I'm probably still a naïve moron, because despite everything I've learned in the past six years, I'm pretty sure I don't know much about the world.

After a bit Gabriel comes back, the glass in his hand much fuller than the glass I originally got.

"Thanks," I say.

"You seem like you could use it," he rumbles. "Cheers."

We clink glasses together, and I take a sip. It's not Jack, and I raise my eyebrows.

"Buffalo Trace," he says, before I can even ask. "You're about to talk about getting a divorce, so I figured you might want the good stuff."

I push one hand through my hair and lean against it, looking over at Gabriel.

"I'm going to try to start at the beginning," I say. "But tell me if I'm not."

"Will do," he says.

CHAPTER TWELVE

GABRIEL

RUBY PUTS her thumb to her lip for a moment, her knuckle against her teeth, staring into space like she's trying to collect her thoughts. I force myself not to imagine my thumb between her lips, her teeth against my knuckle. Her tongue against the pad of my thumb as she sucks it into her mouth, those wicked eyes teasing me.

"Okay," she says, like she's decided something, and I snap out of it. "Lucas Dawson is the oldest son of Russell Dawson, the pastor at the Word of God Apostolic Covenant Church, which my family belongs to."

I nod. The Church is pretty notorious — the only reason they're not as famous as Westboro Baptist, the church in Kansas that protests soldiers' funerals because gay people exist, is they think they're too genteel to wave signs around and make spectacles of themselves.

"The Reverend first found Lucas's stash of gay porn when Lucas was fifteen. I don't remember exactly what happened, but instead of keeping it secret like I think most people would have, the Reverend decided that in order to lead his flock properly, he should make an example of his son."

My blood's starting to run cold. I can't imagine being a gay kid in an environment anything like the Burgess's household. Let alone being *made an example of.*

"The Church might not be quite as regressive about gay people as you'd think," Ruby goes on. She's got her head on one hand, the other splayed on the table, and she's tapping her fingers one by one. "Even though they think homosexuality is caused directly by Satan and is horrible and evil, they have this *hate the sin, love the sinner* policy. Basically, what that means is: if you're gay, and you pray really hard about it, and you never do gay stuff, and you really want to not be gay, you're all right."

"So it's fine to be gay as long as you never actually touch another person of the same sex," I say.

That sounds like hell. The prospect of a few months of celibacy is already wearing on me a little. I can't imagine thinking that I'd never, ever be able to have what I really wanted again.

"Well, no," Ruby says. "That's step one. They're also completely determined that, since gayness is a product of Satanic influences, if you get Satan out of someone, they'll stop being gay."

I have a bad feeling about what's coming.

"How do you get Satan out of someone?" I ask, taking a long drink of whiskey.

"You send them to a re-education facility for a couple months."

We both go quiet for a moment.

"Lucas didn't really talk about what happened there," Ruby says, quietly, looking at her glass. "But they sent him three times before we got married, and I was nineteen then.

I think they kept finding porn, maybe even caught him with someone. I don't know. I couldn't ask. But he had nightmares, even years later. He used to wake up shouting."

"Shit," I mutter. I know how *that* feels, but my nightmares are about roadside bombs and being ambushed out of nowhere. I don't know what happened to Lucas, but I've got the feeling it was pretty bad.

"Meaning, I knew Lucas was gay when we got married," she goes on, her gaze flicking up to me and then back down. "But I also believed everything that my father and the Reverend told me, and I knew he'd basically gone to heterosexuality boot camp."

She's tracing circles in the condensation on the outside of her glass, and she pauses for a moment, like she's gathering her thoughts.

"Lucas wanted to be straight, and I think he wanted to love me and he wanted to be attracted to me, so when our fathers suggested the match, it seemed like a good idea. We could please them and prove that gay people could forsake Satan and become straight."

"And then you got divorced and proved otherwise."

Ruby snorts.

"My father and the Reverend don't think we proved a thing, but most of the world took it as evidence that praying away the gay doesn't work. Because if the Reverend's own son and Senator Burgess's daughter couldn't make it work, who else would even have a chance, right?"

Her voice is practically dripping with sarcasm, a bitter edge to it I've never heard before. Not that I can blame her, but I want to reach out, put my hand over hers. Tell her we all do dumb shit when we're kids.

"You were also nineteen," I point out. "Not that he'd be less gay at twenty-four."

"If I'd been older I might have been a little smarter," she says. "But everything I knew, everything in my entire world was telling me that this was fine, this was a good idea, that I should marry Lucas. And I really really believed that if I tried hard enough, that if I was a good wife, I'd learn to love him, he'd learn to love me, and someday he'd..."

She blows a strand of hair out of her face and looks at the wall.

"I don't know. Want me?" she asks, her voice suddenly quieter.

Suddenly I'm angry for her, so I take another drink to mask it. It's bad enough that she got conned into marrying someone who didn't love her, who was never going to love her. But not to know something as simple as how it feels to be desired?

Love's complicated, but lust is simple. It's not much to ask.

For fuck's sake, *I* want her. If we were in any other scenario right now I'd lean over the table, beckon her in closer, and tell her that all it took to get me rock hard was seeing her in pants instead of a skirt. I'd tell her that if she wanted to, I'd take her into the bathroom of Finnegan's Pub and pin her against the wall.

I'd tell her I'm hard again just thinking about it.

But it's not going to happen. Anyone else, anywhere else, yeah, but not her and not here.

"I guess he never magically became straight," I say.

"He didn't," Ruby confirms, taking another drink, then sighing. "He tried. I know he did. He would bring me flowers, and take me on nice dates, cook me dinner, rub my feet, everything that good husbands are supposed to do. We did like each other, there was just never any spark."

She drinks again.

"Probably because the entire time he wanted to be screwing other men," she says in a very reasonable tone of voice.

"Did you two ever have sex?" I ask.

She smirks at me, her eyes sparkling.

"Have you just been sitting over there, wondering that this entire time?" she asks.

Yes.

"It's the obvious next question," I protest, trying not to smile. "If your husband was gay, could he even..."

I trail off, but point one finger skyward, like an erection. Ruby laughs.

"I'm not a virgin after being married for six years," she says. "Don't worry, I'm not *that* weird."

"I didn't say you were weird."

"You were thinking it."

"I was actually thinking that you're shockingly well-adjusted."

Ruby looks skeptical.

"I really was," I say.

"I don't feel well-adjusted," she admits. "I feel like everywhere I go, everyone's staring at me all the time, because I'm a grown woman who's never had a real job and who got her first checking account last month."

She pauses and taps her fingers on her glass, then glances up at me.

"My father doesn't know about the checking account, by the way."

I mime a zipper across my lips.

"Thanks."

"And after six years, you just got tired of it?"

She leans her chin on one palm again, sliding the fingers

of her other hand along the rim of her half-empty whiskey glass.

"One day I was out running errands," she says. "And, halfway through, I realized I'd left some coupons at home, and I wasn't that far away, so I headed back to grab them."

She takes another long sip of whiskey, her glass half empty. Ruby's starting to get a little more expressive with her hands, her cheeks faintly pinker, the façade she's always wearing falling away.

"And when I got home, I found Lucas and another man having sex in our kitchen."

I let out a low whistle. Ruby looks into her whiskey glass.

"That's a hell of a thing to walk in on."

"It took me *so* long to figure out what was going on, actually," she says, shaking her head.

Then she looks at me and laughs, embarrassed.

"I thought I'd caught him watching porn at first," she says. "That had happened once or twice, and it was always awful because *he* was so ashamed about it and then *I* was ashamed about it, but there were these... you know, grunting noises and squishing noises and this sort of rhythmic slapping?"

Ruby is bright red, but she keeps going, still half-laughing at herself.

"Rhythmic slapping and grunting sure sounds like porn," I agree.

"From the door I couldn't tell where it was coming from, but then he wasn't in the den, and he wasn't in his office, and finally I realize the sounds are coming from the kitchen. And I walk in, and..."

She spreads her hands in front of herself, palms up, fingers spread.

"Surprise! Gay sex, right on the counter. Not porn. I

was so surprised that I just stood there and stared for a good thirty seconds before they realized I was there."

"I'd want a divorce too," I say.

"You know what ended up bothering me the most, for some reason?"

"Besides the part where your very conservative husband was fucking another man in your kitchen?"

"That's it, actually," Ruby say. "He wasn't screwing someone else. He was bent over the counter, *getting screwed*."

Ruby leans back in the booth, then rubs her eyes with both hands.

"I've actually never told anyone else this before," she admits. "Not the details, anyway, just that Lucas couldn't *overcome his desires*."

"I'm honored to be the first who knows about the rhythmic slapping sounds," I deadpan.

That makes her laugh, even as she rubs her face again.

"No one wants to know anything about it," she says. "It's just this embarrassing failure that happened, and the faster it can get swept under the rug, the better."

"I've got all night," I offer. "Tell me as much as you want about the squishing sounds."

I don't particularly want to hear the details of her husband getting railed in the kitchen, but I want to keep talking to Ruby like this, as if we're two regular people on an almost-regular date or something, not a trapped girl and her bodyguard.

"The squishing sounds weren't that bad," she admits. "But Lucas had this look on his face of relief, and bliss, and suddenly it was just so, *so* obvious that I was never going to be what he needed or wanted. There was just no way. So I asked for a divorce a couple weeks later, and now, here I am."

My whiskey glass is empty, and I push it aside, then lean forward over the table.

"You know it's not you, right?" I ask.

She sighs.

"I know," she says, arms folded over her chest, looking away.

"You can't make a gay guy straight any more than you can make a dog a cat," I say. "It's got nothing to do with you at all."

"It's just hard," she says quietly. "I really, really tried, and I couldn't make it work, and then when I finally gave up thinking that maybe I could start over and be happy some other way, that was almost worse. I'm pretty sure my father only took me in because it's election year and he's campaigning. The house where Lucas and I lived was actually owned by the Church, and Lucas got disowned and left to be with his boyfriend, and it's not like I had a job besides *housewife*, so here I am again."

She takes another long sip, and I study the lines in her neck as she swallows, then puts the glass down with a *clonk*.

"And I've got to figure out what I'm going to do before I wind up married to Kyle," she mutters. "Maybe I could arrange to be eaten by an alligator or something."

"A sexy cartoon alligator?"

Ruby snorts, then looks up at me.

"You knew that, but not why I got divorced?"

"Your sister said something about it on the bus, so I got curious," I admit. "Prostitutes are old hat, but the cartoon characters fucking were a new one to me. You'd think they'd run into licensing issues."

"I don't think those likenesses were exactly above board," Ruby says dryly.

"You're telling me Disney didn't grant permission for that stuff?"

"Maybe that's part of the thrill," she says. "Cartoons violating each other *and* copyright law."

I laugh again, and then Ruby starts laughing, too.

We stay at the pub for a while. She goes a little deeper into the details of her divorce—she got left with nothing, surprise—and though I don't exactly tell her why I left D.C., I talk about my time in the military and then working for the Secret Service.

"Do you know any good state secrets?" she asks.

"I only know where the Vice President's wife hides the Oreos she doesn't want the Vice President to eat," I say. "They're in a cabinet behind a toaster oven they've never taken out of the box."

"Sneaky," she says, playing with her empty glass.

I nod at it.

"Another one?"

Ruby shakes her head.

"You'd have to carry me home and pour me into bed," she says.

Sounds fine to me. Fuck, her parents aside, it sounds more than fine.

"I should get going, anyway. I'm always afraid someone will figure out that I'm missing," she goes on.

"I'll walk you if you show me how to sneak back in," I say.

"Deal," Ruby says, smiling.

CHAPTER THIRTEEN

RUBY

I DON'T WANT to leave, but I know I should. Any one of the things I've been doing tonight—going out in pants, being alone with Gabriel, drinking alcohol, reading *The Golden Compass*—would make my father flip out completely, but all of them at once?

I'd never see the light of day again. Just like there are places they send gay teens to turn them straight, there are places they send *out of control* women to make them more pliant. And to the people who run those kinds of places, it does not matter that I'm twenty-six and well into legal adulthood.

But right now? I'm having the best time I've had in months, probably since my little sister Joy and I were supposed to go pick peaches at the orchard, got turned around, couldn't find the orchard, and ended up sitting on the rocks in the river at the state park, just talking for two hours.

We got in lots of trouble when we got home without peaches, but it was worth it.

When we stand, I'm a little wobbly on my feet and Gabriel steps forward, one hand out to steady me, but he stops short.

"Am I gonna be carrying you home anyway?" he asks.

I rest my fingertips on the table and take a moment, looking around until the world straightens out a little.

"I can't remember the last time I had two drinks in one night," I admit. "And I think that second one was more than one drink."

"I'll remember that if I ever need to get important information out of you," Gabriel teases, as we walk for the door.

He pushes it open for me, and as I step through, I feel his fingertips on my lower back. His hand may as well be a cattle prod, because I swear it sends an electric charge up my spine, jolting my back straight.

It's been almost a year and a half since someone touched me that intimately. I know it sounds pathetic, but all I've gotten since the divorce has been handshakes and awkward half-hugs, mostly from family members.

So it's not exactly surprising that my extremely hot bodyguard touching my back *kinda, sorta* like we're on a date does some things to me. Any port in a storm, right?

Well, except I'd be happy to dock the S. S. Ruby in Gabriel Harbor pretty much any time. Sunny days, rainy days, cloudy days, night time, morning time, tea time...

You're drunk and ridiculous.

I take a deep breath of night air, finally cooling off, to try and clear my head. That second whiskey really got to me, though I'd never have accepted if I had to walk home alone. But since Gabriel's here, I think I'll be okay.

We walk along the uneven sidewalk, side by side, *not* touching.

Tell him you're scared and ask to hold his hand, I think.

And then tell him he's gotten something on his shirt and if he gives it to you right now, you can get it off. Maybe his pants, too.

I turn crimson and look away. It's not like I've got a lot of practice in flirting or being coy, so my face is probably pretty easy to read, and right now it's saying *hey, I'd like to see you naked.*

"I should tell you something," Gabriel finally says, as we walk past dark storefronts and houses, the Methodist church with the marquee that says GOD IS LOVE.

My parents don't like that church.

"What is it?"

"I told your father I'd report back to him."

I turn my head too fast, and everything spins for a moment. I stop in the middle of the empty sidewalk and shut my eyes, wait for the world to even out.

"I haven't," he says, before I can ask any of my million questions.

"About me, you mean."

"About anything you do that may be cause for concern, according to him."

I open my eyes and look at Gabriel, several thousand thoughts spinning through my head at once.

"Like I said, I haven't."

"Are you going to?"

"No."

"When did he ask?"

"Friday."

I think for a moment, looking at the GOD IS LOVE marquee and breathing steadily, trying to remember which day Friday was. It's not like I have a job or any reason to delineate weekdays from weekends, so it all tends to blur together.

"You didn't tell him about drinking the vodka backstage?"

"I haven't told him anything."

"*Anything.*"

"I think that's what I just said, yeah," he teases.

We start walking again. I knew that my father would probably ask Gabriel to spy on me, tell him about every single move I make, whether he has any reason to worry about my current moral standing, but I'm a little dumbfounded that Gabriel just told *me*.

If anything, I figured that my father just hadn't asked him the right questions yet, and eventually, he'd spill.

"Why are you telling me?" I ask, suspicious. It's not like I have anything he wants, anything I can trade for his silence.

Gabriel just frowns at me.

"Because I thought you should know," he says. "If your father's asking me to be Big Brother, he's probably asked other people, too."

I consider this for a moment, sneaking a glance at him from the corner of my eye. People never tell me things just because they think I should have information. Well, Lucas did, sometimes, but he wasn't exactly in the habit of it and I don't even know where he is now.

"Are you going to tell him anything?" I finally ask.

What I mean is, *what are you trying to get out of me.*

"That's actually why I brought it up," he says, pushing his hands into his pockets. We come to a street corner, both streets completely empty, but he looks left and then right out of habit.

Here it comes, I think. *This is the part where he tells me what he wants from me.*

"I've got a meeting with him tomorrow morning, and I should tell him something," he says. "If I just told him you'd been a perfect angel for the past week he might get suspicious."

"Okay," I say, still not knowing what he wants.

"But I don't know what to tell him," Gabriel goes on. "I'm not going to tell him that I caught you sneaking out to drink whiskey and read fantasy novels, but I also don't know what would keep us above suspicion without getting you into trouble."

Us. He asked what would keep *us* above suspicion. I look over at him again, and he looks back.

"What?"

"Why are you doing this?"

"Doing what?"

"Lying to my father. Your boss. I can't help you, I don't have anything you want."

Gabriel stops again in the middle of the sidewalk, looking faintly puzzled. We're on the edge of downtown Huntsburg now, the houses getting further apart, stone walls and gates separating them from the sidewalk.

"I know," he says.

"If he finds out, he'll be angry with you, too," I point out, crossing my arms over my chest.

Now Gabriel's starting to smile, one side of his mouth just barely pulling up.

"I know that too," he says. "And I'm familiar with trouble."

"So why lie to him?"

"You want to know the truth?"

I roll my eyes, exasperated.

"Yes, obviously, that's why I'm asking."

Gabriel chuckles, and now he's grinning at me.

"Because your father's kind of a creep and I like drinking whiskey with you," he says. "Most of this security job is pretty shitty and I'd like to keep the few parts that aren't."

I blink at him a few times.

"That's it?"

"You also seem like you've put up with more than enough bullshit and I don't see a reason to make your life harder," he says.

I still don't quite believe him. I'm not used to people doing things because they're nice or because they want to, I'm used to people doing things for gain or standing. After all, my father's a politician who practically runs a miniature police state.

"Is it that hard to believe that I just don't want to rat you out?" he asks, arms still crossed.

I rub my eyes, then frown at him.

"No?" I say. "It's just... unusual. But thank you."

I pause.

"Really."

"Don't worry about it," Gabriel says, and we start walking again. "But I still need something to tell your father."

I think for a moment, because I need to keep my father far, *far* away from my real vices—whiskey, Gabriel, books about magic, wearing pants, Gabriel—and give him something else to worry about. Ideally, something stupid. *Really* stupid.

And I know just the thing. I look at Gabriel and grin.

"Tell him a pale, translucent white rock fell out of my pocket," I say. "And I seemed flustered that you saw it."

"A rock."

"And make sure that you specify it had square edges and came to a dull point on top."

The gate to the house is about two blocks away. I'm starting to get nervous, my palms sweating a little. Every time I sneak back in, I run the risk of someone being awake without my knowledge, or the guards being on alert for some reason I don't know about it.

For all I know, I could have been discovered missing already, the alarm already sounded.

"You want me to tell your father you're in possession of a crystal?"

He looks at me, raising one eyebrow.

"You know that crystal meth isn't actually crystals like that, right?"

I grin, because he's picking up on my general strategy, even if he's got the details wrong.

"Not drugs. Witchcraft," I say. "You know who uses crystals like that? Fortune tellers. Mystics. Psychics. Pagans. And you know who gives all those people their powers?"

"Is it Satan?"

"Bingo."

He looks skeptical, but only because he's a normal person.

"He's really going to worry that you're dabbling in witchcraft if I tell him you've got a white crystal?" Gabriel says.

"He really will," I say, still wandering along the sidewalk, my pace slowing as I get closer to the house. "Has he told you about his war against Satan?"

"He did mention something about that," Gabriel says,

and shrugs. "Witchcraft it is, I'm sure you know much more—"

A circle of light shines on the sidewalk up ahead, right outside the gate to my house, and we both stop short. Someone's standing inside, pointing a flashlight at the sidewalk. Gabriel grabs my arm and pulls me against the stone wall separating another antebellum mansion from the sidewalk where we're standing.

I hold my breath. He doesn't let my arm go, and we're both quiet until the circle of light goes away.

"That's not normal," I whisper. "Usually there isn't anyone else around, I can just get back in the same way I got out."

Gabriel pulls his phone from his pocket and checks the time. It's a few minutes after midnight.

"They might have started doing rounds," he murmurs. "Your father wanted a twenty-four-hour patrol, but last time I was at a security meeting, Ray talked him out of it. I guess he changed his mind again."

He finally takes his hand off my arm, though I think I can still feel his fingerprints.

"That's not so bad, right?" I whisper. "We just wait for them to go around the other side of the house and sneak back in?"

"You make it sound so simple," he teases me. His voice is so quiet and low that I feel like I'm hearing it through my spine, little sparks shooting upwards as he talks.

"It doesn't have to be hard."

"I'd say you should stroll in there and tell them you were taking a walk, but you're wearing pants," he says.

"You mean Satan tubes."

Gabriel gives me a wide-eyed frown.

"I'm kidding, no one calls them that," I say. "But remind me to tell you sometime why women can't wear them."

"You could tell me now," he says, a slight grin on his face.

"Get me back inside without getting caught and I'll tell you later," I say.

"Deal."

Gabriel holds out a hand, and we shake. Then he nods his head toward my house, and leads the way, walking silently against the wall.

When we reach the gate, we stand outside and listen. After a moment, Gabriel crouches down and peeks through the very edge of the wrought iron monstrosity, staying perfectly still.

I'm sweating, even though the night's cooled off. I'm drunk, I've sneaked out, and I'm with Gabriel, who's being nice to me for no reason other than to be nice, and whose biceps I want to lick.

Finally he stands and looks back at me.

"You can get the bar out more quietly than I can," he says.

I step around him, grab the loose iron bar, and pull it just right. There's a tiny scraping noise, but it comes out almost silently. Gabriel squeezes through and I follow, putting the bar back, we duck into the small, dark space between the hedge and the wall.

After about twenty feet, he puts his hand on my shoulder and we stop again. There are branches poking into me, stiff leaves against my face. I hold my breath. Gabriel's hand stays on my shoulder, and then I can barely see his face turn toward me in the dark.

"Wait," he murmurs.

I wait. I lean back slightly, the cool stone wall against my shoulder blades, and I watch Gabriel's barely-visible face and hope that the echoing thump of my heart doesn't give us away.

Through the hedge, I can barely see a beam of light.

Please don't notice the open window, I think. *Please.*

"Probably just a cat," someone says.

"Or a raccoon or something. Did I tell you last week my mama called me nearly in hysterics, something about a bear getting into her outdoor trash can, so I drove over at seventy miles an hour and when I get there ain't nothing but raccoon prints all over the thing?"

"Yeah, you told me last night."

The voices are getting fainter.

"Shoot," the other one says, and then I can't see the light any more, but Gabriel's thumb is stroking my shoulder through my shirt, he's still looking down at me. I feel like all my muscles have liquefied.

I tilt my head up and turn my body toward him. A branch scratches my arm and I ignore it, because all I can think about is *him*, inches away from me, and he's looking at me in a way no one's ever looked at me before.

Even though it's dark, I could almost swear his gaze is hungry. Voracious. So smoldering that I think I might spontaneously combust at any second, and then he leans in, just barely.

I'm going crazy, the air between us charged and electric, the promise of his mouth on mine short-circuiting my brain, and I watch his lips, moving in closer. I'm not really sure how to do this, how to kiss someone for the first time without discussing it beforehand, but this seems right.

Gabriel swallows so hard I can hear it, and then he pulls his hand from my shoulder. My eyes open.

"You should go before they circle back," he murmurs.

The disappointment feels like a brick to my stomach, but I step back again and nod.

"Right," I whisper. "Thanks for walking me home."

I think he smiles, but it makes me feel like I just asked a friend's older, hot brother if he liked me back and he said *no*.

"Of course," he says. "Hurry up."

I take a deep breath and squeeze through the hedge, look around, and make my way for the window again.

CHAPTER FOURTEEN

GABRIEL

HOLY FUCKING CHRIST, I'm sweating. My palms are wet and there are droplets snaking down the back of my neck, all with the sheer force of being this close to Ruby and telling her to leave.

There's another version of me who would have kissed her, pushed her up against the stone wall behind us, wrapped her legs around me and asked her how bad a girl she *really* was. But that guy is the reason I'm here at all, because that guy couldn't keep his dick in his pants no matter what the consequences were.

And I'm not that guy. I'm *celibate Gabriel*, who drinks iced tea on his patio and does nice things for Senator's daughters and doesn't want anything in return, no matter how insanely tempting they are.

Through the hedge, Ruby stops for a moment, looks around, then looks up at the house. She walks the same semi-circle as when she sneaked out, entering the row of rose bushes at the same spot, then sliding behind them.

I see a light around the side of the house. They can't see her and she can't see them, but the flashlight beam wanders lazily, here and there, while Ruby ducks between roses and moves toward the window.

I clench one hand into a fist and put it to my mouth, watching. There's nothing I can do except make it worse if we got caught — I'm almost certain I'd set off the motion-detector lights, and then Ruby's father would be even angrier at her and I'd be fired.

The lights get closer. Ruby reaches the window and slides it all the way open noiselessly, standing on her tiptoes. I take one moment to appreciate the view of her perfect ass in that tight denim, imagine standing behind her right now, my hard-as-iron cock pressed against her while I lick the shell of her ear —

"And then she tells me that..." the voice trails off into something I can't hear, but the guys coming around the house are getting closer.

Ruby grabs the windowsill. She pauses for a moment, then jumps, pushing herself up. For a second she wobbles, my heart constricting as I think *I got her too drunk to get back in, she's going to get caught and it's all my fault*—but she tilts herself forward and hoists one leg over the windowsill until she's straddling it.

She looks dead at me, motionless, her face cool and impassive and unreadable as the two security guys get closer and closer to the corner. I nearly shout *GO!* At her, but instead I clench my jaw silently and after another second, Ruby disappears into the darkness of her house and slides the window shut.

The security guys come around the corner, still talking about a girlfriend or something, the light flicking around. I lean against the stone wall and let out a long, shuddering breath as quietly as I can.

That girl is gonna get you in serious trouble, I think.

And I grin, because if it's *that* girl, I don't mind.

———

SATURDAY, her father's got a rally at a county fair about ninety minutes south of us. For once, everyone in the house is excited about this—because, after all the speeches and the talking, they'll get to go to the fair for a few hours. The Senator will be busy telling teenagers in 4-H not to do drugs and trying to look impressed at prize-winning chickens, but everyone else gets to go on rides and eat funnel cake.

Hell, even I'm excited. My parents took my sister and me to a ton of county fairs when we were growing up, all across the country, since we moved so much. I've still got a soft spot for rigged midway games, dangerous rides, and enormous pumpkins.

The house that morning is complete pandemonium, full of Ruby's family, her father's staff, her father's security, and plenty of people who don't seem to serve a purpose other than standing around.

Still, when the Senator storms in through the front door, glowering like a thunderstorm, everyone notices and gets quiet.

"Gabriel," he growls.

I stand instantly.

"Yes, sir," I say.

He holds up an envelope, glares at me, then walks past, up the stairs. Everyone pretends that they're not watching us as I follow.

Even with just a glimpse, I think I recognize the writing on the envelope. I think it's Ruby's stalker, and my stomach sinks. The Senator stalks into his office, me right behind him.

"Close the door after yourself," he barks over his shoulder, and I do.

He throws the envelope onto the table, then sits heavily in his huge leather chair, glowering at it. I nod at the letter on his desk.

"Ruby's stalker?" I ask.

"Read it," he commands.

I pull the letter out. It's a shorter one, just two hand-written pages in his strange, spidery, all-capital handwriting, but by the second sentence it's turned my stomach, because by now he's really getting right to the point.

He calls her names: Jezebel, Lilith, a fallen woman, things that sound biblical that I've never heard of but that I can tell are bad. He tells her that she's brought sin, plague, and corruption on her father's house and shame on her father's name, and I think it's because she dared to get divorced.

Every letter makes me see red, even before I'd ever really talked to her. This guy's a sick fucking son of a bitch, and I'd love to meet him just so I can crumple his face in.

Then I get to the next page, to what he wants to do to her. It's way, way worse than the last one. Clearly he thinks that Ruby is some sort of kindred spirit to his fucked-up, twisted, dark soul. This time, he doesn't just want to rape her like he did in the last letter.

This one talks about months of abuse. Years maybe. He wants to force her to be his for life, have his children, probably never see the light of day again.

I can't finish the letter. It makes me nauseous, and I've seen bodies cut in half by shrapnel. I'm pacing back and forth, shaking and sweating with rage, and I can't stop imagining this asshole doing these horrible things to Ruby.

And I can't stop thinking about how easy it was for her to sneak in and out.

I keep an eye on the trash can, because I think I might actually vomit.

"I don't want Ruby going to the fair today," the Senator says. "This has escalated precipitously. From now on, she doesn't go anywhere without an escort. She stays with people at all times."

"Actually, sir, I think she might be safer at the fair."

The Senator folds his arms in front of himself, listening.

"In here she'll be a sitting duck. Even though the house is well-secured, it's fairly secluded, back from the road. It would be easier to get her alone here, and it would only take seconds for something terrible to happen. The fair will be crowded, hundreds of people around, and frankly, sir, I'm not a psychiatrist but this—"

—this piece of fucking lowlife scum—

"—person doesn't seem to have a firm enough grasp on reality to pull anything off in public like that."

As sickening as the letters are, I'm still not convinced that the writer is actually planning on doing anything. His revolting plans for her are fanciful at best and seem to change slightly each time he writes. Really, I think he gets off on writing letters and thinking about her reading them.

But I'm not an expert in psychology. And it's not my job to figure out whether he's serious. It's my job to take him at his word and protect Ruby.

The Senator rises from his chair, puts the letter into a drawer in his desk and slams it shut before walking to the window and looking out.

"I've alerted both the Huntsburg police and the FBI to the great evil in our midst, but nothing's been done," he says, and for the first time, he doesn't sound like the Senator. He sounds like someone's father, sad and worried that he can't protect his child.

"There's no return address, no handwriting on file, nothing of the sort. So instead of taking action, we do nothing, and hope to stem the rot at our core."

I don't know what he's talking about, or why Ruby's stalker is the rot at our core, but I feel a sudden stab of sympathy for him.

"I'm sure we'll bring him to justice someday soon, sir," I say.

He walks up to me, hands in his pockets, and looks me dead in the eye, once more the Senator.

"Frankly, son, if I have my way it'll be God's own justice, not the justice of the courtroom," he says quietly.

Then he walks toward the huge door to his office.

"I'll inform Ruby," he says, and I follow him out and down the stairs.

I hang back as he tells her. She's smearing sunscreen onto a kid's face, smiling perfectly and beatifically as she does. The smile only falters for a split second as her father talks and then it's back, beautiful and unwavering.

As her father walks off, she looks at me, steady and unreadable, and then she goes back to smearing the kid with sunscreen.

For just a split second I imagine her, tied down to a dirty bed, terror in her green eyes, and the thought alone sends a spike of fury and rage through my chest.

I'll find him, I swear silently. *I'll find him and I'll fuck him up good.*

THE BUS RIDE to the Holtville County Fair is noisy, tedious, and boring. Ruby's up front while I'm in the back with the rest of security, making innocuous small talk about weather and guns.

When we get to the fair, the bus goes to a parking lot labeled VIP. It's not a real parking lot, just a field with half-dead grass, but we lurch along until we've pulled up alongside a few other buses. The air outside the cool bus is sticky and heavy with the smell of grass, my shirt sticking to my back as soon as I get out.

Ruby's standing off to one side, talking to her mother.

"Good morning, Gabriel," she says, tilting her head and smiling her sweet smile at me.

"Ruby, Mrs. Burgess," I say.

Mrs. Burgess nods. Her smile doesn't reach her eyes.

"It looks like the stage is already set up and ready," I say. "I'm sorry to interrupt, but if you don't mind, I'd like to go over a few final security notes with Ruby before the rally begins."

"Of course," Ruby says.

Her mother's eyes flick from my face to hers.

"I think I'd also like to hear them," she says. "Can never be too careful, you know."

She just doesn't want to leave the two of us alone, not even perfectly visible, just out of earshot. The fuck does she think I'm going to do, throw Ruby over my shoulder and run away with her?

It's not the worst thought, but I'm not a goddamn barbarian.

"Very true," I say, leading them a bit away from the bus, toward the temporary stage behind a tall chain-link fence.

"All right," I say to Ruby. "You remember where the exits are?"

She points.

"There, there, there, and... I think there's one behind the stands on the other side that I can't see."

"Rendezvous point?"

"Ticket booth at the main fair."

"If there's an active shooter?"

"Run in a zig-zag pattern, get behind something."

"If someone grabs you?"

"Raise he—"

She stops, and her mother's head jerks around, eyes wide at her daughter. Ruby swallows, turning pink, but dcesn't look at her mom.

"Make lots of noise," she says quietly. "And if he tries to carry me somewhere, go limp."

I force myself not to smile.

"If he attacks you at close range?"

"Kick him... between the legs."

I'm still not smiling, but we both know that underneath the wide eyes and the sweet smile, she's thinking *kick him in the balls*.

I smile at her professionally, nodding once. Her mother is still trying to smile sweetly, but it's obvious that she's found something wrong here, though I don't even know what. This has all been perfectly above-board, aside from Ruby nearly saying *raise hell*.

Maybe that was it. I don't know.

"I think you're ready," I say.

"Thanks," she answers.

"We should get back to the group," her mother says. "I'm sure they're wondering where we are."

I doubt that, but I follow her back toward the van anyway, Mrs. Burgess leading, Ruby and I two steps behind.

As we walk, her hand bumps mine, and we both pull back automatically.

"Sorry," I say.

"Sorry," she mutters, and we look at each other.

I'm not sorry, her eyes say.

I'm not either, I think.

CHAPTER FIFTEEN

RUBY

I'M PRETTY SURE my parents have resolved that I not be alone with Gabriel again. Since we got back from the lecture at the college last weekend, I've been subjected to a thousand questions about where we were, what we were doing, why I wandered off.

A woman on her own is automatically suspicious. Any time I'm not being watched, I'm susceptible to *bad influences*. Like I'm screwing the whole football team or something any time a family member isn't looking directly at me.

I'm not, obviously, though sneaking out, drinking, and reading *The Golden Compass* is almost as bad.

The day goes as planned. I'm running around again, trying to help set up, corral kids, fix ties, fetch snacks. I didn't even bother to bring the flask.

Gabriel fades into the background, watching everything silently, and I try very hard not to think about how I want to lick the sweat off his neck, or about being in the dark behind the hedge with him two nights ago.

Really, if I could just erase that from my mind, everything would be better. My heart might stop skipping a beat every time we make eye contact. Maybe I could act normal around him.

We say another prayer as we're all about to go on stage. I think it'll be the same speech as last time, only with more drunk rednecks in the audience, wearing sleeveless t-shirts and waving plastic American flags. That just means it'll take longer, since the speeches have to pause for every new bout of shouting and cheering.

Just before I'm set to go on stage, a finger taps my shoulder, and I turn.

"You remember the sniper spots?" he asks.

My mother is ten feet away, giving someone else a dressing-down because the girl's skirt comes above her knee when she sits.

"Top of the stands," I say, pointing. "Roof of the bathroom building, maybe even the top of the barn, but that's probably too far away."

"I don't think this guy has the training for that," Gabriel admits.

This guy? Of course he doesn't have the training, he doesn't exist.

"What makes you think that?" I ask.

"Just a feeling I get from the letters," he says, glancing behind me. He drops his voice. "I'll tell you when I get a chance."

I glance around. For these few blissful moments, no one is even looking at us, so I take a deep breath.

"There's no guy," I murmur, looking away from Gabriel, like I'm not even talking to him. "It's all fake so my father could hire someone to watch my every move."

"Ruby!" my mother shouts, and I turn.

"It's not," Gabriel says, his voice hushed, low, and urgent.

I'm taken aback, and I frown at him for a moment.

"*Ruby*," my mother calls again.

"It's not your father," Gabriel says, his voice almost a whisper. He reaches toward my shoulder but pulls his hand back, like he's suddenly remembered where we are and that there are rules.

I give him one last glance, then turn away, following my mother's insistent voice, Gabriel's eyes on my back.

I've got a smile on my face, but there's a cold chill in the pit of my stomach.

Gabriel doesn't know what he's talking about, I think.

But what if he's right?

———

THIS TIME, while my father talks, I can't stop looking at the top row of the aluminum grandstands, shining in the bright sun. I keep watching the roof of the building with the bathrooms, even the barn. Every time a car pulls into the VIP parking field I look over, nervously wondering if it's the flash of light on a rifle barrel.

Because I believe Gabriel. Or, at the very least: I believe that he thinks the letters are real, and that knowledge sends something cold crawling down my spine.

Maybe my father's hoodwinking him, too. This could be some kind of mind game, some sort of double-cross where he's really working for my father and only pretending to be nice to me. But the urgency in his voice, the way he almost touched me in front of everyone—all that makes me want to believe him.

The speeches last forever. I think my father might never stop talking, all while everyone on the stage behind him slowly melts in the hot September sun. I'm pretty sure the back of my t-shirt is soaked through with sweat, and I can feel it trickling down my pantyhose-clad legs.

And I can feel Gabriel watching me from the side of the stage where he stands, huge and tall and official-looking, arms crossed in front of himself. For once I wish he wouldn't, because by the time I get off this stage I might be a puddle. A disgusting, sweaty puddle, still wearing a shapeless khaki skirt and pantyhose.

My father finishes talking to huge applause and flag-waving. Just like every time I have to sit here and listen to him bloviate, I wonder if these people understand what they're really voting for. They hear *Return to Moral America* and imagine a Norman Rockwell painting of the 1950s: Dad at work, mom in the kitchen, two perfect kids and a Golden Retriever in the back yard.

But the reality is Lucas, who suffered for years and years before finally getting disowned by his own father. The reality is Kyle, who I don't even like, but who ended up going to prostitutes instead of having a girlfriend like a normal guy, or it's Mason, a grown man who can barely make eye contact with a woman.

The reality is *me*, an adult woman who's never had a job, who has to hide her checking account from her own father. It's not that I don't want a job. I'd love to get one, move away from my parents, maybe even go to college. But figuring out how to do all that is gonna be a *task*.

Someone else goes up to the microphone and thanks him. More applause, and then at last, amidst lots of flag and sign waving, we all finally stand and get off the stage. The moment I do, I can feel twin trickles of sweat down the backs of my legs, damp underneath the pantyhose.

It is really, really unpleasant, but I pretend it's not happening and descend the stairs, passing by Gabriel.

"Didn't get sniped," I say as he falls in next to me.

"Nicely done," he says, his voice low. Even this tiny, dumb conversation seems dangerous, because I'm afraid it makes it obvious that we know each other better than we're supposed to.

As if on cue, my sister Grace turns and gives me a look. I just smile bigger and sweeter at her.

There's no real backstage. The stage was set up on the same field as the VIP parking, so besides the building that houses the bathrooms and the attached sheds, it's just grass, an area for us cordoned off with plastic tape.

People mob the plastic tape, shouting things at my father. Some of the people seem angry, but most of them are holding red, white, and blue MORAL AMERICA signs, and he's fully in his element, shaking hands and kissing babies. The whole politician routine.

Slowly, we make our way to the fairgrounds, my father glad-handing the whole way. Someone hands out tickets, and then we finally enter the fair proper.

"This is *great*," Gabriel says.

I look over at him, raising one eyebrow. I hadn't expected him to be the county fair type.

"I didn't know you were a fair enthusiast," I say.

"I have a soft spot for them," he says, grinning. "Where else can you see enormous pumpkins and eat funnel cake?"

I think for a moment as we walk on a wide boulevard between a row of shiny new agricultural equipment—the latest models, all for sale—and a huge red barn, animal noises issuing forth. Someone's kid sprints toward a tractor and starts to climb, only for his mom to pull him off, shouting.

"I don't know that I've seen funnel cake for sale anywhere else," I admit.

Up ahead is a small fenced-off area, and inside it, someone's riding a small tractor around in circles, doing some sort of demonstration.

"That's what makes it special," Gabriel says.

"Maybe there's no funnel cake anywhere else because funnel cake isn't actually—"

There's a huge bang up ahead. Someone screams, and I jump backward, scraping my arm against the tractor.

Then there's another bang, this one bigger and louder and longer. A puff of smoke rises into the sky, and I'm standing there, frozen, mouth open.

"RUBY!" Gabriel shouts, and I realize he's got his hand on my arm, pulling me as the scene breaks into pandemonium. I swear everyone is screaming and running, men shouting and pulling guns out of holsters, pointing them around wildly.

His grip tightens until it hurts but it's effective. I nearly trip over my own feet but I follow as he practically drags me ten feet into the barn, around the wall and into a dark corner.

"Get down," he growls, yanking me again until I half-crumple to the ground, straw and dirt sticking into my knees.

It's dark. It smells like cows and earth and wood, but Gabriel's on his knees in front of me, my back against the rough wall of the barn and he's got one forearm against the wall above my head, leaning over me.

There's *another* bang from outside the barn, and I shut my eyes. More shouting.

Someone's finally tried to kill my father.

My heart just about stops. For all his talk about terrorists and suicide bombers in our midst, I never took him seriously.

"Are you okay?" Gabriel asks, his face inches from mine.

I've still got my eyes closed and I just nod, scraped knees aside, his hand still on my arm.

"What happened?"

"I don't know."

There's a long, mechanical grinding sound outside. The shouting dies down, and I hold my breath, bracing myself for another horrible sound.

Instead, I hear someone laugh.

"Well, shoot," a voice says. "You all right?"

I can't make out the answer, but it gets another laugh.

"...in the tailpipe? What on earth?"

"Must have..."

I release a long, shaky breath and relax against the wall.

Not terrorists. Not an assassin, not my stalker.

Voices rise again, a tangle of people saying *are you okay* and *what on earth was that* and *I got mud all over this shirt.* After a moment I open my eyes again.

Gabriel's face is inches away from mine, his huge form still leaning over me. He softens his grip on my arm.

"Sorry about that," he murmurs. "Are you okay?"

I'm still breathing hard, adrenaline rushing through my veins, but I nod and swallow.

"Yeah," I say. "Yeah, I'm fine."

Gabriel doesn't answer, just looks at me, his eyes searching mine, his face inches away as my heart slams in my chest, the two of us huddled on the ground in this dark corner of the dairy barn. We're frozen like that for a long moment, my breath suddenly caught in my throat as I forget about everything that just happened, about the tractor and my father and the state fair.

All I know is he's here, right in front of me. Closer than he's been, closer than he should be, and this time I don't stop myself.

We both lean in and then his mouth is on mine, firm and soft all at once. A thrill like an atomic explosion sizzles through me, my nerves crackling and jangling, and he slides his rough hand behind my neck and pushes me back until I'm pressed against the wall of the barn.

I snake one hand through his hair, pulling him against me, desperately, *needing* this. I have no idea what I'm doing but it feels so right that I can't stop.

Gabriel pulls away for half a second, tilts his head, kisses me again. I open my mouth under his as he grabs my waist, pulls me in, his big hand sliding around me until his fingers are against my spine, four points of pressure sending an electrical charge through my whole body.

We kiss furiously, ferociously, like this is the only chance we'll ever get. All I want is him, his mouth on mine, his hands on my body after what feels like years of frustration, and he's pulling me into him and pushing me back against the wall all at once, his lips rough on mine as our tongues tangle together.

I shift on the ground, unfold one leg, stretch it out to one side so our thighs are touching. His grip on my back tightens and his hand moves down until it's squeezing my hip, right above my butt. I tighten my hand in his hair, the other on his shoulder.

Gabriel groans. It's barely audible, but the sound sends a thrill through me, from my toes to the top of my head.

"—you seen Ruby?" a voice asks just outside the barn.

We both jerk back instantly. I hold my breath, and for an instant, we stare at each other.

Then Gabriel rocks to his feet. He clears his throat and offers me his hand, helping me off the ground.

"I've got her," he calls as I stand.

For one more moment, we lock eyes, neither of us saying a word. I'm still too surprised to even think.

"You in here?" Ray's voice calls, and then I see his silhouette at the barn entrance.

Gabriel's fingers on my lower back nudge me forward, and then, just like that, it's over. I've got my smile on again, I brush the dirt and straw off myself, I smooth my hair against my head.

"Oh, phew," Ray says when he sees us. "I thought we might have a situation on our hands for a second there."

I swallow, then widen my eyes, blinking as innocently as I can. Like I wasn't just making out with my bodyguard, ready to wrap my legs around him in a dairy barn.

"What happened?" I ask.

CHAPTER SIXTEEN

GABRIEL

RUBY WALKS out of the dairy barn and into the bright sunlight, blinking, her blonde hair gleaming in the sunlight. Her face doesn't have a single hint of what just happened. Looking at her perfect, sweet smile, you'd never guess that I finally just kissed her on the floor of a barn. That I was ten seconds from my hand up her skirt and her legs around my waist.

As we pass Ray, I swear to God he gives me a look. A suspicious look. An *I-know-what-you're-up-to-and-I-ain't-having-none* look.

I nod at him once, professionally, pretending my dick's not so fucking hard I think it might fall off.

"What *was* that?" Ruby is asking her brother, Zeke, who's standing next to a tractor, brushing himself off.

"The terrorists are winning," he says, keeping his voice low so no one else can hear them.

Ruby just gives him an obvious *don't smartass me* look.

"The tailpipe of the bushwhacker someone's demonstrating over there somehow got stuffed with mud and straw," Zeke says, his voice louder this time. "It backed up or something, there was a small explosion, and then everyone carrying a gun pulled it out and started looking for the bad guys."

"Mechanical problems and bad timing, not an assassination attempt," Ruby says.

Or a kidnapping attempt, I think.

"Right," Zeke confirms.

———

WITH A GROUP THIS SIZE, anything takes forever, so we stand around the tractors for another ten minutes at least. Ruby makes nice small talk with her siblings and with the other women of the party, and I painstakingly imagine taking apart, cleaning, and re-assembling every weapon I've ever handled.

It almost does the trick, though every time I look over at Ruby I think of her lips on mine, the way her back arched into me when I put my arm around her, her hands in my hair pulling me in desperately.

And then I have to think about more weapon reassembly. It's a vicious cycle.

The large group does splinter apart eventually, but it's not as if Ruby and I are going to be wandering the Hall of Mirrors alone together. We get stuck with her sister Grace, her husband and two kids, Joy, Pearl, Ruby's sister-in-law Deborah, the Senator's aide Mason and his girlfriend Lilah, and another security guy whose name I think is Danny.

There are no more opportunities to be alone. I can't tell if this is standard or if her sisters are getting suspicious of Ruby. I just know that every time she excuses herself for the restroom, someone else also happens to need to pee.

Even though I was looking forward to the fair, now all I

want to do is get it over with. Instead, we wander down the midway, slowly, watching poor saps get suckered into trying to win their girlfriends giant teddy bears.

For half a second, I think about trying to win Ruby a giant teddy bear. I probably could. But it wouldn't exactly ease suspicions.

We watch a wool-spinning demonstration. We visit prize chickens. We get funnel cake and have to say a blessing before we can eat it. We look at very large vegetables. Ruby and I have scintillating conversations along the lines of:

"Gosh, that prize-winning rabbit is very fluffy, isn't it?"

"That *is* a very fluffy rabbit."

When we get to the roosters, I consider asking her whether she likes big cocks, but I don't. I just walk along, a respectful two feet away from her, while she explains birds to her nephew.

It's torture. It was bad enough having to stop earlier, but wandering around this fair, surrounded by her suspicious family, looking at farm animals while wanting nothing more than to pull her into a stall and put my hands under her skirt?

Excruciating.

Then, toward the end of the day, we visit prize-winning quilts. Ruby takes her time, looking at each quilt slowly and methodically, each one hung on scaffolding, making enormous quilt-lined cubicles of the building we're in.

I follow her. She points out the different techniques and stitches used in each one, speculating on why they won. Since I don't know the first thing about quilts, it's actually kind of interesting.

We walk around the corner of a quilt-cubicle, and then suddenly, we're alone again, facing an enormous quilt that the plaque says is made entirely from neckties, gathered into a starburst pattern.

"So," she says, looking at the quilt and not at me.

I can hear her sisters talking, maybe fifty feet away. I clear my throat and look at the quilt as well.

"Sorry if I got you dirty earlier," I say, keeping my voice low and even, like we're talking about nothing. "In the dairy barn."

"I don't mind a little dirt."

My eyes are practically boring holes in this damn quilt, but I'm thinking of her leg against mine, the noise she made as she shifted her hips against me, and my insides feel like a furnace.

"Good," I say, as steadily as I can. "Because I can't guarantee it won't happen again."

"I'll make sure I'm prepared," she says, her eyes still locked on the quilt with laser-like focus. "Just in case I get even dirtier next time."

My mouth goes dry. I swallow, and from those two sentences I can feel the blood rushing to my dick. Ruby glances at me and we make eye contact, quickly.

She blinks once, as innocent as can be.

"Isaac, get *over* here!" her sister Grace scolds from somewhere else in the building.

"Gabriel," Ruby says, her voice low.

I raise both eyebrows.

"Why do you think my father didn't write the letters?"

"Isaac, stop that or Daddy's going to give you a spanking. I'm counting to three. One. *Two*."

"Because they're way too fucked up," I say quickly, hoping everyone else is preoccupied with Isaac's bad behavior to be listening to us. "I know your father has a lot of problems, but not like this. This is way, way beyond anything like that, Ruby."

She looks back at the quilt.

"He would go pretty far to keep me in line if it made him look good," she says.

"Not this far," I say. "And if it got out that he'd written them? He'd be done. It wasn't him. Believe me."

"I want to."

Just as I open my mouth, Grace appears around a quilt, her baby strapped to her in a sling, Isaac attached to her hand, his chin quivering.

"It's the hand-stitching on the details here that's really impressive," Ruby says without missing a beat, pointing to something or other on the quilt in front of us.

"We're going," Grace interrupts. "Can you take him for a minute? Emma's about to get fussy, too."

Across the way I see her husband, talking to another man, not even looking in Grace's direction, totally oblivious to the double-meltdown that seems imminent from his children. But Ruby swoops in, takes Isaac's hand, and crouches down in front of him.

"Okay, buddy," she says very, very seriously, her face scrunching into a goofy frown. "What seems to be the problem here?"

He stares at her for one second, frowns, and grins.

"Silly," he says.

———

WHEN WE GET BACK to the house that evening, the men all head to the living room while the women all go into the kitchen. Even though they've been on their feet all day, walking around, and half of them are sunburned, food production kicks into high gear anyway.

I don't get to talk to Ruby again, at least not alone. I'm perfectly free to share my thoughts on which bunny was fluffiest as I stand next to her, peeling potatoes—not a man's job in this household, but I was raised to be useful—but we can't talk about anything real.

Like how dirty I might get her next time I see her alone.

After dinner, the hangers-on finally leave, the family retires to bed, and I walk across the back yard to the carriage house, tired, dusty and sweaty from the fair, but still wound up as fuck.

My head is swirling as I open the door and turn on the lights, open my fridge, and pour a tall glass of unsweetened iced tea, my new bedtime ritual. If this stuff has caffeine in it, I sure can't tell.

I don't go outside to the patio, I just lean against the counter. The downstairs of my apartment is open-plan, so it's all just one big room: a couch pointing at a TV, a square dining table, a small kitchen with a few feet of counter space, a stove, an oven, a dishwasher, and a fridge. Stairs leading up to the second floor, which has two bedrooms and another bathroom.

As I'm standing there, lights illuminate the second and third stories of the big house. Most have curtains over them, and if I can see anything, it's just blurry ovals, though even that feels strange and creepy.

I walk to my own front windows, one hand on the curtains to pull them closed, when someone in the big house yanks the curtains open in Ruby's room.

Of course I know which room is hers. It's my job, but my hand freezes, my blinds still up.

She's standing there, both hands on the windowsill, and

though she's backlit I can tell that she's looking at me across the yard. I look back, taking a long drink of iced tea and wishing for the millionth time that it were something a whole lot stronger.

It's just this situation, I tell myself. *If you were back in D.C., not this weirdo hyper-strict practically-Amish compound, you'd be getting laid somewhere else and you wouldn't be worried about Ruby at all.*

I don't know that I believe myself. Ruby's motionless for another moment, and then she pulls her curtains closed again. I let my blinds drop, finish the rest of my iced tea, and hit the shower before bed.

I jerk off thinking about her, yet again, except this time I've got something to really go on as I imagine her body underneath me, on top of me, her green eyes half-shut with pleasure. Her gasping and shouting my name as I lick her again and again, her thighs around my ears.

When I come into the shower drain I grunt, the sound echoing off the bathroom walls, and I lean against the tile, breathing hard.

There are a million ways to solve lust, I tell myself. *That's all this is: she's the only cute girl anywhere around, and you're still getting used to this celibacy thing.*

You can do anything for a couple of months, Kane. You've done way fucking harder.

I don't quite believe myself, and exhausted as I am, I don't sleep well at all that night.

———

MORNING BRINGS ANOTHER CONUNDRUM: the letters.

I need Ruby to believe me about them. She's in danger

and she deserves to know exactly how, her father be damned. I can't blame her for thinking he's behind them, either—for any other situation it would be a crazy, paranoid leap, but for her?

If I hadn't read them, I might agree with her.

Today's Sunday, so it's the Sabbath. That means church from eight in the morning until three in the afternoon: Sunday School, which Ruby teaches and I therefore attend; Bible Study, in which we read seemingly random passages aloud and then discuss them; a sermon by the Revered Dawson; Worship Team, which involves singing; lunch break; more sermon; more Worship Team.

In short, way more church than I'm used to, even though I also went last week. It's also way more intense than the churches I attended growing up. We didn't take the Book of Revelation literally, for instance, but the Word of God Apostolic Covenant Church certainly does.

After church, we all go back to the house. The Sabbath is supposed to be a day of rest, but apparently that doesn't apply to housework, so the moment we get back, the women head into the kitchen. I'm about to follow when the Senator calls my name, and my back goes ramrod straight.

"Yes, sir," I answer.

"Could I talk to you for a moment?" he asks. "I think she's pretty safe for the time being."

I start sweating instantly.

He knows. Ray saw, someone saw, and I'm about to get fired.

I tell myself that if he knew, if he even *suspected* what happened yesterday I'd already have been sent packing in disgrace, never to have my real job back. Or, given how powerful Burgess is, any job within spitting distance of governmental security.

In his office, I close the door behind myself. The Senator gestures at me to sit in a chair, facing his desk, and then leans back in his own chair, looking at the huge cross on the wall to my right.

"I've been worrying more and more for Ruby's soul of late," he starts, and it's a hell of a way to start a conversation. "Tell me, Gabriel, have you noticed anything that might worry a father?"

Well, sir, she sneaks out regularly to read books and drink whiskey.

She owns pants.

We kissed in the barn, and if someone hadn't come in, I don't think we would have stopped.

Instead of saying any of those things, I sigh and furrow my brow.

"To tell the truth, sir, I'm not exactly sure what I'm looking for."

He nods thoughtfully, still looking at the cross.

"I suppose I'm asking for your thoughts on a spiritual level. Whether you've noticed anything about my daughter to make you think she might not be pure of heart. If she's acted sly or suspicious in any way, if she seems secretive, that sort of thing," he says, steepling his fingers together.

I could just tell him. He's got the keys to my future in his hands, and it's what he wants. I could throw Ruby under the bus, get my job back, and get laid plenty when I'm back in D.C. after a few more months.

It'd be a whole lot easier, and I'd be a whole lot less likely to find myself in trouble.

"Well, sir..." I say, letting my words fall from my mouth slowly. "There was something."

He looks over at me, and suddenly I realize he's got

Ruby's eyes. Or maybe she has his. I guess I know where she gets that piercing, commanding stare from.

"Yes?" he asks, his voice quiet and dangerous.

"I'm sure it's nothing," I say, leaning forward.

I'm not much of an actor, but I'm really swinging for the fences right now.

"The other day, we were speaking, and when she went in her pocket for something, a white stone fell out."

Ruby, you better be right about this or I'll seem like an idiot.

The Senator frowns.

"Go on."

I shrug.

"It was fairly small, kind of blocky, pointy on top, and maybe a milky, translucent color? The only reason I remember it at all is that she seemed pretty flustered that I saw it. Picked it up right away, shoved it into her pocket, turned bright red. But it just looked like a rock to me," I say, shrugging.

His eyes are just about burning holes through me now. I think that means it's working.

"Is that all?" he asks, his voice quiet.

I shake my head and smile, like I'm apologizing.

"Sorry, sir," I say. "Your daughter's remarkably well-behaved."

He looks at the cross again.

"I'm not so sure about that," he says, his voice darker. "Gabriel, I'm going to need to ask more from you. From now on—"

There's a knock on his office door, and he stops. The door opens slightly, and Mrs. Burgess pokes her head through.

"Darling, I'm so sorry," she says. "But the Reverend's downstairs. He said he stopped by to give you something?"

He frowns, then smooths the front of his shirt.

"Did he say what?"

"He didn't."

The Senator thinks for a moment, then nods his head once.

"I think I know what this is," he says. "I'm so sorry, son, if you'll excuse me for just a moment."

The Senator and Mrs. Burgess leave me alone in the office, the door still open.

As I hear them going downstairs, I have an idea.

It's a dangerous idea, and I definitely shouldn't do it. I think I might already be on thin ice.

On the other hand, it can't be a worse idea than making out with Ruby in public.

Quietly, I stand. I walk to the desk, crouch behind it, and pull on a drawer. Ruby said that he kept them here, somewhere, and this is the best way I can think of to get her to believe me—just show her.

I pull open drawer after drawer, but there are no letters. I hear loud male voices downstairs and hold my breath, still pulling them open.

The Senator invites the Reverend to stay for dinner. The Reverend says he can't stay, he's got to get going, and the front door opens.

I pull on another drawer and *there's* the stack of letters, finally. I grab the top few, fold them in half, shove them in my pocket, and shut the drawer. The Senator walks in just as I sit in the chair again, hands behind my head like I've been perfectly still and relaxed this whole time.

"My apologies," he says. "Where were we?"

CHAPTER SEVENTEEN

WATCHING Gabriel ascend the stairs after my father, my heart just about stops. I know he's about to be quizzed on my behaviors again, and it gives me a raw, ugly, vulnerable feeling in the pit of my stomach.

It doesn't matter that, at this point, Gabriel's got as many secrets from my father as I do. He's not me. If he has an indiscretion, it doesn't reflect poorly on my father the way mine do.

Besides, Gabriel's a man, and in my father's reasoning, men aren't to blame when they give in to temptation. Women are to blame for tempting them in the first place, which is why I wear ugly sacks, pantyhose, and extra-large t-shirts everywhere I go.

My father's got money and power. I don't know why exactly Gabriel is on leave from the Secret Service or how that led to him being here, but I know my father's influence is the ticket to him getting his old life back.

All I've got, to put it very bluntly, is a vagina, and I'm pretty sure someone who looks like Gabriel can find a willing one of those just about anywhere he looks.

I want to trust him. My gut says to trust him. But I don't know if that's smart.

They're up there for twenty minutes. I take out my frustrations on bread dough, kneading it until my arms ache and my face is red from exertion. My little sister Joy looks at me funny, but she doesn't say anything. No one else seems to notice.

I shove the bread dough into three separate bread pans, open the hot oven, and shove them in. Just as I'm putting the last loaf in, there's a voice behind me.

"Need help?" Gabriel asks.

I jump, stand too fast, and my left forearm just above the oven mitt touches red-hot metal.

I yelp in surprise and pain, and everyone in the kitchen turns and looks at me.

"Are you okay?" Joy asks, standing at the sink, the water running.

I just look at the shiny, burned patch of skin, still surprised.

"I think so?"

"You need to run cool water on that," Gabriel says, and gently takes my other arm. He pulls me away from the oven and closes the door. As I walk to the sink, Joy backing away, it finally starts to hurt.

I'd almost forgotten how bad burns hurt, and I bite my lip, shaking the oven mitt off my hand. Gabriel's still got a hand on my shoulder as he adjusts the water temperature, checks it, and I plunge my forearm under.

I exhale with instant relief. Gabriel takes his hand from my shoulder, and my mom and other sister go back to what they were doing. Joy's still standing there, eyes wide, like she's not sure what to do.

"I'm so sorry," Gabriel says, his voice low. "I didn't mean to surprise you like that, I thought you heard me."

I shake my head, turning my forearm back and forth under the water.

"Just jumpy," I say, and glance at him, even though Joy's watching.

I think Gabriel knows why I'm jumpy, but neither of us says anything. After a few minutes, he grabs a kitchen towel and runs it under the cool water, then sits me down at the kitchen table, the damp towel on my burn.

My mother glances over, and maybe I'm imagining things, but I think she looks suspicious. I straighten my back and make sure I'm not within a foot of touching Gabriel.

"I'm so sorry," he murmurs again. "I really didn't mean to frighten you."

"It was just clumsiness," I say, glancing up at his face. "Not your fault. You didn't push me into the oven, you know."

"But I can still apologize, right?" he asks. There might be a hint of a smile around his eyes, or I might be imagining it.

"Well, have you got something to apologize for?" I ask.

I don't think we're talking about the accidental burn any longer.

I glance over at my mother and sisters, but my mother is scolding Pearl for making lumpy gravy, and Joy has the water in the kitchen sink running as she stares out the window, daydreaming.

"Only for scaring you," he says, the smile around his eyes deepening, his voice lowering even further. "Like you just said, I didn't actually *do* anything."

Relief washes through me. He didn't tell my father what I've been up to, even though it probably would have been good for him.

"If you didn't do anything, don't apologize," I say.

"I did get you something," he says.

I glance over. They're still scolding, sulking, and daydreaming.

"You did?"

Gabriel just nods.

"That feel any better?" he asks, his voice louder now. I've got a feeling he's not just asking about the burn.

"I think I'll be okay," I say.

"*RUBY*," my father says, his voice carrying down the table. From the way he says my name, I can tell it's not the first time he's tried to get my attention, but I've been spacing out for the past few minutes.

I swallow green beans and smile.

"Yes, father?"

"Kyle Pickett approached me today after the sermon," he says, cutting a chunk of roasted chicken and stabbing it with his fork. The motion is technically polite and genteel, but there's a force behind it that's anything but.

I rest my hands on the edge of the table as my stomach begins to twist inside me. Any time Kyle talks to my father it can't be good for me.

"Did he?" I ask, voice neutral, since he's clearly waiting for a response.

"He asked my permission to take you to Rosalie's for dinner on Tuesday night," he says, and puts the bite of chicken into his mouth.

It feels like everyone at the entire table holds their breath as he chews.

"I accepted on your behalf. Kyle's a godly, upstanding

man, the missteps of his youth aside," he goes on, slipping into lecture mode. "He has many good qualities to recommend him, and I think he could be an excellent match for you."

I look down at my plate of food, cheeks flaming. Everyone here knows what my father really means, even if he won't say it in front of everyone.

When he says *Kyle could be an excellent match*, he means *Kyle's the only one willing to take you, and a woman of your age should be married.*

I force myself to smile and look my father in the eye. He can probably tell that it's fake, but it's the best I can do right now.

"Thank you, father," I say, keeping my voice soft. "I'm so glad to have you looking out for me."

I don't mean a single word of it, but I'm doing what I have to. There are options besides going on a date with Kyle, sure, and believe it or not they're all much, much worse than suffering through nachos.

I lift my hands to my plate again and keep eating mechanically. I'm not hungry at all, but I have to act normal right now, so I keep chewing and swallowing the suddenly-flavorless meal.

My father changes the dinner topic to politics. Specifically, he and my brothers James, Jr. and Daniel discuss whether the U.S.'s most recent talks with Israel are likely to usher in the End of Days and the Rapture. They hope so. I don't.

As they talk, I glance over at Gabriel by accident, and his eyes flick to me for just a second. I wish I could tell him that I'm sorry about Kyle, that going on a date with him is the last thing I want. That I'm just doing this for survival and I'd just rather be with him on the dirt floor of a barn, but I've got no idea what Gabriel thinks about all this.

For all I know, the kiss was a mistake and he doesn't want to get involved in this mess. If he didn't, I wouldn't blame him.

———

AFTER DINNER, I'm so preoccupied with Kyle that I almost forget that Gabriel has something for me, and I don't know what. It's not until I'm alone in the kitchen with my mother, doing the dishes and tidying for the morning, that I remember.

And I have an idea. I straighten the tablecloth on the kitchen table, then put my hands on my hips, frowning theatrically at the vase of flowers sitting on it.

I sigh. My mother finally looks over.

"These are getting old," I say, sounding as displeased as possible.

She glances at them.

"I'll send Pearl to get fresh ones from the garden tomorrow," she says.

I grab the vase instead and examine the flowers like I'm a jeweler looking for imperfections.

"I'll go get new ones now," I say. "These are dying, and they smell funny, and it's a nice night. Besides, I could use some practice with arranging them."

My mother looks very, very skeptical, so I smile at her and hope it works.

"You know, if I'm going to be going on dates with Kyle," I say, hoping she picks up on my hint.

Dates mean a relationship, an engagement, and—sooner rather than later—a marriage. And, above all else, my mother tends to blame my poor household management skills for my failed marriage.

As if being able to arrange flowers well would have made Lucas less gay.

Finally, she nods once and turns back to polishing the kitchen counters. I grab some shears and a basket, push the kitchen door open, greeted by the cool night air, and take a deep breath. It's starting to smell like fall, just the barest hint of brittle leaves and wood smoke in the air.

I toss the flowers into the compost, dump out the water, and then stroll into the garden. I don't actually give a crap about whether the flowers were old or not, but it's dark outside and Gabriel has already headed to the carriage house for the night.

I saw him looking at me last night from his window, so I know he watches sometimes. Hopefully he's paying attention now and he'll come out, say hi, and we'll have a perfectly dark-but-above-board conversation.

Roses, snapdragons, marigolds, zinnias. A whole bunch of flowers I can never keep straight, except they're mostly pretty, and my mother and sisters all seem to know how to make them look fantastic and I don't.

I turn the corner into the vegetable garden, around some tall-but-nearly-dead tomatoes, and I hear a door shut, so I kick the tomato trellis, making it shake a little.

It works, because a few moments later, Gabriel's standing at the end of the row, his hands in his pockets. He's out of his work clothes, just wearing jeans and a t-shirt that says Great Smoky Mountains National Park on the front, his muscles practically bulging out of it.

I swallow hard, fire suddenly snaking through my body, winding lower and lower. With everything that's happened I'd somehow forgotten the sheer, total lust he unfailingly inspires in me. I'd somehow forgotten how hard it can be to talk to him alone without wanting him to push his hands up my skirt, his lips on my neck.

"Lovely night," I say, nervous again, but for a completely different reason this time. "Nice time to pick flowers, don't you think?"

He glances up at the house, searching the windows for activity, then reaches into his pocket and pulls out a few envelopes, steps closer to me, and holds them out.

I can barely read the writing on them, but I can tell they're from my stalker. The handwriting matches.

"I already stole some," I admit, not taking them.

"Not these," Gabriel says, his voice low and gravelly. "If you think it's your father writing them, you haven't read these."

He sounds so grave and serious that I believe him completely. I take the letters, glance back at the house, then lift my shirt slightly above the waist of my skirt.

"Don't watch," I whisper, teasing. "I'm being indecent."

I push them into the top of my pantyhose, half an inch of my stomach exposed. Gabriel doesn't look away, just grins, watching me.

"You're probably going to Hell now," he deadpans.

"If I am, this wasn't the tipping point," I say, smoothing my shirt back over the envelopes squashed against my skin. If I have to wear the uncomfortable, deeply unflattering combination of pantyhose and extra-large t-shirts, at least it's a good outfit for hiding contraband letters.

"The witchcraft was probably the tipping point," he agrees, crossing his arms in front of him. "Or whatever you use white, translucent crystals for."

"They're how I get men to lie to my father on my behalf, apparently," I say. "The spells seem to be working."

I pause for a moment. Gabriel smiles.

"Thanks, by the way," I say.

"I already told you, I'm not gonna make your life harder," he says. "Though, Ruby, I should warn you. Those letters have some fucked up shit in them. Fucked up shit about *you*. I understand why your father doesn't want you to read them, and I hate being the one to give them to you, but... you should. You deserve to know what's happening."

I swallow.

"That bad?" I ask.

"Pretty bad," he admits, his hands back in his pockets. "Ruby, I'm sorry."

"Don't be."

He raises one eyebrow slightly, a hint of a smile on his face.

"I'll be as sorry as I want," he says, and I laugh quietly.

"This is where you make your big stand?" I tease. "On feeling bad that I've got a stalker?"

Gabriel glances quickly at the big house, then back at me, still smirking.

"I feel like a neutered housecat around here and it's driving me crazy," he says, his voice gone low and growly. "I've got to stand firm on *something*."

I raise both eyebrows.

"Neutered?"

The second that's out of my mouth, my face heats up, and Gabriel grins.

"Just metaphorically," he says. "But you knew that."

I swallow, anxiety writhing in my chest, because as much as I like this and want him and have desires I'm not sure I completely understand, I don't know what I'm doing. Flirting with men like this just isn't in my repertoire.

"I had suspected as—"

I hear a door open, and we both turn our heads, my heart seizing. We're not doing anything, just talking, but I know that nothing I do is above suspicion, ever.

My mother comes out of the kitchen door, glances around, and finds me. She walks over.

"Ruby!" She says, her usual smile perfectly in place, even as she takes in Gabriel's muscled, t-shirt-clad form. "Will you make sure to get some camellias? I'm afraid they'll stop blooming soon and they're *so* lovely. Hello, Gabriel."

"I'll make sure to get some," I say, and I know I'm talking a little too fast, but I can't help it. "Gabriel just saw that I was out here alone and wanted to make sure I was okay."

My mother's smile tightens a bit.

"You're so sweet for your concern," she says, honeyed sweetness dripping from every word. "But I'm sure Ruby is just fine."

Gabriel ducks his head.

"Of course, ma'am. Have a good night Mrs. Burgess. Ruby."

"Good night," my mother says.

He turns and goes back to the carriage house. My mother turns to me, a hardness behind her features that I recognize a little too well.

"Which flowers were you thinking, dear?" she asks.

CHAPTER EIGHTEEN

GABRIEL

I HAVE a full day to wonder if giving Ruby the letters was a mistake. I see her, of course, but we don't talk again until Tuesday. That gives me plenty of time to wonder whether she's been caught with them, whether we're now under suspicion because we were seen talking in the garden.

I swear to God, this house is making me crazy. Before I started this gig I wouldn't have believed the sheer level of scrutiny I'd be under here, from her family alone.

But Ruby's siblings, their friends, her father's aides and employees all do a good job of keeping me paranoid. I don't know if one of them might overhear something and tell her parents. I feel like I'm living in a very small police state.

Monday afternoon I follow her into the laundry room. I know that Ruby's probably desperate for a few minutes alone most of the time, so I don't follow her every step: as long as I know where she is and that I can get to her in seconds, I'm fine. This house is well-secured already. She doesn't need me three feet away at all times.

When I enter, she looks up, then glances through the

door behind me, still taking clothes from a laundry basket, shaking them, and pushing them into the washing machine.

"There's no one in the hallway," I say, meaning *no one saw me come in.* "I just had a question about getting a stain out of a shirt."

"Just let me get this started and I'll tell you anything you want to know," she says, shaking a man's shirt until the cuffs come unrolled, then shoving it in.

"It's a mud stain," I say, just to keep talking. "You know that bright red clay they've got around here? That stuff stains like there's no tomorrow."

She pours detergent into the tray of the washer, closes the lid, cranks the dial, and the machine starts.

"It's the bane of every gardener in the state," she confirms, leaning against the washer and folding her arms. "What kind of fabric did you get it on?"

The machine hums, half drowning out her last few words. Good to know I was right about talking in the laundry room.

"You read them?"

She swallows and looks at the wall in front of her, face stony.

"I did," she says. "You were right. They're bad."

"I'm—"

"Gabriel, I swear if you apologize again I'll tell my father you've got the Satanic Bible hidden in your apartment."

"It was the one thing I had left, Ruby," I tease. "Now I'm a broken shell of a man."

She glances at me, swiping me up and down with her eyes. I lean against the doorway, inviting her to look as long as she wants. She's more than welcome.

"I think you'll be okay," she says. "The letters are still in my room, though. I didn't want to risk walking around with them stuffed into my undergarments all day."

I swallow.

"And?"

The washing machine pauses its hum for a moment, then kicks into the next part of the cycle, water swishing back and forth inside it.

"And I think you're right," she says, her voice nearly a whisper. "I must have stolen the wrong ones last week, because they were way tamer—he called me a Jezebel and a harlot and all that, but they didn't go any further. They didn't threaten anything... *specific*."

"Ruby," I say.

She looks over at me, and I realize that her green eyes are shiny with tears. My stomach clenches, with sympathy, but also with rage. What kind of father is the Senator that him faking a stalker is a reasonable possibility?

Before I know it, I've got Ruby in my arms, in front of the washing machine, her head against my collarbone, and I'm holding her tight.

"Don't," she whispers, but she hooks one arm around me, her hand tentative on my back.

"No one is going to hurt you," I murmur into her hair. "I promise."

Ruby doesn't say anything, just leans into a little harder, just for a moment.

I know full well this is stupid, that I shouldn't be holding her like this, here, in the laundry room. Anyone could walk in and I'd be permanently screwed out of a job, and she'd probably be sent off to some sort of boot camp for misbehaving women.

But there are some things I can't fucking do. I can't see

Ruby frightened and about to cry and not hold her, tell her everything will be okay.

I protect people. It's what I do, what I've always wanted to do, and right now I especially protect Ruby.

She takes a deep breath. She squeezes me tight, with both arms, and then she pulls away from me, cold disappointment slithering through my veins.

Footsteps sound in the hallway. The washing machine swishes and hums.

"Go," she says. "I'm fine."

I frown, because I don't believe her, but she turns away, picks up another basket, and starts unloading the dryer, glancing over her shoulder at me.

"Don't do all that only to get me in trouble by standing there," she says, almost playfully. "Go on. Get."

"Yes, Miss Burgess," I tease, then walk out of the laundry room.

———

BETWEEN THE LETTERS, the barn, and the laundry room, I nearly fucking forgot about Ruby's date with Kyle. It's probably because Kyle is completely forgettable, even as the guy who's taking Ruby on a date.

I'm reminded when her father calls me into his office Tuesday morning and informs me that I'll be accompanying them, along with her sister Pearl. I'm Ruby's bodyguard—obviously—and Pearl is their chaperone.

"You'll also be functioning as their chaperone, of course," the Senator says, standing tall in front of his window, gazing out, hands locked behind himself. "Ruby is well aware of what's expected of her, but there's to be no touching above the wrist, no sultry talk of any kind, and no salacious mannerisms from either of them."

Somehow, I keep a straight face, even when he says *sultry talk.*

It's not going to be a fucking problem, I think.

"Furthermore, Mr. Pickett and my daughter are not to be left alone. At least one of them should be within your range of vision at all times. If Ruby uses the ladies' room and Kyle says he needs to use the men's, you follow him. Also, you are to sit at a table, not a booth. No alcohol. No excessively spicy food."

I desperately want to ask him if booths are the seating arrangement preferred by Satan, but I bite my tongue.

"Yes, sir," I say instead.

"They are to be home by 9:30 sharp, barring an act of God," he says, and I'm positive he means that literally. "To put it bluntly, Gabriel, Ruby's virtue is already quite suspect within the community due to her past, and it's my job as her father to see that her reputation is pure."

The hairs on the back of my neck are standing up, because every word he says just makes me angrier. I'm pretty fucking sure it's Ruby's job as an adult woman to see that her reputation is whatever the fuck she wants it to be, but I don't say that.

"Of course, sir," I say.

"Thank you, Gabriel," he says, dismissing me.

EVEN THOUGH I forgot about Ruby's date with Kyle to begin with, by 6:05 pm I'm fucking pissed. Pearl and I are sitting downstairs, on opposite ends of a very fancy couch in the sitting room.

Yes, this house has a sitting room.

Kyle's late. He was supposed to pick up Ruby at six, and it's been five minutes. What kind of asshole is late for his first date with a girl?

And what kind of asshole is late for his first date with Ruby?

I've had the whole day to stew about this, the fact that some perverted prostitute-fucking unwanted-dick-pic-sending asshole gets to go on a date with Ruby, sanctioned by her father, and I have to chaperone.

Meanwhile, if I make too much eye contact with her in public, it makes her whole family suspicious.

I'm jealous. Not jealous of Kyle, really—he's a dopey sad-sack who's always going to be known as the guy with the cartoon porn, who I don't think could find a woman to date without paying for her or arranging it through his father— but I'm jealous that he gets to do this.

On the other side of the sofa, Pearl sighs. She's just sitting there, not doing anything, staring ahead blankly while I impatiently flip through the pages of *Helpmeet* magazine. This month's issue has a feature called "Should You Let Him Decide?" with a list of important household and life decisions listed below it.

Surprise: the magazine advocates giving your husband complete and total control over every decision it lists, including what kind of house to buy, what to wear, and how many children to have.

At 6:07, the doorbell finally rings. I've been informed that the Senator will be answering it, but I'd fucking love to do it myself, let Kyle see what he'll be dealing with tonight.

"Good evening, Senator," I hear Kyle's reedy, wimpy voice say.

"Hello, Kyle," the Senator says. I can hear the frown in his voice. "I thought you said six."

For the very first time, I feel a tiny glimmer of affection for the man.

"Sorry, sir," Kyle whines on. "You know how that stoplight at Courthouse road doesn't have a left turn lane, and so sometimes if there are a couple of people making a left turn there it takes a few light cycles because the traffic from the opposite direction blocks it? There was this car making a left there and this guy just would *not* go..."

That's why you give yourself extra time, you dumbass, I think. *You're on a fucking date. Do it right.*

Still talking about this stoplight, the Senator walks Kyle into the sitting room. Out of politeness, I stand, and after a moment, so does Pearl, still looking dour.

"Kyle, this is Gabriel, Ruby's bodyguard, and you know her younger sister, Pearl." the Senator says. "They'll be accompanying you tonight."

Kyle sticks one hand out.

"Nice to meet you," he says, in a tone of voice that makes it clear he thinks it's anything but.

"Likewise," I say, matching his tone.

"Pearl," he says, nodding.

"Hi, Kyle," she responds.

Then we just stand there. He's got grocery-store flowers with him, still wrapped in cellophane, the rubber band around the bottom, packet of flower feed attached, and it crinkles every time he moves.

Take the plastic off, I think. *Fucking pretend you tried.*

After a moment, the Senator clears his throat and gives Pearl a look.

"I'll go see if she's ready," she finally says, and leaves the room.

The Senator turns to Kyle, his hands in his pockets. Kyle suddenly looks like a deer in the headlights, and in this moment, I don't pity him. I've felt the full brunt of the Senator's glare before, and it's not a good place to be.

I stood up to it better, though.

"Son," the Senator begins. "I didn't want to say this in front of my daughter, but now that we're in the company of men, I don't mind telling you that I'm well aware of your problems with pornography and prostitutes, and if you dare to bring any of that near my daughter, you'll think you've been struck down by the Lord God himself."

Kyle turns white, then bright red, his mouth opening and closing like a fish. I feel another tiny glimmer of affection for the Senator, despite myself.

"Yes, sir," he finally manages to get out.

"You are not to speak inappropriately to her tonight," he goes on. "You are not to touch her. As far as she's concerned, pornography and prostitution do not even exist. I'm fully aware that my daughter is no longer pure, and in the past she has been bedeviled and led down the wrong path, but you are to treat her as if she is untouched as the driven snow. Is that clear?"

"Yes, sir," Kyle says, his voice a whisper-squeak.

On the stairs, we hear voices, and all three of us turn. Pearl appears, still sullen, followed by Ruby, dressed for her date.

Jesus *Christ* she's a knockout. Even though she's wearing a dowdy skirt that falls below her knees, a shirt that's at least one size too baggy, and a black cardigan that comes down to her wrists, none of it can hide how fucking beautiful she is, how tempting her curves are, or the way I can see her body move, graceful and lithe and full of secret promises, below her clothes.

Kyle steps forward, holding out the flowers. The Senator and I both watch him, and for this one short second, I feel oddly united with the older man.

"Hi," Kyle says. "I brought you these daisies, because I'm sure we both remember the sermon from Valentine's day when the Reverend discussed the appropriate types of flower..."

Ruby's smile stays frozen on her face as she listens to Kyle prattle on, but after a moment, she glances at me.

I don't say anything. I don't do anything. I just lock eyes with her while the man who's actually taking her on this date makes a total ass of himself.

It's a fucking stupid situation that I've gotten myself into, going along on some other man's date with this girl I've kissed once and talked to a handful of times, but who I want like there's no fucking tomorrow. I don't know how I got myself here and I've got no clue how the fuck I'm going to resolve it.

But when she looks at me like that, like she's thinking of the secrets we share instead of listening to him, my jealousy fades into nearly nothing, because if I were jealous, it would mean that I thought Kyle was some kind of threat. That he actually had some chance of winning Ruby tonight.

I'm not jealous of Kyle. There's no point.

Still looking at Ruby, I wink.

CHAPTER NINETEEN

RUBY

KYLE CROSSES his arms in front of himself, trying to stare down the hostess at Rosalie's Mexican Kitchen.

"I very specifically made a reservation for a *table*," he says.

The poor woman looks baffled.

"I can also seat you in the other room," she offers.

"Is it also a booth?" he says, starting to get snappy with her.

"Yes."

Kyle sighs and rolls his eyes. I have to look away out of sheer embarrassment for him.

"Sitting in a booth is completely unsatisfactory," he says, a whine creeping into his voice. "When I called to make a reservation for tonight, I asked for a *table*, and now I've arrived only to find out that you don't have one available."

"I'm afraid that wasn't noted on the reservation, and I'm very sorry," the hostess says. "If you'd like to wait, I think a table will be opening up in about twenty minutes."

I swear Kyle almost stamps his foot.

"The standard of service here is—"

I touch his shoulder lightly, because people are starting to stare at the four of us, all gathered next to a big, empty booth while a grown man complains.

"I don't mind sitting in a booth," I say softly. "It's okay, really."

I glance behind us at Pearl and Gabriel. Pearl's glancing around the room, like she'd rather be anywhere else, and Gabriel has his hands in his pockets and looks like he's doing his best to pretend this isn't the most awkward thing he's ever been a part of.

"Ruby," Kyle says, his voice quieter but still much too loud. "I don't know if you've read the Reverend's pamphlet series on Godly dating, but he very specifically says that booths in restaurants are simply an invitation to—"

"I trust in your better nature," I say, smiling sweetly at him. "I'm sure you can resist a little temptation."

Kyle frowns. He huffs. The hostess is trying very hard not to make a *these people are crazy* face.

"All right," he says. "We'll take the booth, but I'd like to speak with your manager."

As the four of us all slide in, I think *what a good date this is going to be.*

———

THE MANAGER IS VERY, very apologetic, and Kyle is very, very self-righteous. Rosalie's Tex-Mex kitchen is owned by fellow members of our church, and although I don't recognize the manager, I'd bet he knows who I am and probably who Kyle is.

"The service here has really gone downhill," Kyle says, still a little too loudly, when the manager walks away.

"I think they made an honest mistake," I say. There's a

bowl of free chips and salsa, and I take some. "Isn't *table* usually a generic term meaning *somewhere to sit* when you make a reservation?"

Kyle frowns, like he's got a problem with me correcting him.

"I used to come here sometimes with Lucas, and they were always *so* nice," I go on. "Really, I think it's just a miscommunication."

I mention my ex-husband specifically to make Kyle uncomfortable, because God knows he's spent the last twenty minutes making *me* uncomfortable. I know it's not nice, but I don't feel particularly nice right now.

"It's owned by Godly people," he mutters. "Any good business owner would have read the pamphlets..."

I eat more chips and salsa and tune Kyle out. Eventually he reaches for one as well, just barely touching the chip to the salsa.

When he eats it, he frowns.

"That's kind of spicy," he says. "I don't know if we should be eating it."

I take a big scoop of salsa on a chip, put it into my mouth, and chew, making eye contact with Kyle the whole time. It's barely spicy, and I'm not big on spicy food.

"Tastes fine to me," I say, wiping my lips daintily, then look over at Pearl and Gabriel. "Is this too spicy for you?"

Pearl shrugs.

"I'm alright with it," Gabriel says, folding his hands together on the table and leaning forward.

Kyle acts like Gabriel doesn't even exist. I can't even blame him, because just looking at the two of them from across the table, there's no contest. Kyle's wearing a mint-green polo shirt tucked into pleated khakis, his shoulders shrugged forward, the same haircut he's probably had since he was five, a perpetual petulant scowl on his face.

Gabriel, on the other hand, is wearing a chambray shirt with the sleeves rolled up to his elbows and gray slacks that make me unable to quit staring at his ass. He's sitting at the table perfectly relaxed, glancing at me every so often like we're in on the same joke.

Which we kind of are.

After a few more false starts, Kyle quits whining. He orders nachos for all four of us—no jalapeños—and after we all eat a bit, he seems to mellow out a little.

I ask him about his work with the Reverend, and he asks how I've been enjoying my return to my father's house, though he side-steps mentioning the reason why I've returned to my father's house.

I don't lie, but I don't tell him the whole truth.

"It's been a challenge," I say, hands folded neatly on top of the table. "It's taken some time to learn to submit to my father's authority again after submitting to a husband's authority."

Across the table, next to Kyle, Gabriel's eyebrows go up for a split second.

That must sound really strange to someone not in the church, I realize.

I feel myself blush, and I take a sip of water to cover it up. In my world submitting to a husband's authority just means doing whatever he says with a smile—and, at least in my experience, it's never sexual. When I submitted to Lucas's authority, it usually meant letting him get the curtains that *he* wanted for the living room, or laundering his shirts the way he liked.

It's not like he ever pulled out whips and chains or something. When he did initiate sex, which happened bi-monthly at best, he did it by climbing on top of me after we were both in bed already, doing some half-hearted kissing until he was hard enough for *the act*, and then I had about three more minutes until it was over.

For a split second I think yet again about the barn, up against the wall, Gabriel's mouth practically devouring mine. I have to take another sip of water.

Kyle just nods, then pauses, and finally looks at me.

"I'm sure it's a difficult adjustment," he says. "And I don't think I've ever said this, but I'm sorry for what you went through."

I think it's the first empathetic thing he's said to me, and it catches me by surprise.

"Thank you," I say.

"Several people have told me that I shouldn't be thinking of courting you because of your failed marriage," he goes on. "But you seem like a clever, thoughtful enough woman, so I trust that you're able to learn from your previous mistakes and carry on."

Kyle smiles warmly at me, and I realize that he means this as a compliment.

I smile back. It's my default facial expression, though to Kyle's right I can see a muscle tense in Gabriel's neck as he looks at a picture on the wall with a great deal of interest. My stomach twists, and I swallow, getting ready to do something I've never done before.

"My biggest mistake was marrying someone I wasn't suited to," I tell Kyle, tilting my head slightly, still smiling.

"Marriage is a marathon, not a sprint," he says, parroting one of the Reverend's favorite lines. "What happens at the beginning is only a small part of the entire experience, and a great many things can be overcome with faith and commitment."

Kyle's never been married, of course. He's never tried to make it work with someone who would never be interested in him, no matter what.

"They shouldn't always be overcome," I say bluntly.

Kyle regards me suspiciously. The muscle in Gabriel's neck twitches again, and I sit up a little straighter. Normally I'd just smile and agree with whatever Kyle said, because I want this conversation over with, but with Gabriel here I've got the urge to argue with Kyle.

"I disagree," Kyle says, frowning. "Marriage should be an unbreakable covenant, entered into with thought and seriousness."

"Then perhaps we shouldn't let nineteen-year-olds enter into that covenant," I say.

I've dropped my smile. I'm still speaking softly, and Kyle looks taken aback and confused that I'm saying any of this.

"People need to marry before they're tempted into sin," he points out. "And nineteen is more than old enough."

I take a deep breath. Kyle's parroting the stuff I've heard all my life, but after walking in on my husband like I did, let's just say my opinions have changed a little.

But I've never argued about this with anyone before, as strange as it sounds. I'm not sure what to say—*maybe sin's not that bad?*

Maybe it's a worse sin to make yourself miserable for a lifetime than to lust outside of marriage a little?

"But people are perfectly capable of—"

"Who got the chimichanga?" the waitress asks over my shoulder.

Pearl raises her hand, and I take a deep breath of relief.

Once we all get our food, Kyle says grace over it, and then we're all too busy eating to talk.

I'm relieved, because I know better. If I argue with Kyle, it'll only get back to the Reverend and my father, and that would be pretty bad.

Keep sweet, I remind myself. *No need to make this too hard on yourself.*

CHAPTER TWENTY

WE EAT IN NEAR-TOTAL SILENCE. Kyle and Ruby don't ask how the other's food is, don't make small talk, hardly even look at each other. It's probably the worst date I've ever seen, and it's made ten times weirder because I'm chaperoning.

Not to mention that every thirty seconds for the past couple days I think about Ruby, in the barn, my mouth on hers, her body arching into mine, or the way she felt in my arms in the laundry room. The last thing I should be thinking about right here, right now, but it's satisfying as hell to remember while she's on a half-assed date with someone else.

Kyle shoves his plate away.

"Give me your hands," he says, a slight, impatient whine in his voice.

Ruby does, and he clamps his fingertips around hers like he's some sort of alien who's never held hands before, but I'm suddenly jealous anyway. That he gets to touch her and I don't, even though I'm the one she wants to touch.

"Ruby Burgess," he says, then looks at her and waits.

"Yes," Ruby says after a long pause.

"I want to make my intentions toward you perfectly clear," he begins.

I've met the guy twice and even *I* can tell he's about to begin another self-righteous monologue. Ruby's face is carefully, perfectly blank, and I'm pretending I'm not paying attention while hanging onto every word this slimy fuckwit says, my hands locked together on the table.

God, I hate that he's touching her. I know she doesn't like it and I still hate it.

"After careful study, prayer, and consideration, I believe that our personalities, interests, and beliefs are well-aligned. Both of us have certain black marks in our past, but I think that together, with faith and perseverance, we can both overcome these things and join together someday in the sight of God," Kyle says.

My back straightens and one hand tightens into a fist on the table.

Is he proposing? He can't be fucking proposing.

"I believe that our union may take more spiritual work, guidance, and patience than others, but as I stated earlier, a marriage is a marathon and not a sprint. Therefore, Ruby, I intend to ask your father his permission to begin an engagement."

Engagement.

I think I'd be angry if I weren't just fucking confused, because it's the worst proposal I've ever heard.

Was that really it? This douchebag just said *we don't really like each other but let's get married* to Ruby, of all people?

My knuckles are all white. There's a muscle twitching in my neck, because I want to take him by the collar, drag him out of this restaurant, and give him a good hard lesson in treating women right.

Ruby clears her throat.

"I don't think I'm ready for that sort of commitment," she says, her voice perfectly neutral, her ever-present smile soft and sweet. "It hasn't been very long since my marriage to Lucas ended, and I just don't think that I'm ready to take that step with someone else yet."

Kyle frowns slightly.

"It's been six months," he says. "And I don't mean to be rude, but you're already twenty-six."

Ruby's eyes flash, and her smile falters for a moment.

"For right now, my place is in my father's house, with my family," she says, her voice syrupy-sweet. "I've prayed this over quite a bit, and the Lord is clear that he wants me to wait."

Kyle nods, stiffly.

"I see," he says. "Well, I hope the Lord hasn't laid it on your heart to wait too long! Ha!"

Ruby pulls her hands away like she can't do it quickly enough, and something relaxes in my chest, just a little. Kyle frowns, then looks around.

"The service here has gotten terrible," he says. "Maybe I should talk to the owners about this..."

Ruby looks at me, almost like she's laughing. Like we share some dark joke, just between the two of us. Maybe we do.

"*Ugh*," Kyle says, and stands, flinging his napkin back into the booth. He rises and stomps away, looking for our waitress, and I take a deep Kyle-free breath.

"You should have said yes," Pearl says with the air of a teenager who knows everything.

"I don't need this from you," Ruby says without changing her tone.

"Look how angry he is. He might not ask again," Pearl points out.

I bet Ruby would be heartbroken, I think, and there's the almost-smile from her again. Pearl turns to me imperiously.

"You wouldn't ask again, right?" she says. "If a girl rejected you like that?"

That's not how I'd propose a date, let alone a goddamn marriage, I think, but I don't want to get into it with Ruby's little sister.

"It depends," I say, trying to sound as neutral as possible.

"That means no," Pearl proclaims.

That means I'd do it right and fuck yes I'd ask again if I thought it would work.

"It means it depends," I tell her.

She turns back to Ruby.

"You're not going to get to pick and choose," she says, and for a moment she sounds exactly like their mother.

"You're here to chaperone, not give me life advice," Ruby says, sounding bored and irritated.

"You'll remember this when you're an old maid," Pearl says smugly. "Let me out, I need to use the ladies' room."

Ruby lets her out of the booth and then slides back in until she's almost across from me. There's still no sign of Kyle.

"For your sake, I hope this is the worst date you've ever been on," she says.

I want to take her hands, lean over the table, and kiss her. For fucking once I want Ruby to know that someone's excited about her, that someone wants her like fire in his veins, that someone jerks off twice a day thinking about her.

"If I go now I could take that little motherfucker to the

alleyway out back and fucking teach him how to talk to women on dates," I offer, my voice low and quiet. "I won't even leave a mark."

Ruby turns bright pink.

"Please don't," she whispers.

I just shake my head. I'm not an idiot, and I know that beating up Kyle right now would only land Ruby herself in trouble or worse. Doesn't change how badly I want to, though.

Something else occurs to me.

"Ruby, have you ever been on a real date?" I ask.

"You mean alone with someone? No chaperones?"

"Right."

"Sure," she says. "Plenty of times with Lucas after we got married, and last week when you found me at the pub. Though I guess that wasn't really a date, that was..."

"I bought you a drink and took you home," I point out.

"You're my bodyguard and it's your job to know where I am."

"It's my job to keep you safe, it's not my job to enjoy your company."

We look at each other. Her eyes flick to my lips for a split second, and I swear it takes every drop of self-control I have not to lean across the table and crush her mouth against mine, right then and there.

"Is it your job to offer to beat up my suitors?"

"Suitors, plural? Are there more of these assholes somewhere?"

Ruby looks at me, looks down at the table, looks back at me like she's trying not to smile.

"There's only the one official suitor," she says. "And I think you just heard him bring his romance A-game."

"Sounds like you need an unofficial suitor."

"I'm not sure I need a suitor at all," she says. "I think I just need someone whose company I enjoy and who walks me home. I've had it with suitors, Gabriel."

"We could just leave this restaurant right now," I murmur. "We'll go somewhere else for an hour. I don't care where, and I'll tell your father that I thought there was a threat and I needed to get you out and keep you safe."

"Please don't get fired," she whispers.

I nearly reach across the table and take her hand in mine, but instead there's an annoyed sigh off to the side, and Pearl appears. Ruby lets her sister back into the booth, my heart still hammering.

The moment's over, my heart pounding at Pearl's sudden arrival because Ruby makes me a little crazy, a little reckless. I know better than to flirt with my charge while she's on a date with someone else, but here I am.

I can't stop thinking about it: Ruby, the barn, the space behind the hedge, backstage at that first rally. I'm thinking of the flash of belly I saw the other day as she hid the letters, how nearly impossible it was not to grab her and kiss it, or of her in my arms.

Kyle's hot on Pearl's heels, looking smug, and he sits next to me, across from Ruby.

"I had to speak with the manager again, but I think he understands my concerns about the level of service here," he says. "Simply put, to keep up in today's society, a restaurant needs to be..."

Something bumps against my ankle. I move my foot away out of habit, but a split second later, Ruby catches my eye.

Slowly, I move my foot back. A shoe bumps my ankle again, then nuzzles along my foot, and I have to force myself not to smile as I nuzzle back.

Kyle drones on, waiting for the waitress. Ruby watches him intently, her green eyes practically boring holes through him, as she plays footsie with me and I play back.

It's probably the stupidest possible way to get caught with her, but I'm not about to stop.

CHAPTER TWENTY-ONE

RUBY

WHEN THE DATE is finally over, Kyle walks me from his car to my front door. Pearl and Gabriel follow, twenty feet behind, both looking on.

Kyle's goodbye is mercifully brief. He tells me, more or less, that I was a very suitable, respectable date, and that he found my company very proper and Godly.

Or something. I'm not listening, I'm smiling and trying to pretend that Gabriel's not standing next to my sister, where I can feel his eyes on me like fingers down my spine.

"Thank you for a nice time," Kyle finally says.

For one second, I think he's about to shake my hand, but he just nods.

"Thank you," I say, because I can't think of another response.

He walks away. Pearl and Gabriel approach, and Pearl's through the front door first while Gabriel holds it, gesturing us through.

As I pass him, his fingers brush my lower back again, like he's teasing me: *here's what dates could be like.*

My mother bustles into the entrance hall, *beaming.* I try

to arrange my face to look more excited, and I have no idea whether I succeed.

"Well?" she asks, all smiles. "How did your date go?"

I got proposed to by someone I don't like, and the best part was the two minutes I spent alone with my bodyguard, I think.

"It was nice," I say.

"He proposed and she turned him down," Pearl says, walking past my mother and toward the kitchen.

Her face freezes.

"Oh?" she asks.

I clear my throat, straightening my spine and girding myself because I don't have a lot of experience standing up to my parents. This is all kind of... new.

"I told him it's too soon," I say, twisting my hands together in front of me. "I've only been divorced from Lucas for six months, officially, and I don't want to rush into something else right away."

She keeps smiling and turns to Gabriel.

"You're welcome to head to your own quarters," she says, and even though she sounds friendly, it's clearly a dismissal. "Thank you *so* much for chaperoning."

"Yes ma'am," Gabriel says, nodding his head at her. "Any time you need me."

And he walks away, leaving me with my mother, whose smile fades with Gabriel's footsteps.

"Let's talk," she says, and pulls me away.

———

MY MOTHER'S talk is more of a lecture, and it's the same thing I've been hearing for almost a month now: my options are Kyle or spinsterhood; I'm not going to get a better offer; a woman's place is married and raising children; it's unseemly for me to be even in this position, living at home at such an advanced age.

The second I can get away, I retreat to my bedroom and flop dramatically on my bed, still clothed, and try not to cry.

I've had *six months* to figure something out. Six months since my divorce was final and I came back home, and all I've done is open a checking account that's got fifty bucks in it. I could have been coming up with a plan, some third option that wasn't Kyle and wasn't living with my parents forever, but instead I moped around and didn't do crap.

Not that I know what to do. I've got an idea of what the end goal is—a place to live and a job that pays for it—but I don't know how to get there. I have a GED and was home-schooled by my mom, who prefers sewing to math, so I'm still not exactly sure what trigonometry is.

And I can't get a job without my family figuring it out, so I need a place to live, but a place to live requires money, which people tend to get from jobs. That's not even the worst part.

The worst part is, if I leave on my own, I'm leaving my family. That's all there is to it. If I do this, I'm out of the church, out of my family unit, out of nearly everything I've ever known. I'd escape my parents, sure, but no more Grace, no more Isaac who thinks he's a helicopter and Emma with her toothless smile, no more throwing rocks into the river with Joy or smart-ass comments from Zeke.

But then I think again of Kyle's cold, clammy hands clutching my fingertips, and my stomach turns. I think of him saying, basically, *we don't like each other but we're desperate.*

I remember sex with Lucas, which is all the sex I've ever had: under the covers, in the dark, totally silent while he pumped away, eyes closed against the fact that I was never what he really wanted. After the first few times it didn't hurt any more, but it was about as erotic as brushing my teeth.

And of course, from there my mind goes to the barn, *again*, which feels like the only thing I think about sometimes, and I close my eyes and take a deep breath, trying to stop the white heat that's slithering though my body already.

Kyle. Barn. Kyle. Barn. I'm still lying on my bed where I flopped, arms over my head, as the rest of my family comes upstairs one by one. I listen as they all get ready for bed and then, after a little while longer, it's quiet.

I sit up. The light underneath my door is gone, so I stand up and turn off my light too, and suddenly I can only see by the sliver of moonlight coming in through the window.

And the very faint lights in the carriage house.

All at once, my mind's made up. Screw horrible dates with Kyle, screw Pearl telling me I'm going to be a old maid, screw being damaged goods.

I know what I want, and for once, I'm going to go after it.

I still stand there, by the window, for a few more minutes, pretending like maybe I'll talk myself into behaving. I don't.

I close the curtains and turn away, open a drawer, reach in, and grab the vodka. I take one big swallow for courage, but it feels like my insides are doused with gasoline and I just held a match to them and now my body's enveloped in this sinuous, writhing heat.

This is stupid. It's easy to get caught, and in the best case scenario, my parents throw me out of their house with nothing.

But for the first time since I asked Lucas for a divorce, I'm doing something. I'm not smiling and nodding and going along, I'm acting like an adult and taking charge.

I'm opening my bedroom door, tiptoeing down the stairs, sneaking to the pantry with the window, every muscle and nerve on high alert, the vodka snaking through my veins and whispering *go on, go on* in my ear.

And I open the window and drop through into the cool night air, leaving my father's house.

CHAPTER TWENTY-TWO

GABRIEL

I'VE JUST POURED my nightly iced tea when there's a soft knock at my door, and I'm so surprised I nearly drop it. Instantly, my hand goes to where my holster should be, but I'm not wearing it because I'm at home.

Bad guys don't knock, Kane, I tell myself.

But I know who would. The knowledge makes my pulse race as I cross the kitchen and the living room, iced tea in hand, to the back door.

For a split second I imagine who else it could be: the Senator, here for yet another chat. Kyle, in some sort of misguided attempt to prove himself.

Or one of the other Burgess women, lonely and after the only non-related man in the house. The thought makes me wrinkle my nose.

But I open the door and it's her. Of course it's her, blonde hair floating gently in the breeze and eyes bright green, even in the dark, piercing right through me like always.

Then she tilts her head to one side, and I think she's nervous but she smiles anyway and it's not her regular, sweet smile. It's mischievous and coy and devious and I swear to God that smile is promising me things I've only ever dreamed of.

"Invite me in?" she says, keeping her voice quiet.

I hesitate for a split second. If she gets caught in here, even if we don't do so much as kiss, my old life is gone. My career in the Secret Service is officially over, the end mired in scandal, my name blacklisted in Washington, D.C. forever. I'll be lucky to play rent-a-cop to state assemblymen after this.

And in this moment, I couldn't fucking care less.

"Welcome to the carriage house," I say, stepping back from the door.

Ruby steps in quickly and I shut the door behind her, already nervous that she's been seen. She glances around my apartment, taking it all in, suddenly seeming a little uncertain, like maybe she hadn't planned this far.

It's all right. I've got some ideas, so I lean back against the kitchen counter, just watching her, every nerve in my body singing.

"How can I be of service?" I ask, my voice low and slow.

Ruby lifts her shirt, and for a moment I think she's just going to take it off right then, right there, no preamble. My dick practically leaps out of my pants, but instead she lifts it an inch above her waist and pulls three letters out of her pantyhose.

"I came to give these back to you," she says, holding them out.

I just grin, and Ruby frowns.

"What?" she asks, still holding them.

"Those were in your bedroom, down the hall from your father's office, and you brought them all the way out to my apartment to give them to me to put back?" I ask, taking a step toward her. "Sure, Ruby."

I swear she turns three different shades of pink, but she cocks her head at me defiantly, and after a moment, a smile starts gathering around her eyes. A real one.

"I don't know what you're saying," she says, teasing me.

"I'm saying you're a whole fucking lot craftier than bringing the letters to me when it's miles easier to put them back yourself," I say, moving toward her.

Now there's only a foot between us, and it feels like the air itself is charged with electricity.

"Then I must really be here for some other reason," she murmurs.

I grab the letters, toss them onto the kitchen table, and take her hand, lacing our fingers together as I walk her backward. Ruby stumbles a little but I steady her with my other hand on her back.

"Is it this it?" I growl once she's against the wall. "Any chance you're here to finish what we already started?"

Her hand is still in mine and I press it against the wall, over her head, our faces almost touching. I feel like I could almost jump out of my skin right now, and I can practically feel Ruby's pulse beating through the air.

She doesn't say anything, her eyes wide, and I dig my fingers into her spine, through her ugly t-shirt.

"If you're here for something else, Ruby, say the word now because this is *all* I've been fucking thinking about for three days straight," I say, my voice low and rough with desire.

"This was it," she whispers.

I squeeze her hand, push it harder against the wall, and kiss her. I can barely force myself to hold back but I do, make myself kiss her slowly and carefully this first time, swiping my tongue along her lip until she opens her mouth under mine, gently curling our tongues together as I try not to growl.

The sheer effort of holding back has me trembling, and I pull away from her by millimeters until our lips are barely touching, my hand gripping hers so tightly my knuckles are white.

Go slow, I command myself. *Ruby's not like the other women. Slow down.*

But as I'm admonishing myself, her hand closes around the back of my neck and pulls me in toward her with surprising force. My mouth practically crushes hers, our tongues tangling together instantly and I groan because I can't help it, pressing her hips against the wall with mine, our bodies flush together.

Ruby arches her back and rolls her hips and I growl at the friction against my cock, the fucking delicious heat of it all. Now my hand's moving down, from her spine to her ass, perfect and round and squeezable as fuck through her ugly denim skirt.

So I squeeze. Ruby gasps, and I let her hand go so I can grab her ass with both of mine and I pull her against me, my erection tight against her belly.

She doesn't pull away. She pushes her hips into mine with a ferocity that takes me by surprise, and I grunt because I can't help myself.

"Jump," I tell her, pulling back.

She blinks, breathing hard.

"What?"

I grab her arms and throw them over my shoulders while she looks confused. Disheveled and fucking beautiful, but confused, so I grin.

"Hold onto my shoulders and hop in the air," I say.

She frowns, but after a moment she hops into the air and I grab her upper thighs, pulling her legs around my hips and pinning her against the wall my aching erection pressed right up against her heat, her skirt wide open.

"Oh!" she yelps, laughing.

"There you go," I say, grinning. I run one hand over her knee, smooth with nylon, and Ruby keeps laughing and kisses me again, hard, her tongue in my mouth.

It's taking everything I've got not to tear her pantyhose and underwear off and take her right here, just like this. Her legs tighten around me as her hands wander through my hair, down my neck, over my shoulders, leaving tingling trails wherever they go.

I pin her against the wall a little harder with my hips. Ruby gasps into my mouth but moves her hips against me again, the friction nearly overriding my system as I move my hands down her body slowly, palms open over her shoulders, her collarbones, her high, full breasts.

I pull back and look into her wide green eyes as I touch her for the first time, letting my hands linger over her ugly t-shirt, feeling the heat of her body underneath as her chest heaves with every breath.

As desperately as I want her, *now*, I need Ruby to be okay, to want this herself, so I pause for a moment, just watching her.

She grabs my hand by the wrist and holds it to one breast, the perfect mound filling my palm as I grin. I'm not sure I've felt a girl up outside her clothes like this since I was a teenager, but I like it. Somehow being with Ruby makes this all feel brand new, exciting, like I'm touching a woman for the first time.

I grab both her breasts, still through her shirt, and she kisses me again so I run my thumbs over where her nipples should be, though the bra she's wearing is too padded to tell. Ruby bites my bottom lip and I groan into her mouth.

"Sorry," she whispers, putting one hand to my mouth.

I grab her ass again and hoist her higher, since she's starting to slide down the wall.

"What for?" I ask, kissing her jaw, one hand moving under the hem of her shirt, finding denim and pantyhose.

"The noise," she whispers.

"The noise was a good noise," I say into her ear. "Don't worry, it takes more than a nibble to hurt me."

I close my teeth around her earlobe gently and she gasps. My hand finds the edge of her hose and above it the warm, smooth skin of her belly, and I run one thumb just under the bottom of her bra, feeling her thighs tighten around me.

It's delicious. Better than I'd imagined, and I'd imagined that pushing her against the wall like this would be pretty fucking good. But she's starting to slip down again, so I kiss her neck one last time, grab her ass, and pull her away from the wall.

"Oh!" she says, softly, wrapping her arms around my neck, but I'm already halfway across the small kitchen, putting her down on the table, her legs curling around me again as I grab her shirt with one hand, about to pull it over her head.

But Ruby pulls back, one hand on my chest.

"Wait," she gasps.

We're both panting for breath, our bodies pressed together, every muscle in my body crackling with her electricity. But Ruby looks a little nervous, uncertain, so even though it's the last thing I want, I stop.

"Waiting," I say, lifting my eyebrows, twisting the hem of her shirt in my hand.

Ruby swallows and looks up at me again.

"I've never done this before," she says quickly, the words coming out in a nervous rush. I wait a moment, expecting more, but she just looks up at me like she's waiting for a response.

A smile tugs at my lips, and I can't help but laugh softly.

"And?" I murmur, my fingers still playing with the hem of her shirt.

"And... I don't know what I'm doing?" Ruby says.

I pull on her shirt and lean in closer, my other hand sliding up her denim-skirt-covered thigh.

"What you're doing is driving me absolutely fucking crazy every time you so much as look my way," I tell her, my voice getting gravelly and dipping low. "Any further questions?"

CHAPTER TWENTY-THREE

RUBY

I'M NOT sure what I was expecting Gabriel to do, but *start laughing* wasn't it. I'm holding my breath, sitting on the kitchen table with my legs wrapped around him, and he's grinning and chuckling.

"Any further questions?" he murmurs.

God knows I have plenty, but not for right now.

"It just seemed like you should know what you're dealing with," I whisper. I'm nervous because I don't want Gabriel to think I'm some sort of super-erotic sex goddess or something, because there's nothing further from the truth.

"I've had sex before but that's it," I say, feeling more and more awkward with every word. "I've never really done the, um, the foreplay parts, or any of the other stuff, just the actual..."

I trail off, my face blazing red, but Gabriel's still grinning.

"So you've never done *this* before," he says, his voice low and rough as he grabs both my knees and pulls me hard against him, his massive erection rubbing hard against my most sensitive parts.

I shake my head.

"And you've never done *this* before, either," he says, leaning in, taking one breast in his hand and running the pad of his thumb right over my nipple. Even through my extra-padded bra, I shiver.

"No," I whisper, though I'm getting less nervous with every moment.

"This?" he growls in my ear, sending a cascade of tingles down my spine, and then kisses my neck right below it. "Or this? Or this?"

Each question's punctuated with another kiss, lower on my neck, flooding my senses and making my eyes shut with pleasure. He slides his hand up my shirt again as he covers my neck with kisses, long and slow, short and rough, everything in between.

"I don't care what you haven't done before," he finally murmurs against my other ear. I'm half-delirious, leaning back on my hands and panting for breath, tingles down my spine. "I only care that you want to do it now."

I don't trust my voice so I turn my head and kiss him hard, pushing one hand through his hair. When he pulls back he lifts my shirt over my head and before it's even off I'm already sitting up straight, undoing my bra and letting it fall to his kitchen table.

He grabs me roughly, the fingers of both hands digging into my spine, and pulls my body against his, the fabric of his t-shirt soft against my skin, and I shiver as it rubs against my stiff, sensitive nipples.

He's practically devouring me, his tongue in my mouth and my hands in his hair, clutching his neck like I'm falling and he's all that's holding me up.

I squeeze him tighter with my legs and he slides his hands around my rib cage, the rough pads of his thumbs tracing the curves under each breast, finally sliding up to my nipples and circling them, slowly.

I moan in surprise, the sensation sending a bolt of heat straight downward. Gabriel chuckles slightly and bites my lower lip just hard enough.

"You have to stop laughing at me," I tease, gasping.

"I'm not laughing *at* you," he rumbles, his thumbs still moving deliciously. "I'm laughing with sheer fucking delight at the noise you just made."

He pinches them, rolling both nipples at once between his fingers and thumbs. I bite my lip, run my hands down his chest, and slide them under his shirt, slowly savoring his warm skin and hard, rippling muscles underneath it.

"Take it off," he says. "I'm not shy."

I reach up and pull his shirt over his head he flings it away, and good God is it a beautiful sight as he leans in again, the muscles in his shoulders and arms bunching. I run my fingers over them at last, feeling him flex and move, and I can't help but dig my fingernails in a little as he kisses me again, his skin against mine, pushing me backward onto the cool wood of his kitchen table as he leans over me, his lips trailing down my neck.

Gabriel takes one nipple between his teeth, just barely biting it as he runs his tongue across it. I grab his shoulders even harder and gasp, my teeth clenched together because even though the carriage house is probably far enough away that no one can hear, I don't need to take even more chances.

The fingers of his other hand slide beneath the elastic waist of my pantyhose, pulling on them gently, and he switches nipples, flicking his tongue across the other one. I'm practically squirming on the table, breathing hard, my legs locked around his waist, absolutely aching with desire.

Then Gabriel plants a single kiss on my upper belly and stops, looking at me. I look back, and he stands up straight and offers me his hand, pulling me upright.

"The kitchen table's only good for so long," he murmurs. "Come on."

He grabs my ass as I hop off the table, then leads me up the stairs and into his bedroom, shutting the door behind us, then turning to slide an arm around my half-naked waist.

I lean back against Gabriel, my eyes sliding closed as I savor the feeling of his warm skin against mine, his lips on my hair, his hands moving over my body. I arch against him as he grabs my hips in both hands and practically drags me against him, the huge bump in his jeans grinding against my ass as I exhale hard.

I think my insides might be melting, heated by the liquid desire that's flowing through me, hot and insistent. Gabriel leans down and kisses my neck again as he pulls me in harder, and a soft moan escapes me as I stand on my tiptoes and reach behind myself, running my palm over his denim-covered erection.

He grunts into my neck, and this time I don't apologize. I smile and don't stop. The grunt turns into a growl and I close my fingers around it as well as I can through his pants, stroking him from tip to root.

Gabriel's panting for breath, and he leans over me again, one hand in my hair pulling my head around, and gives me a long, deep kiss. Then he undoes the button and zipper on my denim skirt and puts his hand inside, underneath my pantyhose and underwear.

"Ruby," he says, his voice a rough whisper. "Has anyone ever made you come before?"

I swallow hard.

"Just me," I whisper back.

"Jesus, that's a shame," he murmurs, his fingers slipping downward and skimming along my lower lips. "Because you're wet as hell and I bet watching you come is fucking incredible."

I'm bright red, not that it matters since it's dark and I'm facing away, but Gabriel pushes a finger between my lips and to my entrance as I gasp and lean into him harder.

His fingers start circling my clit, slowly, and I sigh as the heat begins to build. This, at least, is a little familiar, since it's what I've been doing under my covers in the dark for a long time now.

Well, and for the past week, I've been doing it and pretending it was Gabriel, though this is even better than I imagined. It doesn't take long before I'm biting my lips together and trying not to moan, shocks zapping back and forth through my entire body. I'm standing on my toes and leaning against him, one hand slung backward around his neck, bucking and rolling my hips because I can't help myself.

But then he stops. I hold my breath, but Gabriel pulls his hand away, and in one quick motion spins me around, pulls my skirt off, and pushes me backward until I'm stumbling onto the bed, legs wide.

He's right behind me, kneeling, and he grabs the waist of my pantyhose and pulls down. They half stick to me, and so I grab them too, yanking and peeling and doing my damnedest not to poke a hole through them with a fingernail.

"I hate these stupid things," I mutter. "They're basically torture."

"I hate them too," Gabriel says as he slides them down

one leg. "Can you imagine the thoughts I'd be having if I saw you bare-legged?"

I finally get them off my right leg, and seconds later, Gabriel pulls them off my left and flings them to his bedroom floor in irritation.

"No," I say, and swallow, because I'm about to talk *sexy*. "But you could tell me."

He grins, grabs my panties, and pulls them off with one hand. Then he's on his hands and knees over me, reaches back, and grabs one ankle in his hand.

"I'd probably think incessantly about getting you alone and putting my hands up your skirt," he says, and kisses my ankle, putting it over his shoulder. "I'd fantasize about how soft you'd be, how I could wrap your thighs around my head."

He kisses the inside of my knee, and I'm holding my breath because I have a feeling I know what he's going do and—surprise—no one's ever done it to me before.

"I'd think about—" he kisses my inner thigh hard, his lips a little rough against my skin, "—what you smelled like, what you *taste* like," —two more kisses— "how you sound when you moan my name."

He kisses my thigh again slowly, but this time he sucks on the soft, tender skin there for a moment, just long enough that I can really feel it.

"So the pantyhose were effective?" I gasp, because now he's kneeling on the bed, his head between my legs, one knee over his shoulder and my whole body is wound like a spring, a combination of nerves and desire.

"Not exactly," he rumbles, his mouth so close to me I can feel the vibrations. "I thought about all those things anyway."

Before I can respond something touches my lower lips

and pushes them apart, delving between them and grazing my entrance, something flexible and strong.

It's his tongue, I think, both hands clenched tightly on the comforter. *It's his tongue, this is normal, everyone does this all the time and there's nothing to be—*

His tongue reaches my clit and I gasp as pure pleasure bolts through my body. I nearly knee Gabriel in the head as my entire body jolts, his fingers closing around my thighs even harder as he circles my clit slowly with his tongue.

I can't even believe how good it feels. He keeps going, moving faster and faster, and I have to clench my teeth together to keep myself from shouting. My whole body is bucking and writhing, my hands and toes clenched, and I feel like I can barely control myself but I couldn't care less.

This is spectacular, incredible, and Gabriel keeps flicking his tongue over my clit perfectly and sending me higher and higher until, with a gasp, I crash down and come so hard it feels like a religious experience.

Gradually, it fades. I open my eyes. Gabriel's tongue circles me one more time, sending a quick jolt through my muscles, and then he kisses me on the thigh again. I just lie there for a moment, staring at the ceiling, until I feel his hand on mine, gently pulling at me.

I look down. Both my hands were clenched in his hair, and I release him instantly.

"Sorry," I whisper, but he's grinning.

"I was right," he says, and pushes himself to his hands and knees, planting a kiss on one hip. "Watching you come is pretty fucking incredible. Even if you did nearly scalp me."

"I didn't mean to," I say, as he kisses the spot right above my belly button, the bottom of my ribcage.

"Did you mean to shout *oh my God* over and over

again?" he asks, his tongue dipping into the hollow of my throat.

I blink.

"No?" I say, my hands on his shoulders again, my knees around his hips. I'm acutely aware that I'm totally naked and he's not as denim slides along my thighs.

"You could have been quieter," he murmurs, kissing my jaw. He smells musky and kind of odd, and it takes me a second to realize me smells like... well, *me*.

"Apparently not," I say, trying not to laugh. "I thought I was being quiet as a church mouse."

He kisses me, hard and slow, and even though he tastes like me it's kind of hot, a reminder of what we just did. I'm sure there are church doctrines against this but I couldn't care less as he winds our tongues together, my legs wrapped around his waist again, his thick erection pressing up against my clit even through his jeans.

I reach down, between us, and grab his belt buckle, pulling at the leather while he groans into my neck.

Downstairs, a sharp knock sounds.

We both freeze.

In an instant, Gabriel's rolled off of me and is standing, at the door, listening while I sit up on his bed in sheer terror.

It's my father, I think, my insides constricting in horror. *He heard and he knows what I'm doing and oh God I'm going to be sent to reeducation camp and married to Kyle and he'll impregnate me a dozen times and I'll never escape and I'll never see the light of day again.*

Unless I run, right here, right now, though I've got nowhere to go—

Gabriel looks back at me, puts a finger to his lips, and opens the door. My heart is racing so fast that I'm afraid it's audible all the way downstairs, but I just nod mutely and watch him as he leaves the room and shuffles down the stairs, making plenty of noise.

The front door opens.

"Everything alright?" I hear him say, yawning theatrically.

"We were just comin' here to ask you the same question," an unfamiliar voice says. It must be one of the new guards my father hired to patrol the grounds at night. "We heard some grunting and wanted to make sure you didn't have an intruder or nothin'."

They heard it outside. Oh my God.

For a second I forget all about re-education camps and running away, and I'm just mortified.

"Aw, shit," Gabriel says.

There's a pause, and I can hear the man outside shuffling.

"That was me," Gabriel goes on, like he's confessing something. "I hate to talk about it, but I served a tour in Afghanistan and I've still got... you know. I dream about it sometimes. Wake up drenched in sweat."

He does?

The other man sighs.

"Sorry to hear that, brother," he says. "Glad you're alright."

"Don't apologize," Gabriel says. "Thanks for checking. Have a good night."

"You too," the other guy says. The door shuts. I finally exhale, my body coming unfrozen, and I glance over my shoulder at the big house.

Almost every light on the second floor is on, the floor below where I'm supposed to be asleep in my bed, and for the second time in about sixty seconds, I freeze.

Then I practically dive for my skirt and pantyhose as

Gabriel's steps cross the floor. I don't bother getting the hose on, just shove them in one pocket as I pull my skirt up, then search for my underwear on my hands and knees.

There's a sigh from the doorway, just as I grab my panties, and I look over. Gabriel's standing there, leaning against the door frame with my shirt and bra in his hand, watching me with a giant bulge in his jeans.

"Someone's awake in the house," I whisper, getting to my feet.

"Yeah, I saw the lights," he says, his voice slow.

I sit on the bed and pull my panties back on. I'm still naked from the waist up, and Gabriel tosses me my bra, then my shirt.

I feel awful. I mean, I feel great but at the same time I'm so nervous I'm almost sick to my stomach, plus I feel awful that Gabriel just did *that* for me, and I haven't reciprocated in the least.

When I finish getting dressed, I sit on the edge of his bed and look at him for a few seconds, because I have no idea how to end this particular meeting, even though I need to go, now, before someone realizes I'm gone.

"I'm sorry," I finally say, my eyes flicking to the lump in his jeans. "That we didn't get to..."

I trail off, because I have no idea how to phrase *do stuff with your penis*, but Gabriel just grins and offers me his hand, pulling me off his bed.

"Don't be," he says, kissing me, his mouth still musky. "I had a great time tonight."

I stand on my toes and kiss him harder, because whether or not I'm about to get in a lot of trouble, hot, silky desire is snaking through my body again and I just want to touch him, get close to him.

Gabriel pulls my skirt up and grabs my ass, giving it a good, long squeeze.

"Get outta here," he says. "Stay out of trouble so we can do this again."

"Right," I whisper. "Sorry."

One more squeeze, and then I'm down the stairs.

I grab my shoes from the kitchen, slide them on, and slip out the back door.

CHAPTER TWENTY-FOUR

GABRIEL

HOLY SHIT, I can't believe I just did that. There was a naked girl in my bed—fuck, a naked girl who'd just *come her brains out*—and I just told her to go instead of getting herself into trouble.

A couple months ago, I'd never have done that. Hell, a couple of weeks ago I wouldn't have turned down more sex. I didn't do that, one of the dumbest decisions of my life, which is why I'm here in the first place.

I walk to my bedroom window and angle myself so I can see through the blinds without moving them. Ruby's a dark shape walking across the lawn in a wide circle, and as I watch her head for the pantry window, shoulders straight, hair moving in the breeze, I think: *maybe I don't regret coming here quite so much any more.*

She ducks around the side of the house and I can't see her anymore, but I'm holding my breath. I'm still hard as fucking iron, and I clench my hands into fists, determined to wait until I'm sure she's okay before I jerk off thinking about Ruby for the thousandth time.

Ruby, half-naked on my kitchen table, her breasts full and her nipples stiff under my hands. The way she gasped when I touched her.

Ruby, naked on my bed, her legs around my waist. The noise she made as I kissed my way down her leg, her hands in my hair as I licked her.

The way she moaned, pussy clenching, when she came, every ounce of her self-control gone out the window.

I swallow, teeth clenched, cock throbbing in my pants.

Not until she's okay.

I keep waiting, powerless, and I fucking hate it because I've always been terrible at sneaking and subterfuge. I'd rather go in, guns blazing, and get the job done once and for all, but that's not how it works here.

Finally, just as I'm starting to get nervous for her, a curtain moves in her bedroom, and a sliver of darkness appears, Ruby's face in the middle. I lift a single slat in the blinds, and I can't see her face that well, but I'm almost certain she smiles.

Then she waves. I stick my fingers through the blinds and wave back, and she closes the curtains.

In seconds I'm on my bed, cock in my hand, the memory of Ruby's moans filling my ears as I pump my hand hard, desperate for some kind of relief. I think of her naked, on the bed, of her fingernails on my back as I tease her slick folds, the way she'd moan as I enter her. The expression in her eyes as she gets close, the way she'd feel as she came with me inside her—

I erupt in seconds, faster than I've come in years, clenching my jaw so I don't shout. Afterward I take a deep, long, shuddering breath, stand, and head for the bathroom, dick still hanging out of my pants since I'm alone here, after all.

It didn't scratch my itch. It didn't come close, but at least I think I can sleep tonight.

––––––

IN MY SHOWER the next morning, I wash my face about twenty times. Not because I mind smelling like Ruby, but because I can hardly walk around the Senator's house with the smell of his daughter's pussy on my face. Even if the thought makes me smile.

Besides, I've got a suspicion that the Senator couldn't identify the smell of pussy if there was one right in front of him.

When I walk into the kitchen, Ruby's right there, stirring together a big bowl of fruit salad. She looks over at me and for half a second we both stop, and I swear to God something about the way the morning sun lights her hair makes her look like some sort of angel.

The urge to walk over, wrap her in my arms and kiss her good morning is so strong that I have to clench my fists in my pockets. But then Mrs. Burgess bustles in, carrying a pot of coffee, and breaks the spell.

"Morning, Gabriel," Ruby says, exactly the same way she does every morning.

"Morning, Ruby," I respond, and Mrs. Burgess hands me a cup of coffee.

"Go on in to breakfast," she says, in the polite voice she uses for orders. "The food will be right in."

"Thank you, ma'am," I say.

I give Ruby one last glance, force myself not to think of how soft her thighs were against my lips, and go into the dining room to join the rest of the men.

———

AFTER LUNCH, there's a meeting of the Senator's security staff. Thank God, no one mentions the strange noises from last night. Even though I sometimes do wake up shouting, I'm pretty sure it doesn't sound anything like Ruby whisper-shouting *oh my God* over and over again, so I was kind of surprised the guy bought it.

The meeting feels like it lasts forever in a stifling hot room right off the Senator's office. The air conditioning doesn't work too well in a house this old and this big, and Ray, who's a little paranoid, won't open a window. So I sit there, sweat, and think about Ruby's legs wrapped around my waist.

As it's ending and I'm leaving, distracted, I hear the Senator clear his throat pointedly, and my stomach clenches.

"Gabriel," he says.

I snap my head up and look him in the eye, thinking *I've never seen your daughter naked.*

"Sir?"

He buttons one button on his jacket, waiting for the rest of the security staff to trickle out. Then he nods at the door to his office, indicating that I should follow him.

"A word," he says.

I steel myself, nodding, and follow.

Don't take it out on Ruby, I think. *Make sure I never work again, just don't take it out on her.*

He sits as his desk, waving a hand at the chair opposite, and I follow suit. Wordlessly, he takes an envelope from a drawer and tosses it across his desk.

I'm relieved but angry, all at once, one emotion traded for the other as I pick up the latest missive from Ruby's stalker and start praying, wordlessly, that this is one of the harmless ones.

"It came today," the Senator says, his voice listless. "Postmarked yesterday from Atlanta, just like all the others. Nothing in the envelope. It's the same notebook paper, the kind you get at Wal-Mart for fifty cents a ream."

Everything about this letter is untraceable, he's saying. They all are: envelopes and paper and ink used by millions of people; postmarked Atlanta, one of the biggest cities on the east coast. He told me during one of our meetings that he had the FBI run the DNA from the envelope sealant, but it didn't match anything in the system.

Besides, *just letters* is pretty low on the threat scale for law enforcement. Even letters like these.

I open it without saying anything, the Senator's eyes on my face, and start reading.

About two paragraphs into the spindly handwriting, I start frowning.

"This is..." I start, trailing off. I turn the page over and skim the other side, alarm bells ringing louder and louder.

"Sir, as far as I can tell this is an exact account of her activities at the Holtville County Fair last Saturday," I say. I feel like I've been punched in the gut.

I was there. I was with her, the whole time, and I didn't protect her from him. This fucking creep was there too, watching her every move. Noting it down for later use, and now he's goddamn taunting me with that knowledge.

"This has escalated," the Senator says darkly.

I read it again, practically seeing red. I can't believe how wrong I had this guy, thinking that he would never try anything, thinking that he just got off on writing her creepy letters and nothing else.

He followed us. He followed *her* and I had no idea. Cold sweat starts tracing down my body as I think of every time that day that she left my sight, that she went to the ladies' room, that she turned a corner before I did.

Everything. He saw everything, and this message is crystal fucking clear: if he wanted to, he could hurt her.

I could flip the Senator's desk over right now, my whole body nearly vibrating with raw rage even as I try to collect myself and act as though I'm professionally upset, not fucking murderous.

"We need to go after him," I say. "There has to be something. We know he was close last Saturday, and chances are, he'll be close again. He'll want to try something, and when he does we'll—"

I stop short, because I nearly say *rip his fucking arms off and beat him with them.* I clear my throat.

"—See that he's arrested," I finish.

"I agree," the Senator says curtly. "I'll be adding to her security detail during events that require her to leave the estate, and I'm increasing patrols around the house itself."

He leans forward at his desk, eye glinting dangerously. I'm strangely glad that, as differently as we feel about everything else, we're both fucking furious about this. We have exactly one thing in common, and it's our desire to protect Ruby.

"I've spoken again with my contacts at the FBI and exerted a little pressure," he says. "Right now, they've got a handwriting analyst working on this, as well as a few agents going through the security cameras from the post office where this was postmarked. It's a long shot, but I had to do something."

"Are there records of who attended the fair?" I ask, though I'm sure he's thought of it.

The Senator shakes his head.

"FBI and Holtsville PD have gone over what they could already," he says. "Someone just walking around the fair wouldn't have set off any alarms."

But he was there, I think. *He was right there. I must have seen him.*

We might have made eye contact. Jesus, I could have spoken with him.

The thought turns my blood cold.

"I'd like you to put together a security plan for our overnight visit to Charleston to attend the Patriots for America rally," he says. "Any resources you need are yours."

"Thank you, sir."

There's a knock on the side door, and Mason sticks his face in.

"Your daughter, sir."

The Senator sighs.

"Yes, send her in."

The door closes, and he leans across the desk, hand extended. It's a clear *we're done here*, so I stand and shake his hand as the door opens again and Ruby walks in.

I swear every inch of my skin prickles.

"You wanted to see me, father?" she asks in that clear, honey-sweet, fake voice.

"Thank you, Gabriel," the Senator says, and I head for the door.

Just as I step through, I hear him say, "Ruby, I heard you refused Kyle Pickett's offer of marriage."

The door shuts behind me, and I stop short.

That's what he's fucking talking to her about?

Every nice thought I had about the Senator wanting to protect his daughter flies out the window. I nearly open the door again to give the man hell, but instead I clench my teeth and stop myself. Getting fired won't make Ruby any safer.

In the side office, Mason is watching me from behind his desk, but he quickly looks away when I make eye contact. Still fuming, I let myself out and head downstairs to start planning for our trip.

CHAPTER TWENTY-FIVE

RUBY

I SEE Gabriel all day long, but we never mention what happened last night. We can't. We've graduated from *isn't that bunny fluffy* to the broad outlines of our lives: how he grew up an Army brat, never in the same place for more than a few years; how I used to have a dog named Goldie. But I can't say *I'm coming back tonight.*

Still, even though our conversations are short and scrubbed clean of anything salacious, I like them. I feel like I'm finally starting to put together the pieces of Gabriel.

On one hand, there's the polite consummate professional who quizzes me on exits and vantage points, who's constantly on the lookout, who's always close and protective and ready to take down a threat. Who makes me feel safe, no matter what.

And on the other, there's the Gabriel who gets me wet with a glance, who pushes me against a wall and makes me moan. The Gabriel who left a light purple hickey on my inner thigh last night, which I found when I took a shower this morning.

That Gabriel finally finds me folding laundry in the

family room, and as he leans against the doorframe, I can't help but blush, even though I can hear my mother talking from the next room over.

He doesn't say anything, but he raises one eyebrow and just looks at me, questioningly.

My mouth goes dry, but I nod once, doing my best not to smile.

Then Gabriel winks. I wink back. My mother appears behind him, and he steps out of the doorway as she asks if I've starched my father's shirts properly this time.

Just then, I don't even remember what starch *is*.

———

THAT NIGHT, it feels like it takes forever for all the lights in the house to go out. I've already got my stupid pantyhose off, wadded up in a ball in my underwear drawer, and there's nothing I can do but lie here until it's finally time to sneak out to the carriage house.

This is stupid. I know it's stupid. I'm a grown woman— I'm divorced for Pete's sake—and I'm sneaking out of my parents' house through a window to go meet a man.

I need to leave. I've known that much for months, but I haven't got anything in place yet, so for now, it's all tiptoeing past floodlights and holding my breath every time I come back in.

Once it's quiet, I grab my shoes in one hand and head down the back stairs, barefoot, treading to the far-right side where they're less squeaky. I skip the sixth from the top and the second from the bottom, and I get to the hall between the laundry room and the kitchen without any sound.

And then I freeze, because there are voices.

I hold my breath and will myself silent and invisible,

trying to shrink so I fit into the deepest shadow the stairway has to offer, just listening.

Say you came down for a drink of water. No one will suspect anything…

"But I can't," the first voice whispers, and I frown. "It won't work, they'll find it, they found the first one…"

It's my youngest sister, Joy, and my heart tightens in my chest.

Joy, what are you getting up to?

"So hide this one better, dummy," says my brother Zeke's voice.

"I can't," she whispers, sounding completely miserable. "Pearl will find it again, and this time she'll tell Mom and Dad and she'll probably tell them that I'm worshipping Satan or something because she's way too dumb to know what imaginary numbers are, and…"

In the dark, I raise one eyebrow.

"You're telling me you're sneaky enough to enroll in a college math class and not sneaky enough to hide a textbook from Pearl?" Zeke says. "Please."

Now I'm grinning. I wish I'd been enrolling in college math classes when I was fourteen, but my rebellion was limited to kissing a boy a couple of times. Math might have actually been helpful.

Atta girl, Joy.

"Okay, okay," Joy mutters. "I just…"

I slip away in the opposite direction, toward the pantry with the window, their voices fading into the background. The window slides up silently, and I get out, go behind the rosebushes, cross the yard in a wide circle. I've done this enough in the past six months that I know the route by heart, though when I get to the wall behind the bushes, I go toward Gabriel's carriage house instead of the loose bar in the fence.

This time, I don't even have to knock.

He pulls the door open before I have the chance and when I see him, I just stand there for the space of a few heartbeats, savoring the moment. Looking at him for as long as I want, as much as I want, not afraid that someone else will catch me and wonder if I'm thinking lustful thoughts.

Which I am. Obviously.

He's in jeans and a t-shirt again, barefoot, the lines of his muscles visible through the thin fabric. My insides turn liquid almost instantly as I stare, wondering how on earth this is happening to me.

Gabriel grins and lets me through his door, shutting and locking it behind me. Before either of us says anything, he grabs me and pulls me close, one hand snaking through my hair as he kisses me hard and slow, our mouths opening, a low growl sounding in his chest.

"Do you know how fucking crazy you drive me some-times?" he murmurs. "I have to make small talk with your mother while she arranges flowers and all I can think about is how wet you were last night."

All the blood in my body rushes to my face.

"She was talking about her dandelions and all I could think about was my tongue in your pussy," he goes on.

I somehow blush even harder and turn my face away, because I have literally no idea how to respond to that, even though I'm already wet and aching. But Gabriel just chuckles and lowers his face to mine, talking right into my ear.

"Let me guess," he whispers. "Nobody's ever talked dirty to you before, either."

"No," I murmur. "And my mother doesn't grow dande-lions, those are weeds."

"I told you I wasn't paying attention."

"Apparently, you've never paid attention," I tease.

"I've paid plenty of attention to the right things," he says. "I know every way an intruder could get into your house, and I know the *exact* shape of your ass when you bend over to get something out of the oven."

He reaches down and gives my butt a good, hard squeeze, and we kiss again, harder and faster, the words *my tongue in your pussy* still ringing through my ears.

Before I know it, his hands are under my shirt. He unhooks my bra and then flings them both off all at once, the cool night air touching my skin. Then he whirls me around, lifts me up, and suddenly I'm sitting on the stairs and he's leaning me back, his hips between my legs again.

This all still feels wild and unfamiliar, like my body is a mess of competing impulses—to kiss him again, grab his hair, moan, grab his shoulder, tear his shirt off, bite his neck, all at once. I feel like a kid in a candy store, except I've broken into the candy store and all the candy is very off-limits.

Also, all the candy is sex.

But then Gabriel kisses my neck again and I gasp, my hands clawing at his shirt, and he nips at me.

"Please don't leave a mark," I whisper.

"I know better," he murmurs, his voice vibrating against me.

"You left one last night."

His hand slides up my ugly skirt—this one's khaki—and his thumb finds exactly the spot where I've got a purple splotch.

"I know," he says. "I couldn't help it, and it's not like anyone else is gonna see it."

Then his mouth is on my collarbone, his hand sliding under my panties and at the exact same time, he brushes his thumb along my lower lips and closes his teeth around one nipple.

My whole body jolts, my hand tightening on his shoulder. He flicks his tongue over my nipple as his thumb slides between my folds and I gasp, toes curling.

I cannot believe what I've been missing out on all these years. Gabriel hooks his fingers over my panties and pulls, so I lift my butt off the stairs and they come off, flying down the stairs to somewhere on the ground floor of his apartment, but I'm not watching them.

My skirt's around my waist now. I grab the banister with one hand as his thumb moves to my clit and starts moving in slow, steady circles, his mouth still on my nipple. I take a deep breath and let it out slowly, forcing myself not to moan or shout or make any noise at all.

Somehow, I'm once again pretty much naked while Gabriel's still fully clothed. And somehow, once again, I'm pretty sure he's going to make me come before I even see his penis.

Because already, the heat's building inside me. I've been on edge all day, nervous and excited and aroused whenever he looks at me, and God knows I've been thinking about this constantly. So it's no surprise that I'm already close, lying back on the stairs as he licks me and fingers me and I hold onto the banister for dear life and try not to make a peep.

A whimper escapes my mouth. Gabriel bites down a little harder on my nipple, and I gasp.

"Shh," he teases me.

"I'm trying," I whisper, panting for breath, but he just laughs and sucks my other nipple into his mouth.

As he does he strokes my lips with another finger. My

fingers and toes tighten and then he slides the finger inside me, into my tight entrance, and moves it against my sensitive front wall.

I nearly shout, gritting my teeth together, but Gabriel just moves his hand harder, faster. He adds another finger and I clap my other hand to my mouth just in time, because seconds later I come, flying over the cliff's edge and into the abyss below.

Gradually, it stops. Gabriel takes his fingers out of me and slides his hand around my thigh, kissing my neck again, nipping at my earlobe.

"There's no windows in the stairwell," he murmurs into my ear. "I thought maybe you could get all the noise out of your system."

I'm still gasping for breath, my head back against the stairs. I don't have a response, but he kisses me again, his hard body against mine, and finally I've got the presence of mind to pull his shirt off, tossing it down the stairs behind him.

Then we're skin-to-skin, and he scoops me up off the stairs and half-carries me the rest of the way into his bedroom. My skirt's off before the door is even closed, and I'm pulling at his belt, finally getting it undone as his hands drift down my back.

Gabriel groans when I pull the zipper down on his jeans, and then his cock springs out into my hand, long and thick and hard as rock. I hesitate for one second—*oh my God what do I do*—but then I take it in my hand and stroke him once, hard, from tip to root and back.

He grabs my ass harder and grunts, his eyes closed, so I do it again, then again, and then I stand on my tiptoes and kiss his neck. I can feel his pulse under my lips as I do, still stroking him hard, our bodies pressed together. I move my mouth lower, to his collarbone, then his chest, and then Gabriel groans *again*, a little louder, and I realize what I'm about to do.

And I don't think. I let my body, throbbing with desire, take over, and I get on my knees, trailing kisses along his hard stomach, down his light treasure trail, until there it is right in front of me.

It's big. Bigger than normal, I think, though what the hell do I know since all my information comes from my gay ex-husband and the porn I used to catch him watching. And I'm nervous, but I'm wet and I'm aching and dear God, more than anything I want to hear him make that noise again, I want to make him feel as incredible as he's already made me feel.

Twice.

So I stick out my tongue and lick the rigid underside of his shaft, my heart beating so fast it's practically a hum, and Gabriel gasps, so I do it again.

This time he groans, and I take his head into my mouth, moving my tongue around it, careful to keep my teeth away. I swear I can feel him get even harder in my mouth, a deep growl coming from his chest as I pull back, my lips sliding over him.

"Fuck, Ruby," he whispers, and I curl my toes.

With the next stroke I take him deeper, then deeper, until his breathing is ragged and his cock is hitting the back of my mouth before I pull him out with a slurp, my tongue sliding along the underside. I bob my head up and down his shaft slowly, still getting used to this, but his breathing's getting faster and he's leaking pre-cum into my mouth.

"Jesus, that feels good," he growls. "You like that?"

I do. Even if I've been told my whole life that this is dirty, wrong, something that sluts and whores do. I've got

Gabriel in my mouth and he's panting and moaning. He's hotter than hell and I'm doing this to him.

He slides one hand over my head and just keeps it there, gently, while I keep going. Now he's grunting with every stroke, his cock starting to twitch. I pull him from my mouth and suck at the tip slowly, and even though I feel completely dirty doing this, I don't mind.

"Stop," he finally gasps.

I ignore him and suck the tip of his cock into my mouth again, start to slide my lips down his shaft but then his hand locks into my hair and pulls me back with surprising force.

"I'm gonna come if you don't stop," he growls, releasing me.

I swallow.

"And?"

Gabriel takes a deep breath and then looks down at me.

"And," he says, pulling me to my feet, "what I really want is to feel you come while I'm inside you."

He kisses me hard, even though I'm sure I taste like him, as he winds his hands through my hair. Then he pulls away, a teasing smile crinkling the corner of his eyes.

"If that's okay with you," he says.

He walks me backward a step, his hardness practically throbbing between us. I'm wet and aching again, and even though part of me is quietly whispering *you can't have sex with someone you're not married to,* I ignore it.

"It's okay," I gasp.

I think that's the least sexy possible response, but Gabriel just grins and keeps walking me backward, toward his bed.

"So you don't mind if I just keep getting you off, then," he teases. "It's perfectly fine with you."

I open my mouth to reply, but then we're up against his

bed. He grabs me and tosses me onto it and then he's on top of me, laughing into my neck as he nuzzles me, one hand skimming along a nipple, his hips between my legs. I swallow hard.

"Right," I whisper.

"Good," he says. "Because God knows I've been thinking about it since the moment I saw you buying vodka at eight in the morning."

He reaches into his bedside table and I reach between us, taking his cock in my hand again, my back arching and my hips digging into his. Everything I've ever learned is telling me that I should *not* be doing this, but I couldn't care less.

How could something that feels so right—so, so right—be wrong?

"Shit," Gabriel mutters, shutting the drawer of his bedside table. "I forgot I hid 'em like a porn stash."

He rolls off the bed and crouches next to it, reaching under the mattress. I raise myself up on my elbows and raise my eyebrows as he pulls out one foil packet and then winks at me.

"Police state," he teases, leans over the bed, and kisses me hard again, rolling me onto my side.

He tears the package open and rolls the condom on, climbing back onto the bed, pulling my legs around his waist. The tip of his cock bumps against me, sliding between my lips and then up to my clit, and I grab the back of his head and sigh explosively, pressing our faces together.

"Come on," I whisper as I roll my hips, trying to guide him back to my entrance. I need this right now, because otherwise I think I might actually lose my mind.

Gabriel kisses me, guiding himself back to my entrance.

I tighten my legs around his waist and then gasp as he enters me slowly.

Sweet Jesus, it feels good. He groans into my ear, his hand closing around my shoulder, every muscle in his back tensing, like he's trying to hold himself back.

"You okay?" he whispers roughly.

"Don't stop," I gasp. He doesn't respond, just grunts and sinks himself into me faster. I can feel every millimeter of him as he enters, every sensitive spot inside me lighting up with pleasure as he does.

All I can think is, *so this is what the big deal is all about.*

Then he's all the way in and I'm panting for breath, filled and stretched because he's way bigger than my ex, but oh my God does this feel good as we start moving together. There's something completely intoxicating about it as he thrusts slowly at first and I can feel every single muscle in his body working, hear his ragged breathing as the heat inside me pumps and writhes, threatening to burst free at any second.

After a moment he pauses, then grabs my hips and pushes himself to kneeling, my hips suddenly off the bed, his cock still buried deeply inside me, and I nearly shout.

"Shh," he teases me, pulling one knee over his shoulder.

"I'm try—" I start, but I just gasp again as he starts thrusting even deeper, reaching one hand up to tweak a nipple. The new angle has me seeing stars, and I bite my lip, eyes closed, hands locked on the sheets as I do my absolute best not to make noise.

I'm right on the edge, Gabriel moving slow and steady and hard and deep. I can hear myself whimpering, because nothing has ever felt like this and I had no idea it could, and then he's got one thumb on my clit and rubs it in a slow circle.

That's it. I come explosively, shoving one fist to my mouth as I half-grunt, half-shout, my toes curling as I surrender completely to the pleasure rocking through my whole body. I think I might be melting it's so intense, but I don't care.

Then Gabriel grunts, holding his breath, and even through the haze of pleasure I can feel him jolt inside me, again and again.

I don't want this to end, but gradually, we both slow. I take my hand away from my mouth and my eyes open as he leans over me again, still inside me, and kisses my neck, my ear, my lips. We kiss for a long time until finally, he pulls out and rolls over, flopping next to me on his bed, his erection still at half-mast.

"Was that also okay?" he teases.

CHAPTER TWENTY-SIX

GABRIEL

I'M EXPECTING Ruby to roll her eyes, but she just exhales and smiles, still on her back. It's a real smile, maybe the most genuine one I've ever seen her make, just pure, unguarded happiness.

"Yeah, that was fine," she says, turning her head toward me. Her green eyes are sparkling, even in the dark, her hair wild on the pillow. "Completely acceptable."

I pull her in and kiss her one more time, lazily, our faces both half-smashed into the pillows below us. It's slow and almost sloppy, but there's something intensely intimate about this, kissing just because even though I'm totally, utterly, and completely sated, I like the feel of her lips on mine.

When it ends, I heave a deep breath, then sit up on the edge of the bed.

"Be right back," I say, and head into the bathroom, condom bobbing at the end of my mostly-floppy dick. I wrap it very carefully and toss it into the trash, figuring that the plumbing in this place is probably pretty old, and if it gets clogged with a condom, there will be some serious questions.

When I get back to the bathroom, Ruby's gone.

My heart squeezes and instantly I think *she's been taken, he got her, he was watching even here and all it took was for me to leave for one second* but then I hear a quiet noise downstairs, and some of the tension unfurls.

I rush down, and she's there, of course, sitting on a chair and putting her shoes back on, wearing her skirt and bra, totally un-kidnapped. As I walk in, she looks me up and down, then looks away like she's embarrassed.

"I should go," she murmurs. "Have you seen my shirt?"

"Don't," I say.

She looks at me, that guarded expression back in her eyes.

"Gabriel," she says. "I can't—"

"Twenty minutes," I say, and I grin at her so I don't sound like I'm begging.

Which I'm not. I'm not begging, I'm just asking her to stay because I want her to stay. I want twenty more minutes of talking together like two adults, of real, raw, unguarded Ruby who doesn't have to please anyone or think about who's listening.

She bites her lip and looks away, at the front of my apartment. It's dark outside except for the faraway streetlights: no lights on in the house, no sign of life.

"I got whiskey," I say, and that gets a smile out of her.

"I swear you think I'm an alcoholic," she says, but she takes her shoe back off.

"I met you at a liquor store at eight in the morning when you had a toddler in tow," I point out, walking naked through the downstairs of my apartment toward a cabinet.

"There were special circumstances," she laughs. "And I'm not even the one who nearly puked on a two-year-old."

"I've got better aim than *that*," I say, kneeling on my kitchen floor.

I pull pots and pans out of a cabinet, all unused, until I can grab the bottle of Four Roses I've stashed back there. I feel pretty ridiculous hiding whiskey like a seventeen-year-old, but if I'm going to be fucking the Senator's daughter—which I absolutely intend to continue doing—I should probably be as squeaky clean as possible otherwise.

"Has it been as bad as you thought it would be?"

I close the cabinet, bottle in hand, stand, and turn to stare at her like she's crazy.

"I'm pouring you a drink still stark naked," I say, bafflement in my voice. "No, it's not as bad as I thought it would be."

"Well, not that part," she says quickly. "But everything else."

As far as I was concerned, two weeks ago the worst part of this was going to be not drinking or getting my dick wet for a couple of months, and here I am, wet-dicked and pouring whiskey into tumblers. But I don't want to say that to Ruby, because then the rest of the truth is gonna have to come out, too.

That there were women, all the time. Lots of them, mostly political types who were in town for a few weeks looking for a little fun before they went back to wherever they were from, and I was always more than happy to provide a night or two of good times.

I'm not an asshole. I knew their names and the basic details of their lives. Sometimes I'd even call the next day, see if a woman wanted to get together again. But all I ever wanted from them was sex, and they were more than happy to oblige.

Harmless, until it wasn't. Until I wanted sex from one particular woman, and *that* ended in disaster.

But that's not how I feel about Ruby. Even though I barely know her, it's just *not*. This feels different, strange, like she's somehow gotten a hold on something deep inside me and isn't letting go of it.

So I don't want her to know that I've got a past with dozens of women, and I really don't want her to know why I'm here now. At least not yet. Not now, when we're sated and drinking whiskey in the dark and this moment is just about as perfect as it can be.

I grab ice from the freezer, plop it into the glasses, and hand one to Ruby.

"Everything else has taken some getting used to," I admit.

She looks at me, then down at my dick. She stares at it for a few seconds, then looks back up at me, and I can't help but grin.

"You're gonna have to wait about thirty minutes for round two, so drink up," I tease.

Ruby smiles and shuts her eyes, shaking her head.

"Sorry," she says. "It's just, like, *there* and..."

I take a long sip of my drink, my other hand on my hip, dick totally exposed.

Ruby starts giggling, and I grin.

"You're not supposed to laugh at someone's dick," I tell her, giving it a slight wiggle.

She laughs so hard she snorts.

"My self-confidence is gonna be ruined now," I tease her. "I'm a broken man, Ruby, and it's all because you laughed at my dick."

"I'm not, I swear," she gasps. "It's just, I don't know, it's right there?"

I lean down and give her a kiss.

"I'm gonna go find my pants so you stop mocking me," I say.

"I'm sorry," she says again, but she's still laughing, and I head upstairs and get half-dressed, sticking another condom in my pocket just in case. The whole time I'm grinning like an idiot.

I get it. Dicks are funny. Besides, it just made her come so hard her eyes rolled back in her head, so I'm feeling pretty confident about it right now.

When I get back downstairs, she's sitting on the couch, feet tucked under her, looking at the curtained windows to the yard. I grab my drink and sit as well, one arm around her. I've got jeans on again but no shirt, and apparently, she hasn't found hers either, so we sit there skin-to-skin, and for a long moment, we just sip our drinks without saying anything.

"My father said you're tightening security," Ruby says, all of a sudden. "I meant to ask you about it earlier, but I got... distracted."

"He didn't say why?"

She snorts.

"He went into excruciating detail about the many reasons that I should put aside my pride and personal preferences, suck it up, and have ten children with Kyle, but no, he didn't elaborate at all on what happened with the man who's stalking me," she says. There's a bitter edge to her voice, but it's not like I can blame her.

But I do hate being the one who tells her this stuff, the only one who'll bother to tell her the truth she deserves to know.

"He was at the county fair," I say, and then explain everything. Ruby looks into her drink the entire time without saying anything. I try to sound as professional as I can, the fact that we're both half-naked aside, because the last thing I want is for her to be scared.

Cautious, yes. Alert, aware, maybe a little nervous, fuck yes. Those things are useful.

I finish, and she's still leaning against my chest, quiet, swirling the ice in her glass.

"You've read most of the letters, right?" she asks.

"Right."

She thinks for another moment.

"What's his deal?" she finally says, and looks up at me. "Why's he doing this?"

"I have no fucking clue," I say, taking a sip of whiskey.

"Does he want something?" she asks.

"Most people who do this sort of thing want control," I say, slowly. I've got half a degree in criminal justice, even though I stopped going to classes when I got hired for the Secret Service. "It's a power trip thing. I think he likes making you afraid, and he likes watching us all scramble to protect you and keep you safe."

I take a deep breath.

"And I think he likes knowing that if he can't have you, he can dictate what you do anyway," I say, and take a drink before I say this next sentence. "I think he's incredibly attracted to you, but I think that because—as he puts it—you're no longer pure, he feels guilty about it and it gets all twisted in his head. So, he wants you but doesn't want to want you, and he's ended up writing a ton of fucked up letters about it."

"I wish he wouldn't," she says, sighing. "It'd be nice if he would just... go get laid or something."

"Yeah, but then you wouldn't have your own personal bodyguard," I point out.

She looks over at me, a smile in her eyes.

"I wouldn't constantly be *this* close to a re-education camp for proper ladies," she says. "I've heard lesson one is *don't drink whiskey half-naked with men you're not married to.*"

"I doubt re-educated ladies are supposed to do that with their husbands, either," I say. "As far as I can tell, based on my time in your household, ladies are supposed to make jam, take pretty pictures of jam, have a dozen children, and wait on their husbands."

"You've been paying attention," Ruby deadpans. "Clearly, it's no wonder I got divorced, since my pictures of jam all turn out terrible."

"That's what turns men gay," I agree. "Bad jam pictures. We see 'em, and bam, next thing you know we love dick."

Ruby snorts, laughing.

"I honestly wish it were that simple," she says. "I can learn to take better pictures of jam, but I don't think I can learn to want what I'm supposed to want."

She drinks the rest of her whiskey in a gulp, then leans across me to put it on a side table, getting onto her knees. I let my hand skim down her back, and my dick twitches as she kneels next to me, on the couch.

"What are you supposed to want?" I ask.

Ruby rolls her eyes, but puts her hand in my hair, playing with it.

"You know what I'm supposed to want, you see it every day," she says. "I'm *supposed* to want to have a nice, Godly husband who I bless with baby after baby, and I'm supposed to want to submit to his every whim and serve his every need."

I grin.

"Sounds boring," I say.

"It is," Ruby says.

"Doesn't sound like you at all."

"Nope," she says, then tilts her head to one side, eyes crinkling with a smile. "Not that I know what I do want. Just not that."

"Well," I say, sliding one hand up her skirt. "I have some thoughts on what you might want. I'm not sure how useful they'll be overall, but for the next few minutes you can tell me what you think of them."

She laughs and blushes as I run my fingers under the elastic of her panties.

"This is purely to help me figure my life out," she teases, leaning forward until our foreheads are touching. "How selfless."

I run my fingers along her lower lips, and she's soaking wet again, slick and swollen. She kisses me and makes a noise into my mouth, so I bite her lower lip gently as I pull her panties down for the second time that night.

"For example," I say, my voice low and dusky. "You might want to get on top of me and ride my cock, but you won't know unless you try."

Ruby blushes even harder, and I fucking love it. There's something about the combination of her blush and how wet she gets when I talk dirty to her that I can't get enough of.

She swings one leg over me and sits on my lap, her wetness right on top of my still-clothed cock, and I grin, kissing her again, harder, reaching behind her and getting her bra off. Ruby moans quietly when I take both her nipples in my hands, rolling them gently between my fingers, as her hips buck against me.

I unbutton her ugly skirt, and she steps off me for a second, pushing it to the floor. As she does, I undo my belt and jeans, get the condom from my pocket, and pull them off as well, my cock springing free. Ruby looks at it, and I grab it in one hand, grinning at her.

Then she's on me again, rolling her hips against me. She grabs the condom from my hand and tears it open, sitting back to unroll it down my length as I dip one finger into her wetness, making her bite her lip. Despite already coming once tonight, I'm catastrophically hard, my hands all over her as she strokes my condom-covered cock once.

I grab the base and her hip, because she seems a little uncertain as she leans in and kisses me again.

"C'mere," I whisper, pulling her in. She reaches down and puts one hand over mine and then I'm at her entrance and her tight channel is taking me in, pure pleasure coursing through my body. Ruby sinks all the way down until I'm hilted in her and panting for breath, my hands locked on her hips so hard that she might bruise.

We kiss and I can feel her muscles fluttering around me, intense and intoxicating, so I kiss her back and she rolls her hips, just enough to send another spike of pleasure through me.

Slowly, Ruby starts moving, tentatively at first, and I remember what she said earlier, *I've never done this before.* I wasn't lying when I told her I didn't care, because watching her is goddamn magic. The way her perfect breasts bounce right in front of me, the noises she makes when I hit that spot inside her, the way her eyelids flutter.

I don't give a shit if she hasn't done this a thousand times and doesn't have finesse, because watching her learn to ride my cock the way she likes it is one of the hottest things I've ever seen.

Gradually, she gets into a rhythm, one hand on the back

of the couch for leverage. Now we're rocking together, my hands moving her up and down on me. I'm lost in a haze of pleasure, trying to force myself not to come before she does. I lean forward to kiss her neck, lick a nipple, and she wraps her arms around me.

The angle inside her changes and I growl, somehow sliding deeper as she moans, her channel clenching around me as she does, the feeling heady and intoxicating. For once, I'm glad I'm wearing a condom so I don't come too fast.

I grind into her again, my arms wrapped around her waist now, and Ruby makes a noise that's half-moan, half-sigh, her head back as I kiss her throat.

"Was this what you wanted?" I murmur, her skin just below my lips.

"Yes," she whispers. "God, yes."

Ruby leans back with one hand, steadying herself against my knee. Now I'm watching her body as she undulates, eyes closed, her muscles already fluttering and spasming around me. It's fucking intoxicating, and her fingers dig into my knee and my shoulder as she gasps, holding her breath, right on the edge.

I grind my teeth together and bury my face in her neck, keeping myself from coming through sheer force of will as I pull her onto me roughly. She whimpers as I hit *that* spot, and instantly I'm lost and helpless and there is goddamn nothing I can do except growl into her neck and rock her back and forth, again and again until she grabs a fistful of my hair, exhales hard, and clenches around me so tight my vision goes white.

It's glorious. I've never felt anything like it, not in the dozens of women I've had, and I come seconds later, pumping myself again and again into Ruby until I'm completely and utterly spent but we're still just rocking together, arms around each other. I can feel her breathe, her heartbeat, and I don't want to stop, I don't want to leave.

And I don't know what the fuck is happening.

CHAPTER TWENTY-SEVEN

RUBY

AFTER A LONG TIME, I finally unwind myself from Gabriel and stand on shaky legs. I'm still tipsy, but more than that I feel dazed, almost high, until Gabriel also gets up and kisses me again.

I take a deep breath, and suddenly remember where I am and what a bad idea it is.

"I should go," I tell him.

"*Now* I agree with you," he says, sneaking one more kiss.

I put on my skirt and underwear, find my bra, and after a quick search of the kitchen my shirt turns out to have slid partly under the microwave stand. I'm sure I'm disheveled and smell like sex and sweat and whiskey, and I know that I should care, but I can't be bothered.

I'm sated and sleepy, and more than anything I want to stay there, with him, instead of going back into my parents' house where everything I just did comes with a heavy price.

He sees me to the door. We kiss again, and just before I leave he drops a kiss on my hair, and it's strangely different. There's no lust or desire in it, but it's sweet and protective. Almost more of a blessing than a kiss.

"Give me a wave when you're in your room," he murmurs.

"Will do," I say, and leave.

Thank God I've walked this line a thousand times and don't even have to think about it as I head back to the house, creep behind the rosebushes, and get back through the pantry window. After I get in I stay in that tiny, dark room for a long moment, just listening.

Outside, a couple of guards walk by, talking about something or other, but there's no noise inside the house. I exhale, trying to get my breathing under control, and then make my way upstairs to my bedroom. I shut the door softly and creep to the window, parting the curtains.

A single slat on Gabriel's blinds lifts, and I wave at it. The slat jiggles, and I can't help but grin like an idiot as I shut the curtains, put on my pajamas, and then lie down in my bed.

I can't believe I just did that.

And I'm definitely, *definitely* going to do it again.

———

STRANGELY, the next couple of days are kind of fun. Nothing changes, outwardly—we have the same conversations, about yeast rising and our favorite icing flavors when we were kids and what kind of photo filter I should put on a picture of flowers, but there's something charged about them, an undertone of something thrilling that makes me nearly giddy.

We have a secret. We have a really great secret, a secret that no one knows but us, and so we're acting like teenagers around each other no matter how much we try not to.

At the same time, it's even harder. Getting to have him

at night, not just the sex but the being alone, getting to be myself, makes it nearly impossible to keep my hands off him during the day. I nearly drag him in a closet just to kiss him about a thousand times, but somehow, by some miracle, I hold myself back.

I don't think anyone notices. I get a few weird looks from my mother, but she's always glaring at me for one reason or another, so I don't think it counts.

And I go back. Two nights in a row I can barely wait for all the lights to be off before I'm heading out of my room, down the back stairs, through the kitchen, out the window and into Gabriel's apartment, where the second night we don't even make it all the way up the stairs.

Afterward, when we're breathless and sated, we drink whiskey naked together in the dark. I finally ask him about the Marines, about Afghanistan, about whether it's true that he still wakes up shouting sometimes, and it is. He shows me the scar from the tube that drained his punctured lung after an IED went off and broke half his ribs.

He asks about my family, slowly draws out the details of my relationship with Lucas, the complicated entanglements I have here. I tell him that I know I need to leave, that I'm trying, I'm working on a plan.

Gabriel's quiet for a moment, shifting his whiskey glass in his hand. I'm sprawled half across the couch and half across him, because even though this is the fourth time he's even seen me naked, I'm oddly comfortable around him. It just feels right that we're doing this.

"Let me know if you need help," he says.

I bite my lip.

"Thanks," I say. "But I need to do this myself."

He smiles down at his glass.

"I thought you might say that," he says. "Stubborn."

I just shrug, smiling. He's not wrong.

————

I'M JUST DOZING OFF, the rumble of the tour bus finally lulling me to sleep, when there's a delicate hand on my arm.

"You look tired," Lilah, Mason's girlfriend, says. "Are you sleeping okay?"

My eyes fly open and my stomach lurches, because I haven't been sleeping okay, I've been having sex with my bodyguard and then hanging out naked until two or three a.m. for the past couple of days.

"I know the campaign is stressful for everyone," she says, smiling beatifically, taking her hand from my arm.

"I've had a little insomnia lately," I admit. "I'm sure it'll go away."

"Have you tried warm milk and honey?" she asks, tilting her head to one side. "My mom used to give me that when I couldn't sleep."

"Thanks, I'll give it a shot, I say."

"And don't stress so much, I'm sure your father has his race completely locked up," she goes on, softly. "Nothing to worry about. Plus, I heard you and Kyle..." she smiles again and winks.

That's weird, I think, even as I smile back at Lilah with the overly sweet, fake smile that's my default. Lilah's my former sister in law, and even though her family completely disowned and disavowed Lucas, it's strange that she's acting like she doesn't even remember him.

"You know how it is," I say, attempting chumminess, or *something*. "I start thinking about one thing, and next thing you know, I can't turn my brain off."

She nods, her brown hair floating over one shoulder.

"I sure do," she says. "But try the milk, it really works."

On her other side, Mason says something to her, and she turns away. I lean back and close my eyes again, but I'm not about to go back to sleep.

Is Lilah happy about Kyle?

Is it strange that my ex-sister-in-law thinks it's great that I'm allegedly dating again, six months after the divorce?

I take a deep breath. On my other side, Joy squirms in her seat and bumps me, her nose in one of the 'wholesome' mystery books she's permitted to read.

The one time I visited Lucas's family home since he left, everything of his was gone. Pictures—even family pictures with him in them—his things, even his books and DVDs. Like he never even existed, so maybe that's what this is. She's forcing herself to forget that she ever had a brother and that I was ever married to him.

I seriously have to get out of here, I think, and then I drift off to sleep again.

———

THIS RALLY IS PRETTY BIG, and Gabriel's afraid that my stalker might be here, somewhere in the crowd, so we're following a modified version of what he calls the *Outdoor Gathering Action Plan*, or OGAP. It turns out that Gabriel is very fond of acronyms, which he blames on his time in the military.

"All right," he says, ten minutes before the rally starts, crossing his arms. "Give it to me."

People are swirling around us, but I raise one eyebrow anyway. Gabriel frowns.

"OGAP," he says, all business.

I clear my throat, because apparently, this is no time for flirting.

"Exits throughout the hall, the usual places, with the exit signs," I say. "If there's a riot, get to the bus, which will have a guard and can be locked. If I get grabbed, fight back. If I'm being carried, go limp. If he's got a weapon, do what he says to buy time."

Gabriel nods once, officially. Right now, he's perfectly serious, completely professional, and not even checking me out a little. I'd almost be offended, but my life might depend on this, so it's fine.

"Active shooter?" he says.

"Hit the ground, get behind something if I can," I say. "When he's apprehended, get to the bus."

The bus is bulletproof. My father's had a few death threats over the years, though none were ever serious.

"If we get separated?"

"We meet at the stage door past the stairs."

"If I'm down?"

A chill runs through me, but I ignore it.

"Stay low, get to the bus."

Finally, Gabriel smiles at me, a sparkle in his eye. There's a gap in the people rushing around, and for a few seconds, no one's in earshot. He steps closer and suddenly he's towering over me and my stomach flips, heat rushing through me.

"And if you get lonely and want someone to make you shout his name?"

I do my best not to smile and fail.

"Why would I get lonely?" I murmur, looking up at him. "You're perfectly good company, and you live in my back yard."

Good *lord* I want to kiss him, but the moment is over,

people are walking by again, and he takes a step away from me, back to perfectly professional.

"I think our bases are covered," he says, nodding once.

You can cover my bases if you want, I think, my pantyhose feeling extra warm and uncomfortable.

Ruby, that doesn't even mean anything.

"Sounds good," I agree, making myself look at his face, and not the way he fills out his suit. Which is *well.*

"And don't forget, I'm right here if anything happens," he says, his voice dipping to a lower register. "Anything at all, I've got you."

I have the feeling he doesn't just mean *because I'm your bodyguard*, but I don't know what to say. Then we get called to prayer anyway, so it doesn't matter.

———

THE RALLY ISN'T INTERESTING. It's a whole bunch of people waving signs in the audience while I sit dutifully behind my father as he preaches about his good, wholesome American values and how great America is, how we need to get back to our real American moral center, etc.

A couple months ago I actually listened once or twice, and I was kind of surprised when I realized that nearly everything he says at these rallies—everything that makes the crowd lose their minds—is basically meaningless. He never says what he means by a moral America, or what he's gonna do to get us there. He just says it should exist and everyone loves him for it.

So I do what I usually do: tune out and try not to ogle my bodyguard. Did I mention that he's wearing a suit, and that he's wearing the hell out of it? He is.

After the speeches, my father takes questions. I'm half

thinking about sitting on Gabriel's lap as I take his tie off, half thinking about whether I could somehow use my mom's Perfect Wife blog to somehow make enough money on the side to move out.

And then I hear my name.

"—has moved on and found someone new in her life already, is that true?"

My heart slams into my throat, and I sit bolt upright in the second row. Why the hell is someone asking questions about me?

Unless that's *him*.

At the exact same time, my father and I both glance to the side of the stage, where there's a flurry of activity, just out of sight of the audience. The security guys are all rushing around, Gabriel pointing and telling them where to go. He's clearly taken charge of the situation, and I take a deep breath, calming a little.

My father turns back to the audience, folksy smile in his voice, his drawl suddenly exaggerated.

"Now, y'all know I prefer to keep my family's business private since they didn't ask to be a part of this," he says, politician smile wide as can be. "So all I'll say is that my daughter Ruby is very happy, and may have some big news soon."

What?!

For a split second I lose control of my face, and my mouth drops open. I don't know what he's talking about, unless he's somehow known about Gabriel and me the whole time and is telling everyone, right now, except that doesn't make any sense because I don't know what news...

Kyle. Obviously. Jesus, I'd nearly forgotten about Kyle but that has to be what my father means.

He just told a crowd of people that he thinks I'm getting engaged soon, and he *has* to mean to Kyle.

I think my own lungs are trying to strangle me, because sitting on that stage, perfect smile on my face, I can barely breathe. I feel like I've turned to stone or something, only I have to force myself not to rage-cry, and I don't think stone ever does that.

I hate him, I think, over and over again. *I hate this. I hate him.*

And if he thinks I'm marrying Kyle, he's as wrong as he's ever been.

CHAPTER TWENTY-EIGHT

GABRIEL

I POINT at two security guys—Marcos and Nate, I think, but I'm not 100% on that—and start issuing commands.

"You and you, go get him. Don't make a fuss, just escort him out. You—" I sweep my hand across four more security guys, all standing around "—make sure he doesn't leave. Watch the exits. Anything happens, de-escalate the situation to the best of your ability. He has a weapon, take him down."

They scatter. Ray, the Senator's head of security, is already on the phone with the county police, and I look back at the stage, heart hammering.

She's there. She's fine. She's sitting bolt upright, her frozen smile nervous, but she's fine.

The guy who asked the question about Ruby goes to sit down, but the two security guys come up to him instead.

Don't fuck this up, I pray, glancing at the stage again.

She's still there. Still fine, though now she looks *pissed*. The security guys seem like they're reasoning with the guy who asked the question, and I watch, every muscle tense, as he shakes his head, arguing with them.

Don't argue. Don't make a scene. Just go.

My gut's telling me it's not him, because my gut's telling me that the bastard who's stalking Ruby isn't brave enough to actually get up and say her name out loud like this. But I've still got every intention of making sure that this guy *isn't* him.

I glance at the stage. I glance back at the security guys, and after a long moment, the guy finally shrugs and starts walking for the auditorium door. I take a deep breath of relief.

No scene, no fuss, no dramatic takedown.

Ray puts his phone in his pocket and nods at me once, curtly.

"County Sheriff is sending somebody out to question him," he says. "Want me to go babysit and you stay with her?"

"Sounds good," I tell him, my voice clipped. "Keep me updated."

There's no fucking way I'm gonna do anything but stay here, Ruby firmly in my sights, where I can protect her. Other people can interrogate the guy who asked the weird question.

My breathing slows. My heartbeat slows. Ruby's still sitting in her folding chair on the stage, and she's got her fake smile on again, though her back is still perfectly straight. I half watch her and half scan the audience, the catwalks above, the exit doors.

I'm on high alert, since I'm more than aware that distractions are dangerous, and even more dangerous if we think we've caught the guy, but nothing else happens in the auditorium. Audience members ask more boring questions about taxes, the Senator answers, walking back and forth across the stage, Ruby smiles, jaw tight.

It feels like forever, but at last they finish. The Senator walks offstage and straight for me, followed closely by his wife and Ruby.

"Update," he says through clenched teeth.

I tell him everything that just happened: the guy is being questioned, the County Sheriff is here, the perimeter is being patrolled in case he's got an accomplice. I keep talking, telling the Senator more and more minor details until his face has gone from purple to red to tan again, the knots in his jaw worked out.

I learned early in my Secret Service career that it can be valuable to talk until someone's no longer furious. If the Senator walks in there and punches a perfectly innocent man who asked a nosy question, that's not good for anyone.

"I want him in custody," he growls at me. "Not just being questioned. *In custody*. I want this on the record. I want him strung up and made an example of, by God."

"*Jim*," Mrs. Burgess says.

He exhales hard, through his nostrils. On his other side, Ruby's practically glaring a hole through him.

"Sorry, Edith," he says. "Gabriel, thank you. I'm going to go check in with Ray. Ruby, I think it's best if you stay here with Gabriel."

With that, he and his wife walk away and I'm standing there with Ruby, people drifting by.

She's furious, her eyes bright and her jaw clenched tight, just like her father's was. Ruby doesn't even look at me, just glares at a spot in a curtain somewhere behind my head.

"Ruby," I murmur, and she looks at me. Then she looks away. She takes a deep breath.

"I can't," she says, and starts walking.

She shoves her way through curtains, through an exit

door, into a dusty, unused hallway, and I follow her every step.

As she walks down the hall, I hear her gasp strangely. She's crying, walking so fast she's practically running down this hall.

"Ruby," I call out as she shoves her way through a door that says WOMEN.

I hesitate for a second, then follow her, hoping there's no one else inside.

It's a dressing room, and she's leaning against the wall in the narrow entrance hallway, eyes closed, chest heaving like she's trying desperately not to cry.

We're alone. Thank fucking God, for once we're alone, so I wrap her in my arms and hold her close.

"We got the guy," I tell her. "The Sheriff is here, and they're taking him into custody and questioning him right now."

She takes another long, shuddering, deep breath, then clears her throat.

"He just told thousands of people that I'm going to marry Kyle," she says.

I'm startled speechless. That must have happened when I was issuing commands instead of paying attention to what was on stage.

"He did?" is all I can say.

Ruby pulls back, leaning against the wall. Even though her eyes are still glassy, she's not actually crying yet, and she snorts.

"'Ruby's gonna have big news soon' sure doesn't mean I'll be heading off to college," she says, her voice bitter and sarcastic.

I completely missed that aspect of all this, totally focused on getting the guy, making sure he didn't escape.

"This is what he does," she says, her voice quiet and steely. "He thinks that he can control everything, he thinks he can tell people what they're going to do. He thinks he has the final say in everything, in all of our lives, that if he just says *you're gonna marry Kyle* then it'll come true through sheer force of will."

She takes another deep breath.

"And I am fucking tired of it," she whispers. "I'm tired of being told what to do, where to go. Who to marry. I'm tired of fucking pantyhose and being watched all the time and having to *keep fucking sweet* and take pictures of jam and never getting to choose what I do or where I go and goddamn everything. I'm tired of goddamn *everything*."

She leans her head back against the wall and her green eyes look at me defiantly, sparking in the low light.

"You're not gonna offer to rescue me again?" she asks, her voice still tight, though there's a strange, new note in it.

"I didn't offer to rescue you," I say, stepping closer. "I said I'd help you. I know better than to think you need rescuing."

Ruby reaches out and takes my tie in one hand, her eyes flicking up to mine. There's something unreadable and intense in the way she looks at me, something almost dangerous, and I hold my breath.

"Good," she says, running her fingers down my tie. "I'm glad someone doesn't think I'm a helpless damsel."

She pulls on my tie a little, and I put one hand on the wall over her shoulder. I have no idea where this is going, whether she's angry or seducing me or both or neither, but I *am* pretty sure this can't be a good idea.

"I don't think a helpless damsel would get through what you did and still be this feisty," I say, and she smirks.

"Feisty," she murmurs, half to herself. "I like it."

Ruby yanks hard on my tie, jerking me forward and crushing her lips against mine. I still don't know what's happening, but she grabs my belt and pulls me forward until I'm pressed against her, the wall against her back.

She bites my bottom lip as I pull away, and I swear to God she growls as she does.

I'm hard already, so fucking hard, every nerve in my body alive and electric because I think she's angry-seducing me and lord almighty do I like it.

But I clear my throat and take a deep breath.

"They're gonna notice we're gone soon," I say. "If they didn't already."

"I don't care," she says, and pulls on me again, but I resist her.

"Ruby," I whisper.

With her other hand, she reaches out and hits the lights, plunging us and this dressing room into total darkness. Suddenly every touch is intensified, and I can feel the body heat pulsing off her, every breath she takes, every movement of her hips.

Shit.

"There's one thing in my life right now that I chose," she says, her voice low and intense. "Everything else gets decided for me, but I show up at your door every night because I want to."

Her hand trails down my chest, and I slide a hand around her back, digging my fingers in.

"And right now, I could really stand to do something because I want to, not because I was told to," Ruby whispers.

Now she's got both hands on my belt, our hips pressed together. I'm hard as fuck and I know she knows this is working.

Get caught and you're never going back to DC, I remind

myself. *This is already fucking dangerous, but if the Senator knows that you're...*

As I'm thinking that, I realize something.

I don't care.

I kiss Ruby again, harder this time, and she pulls at my belt and wraps a hand around the back of my head, our tongues tangling together as she bumps against the wall, her back arched.

She undoes my belt, unzips my pants, and a second later, she's got her fist around my cock as I pull her against me, forcing myself not to groan.

"You're a very bad influence," I whisper into her ear.

Her fist tightens, and I gasp.

"I'm not sorry," she whispers back.

I kiss her neck and slide one hand up her leg, my fingers practically whistling against the nylon of her pantyhose as she groans quietly and pushes her hips against me.

I want her. Holy fuck do I want her, here in the dark where everything feels urgent and desperate and almost cataclysmic.

Ruby puts her arms over my shoulders, I grab her ass, and then I hoist her into the air as she wraps her legs around me, cock nestled against her heat as her skirt folds over her hips. She writhes against the wall and we kiss, so hard that her teeth are on my lips as her tongue's in my mouth.

I punch one thumb through her pantyhose, and in a second the hole widens and I shove her soaked panties aside, stroking her lips. My thumb finds her clit and I slide two fingers inside her, the muscles of her channel clenching around me as I crook them into her most sensitive spot, the one that makes her eyes flutter closed.

"Gabriel," she whispers.

Jesus.

"I wish I could resist you just a little," I murmur into her neck, moving my fingers inside her as she grabs my hair in one fist, gasping against my ear. "But I try, and next thing I know you're up against a wall and wet as hell."

"That's your fault," she whispers, closing one hand around my cock.

Ruby wriggles against the wall, and I pull my hand out of her. My eyes have adjusted enough that now we can barely see each other, her eyes two deep pools inches in front of my face.

As she watches me, I lick my fingers off and her eyes widen.

I grin at her, sucking her juices from my fingertips, and she looks faintly horrified.

"You just seduced me into fucking you against a wall at the Hartley County Convention Center," I growl. "You don't get to look shocked when I lick you off my fingers."

I grab her ass again, holding her up, and kiss her hard.

"See?" I whisper. "You're fucking delicious."

She strokes me in her fist, nudging the head of my cock against her entrance.

I take a deep breath and pull back.

"I don't have a condom," I say.

"It's okay," she murmurs.

"I can't—"

"There's a reason Lucas and I didn't have kids," she says, and kisses me again, slowly, her tongue in my mouth. "I've got an IUD. Please?"

"You're fucking dangerous, Ruby," I tell her, but she just said *please* and I'm completely fucking powerless against her.

I slide into her, bare, just her against me, and in a second I'm inside her to the hilt and it feels so damn good for a second I think I'm about to come, there and then, with almost no warning.

After a moment, it passes, and Ruby's legs tighten around me. The movement shifts me inside her, skin against skin, and I can't hold back any longer.

I drive myself into her, hard, and I'm rewarded with her fingernails in my shoulders, raking down my back, so I hold her up and keep going. It's not romantic and it's not tender, but Ruby keeps making small, soft noises of pure bliss and she holds me tight, her fists in my hair, her nails down my back, her legs locked around me.

"Don't stop," she whispers, her voice barely audible as she chants it like an incantation. "Don't stop, don't stop, don't stop."

As if I could, because I can feel her fluttering and clenching around me, like she's losing control, close to the edge.

I thrust even harder, my fingers digging into her ass as I hold her up. Ruby grabs my hair and holds my face to hers, her breathing quiet and ragged.

"Gabriel," she says, so softly I can barely hear her, and she comes. Her muscles clench around me with a power I didn't know she had. I'm bare inside her and seconds later I come too, burying myself as deep as I can, shoving her against the wall even as she moans because I want—I *need*—to have her, possess her, make sure that she's mine in every way, as much as she can possibly be, so she'll always be mine and no one else's.

I come unbelievably hard. I think my ears pop. I slam one fist against the tiled wall of the changing room, over Ruby's shoulder, as I clench my jaw, trying not to make a sound but she feels so fucking good and right that I almost can't help it.

When I finish, I'm panting for breath, sweat trickling down my neck, and I kiss Ruby. I kiss her desperately, like I'm drowning and she's a lifeboat, like she's the air I need.

"Sorry," she finally whispers, but I just start laughing.

"You should be," I murmur back, kissing her again. "You absolutely fucking should be."

CHAPTER TWENTY-NINE

RUBY

I CAN'T BELIEVE I just did that. I almost feel like someone else completely took over my brain and my body, except she did exactly what I wanted to do.

"I know," I say, keeping my voice low. "I couldn't help myself."

He kisses me again, slowly, like he's thinking, and puts one hand on my cheek, brushing my hair back. Even though I think I might have bruises from what we just did, this gesture is so gentle and tender that I close my eyes, tilting my head into his hand.

"It doesn't have to be like this," he says. "It doesn't have to be secret, in the dark. Let me help you."

He's right. I know he's right. My dumb schemes aren't going to work, and the only other person I could think of to help was my ex-husband. And I think he'd be willing to help me get out, but it would be...

Well, weird is kind of an understatement. I take a deep breath.

"I don't want to be your problem," I say, taking his wrist

in my hand. I kiss the inside of his palm, and I can see his eyes tracking me, even in the dark.

"You're not a problem," he says, and he sounds like he's amused. "You think that was problematic?"

I grin, despite myself.

"You think it wasn't?"

He twists our hands together and puts his forehead against mine.

"If I didn't want to help you I wouldn't offer," he says. "I'm dead serious, Ruby. Come with me. We could go right now, just leave from this convention center."

I swallow hard. I'm tempted. I'm tempted as hell to just walk away from all this, to leave this dumb building and never look back, but he doesn't even have a car here. We'd literally be walking, we'd have nowhere to walk to, and I don't even have a change of clothes with me.

Not to mention we've been sleeping together for a grand total of four days. It's probably been the best four days of my life, but even so, I'm a little gun-shy at the moment, a little skeptical of men who think they can fix my life or even help.

It hasn't exactly worked out great in the past.

"Not right now," I say, because I don't know what else to say, because I want to trust and believe him but I don't know if that's smart.

"I knew you'd say that," he murmurs.

"I thought you wanted your job back," I point out.

Gabriel runs his fingers through mine, quiet for a moment.

"There are a lot of jobs," he says.

"Not a lot of Secret Service jobs," I say. I don't know why I'm arguing with him about this, but I can't help it.

"I'll figure it out," he says, shrugging. He's got a hand on my hip and he's stroking my side absentmindedly with his thumb, in this way that he does when he's not really paying attention to what he's doing.

"We have to go," I say, even though it's the last thing I want.

Leave, I think. *Leave now, just walk away, don't look back. It could work out.*

"You're gonna have to put on one hell of a damsel-in-distress act," he says, teasing me. "Which is what you deserve for pulling this, by the way."

"I was just *so* scared that I couldn't help but run away and cry hysterically, and you had to calm me down before I'd come back," I say, blinking up at him innocently.

Gabriel chuckles.

"Absolutely, positively terrified of that guy," I say, trying not to smile.

He kisses me one more time. I smooth my my hair, pull my skirt back down, and make some attempts at adjusting my ruined underwear and pantyhose, praying that the runs don't show below my skirt.

Then Gabriel opens the door, holds it for me, and smacks my ass as I walk through.

———

RAY, my father's head of security, pats my shoulder awkwardly. I pretend to hiccup, doing my level best to force some tears out of my eyes. It's not going great.

"You're okay," he says, over and over again. "We got you, and ain't nothing going to happen, all right?"

I sniffle—or I try—and nod. We ran into Ray first, standing backstage. My father is still glad-handing his fans, posing for pictures and kissing babies and all that, and I have no idea where my mother is. Probably lecturing one of my siblings about something.

"Thanks, Ray," I say, keeping my voice a whisper so it doesn't betray me. "It's just so scary."

He pats me again, standing arm's length away. It's the least comforting shoulder pat I think I've ever felt, but at least he's trying. Ray's always at least meant well. Gabriel stands next to us, looking professional and serious, his hands in his pockets.

A minute later, my mother bustles through a curtain and makes a beeline straight for me. She's smiling, but I know better than to think she means it.

"Where *were* you?" She exclaims. She's overacting, but so am I.

I take a deep breath and bite my lower lip, hoping I look pathetic instead of annoyed.

"I'm sorry," I say. "I just—I couldn't—when that man asked, and then they went and arrested him, and—I can't believe he was *here*."

I'm hoping my nonsensical, broken English helps sell it.

"Sweetie," my mom says, giving me an awkward hug. "They've got him. You're fine."

"I just had to go where he couldn't find me," I whisper. It's more nonsense, but I've got a part to play.

"They've got him locked away now," she says, petting my hair. "He can't come get you any more."

In that moment, I feel awful. She's my mom, and I'm lying to her and sneaking behind her back, going against everything she's ever taught me. I'm disrespecting her in her own home, the woman who gave birth to me and nursed me and stayed up with me when I was sick.

She hugs me for another moment, then pulls back, holding me by the shoulders.

I'm sorry, I think. *God, I'm sorry.*

"But you can't just disappear like that," she goes on, a hard edge in her soft voice. "Especially not with—"

Her glance flicks to Gabriel, then back to me, and now there's something steely and suspicious in her gaze. She clears her throat.

"The bad guy is locked away, but we can't have any questions about you. Not right now," she says.

I stare, my breath caught in my throat.

Did she really just say that? Seriously?

Every nice thought I just had about my mom flies out of my head. I feel suddenly like I'm suffocating, trapped in a tiny, invisible cage, so small I can't even move my arms or scream for help.

Tears prick at the backs of my eyeballs, hot and angry and indignant at my helplessness, and I do the only thing I can.

I start crying, my whole body nearly vibrating with sheer rage.

"Shhh, shhh," my mother says, hugging me again. Automatically, I embrace her back, letting the tears roll down my cheeks.

Over her shoulder, Ray looks away uncomfortably, but Gabriel looks back at me, steadily, and cracks one knuckle.

I sniffle.

"You're all right," my mother says, as comfortingly as she can muster. "Come on, let's go find your father and get out of here, go back home."

I just nod into her shoulder, swallowing. After a moment she pulls back, takes me by the arm, and starts leading me away.

As I pass Gabriel, he catches my eye, the muscles in his jaw working. He doesn't have to say anything for me to know what he's thinking, that he heard what she said, that he's furious and indignant too.

And it makes me feel better. My life may be pretty fucked, but I've got one person on my side.

———

MY FATHER'S NOT HAPPY, but I've seen him angrier, and my mother doesn't mention that Gabriel and I both disappeared for a while. Or, at least she doesn't mention it in front of me.

Maybe she's actually protecting me for once, shielding me from my father's certain wrath. Or maybe she's waiting for more proof. Or, hell, maybe she's just waiting until I'm gone so they can discuss it in detail.

I don't risk going to Gabriel's that night. I'm tempted, crazy tempted, because even more than I want him I want to be with him.

But I don't. Instead, I get myself off quietly, under the covers, and eventually I fall asleep, dreaming of tigers pacing in gilded cages.

———

TWO DAYS LATER, I'm sitting in my father's waiting room, in front of Mason, watching him fidget. He keeps glancing from me to the picture of Lilah on his desk, like looking at her will somehow erase the Fallen Woman image I'm burning into his retinas.

I feel like I'm torturing the poor kid, but I don't even have to do anything. My presence in the same room as him clearly makes him uncomfortable. It's not my fault.

I uncross and re-cross my legs, because my foot is starting to fall asleep, and adjust my skirt down over my knees. I swear Mason leans closer into his computer monitor and turns faintly pink, and I have to resist the urge to adjust my bra too, just to see how he'd react.

Finally, the door to my father's office opens, breaking the incredibly awkward silence, and he gestures me in. Behind me, Mason looks relieved, even as he glances at a picture of Lilah again, like she's somehow supporting him through this difficult time.

"You needed to see me?" my father says, checking his watch.

I gather my wits, straighten my shoulders, and get right down to business.

"I think I should have a job," I say. "And Rosalie's is hiring wait staff."

My father stops mid-sit, hovering over his chair, and just looks at me for a moment.

Then he falls heavily onto the leather, eyes narrowed, like he doesn't think he just heard me right.

"Only part-time, of course," I go on. I've rehearsed my reasoning a dozen times over the past two days, and it's coming out flawlessly. "But I need to be useful somehow, and learning to serve others with a smile on my face would be excellent practice for another marriage."

He frowns.

"Besides, you know that Rosalie's is owned by Godly people," I go on. "You wouldn't need to worry about that, and I'd like to have something to do. A way to meet new people. Learning homemaking is fine, but if I'm going to be helpful to my future husband, I need to know a little more about the ways of world."

He watches me, tapping a pen on his desk, his forehead knitting together.

He's thinking about it. He's really actually thinking about it, and I can hardly believe it.

None of what I said is true, obviously. I couldn't care less about serving others with a smile on my face, but I do care that a big portion of a waitress's income is cash tips.

I've got zero doubt that, should I actually be allowed to get a job, my paychecks would be monitored somehow. But cash can be squirreled away, hidden in underwear drawers and beneath mattresses.

Last night, I spent a little while pretending to 'update the backend' of my mother's homemaking blog, and I looked at apartment rental prices in the towns nearby. If I could find a roommate, I'd be looking at about $400 a month.

It's $400 a month more than I make now, but it's not impossible.

"I don't know," he says slowly. "You know the man we detained last weekend wasn't your stalker, so he's still out there."

"Has he sent any letters recently?" I ask, as innocently as I can. I know he hasn't, not since the letter about the county fair, because Gabriel would tell me.

"No," my father says. He taps the pen a few more times. "Actually, I've been meaning to talk to you. In light of the events of last weekend, I've decided that you need an extra security detail."

My stomach drops. I swear my blood runs cold for a split second, and I feel a little dizzy before I return my face to its normal, sweet expression.

"Why?" I ask, trying for a puzzled smile. "If that wasn't him, then..."

He gives me a long, long stare, like he's trying to decide exactly what to say.

"I don't think it's appropriate that a single man is your sole minder," he finally says. "Frankly, Ruby, I have some concerns regarding you and Gabriel. It's inappropriate for him to be so familiar with you, so I'll be adding a second guard, just to see that there's no impropriety."

I think I might puke. Right here, on this rug, in front of my father the Senator, *I am going to puke.*

I swallow. I don't puke, even though I'm sure my face is giving me away.

"Father," I say, like I'm shocked. "There hasn't been... with Gabriel... he would never..."

I trail off, like I'm too shocked to say *look at me with lust in his heart* or *bend me over his kitchen counter while I moan his name.* He's done both, after all.

"Right now, neither you nor I can afford the appearance of impropriety," he says. "This race is much closer than I would prefer, and your reputation isn't exactly pristine."

You have no fucking idea, I think.

I feel like I could shoot flames from my eyes.

"We'll discuss your employment prospects when we return from Charleston," he says, standing again.

It's not no, I think, and force another smile.

"Thank you, Father," I say.

He nods once, dismissing me, and I leave through the heavy wooden door to the hallway, then go straight to the bathroom, the only place I can really be alone during the day.

I sit on the toilet lid, fully clothed, cover my face with my hands, and take a couple of deep breaths.

He knows, I think, over and over again. *He knows, he knows, he knows.*

Maybe he doesn't know for sure or he doesn't know the specifics or he just thinks that I might be interested in Gabriel, but he knows there's something.

We should stop. Just for a little while, throw them off the trail, and maybe they'll stop watching so closely and I can have a job and then get an apartment and leave finally and we can...

I don't know what. I don't know what the next step is, beyond *get out of here*, and I feel like I can barely think two steps into the future right now. I take another deep breath and try to calm myself down and not start panicking.

Step one, cool it with Gabriel for now. Just for a few nights. It'll be okay.

Step two, get this job at Rosalie's or skim from your mother's blog or something. Just figure it out.

That's all. Baby steps. It'll be okay.

I sneak out that night any way, and I practically launch myself at Gabriel. We don't even make it to the couch.

Afterward, I tell him everything. We agree that I shouldn't come back for a couple of days, that it's worth missing out on *this* to figure things out.

"My offer's still open," he says, lying across me, his head in my lap as I stroke his hair.

"Which one?" I ask, sated and sleepy and teasing. "You make me a lot of offers."

"To leave with you. Now. Tonight."

It's tempting. Holy God is it tempting, but there's something holding me back, because I'm sick of being tossed from person to person and told what to do. I'm sick of other people having control of my life, and even though it's Gabriel, and even though he's different from everyone else I've ever known, I need to fix this myself.

"It's not that I don't want to," I say quietly. "It's just that..."

He smiles, eyes closed.

"Don't worry, I get it," he says. "This is why I like you."

Right then, I think my heart might explode.

CHAPTER THIRTY

GABRIEL

IT'S NOT *NO*. It's *not yet*, it's *not like this*, but it's not *no*, and I should be giddy and pleased with it, but something's still prickling at me.

Tell her, I think. *If you're going to talk her into running away with you, tell her.*

I don't really know how, because all I can think is *I should have already told her* and *I should never have done that*. I'm a little afraid of the way she's going to look at me now.

But this is Ruby, and everything we have is based on me being absolutely fucking truthful with her, even if I don't want to. Even if I don't know how to say it.

So I take a deep breath and man up.

"There's something you should know," I start, something cold and heavy weighing in my stomach. "About why I'm on leave from the Secret Service."

She frowns slightly, her hand still circling through my hair, distracted and sleepy.

"Gabriel, what did you do?" she asks, her voice light and teasing.

There's an iron band around my chest, squeezing.

"I had an affair with a married congresswoman," I say.

Her hand stops.

"I wish like hell I hadn't," I go on. "But I did."

"Did you know?" she asks, her voice soft, her hand still.

I swallow hard.

"Not at first," I say, my eyes closed. I'm afraid to look at her right now. "I know I could have found out, I just didn't. I had a bad habit of thinking with my dick."

"But you knew later," she persists.

"I did."

"And you stopped sleeping with her?"

Here it goes. The worst part.

"No," I say. "I figured, what was done was done, so I kept it up. Until we got caught by one of her aides one night, and the whole thing blew up."

She thinks about it, quietly, for a long time. After a while, her fingers start weaving through my hair again, and I relax a little. At least she hasn't stormed out, hasn't started crying.

"I thought you got in trouble for sleeping around too much," she finally says.

My eyes fly open.

"That was the next thing I was gonna tell you," I say.

"I overheard some of the other security guys talking, and I'm nosy," she says. "And just... I don't know."

I roll over onto my side and take her hand in mine.

"Don't know what?"

"I don't know if I care," she says. "Did you offer to run away with all your other women?"

"For the most part, I didn't know their last names," I say. "Ruby, I know there's no reason you should believe me, but this is different. I've never..."

I have no idea how to phrase what I'm going to say.

"I've never spent an hour thinking about how to make another girl smile," I say. I'm not even thinking about it, just talking, because we're in this pure, raw moment. "I've never thought I'd give a testicle to be able to hold someone's hand in public before, I've never wanted to just hang out and drink whiskey and talk for hours to someone before. You don't have to believe me, but this is…"

I take another deep breath.

"I don't know what this is," I say. "This is new."

She rubs her thumb along the back of my hand.

"Then at least something's new for both of us," she says, almost smiling. "And you know something else?"

"What?"

"If you having that affair brought you here, I don't know how mad I can be."

I grin and kiss her hand, because she's got a point.

"Then I don't completely regret it," I say. "Only mostly."

———

I DON'T KNOW what wakes me up, but it's just barely light outside, the sky outside my blinds just a shade lighter than the darkness inside. I lie in bed, my face half-buried in my pillow for a moment, trying to remember what was it *was.*

Not a dream, I think. Those have been happening less and less over the past few years, but every time I have one — the blast, the screams, falling to the dusty ground, gasping like I'm trying to breathe through a straw — I'm sweating and thrashing, usually woken up by the sound of my own shouting.

Maybe it was nothing, I think, but I have the distinct feeling that *something* woke me up, so I push myself up.

To my right is a soft snore, and I freeze. Ruby's lying there, mouth slightly open, both arms over her head, dead asleep and snoring.

"Shit," I say out loud.

Her eyes flicker open, and for a long moment she just looks at me, totally uncomprehending, like she's confused about where she is and how she got here.

Then she gasps, her eyes fly open, and she scrambles out of my bed, totally naked.

"What time is it?" she hisses, grabbing her skirt and pulling it on as she looks at my bedside clock and answers her own question: it's 5:05am.

Even in the dark, Ruby goes white.

"Go now," I say, also getting out of bed. I look around the floor and find her bra, tossing it to her. "You've got time, you can get back in before anyone's awake, maybe say you couldn't sleep so you got up early to practice being a good wife or whatever bullshit they want to—"

"Charleston," Ruby says.

It takes me a minute to process.

"*Fuck*," I say, finding her panties in a ball near the door. "Is the bus here already?"

She peeks through the blinds very, *very* carefully.

"I don't think so," she says, grabbing her panties from me and pulling them on. "Where's my shirt?"

"Couch?" I say, but she's already out my bedroom door, practically sprinting down the stairs. Her shirt's on my coffee table, and she pulls it on, flips her hair out, finds her shoes.

I kiss her quickly, a half-kiss, and grab her hand before she can run out the door.

"You've got the plan?" I ask.

She blinks, staring at me blankly for a second, and then grins.

"Right here," she says, and taps her temple with one finger. "Tonight."

Then she's flying out the door, power-walking across the lawn, avoiding the motion sensors. I watch her until she gets around the corner of the house, and I slump back down onto the couch, rubbing my eyes.

I can't believe I fell asleep, I think. *There's one thing you can't do, and that's it.*

Though maybe if she gets caught, she'd run away with me.

I get why she keeps saying no. We've known each other for a couple of weeks at this point, and Ruby's anything but stupid; besides, if I were her, I'd be hesitant to depend on anyone but myself, too.

But I want her to. I want her to come away with me, I want her to grab a backpack full of her stuff and we'll drive away from her father's house and from Huntsburg in my shitty car and drive somewhere else. *Anywhere* else.

I've got a couple thousand dollars in savings, and even if I'm not going back into the Secret Service I spent eight years in the Marines and three in D.C., so I can get a job somewhere. Ruby could work part-time, go to college, figure out what she wants to do with her life.

We could get a place together, maybe somewhere out in the country. At night, we'd sit outside and drink whiskey while we watched the lightning bugs and in the morning I'd wake up with her in my arms.

"Jesus," I mutter to myself, shaking my head. I'm still half asleep and just daydreaming, but there's no way I'm going back to sleep, so I make coffee, get dressed, and pray that Ruby doesn't get caught.

———

I GUESS SHE DOESN'T, because I make it through the entire day without getting called on the carpet and fired. An overnight trip with the Senator and his huge entourage is at least three times the insanity of a regular day trip. There are two buses, both *overflowing* with people and their stuff.

As I watch everyone load up, one eye *always* on Ruby, I can't help but think: *if I were going to take her, I'd do it now.* But no one takes her, of course.

On the bus, I sit behind her and her sister Grace, sharing my row with Steven, her new, second bodyguard. He's young, twenty-four, and has that fresh-out-of-the-military twitchiness that I remember so well.

He also won't stop calling me *sir*, no matter how many times I tell him not to during the hours-long briefing on the bus ride.

I try to sound professional. I try to say *keep her appraised of her situation*, not *tell her everything, she deserves to know.*

I try to say *sometimes she forgets she has bodyguards and wanders off*, not *she's probably smarter than you and can escape if she wants.*

I don't tell him that she likes peaches better than pears but strawberries better than peaches; I don't tell him that she thinks funny-looking chickens are exceptionally hilarious; I don't tell him that if she had a dæmon it would be a fox.

Nothing happens at her father's town hall meeting, or on the bus ride, or at the diner where her father has a dinner-slash-photo-op. Nothing happens when we get to the hotel in charming downtown Charleston where we have two entire floors.

We settle in. Ruby and Grace go to the pool, though they don't swim, they just watch the kids splash in the kiddie pool while Steven and I sit by. After a while they head back upstairs, Grace to her room, Ruby to the one that she shares with Pearl, and we walk her to her door. It's ten.

"Will you be going anywhere else tonight?" I ask, hands folded in front of myself.

Steven looks on, face as blank as a stone wall. Ruby smiles, and even though it's the fake, sweet smile, something in her eyes sparkles.

"I don't think so," she says. "Don't worry, I'll be sure to lock the door and call you if I go somewhere."

"Sleep well, ma'am," Steven says, twitching his head once. I think it's a nod.

"Thank you," she says.

"We'll be here at seven to escort you to breakfast," I tell her.

Down the hall, someone opens a door, leaves a room, and knocks on another one. The whole floor is still bustling with activity.

"That sounds lovely," she says. "Good night!"

She turns away, and at the last second, she winks at me.

It's everything I can do not to smile.

CHAPTER THIRTY-ONE

I'M LYING awake in my bed, listening to Pearl's breathing. I've *been* lying awake and listening to Pearl's breathing for the better part of an hour now, not daring to move a muscle myself, watching the numbers on the glowing green clock in the middle of the room as they tick toward eleven-thirty.

For the thousandth time, I go over the plan. The map of the hotel is pretty much burned into my brain, and I think I've been over it enough times that I could draw it in my sleep.

Pearl snorts. I freeze, even though I already wasn't moving, but then she rolls over and I exhale.

Eleven twenty.

Time to roll.

Cautiously, I get out of bed. Pearl doesn't move, so I grab the tote bag that's buried in the bottom of my suitcase and take it into the bathroom, pull out the clothes I brought, and put them on.

Skinny jeans. A tank top.

A thong, which I bought years ago when I was married to Lucas, then never wore. Before I pull my jeans up, I check it out in the mirror: black and lacy, a total one-eighty from anything Gabriel's ever seen me wear before.

The thought makes me nervous, like maybe I'm being too aggressive and forward, but then I roll my eyes at myself.

You show up at his apartment every night and practically jump his bones, I think. *Don't worry about a thong.*

I stash the bag back in my suitcase, flicking off the bathroom light. Pearl's still asleep, her form one long lump in the bed. I take the keycard from the dresser, pocket it, and then say a quick prayer.

God, I'm sorry that I'm about to do some stuff that you may or may not approve of, I'm not really sure any more, I think. *But please don't let me get caught.*

Then I'm out the door, power walking down the hall.

Just as I reach the elevators, I hear a door behind me open and my heart leaps into my throat but I sprint the final two steps to the stairwell and shove the door open, pushing it closed myself. The click echoes in the concrete space, and then there's silence.

I can't hear anyone walking down the hall. I can't hear anything.

Before I lose my nerve, I'm racing down three flights the of stairs. I take a deep breath and open the door at the bottom, silently praying that there are no surprises behind it.

There's a blank hallway. My skin prickles with relief, and I turn right, down the hall and around to the left. I walk past the bar quickly, hoping that there are no security guys getting a late-night beer, and then I'm pushing open the door to the pool, the warm, humid night air embracing me.

It's technically closed, but there's one woman in a black bathing suit slowly doing the backstroke, lit from underneath as the water and lights ripple around her. I shove my hands in my pockets and keep walking, so nervous and electrified that I don't think I can slow down.

I round the corner, and then, there he is, in jeans and a plaid shirt with the sleeves rolled up past the elbows, grinning like he's just won the lottery.

When I walk up, Gabriel pulls me into a short hallway that leads to the bathrooms. He doesn't say anything, just takes my face in his hands and kisses me, slow and hard, mouths open. I trail one hand down his chest and he finds the small of my back with his fingers, pressing me into him before he grabs my ass.

"You should wear tight pants more often," he teases.

"I'll make a note of that," I tease right back.

His other hand drifts down and cups my ass as well, squeezing slightly, and I laugh.

"You never did tell me why women can't wear pants," he says. "Is this it?"

"I'm sure it's one of the reasons," I say. "But it's not *the* reason."

My butt gets one final squeeze, and the Gabriel takes my hand. We leave the hallway and walk out of the pool area, into a small, dark alley. I'd be nervous if it weren't for him.

"What's *the* reason?" he asks.

"Because the seam where the legs meet rubs against the crotch and might *excite the passions*," I say.

Gabriel looks down at me, and we walk out onto the sidewalk of downtown Charleston. Even though it's a little late, it's still busy.

"No one's ever said that," he says, disbelief in his voice, and I just laugh.

"You know why Kyle keeps bringing me daisies?" I ask as we keep walking.

"I assumed they were the cheapest flower he could find

at the Gas 'N' Go, or wherever he buys those things," Gabriel says.

"They're one of the few church-approved flowers," I say. "Since the petals go out and not up. Most other flowers look too much like the feminine parts."

Gabriel's quiet for a moment. We pass a bar that's full of people, spilling out onto the sidewalk, and for once, nobody looks at me weird.

I'd fit in at a bar, I think.

It's like I'm a normal woman on a normal date with a normal guy. Doing normal stuff.

"I can almost see the point about flowers," Gabriel muses. "Who's that famous lesbian painter who painted all those close-ups of—what's funny?"

I'm laughing softly.

"This is normal," I say. "We're just two people on a date. We're holding hands. No one is gonna tell us about Satan."

"Probably. We're still in South Carolina."

"Probably no one is gonna tell us about Satan," I say. "It's just..."

He squeezes my hand.

"I haven't done this before," I say, shrugging. "And it's nice."

Gabriel brings my hand to his lips and kisses it.

"And I thought I'd feel guiltier," I admit. "When I kissed a boy for the first time I felt awful for months, and I cried and prayed and everything, but now I... don't."

"Well, it's good to hear you don't feel terrible about this," he says dryly. "For the record, I don't feel guilty about two consenting adults enjoying each other's company either."

"You make it sound so uncomplicated," I tease. "It's like you haven't even factored hellfire into the equation."

We walk a couple more blocks through downtown

Charleston until Gabriel leads me to a bar. From inside I can hear a live band, something thumpy and down-home with a banjo, and there's a bouncer who checks our IDs.

He barely glances at Gabriel's, but when I hand over my driver's license — yes, it's a miracle, but I really do have one — he frowns at it for a couple of seconds, shining his flashlight on it from a couple different angles, like he's expecting something to pop out of it.

Then he looks at me, squinting a little.

Do I tell him that's my real ID? Does that just make me seem suspicious?

I mean, it's really my ID.

Is he somehow working for my father?

Just as I'm about to really starting panicking, the guy nods and hands my license back. I heave a sigh of relief, and Gabriel leans over my shoulder, looking at it as we walk into the bar.

And he grins.

"How old is that photo?" he asks.

I go to shove it back into my wallet but he reaches over my shoulder and snags it from my fingers, still grinning.

"I don't know," I say defensively. "A couple of years? I know it's not a great picture."

"I think you were hypnotized into taking it," he says as we walk toward a small booth along the wall. He's holding my license just out of my reach, and even though I'm not about to make a big fuss in public, I'd really like it back.

"Okay, now you're just being mean," I tease as we slide into a round booth. "Give me that back."

"You're cute when you're hypnotized."

"I wasn't hypnotized, just at the DMV!"

"Or maybe you're on the really good drugs in this picture."

I make a grab for my license, but he avoids me smoothly, hovering it just out of my reach. Now I'm giggling, and I cross my legs and smooth my shirt down, trying to pretend that we're not flirting like middle schoolers.

He shows me my license, still grinning, and I'm finally forced to look at my own seven-year-old picture.

He kinda has a point, because my mouth is smiling but I'm wide-eyed, like something really amazing and mind-blowing is happening behind the camera. Also, I think I was eighteen or nineteen when the picture was taken, so I'm younger, my face a little rounder.

"No one looks good in their DMV photo," I say, finally grabbing it back. "Let's see yours."

"I don't think so."

"That bad, huh?"

Now he's laughing too, and he puts one arm around me.

"It's just such a good picture that I don't want you to feel worse about yours."

"Let me see it."

"Nope."

"Gabriel."

"Can I get you two some drinks?"

A man with a beard, suspenders, and a flannel shirt has appeared at our table. I sit up straighter, slightly embarrassed, and order an Old Fashioned while Gabriel gets straight whiskey. When the waiter's gone, I turn back to him.

"Come on."

"You're looking at my face now, why do you need a picture?"

I bite my lip, tilt my head, and consider my options. Gabriel's still grinning as he watches me, one arm slung around my shoulders, relaxed and sexy as hell and confident that his driver's license photo is completely safe in his pocket.

So I make a grab for it.

"Hey!" he says, and gets my wrist in his hand. I squirm, laughing, but he doesn't let up as we struggle quietly in the booth, trying not to make more noise than we already are.

"What do you think you're doing?"

"You're obviously hiding a terrible secret," I say, trying to get my hand free.

"I'm *trying* to have a nice time on a date," he teases.

I squirm again, and my hand bumps against a lump in his jeans.

"Seems like you *are* having a nice time," I murmur.

A few other patrons glance our way quickly, because we're being *that* couple.

"So don't ruin it by looking at my license picture," he says, keeping his voice low and close to my ear.

"That bad?"

He shrugs, my wrist still in his hand. Part of me wants to give it up and just make out until our drinks come, but a bigger part of me doesn't want to let him win.

So I reach my other hand to the very top of his waistband, swiping a single finger softly across his hipbone.

Gabriel *gasps* and sits upright as I hit his ticklish spot, and he unhands me just enough that I squirm loose, get into his pocket, and pull out his wallet.

In a flash, I've got his license out and I'm holding it in front of myself, studying it in the low light.

Next to me, Gabriel sighs dramatically.

"This looks like a mug shot," I say.

It's a *bad* picture. The lighting is awful, he's washed out, he's got stubble and an ugly haircut, and he's glaring at the camera like it just killed his dog.

"What do you know about mug shots?"

"I'm trying to decide what your crime was," I go on, teasing him. "Aggressive loitering? Skulking in an alley?"

"You know neither of those things are actually crimes, right?" he asks, but he's grinning.

The waiter comes back and sets two drinks in front of us. Gabriel and I clink our glasses together and drink, though I'm keeping his license out of his reach.

"I'm just saying, in this photo, you're a teardrop tattoo away from murder one and life in the pokey," I tell him.

"The pokey?" he asks, laughing.

"It's a slang word for—"

"I know what it means," he teases. "But I've never heard anyone use it outside of old gangster movies."

"You can make fun of me all you want, but you're not gonna change this picture."

He grabs for it again, and this time I let him get it. By now I'm halfway on his lap, and I'm pretty sure we're making a scene, tickle-fighting in a bar, but I'm also pretty sure that I'm never going to see any of the other bar patrons again and I'm having such a good time that I couldn't care less.

"There, now we're even," he says, shoving it back into his wallet. "I told you your picture was cute and you told me I look like a murderer."

"You said I look hypnotized."

"I said you looked cute hypnotized," he says, his eyes dancing.

"And I said you *almost* looked like a murderer," I tease right back.

"Can we just agree to never look at driver's license photos again?" he asks. "Maybe enjoy our first date?"

I laugh and settle back against his arm, taking another

swig of my drink. Gabriel kisses the side of my head, and a whole pile of warm fuzzies settle in my stomach.

We talk about country music. We talk about whether banjos are making a comeback and whether the washboard has a future as a musical instrument; whether The Charleston, the dance, was named after Charleston, the city; why Spanish moss is called Spanish moss when it's neither Spanish nor moss.

I get another drink, and finish it, and then I get another one. Gabriel and I sit in the booth until it's almost one in the morning, drinking and talking about nothing at all, while the bar gets more and more crowded.

I'm drunk, because I've had three drinks in two hours. Gabriel's arm is around my waist, his hand protectively on my hip, and I'm quizzing him about the Vice President's family, who he worked for.

"One of them must have done something weird!" I say, my face inches from his. "He must have had a crazy porn stash somewhere, or she had a trunk in a closet full of really trashy romance novels. Or there was a sex apparatus under their bed, or something."

He laughs out loud and takes the last sip of his whiskey, setting the empty glass on the table in front of us, then settles his hand on my knee, which is slung over his leg.

"What would this sex apparatus look like?" he says, right into my ear.

I have no clue. I'm aware that that sort of thing exists, but God knows I've never seen one. Even the gay porn I used to catch Lucas watching was apparatus-free.

But I don't let that stop me.

"It's got, you know," I start, leaning back against his shoulder. "Straps? To tie someone down with?"

"Sounds pretty sexy so far," he teases.

"And handcuffs?"

"Also to tie someone down with?"

"And maybe a whip or something?"

"Is the whip attached to the apparatus, or is that separate?"

I stick out my tongue at Gabriel, and he grins.

"You describe the sex apparatus, then," I say.

His hand on my leg moves, and I realize it's not on my knee any more, it's way higher. He leans in until his lips are almost on my ear.

"Well," he says. "It's about six-foot-three, brown hair, blue eyes, has the body of a *god* and the—"

"You *know* what I meant," I tease, but the knot of heat that's been in my stomach all night is starting to move downward.

"Oh, sorry," he says, and his grin gets even wickeder. "Fully erect, it's about —"

I turn bright red, yelp in alarm, and slap one hand over Gabriel's mouth, a little harder than I meant to.

"Mmmph phhhmnes," he finishes, his eyes lit up devilishly.

I look down. The apparatus in question is making itself known, and with all the whiskey coursing through my veins, I stare for way longer than I should in public.

Gabriel clears his throat, and I finally uncover his mouth.

"And it's in great working condition," he says, leaning closer. "Currently available for test drives."

His hand rasps along the denim of my jeans right up against me, and a shiver zips down my spine even as I look around in alarm.

"Everyone's drunk, no one's watching us," he says, pulling me in even closer. "I could get on my knees under this table and make you come twice before anyone noticed."

I close my eyes quickly against the thought, but it doesn't work. I'm pretty sure my panties are already soaked through.

"I think *someone* would probably —"

He silences me with his mouth, pressing it to mine, and I give up on talking as his tongue licks at my lower lip and then meets mine. His hand on my hip finds its way under my shirt, onto my back, pulling me in toward him as his fingers between my legs flick back and forth lazily.

I think I'm about two seconds away from letting him get under the table.

When he pulls back, I bite his lower lip softly, and slide one hand along the enormous bulge in his jeans.

"Ruby, we are in *public*," he teases.

"This is your fault," I say, nuzzling his nose with mine.

A few other bar patrons look at us and then away.

"*You* brought up the sex apparatus."

"*You* got me drunk in the first place."

We kiss again, lips and tongues tangling together, and I can't help but move my hips slightly against his hand. When we pull back we're both panting, and now a couple of people are staring.

I close my eyes in an attempt to regain some control.

"This probably isn't a great place to do this," I say, trying to modulate my voice so I sound as reasonable as possible. "Maybe we should head back."

"Ruby," he says, right in my ear. "We're out alone together, we don't know anyone here, and for once we're out of reach of your family. I'm not going back to the hotel where they are."

"Well, we can't—"

He kisses me again. It's a pretty effective way of ending an argument.

Then he grins at me, and it's absolutely wicked, devilish, and if my panties weren't already dripping wet now they are.

"Come on," he says, and slides out of the booth, pulling me along after him.

Seconds after we leave, a group of people gets into the booth themselves, and Gabriel moves through the drunk, dancing crowd. Even though it's crowded he never loosens his grip on my hand, checking back every few seconds to make sure I'm still there.

Finally, we reach a curtain on the other side of the room, and he swishes it open, holding it for me. There are a couple women in the short hallway, all looking at their phones as they wait for the bathroom, and they glance up as Gabriel and I walk past them, past both bathrooms, and to a door marked EXIT. He pushes it open and walks through, and suddenly we're outdoors, behind the building at the end of a narrow, brick-lined walkway.

In front of us there's a tiny courtyard surrounded by the ivy-covered walls of the surrounding buildings. The only thing in the courtyard is a single table and a chair with an ashtray on it. There are no lights out here except for the dim glow of faraway streetlights, and from one corner, the walkway snakes between the buildings and to the sidewalk out front.

Gabriel grins and pulls me closer, the familiar heat of his body intoxicating against the cool night air.

"Not what I was expecting, but I'll take it," he murmurs, kissing me hard. My insides are one tight, hot coil and I stand on my toes, throwing both my arms over his shoulders.

"Where did you think we were going?" I ask.

He pushes me backward until I'm against the table, and he lifts me up onto it, pulling my legs around him until the friction between us is almost overwhelming.

"I had no idea," he admits, kissing me again. "Somewhere at least semi-private where I can do bad, bad things to you."

I grab his belt and tug, sliding my other hand under his shirt and onto the thick, hard muscles of his back. His hardness is right up against me, and even through two layers of denim, I swear I can feel him throb.

"Why would you do bad things?" I tease, tipsily.

"Because you drive me right out of my fucking mind," he growls. "Because I have no self-control around you, because you could say the word and make me do anything you wanted."

He kisses my neck and then bites me, the tender skin between his teeth, and I try to hold back a moan.

"Because the bad things I do to you make you run your nails down my back while you chant my name, and I like looking at your claw marks in the morning," he says, his voice rumbling against me, sending shivers along my skin.

Gabriel pauses for a moment, his lips against the hollow of my throat.

"And because I only feel right when I'm with you," he says, his voice suddenly quiet. "Because when you're here it's like the world is in color and I didn't even know it was black and white before. Fuck, Ruby, I think I'm drunk."

"I like you drunk," I say, and kiss him, mouth open. "I like you all the time."

"So you like me when I make fun of your driver's license photo?" he teases, his hands sliding down my body.

"Less, but yes," I say, tightening my grip on his belt, the short fur of his treasure trail against my knuckles.

"You like me when I pull you into an alleyway and kiss you drunkenly?" he goes on.

He jerks at my jeans, unbuttoning them with one hand, yanking the zipper down, and pushes his hand inside.

"You like me when—fuck yes you do," he says, his fingers sliding through my wetness and between my lips. "*Jesus* you like that, Ruby, you're goddamn soaking wet right now."

"You did promise you'd do bad things to me," I say.

He slides his fingers inside me, already stroking my walls, the heel of his hand against my clit, and I inhale sharply.

"Only because they feel so good," he says.

I pull at his belt and his mouth lands on mine, his hand still inside me. Before I know what I'm doing I'm unbuckling his belt, unzipping his jeans, and then his hard, thick shaft is in my hand and Gabriel is growling deep in his chest, one hand inside my jeans and the other making a fist in my hair.

I squeeze harder, stroking him, and he pulls my head back with my hair, pressing his lips hungrily to my throat. Everything spins and swirls for just a moment, and when it rights itself I'm biting my lip and trying not to moan.

"Tell me you want me," he says.

"I want you," I whisper.

"Tell me how you *really* want me," he growls, his fingers curling inside me. "I know you do, but I want you to open your beautiful fucking mouth and talk dirty to me, Ruby."

Shit. I have no idea how to talk dirty. But I'm also drunk and on a table while Gabriel's got half his hand inside me, so there's no time like the present to try.

"I want you right here and right now," I say, closing my eyes so I can be braver. Despite the whiskey in my system, I can feel myself blush. "I mean, I want you inside me."

"I am inside you," he teases.

"I mean your cock," I say quickly, blushing deeper.

I take a deep breath.

"I want you to bend me over this table and pull my hair and fuck me until I come really hard because every time I'm around you I feel like I'm going to crawl out of my own skin," I say, the words coming in a rush. "And I can't get enough of all the bad things you do to me or all the dirty things you say to me so please *God* don't stop even if I have no idea what to say back."

He's already pulled his hand out and slid me off the table, his lips rough on mine, his hand sticky under my shirt.

"That was a pretty good start," Gabriel says.

"And I really like feeling you come inside me," I say quickly, my voice soft.

In a split second he's whirled me around, my hips pressed against the table as he pulls my jeans down. For a moment, he pauses, and then one finger slides beneath the waistband of my thong and he snaps it against my skin before shoving it down, too.

My fingers curl against the ugly tabletop as I hear his belt buckle clank. Then there's a hand on my hip and I lean forward, arching back, on my tiptoes, and there's a voice in my head saying *this is really immodest* but I push it away, because I don't *care*.

He teases my lips with his cock, sliding the head between them, higher until he's almost at my clit, then back down, his hand holding my hips against the table so I can't push back and take him. I moan and he finally nudges the head against my entrance, just barely sliding in, like he's teasing me.

It lasts for a moment, his breathing rough and heavy, and then Gabriel takes my hair in his fist and slides into me all the way to the hilt, until his hips slap against mine. I grunt, my head pulled back, because I wanted it so bad and it feels so fucking good that I can't even speak, just make noises.

"Every time I fuck you bare like this I think I'm gonna come in ten seconds flat," he growls, his other hand on my waist.

My mind's gone perfectly blank, and all I can do is reach behind myself and close my fingers in his hair, every single sensitive spot and pleasure point inside me are lit up and on fire, the flames already threatening to rage out of control.

We go slow at first, so slow it makes my toes curl as Gabriel's cock hits all those spots again and again. Somehow, he always finds the exact perfect angle to turn me into a helpless, moaning puddle within three seconds and now he's doing it again, fucking me slow and hard until all I can do is gasp for air and hang on.

It doesn't take long. Even though he's still pulling my hair, I arch back into him, taking him as deep and hard as I can with every stroke until it feels almost too good to bear. I think I'm whispering his name, over and over again, and I swear that right now there is nothing in the entire world except the two of us, ours bodies together, his lips against my ear, his cock inside me.

"Come," he whispers into my ear, his voice rough. "I know you're close, and Ruby, I want to feel you come *now*, with me inside you."

I moan. Gabriel's right: I'm there, on the edge.

He thrusts deep and hard one more time and then I'm over, falling, like I'm weightless and floating, every muscle in my body tensing and flexing at once. At some point, Gabriel claps a hand over my mouth and his other hand digs into my hip and then he growls my name into my ear and I can feel him explode inside me, jolt after jolt until it's over.

My eyes are still closed, my head back against Gabriel's shoulder, and I slowly remember where I am and what I'm doing here.

We should go back inside, I think, but I don't mean it. *I should go back to the hotel, make sure Pearl didn't wake up, I should...*

Gabriel wraps both arms around me and nuzzles my ear.

Fuck it, I think.

CHAPTER THIRTY-TWO

GABRIEL

THIS IS IT, I think. *This is what I want, this is all I want. This and this and this.*

I slide both arms around Ruby and hold her close. It doesn't matter that we're half-dressed in a weird alley behind a bar. It doesn't matter that her parents are asleep at a hotel not that far away; it doesn't matter that there's no way I'll ever be in the Secret Service again.

This is what matters.

"Ruby," I murmur, right into her ear.

"Mmm?" she says, leaning into me. She slides her fingers between mine, and I feel like a puzzle piece locks into place.

"Run away with me," I say.

She swallows, not answering.

"Tonight," I go on. "Now. We don't even have to run. All we have to do is *not go back.*"

Ruby takes a deep breath, her body expanding and contracting against me. I know she's going to say no, and I know that her reasons are perfectly good, and I know that leaving in the dead of night is exciting and romantic but probably not a good idea.

But still. But *still*, I want to take her away and never look back.

"Not tonight," she says, finally, and it takes me by surprise.

"Not *tonight*," I repeat.

She lifts my hand to her lips and kisses my knuckles gently, folding my big hand around her small one.

"We need to plan," she says. "If we wait a week, maybe two, it'll be easier. I can bring some things with me, I can find some money."

She pauses.

"I can say goodbye to Joy and Zeke," she says.

Suddenly, I understand, and I feel like an idiot for not remembering that this is still her family, that despite everything, there are people here she loves.

"I don't think this is it!" a voice shouts from the walkway.

I jerk backward, letting Ruby go, automatically turning away from the voice. In seconds, we've both pulled up our jeans and we're smoothing down our shirts, Ruby running one hand through her hair, clearing her throat.

A guy in jeans and flip-flops walks into the tiny courtyard, stops, and stares at it. It's dead obvious in his face that he knows exactly what we were just doing, and he has no idea how to proceed.

"Sorry," he blurts out, then jerks a thumb over his shoulder. "I was just... yeah."

He turns and leaves, and Ruby and I look at each other. She starts giggling, her face bright pink even in the dark, and then I start laughing too as she walks back into my arms.

"That was close," she says.

"Close, but fine," I point out.

"Can you imagine if I got arrested for public indecency?" she says, sighing.

"Just tell your parents that Satan pulled your jeans down, and it was actually his voice saying my name over and over again," I tell her, grinning.

She burrows her face into my chest, and I grin, stroking her hair, because I can tell she's embarrassed and I think it's adorable.

"You'd think Satan would be busier," she muses. "Billions of people on Earth, yet he's got the time to come personally make me sin."

"Great time management skills," I say, and Ruby laughs.

After a moment, we head back into the bar through the back door. A few people definitely give us looks, but I just had the greatest night of my life and Ruby finally agreed to let me help her escape, so I don't give a fuck what *anyone* thinks.

I pay the tab, and we leave, walking hand-in-hand through Charleston. It's almost closing time, so people are spilling out onto the sidewalks, running the gamut from drunk and belligerent to talking quietly. A few times, Ruby flinches away from someone particularly obnoxious but I squeeze her hand and straighten my back a little, and nobody fucks with us.

We stroll back to the hotel, talking about nothing at all. Ruby's half planning her escape and half talking about all the things she's going to do when she's out, like *wear tank tops* and *go places alone.* I tell her I think she should also start wearing really short shorts, and she laughs, wrinkling her nose.

"I don't know if I should take fashion advice from you," she muses.

"There is *no reason* why—"

I glance over Ruby's head, and suddenly, my stomach tightens, pure instinct driving adrenaline through my veins while my brain rushes to catch up.

Something is wrong, I think frantically. *Something's wrong. What? What is it?*

I hold my breath and scan the street, forcing myself to stay calm. Maybe it's nothing, just a weird noise that kicked me into panic mode, a glass shattering somewhere, someone slamming a door.

Everything seems normal, and we're on the edge of downtown, only a few blocks from the hotel. It's quieter here, less crowded, so I'm on higher alert, but there's nothing *wrong,* I'm just...

The car. It's the car. A black minivan, half a block away, its lights off. All at once I realize that it's *been* half a block away since we left the bar, but I'm drunk and didn't notice it, not until now. Not until we're in the quiet part of town, less people around to hear Ruby if she screams.

"Why what?" she asks, looking up at me.

I tighten my hand on hers, instinctively, and look to the front again.

"Gabriel," she says, and she sounds frightened.

I nearly tell her it's nothing, to keep walking, so we can get back to the hotel and I can send her to her room and we'll take care of this. But I don't. It's Ruby. I tell her everything.

"Don't look," I say, my voice dead calm. "That minivan is following us."

She twitches, like she nearly turns her head, but she doesn't and instead she has my hand in a death grip, so tight I think she might break my fingers.

"I'm right here, and you're going to be fine," I tell her, pulling on every ounce of training I have to keep my voice neutral, because the last thing I need is for Ruby to panic and run or something.

Right now, we're in control of the situation. *He's* following *us* down the street, and though it's not crowded, there are other people around. But if we do something unpredictable, all bets are off.

"Here's what we're going to do," I say. "We're going to go back to the hotel like there's nothing wrong, and when we get there, you're going to go back to your room and I'm going to stay in the lobby and call the team, leaving out the part where it followed us home from the bar. Simple as that."

Ruby nods, speeding up her pace, but I pull her back.

"Don't make him panic," I say. "Come on. Slow and steady."

She squeezes my hand one more time, and I squeeze back. I can tell she's terrified, but she's also brave as hell and so she does exactly what I say: we walk the few blocks back to the hotel. We even pretend to chat about something, and she holds her head high and doesn't look behind her once.

It's half a block behind us the entire time, a black shadow at the edge of my vision, creeping along and trying to dodge through the light traffic as it follows us.

By the time we're approaching the hotel, its soft yellow lobby lights practically calling us, something has become very clear: this guy has no idea what he's doing. If you want to follow someone, you don't creep along, lights off, half a block behind them. Maybe he wants to frighten her, intimidate her, and it might work if I weren't here.

But I am, and this motherfucker's trying his bullshit on the wrong guy, because I spend most of the walk back staying intensely aware of the minivan while also fantasizing about the ways I'd like to kick his ass. There's a lot of them, and the tighter Ruby holds my hand, the more creative they get.

And then finally we're there, at the hotel, where it's well-lit, where there are security cameras, other people, and most importantly, a whole security detail. I'm just fucking praying that this guy isn't smart enough to drive away, because I want him gone for good.

I open the door and Ruby steps through, into the lobby, her movements stiff and awkward, like she's really trying to act normal. The only other person in there is a guy at the front desk who's half asleep, and I automatically tick through the plans of the hotel lobby: all doors but this one locked from the outside; cameras behind the desk; alarm system on the windows; someone always on desk duty. It's safe.

Before we get another step, Ruby sinks into my arms, so suddenly that I take a step back. She squeezes me so tight I can hardly breathe, her whole body shaking like a leaf.

"I'm sorry," she whispers. "I'm sorry, just give me a minute."

"Don't be," I whisper back, holding her tight. "You did great. You're fine, you're gonna be fine."

She takes a deep, shuddering breath. I turn my head and look through the glass doors. No minivan.

Please don't let him have gone far, I think, Ruby in my arms. *I want to wring his fucking neck myself.*

"I'm sorry," she says again. "I just couldn't stop thinking about all the stuff he wrote, and what I'd do if he suddenly came for me, and how I'd escape if he got me…"

"Stop apologizing," I say, into her hair. "You're fine. I'm here. I promise. He's gonna have to go through me to get to you, and he's gonna have a rough fucking time of *that.*"

God, I almost want him to try something, just so I've got an excuse to kick his ass.

Ruby straightens up, takes a deep breath, wipes her eyes. I brush one thumb along her cheek, wiping away one tear, and she half smiles.

"Okay," she says. "Okay. I'm fine. I'll see you tomorrow."

"Tomorrow," I say, and a quick pang stabs through my heart, because stalker aside, I liked this.

I liked being out with Ruby, in public, like any regular girlfriend and boyfriend. I liked holding her hand and seeing her in pants and making fools of ourselves by making out in a booth, and I hate—absolutely fucking *hate*—that come tomorrow it's back to polite nods and significant glances.

So I kiss her. Just once, quickly, but fuck this and fuck her stalker and fuck her parents and fuck everything. It's my job to protect her, to make her not afraid, to make sure she doesn't need to be, so I fucking kiss her.

"Thanks," she whispers, then turns and walks away. I watch her until she gets on the elevator, then mentally track her progress as I dial Ray's number: up to the fourth floor; cameras in the elevator; every room filled with people who could hear her scream.

She's fine. She'll be fine. There's nowhere she could be more fine, but still, something nags at me. I wonder if I should have gone with her, even if it would have meant getting caught.

I pick up my phone and call Ray, ready to get this show on the road.

"Gabe," says Ray's voice in a deep croak.

God, I hate when he calls me that.

"We have a situation," I say. "There's a black minivan outside."

CHAPTER THIRTY-THREE

RUBY

I GET INTO THE ELEVATOR, hit the button for the fourth floor, and lean my head back against the mirrored wall as the doors close.

You're fine, I tell myself. *You're fine, and Gabriel's fine, and he might actually catch this guy.*

The elevator reaches the fourth floor, and the doors slide open. I'm still on high alert, my nerves jangling as I make my way to the door of my hotel room. I look behind me about once every step, but it's dead quiet and well lit.

No one jumps out to kidnap me. No one slides out of the shadows. Nothing moves at all.

I reach my room and stand outside the door, just listening for a moment. It's a heavy door, so I don't know what I'm expecting to hear, but there's no noise at all.

She's still asleep, I think. *Just sneak back in, and if she wakes up pretend you were just in the bathr—*

All at once, I realize that our plan is fucked. My hand is in my back pocket, getting the key out, and I just stop moving. I stop breathing, and I wonder if it's too late.

I could just go back downstairs, get Gabriel, tell him,

and we could go. It wouldn't even matter where or how, because everything is about to fall apart and we're idiots for not realizing it.

My stalker's going to spill everything. He wrote me an entire letter detailing my daily activities at the county fair. He's been watching. At the very least, he saw Gabriel and I leave a bar together, holding hands, at nearly two in the morning.

I feel dizzy, suddenly, like I need to sit down, like I need to take a moment and think through what we should do. Because I can't go into this room, not now, not after I finally decided I trusted Gabriel enough to let him help me leave.

My ears are ringing. I feel like everything is crashing down around me, and one last, desperate time, I think about my siblings. Joy and Zeke, whispering about college math in the kitchen.

I put the key back in my pocket, still staring up at the door to the room I shared with Pearl.

Go. Go now, before he calls in the rest of the team, before they catch the guy and he spills everything.

Joy, Zeke, I'm sorry. I'm so fucking sorry.

And then, just as I step away from the door, it swings open, a rectangle of light falling into the hall. I *panic*, wondering what on earth I can possibly tell Pearl that will keep her from sounding the alarm.

But then I look up, and the figure standing there in the doorway isn't Pearl.

It's my father.

CHAPTER THIRTY-FOUR

"NEGATIVE," Steven says into his walkie-talkie. "No movement here. Target not sighted. All's quiet. Over and out."

He's nervous and jittery, too excited, and talking like a he's a Navy SEAL in a bad action movie, but I let him do it. Anything I try to communicate is gonna be too profanity-laced and loud to even get my point across, so I don't bother.

My point being, *let me the fuck at that bastard.*

I pace back and forth again, right in front of the hotel doors. The Kevlar vest Charleston PD gave me is a little too small, digging into my skin, but that's not the worst part.

The worst part is that he's out there, only a few blocks away, and someone else is going to be the one to take him down. Some Charleston police officer is gonna get to grab him, cuff him, be the first one to see his face and tell him that it's all fucking over and he lost, and I'm here, at the hotel.

Just waiting.

I fucking hate waiting.

I get it, obviously. I'm Ruby's bodyguard. It's my job to guard her, and she's here, up in her room, probably pretending to be asleep. Anyone who comes here is gonna have to get through me—and also Steven, sure—before he can hurt her, and he's gonna have one hell of a time doing *that*.

But it doesn't change that I'd love to be the one punching this guy in the face.

The radio they gave me crackles, a rough, tinny voice coming through. I listen tensely, still pacing back and forth like a caged animal.

"Gibson, roger that. In position now, Cartney and Stiles heading Southeast on third street. Target is still moving very slowly, approximately ten miles per hour."

"All right. Moving to block now, nice and easy."

Silence. More silence. I imagine what's happening right now, the plan we laid out not five minutes ago: one police car behind the minivan, one in front, officers with weapons drawn and bulletproof vests on. Ideally, the unarmed suspect gets out of the van, hands on his head, gets on the ground, and it's over.

If anything else goes down, it's ten armed police officers against one lunatic. I don't like his odds.

The radio crackles again.

"Gibson," the man's voice says. "*Gibson.* Shit!"

Over the radio there's the sound of a motor revving so hard it roars, the sound of metal crunching and glass shattering.

"What the hell?" someone shouts.

Steven and both shove through the hotel doors, drawing our weapons, moving in sync. I've got no fucking idea what happened, but it sure as hell wasn't the plan.

We stand on the sidewalk, motionless, the curve of the hotel driveway in front of us. For a moment, there's nothing but the near-total quiet of a quaint town at two-thirty in the morning, the slight hum of the street lights, the occasional rustle of the breeze.

And *then* there's a siren. The sound of crunch, shattering glass, an overloaded engine being driven so hard it's practically screaming.

I tighten my grip and plant my feet, every nerve in my body practically humming. Someone's shouting over the radio, but I can't understand him through the static, and I'm using every muscle in my body to listen for the sound of a minivan careening my way.

Come on, I think. *Come the fuck on.*

Try me. Just fucking try me.

More glass shatters. The sirens get louder. Metal crunches, and then there's a screech, the sound of metal grinding on metal and a dark hulking shape rounds the corner like a drunk turtle on a skateboard, fishtails, and then points itself right at us.

I swear to God I almost smile.

The minivan's engine howls, redlining, and blue lights whirl around the corner right behind it, but I'm not looking at that. I'm looking at the pale shape behind the steering wheel and I'm thinking, *finally, you motherfucker.*

He doesn't stop and I don't move. Instead I tick off the milliseconds, forcing my nerves quiet as I wait until he's in range. I feel like everything is moving in slow motion: the sirens, the van, the spinning lights. Another car's side mirror goes flying, and then the van is there, in range, and I finally fire.

It happens almost instantly. I get the driver's side tire with my first shot, and the van jerks to the left, losing control. He bumps off a pickup truck parked in the street, careens over the curb as Steven and I move out of the way, but the minivan's nose plows into a concrete planter and comes to a dead stop, steam pouring from under the hood, airbags deployed.

Nothing moves inside it. Two police cars pull up, screeching to a stop, sirens howling, but I'm already sprinting for the driver's side door of the minivan, Steven behind me, weapons out and at the ready.

We look at each other. He nods, weapon trained on the driver's door, police moving into position as I yank the door open.

"Hands up!" someone shouts.

I still can't see his face, because he's got long, stringy brown hair that's flown forward and covered it. Slowly, shakily, he holds up his hands, both shaking so badly it almost looks like he's waving.

At the same time, we all pause, just for an instant. There's something wrong here, wrong about the man behind the wheel, about the small, delicate hands he's holding up.

"Now get out slowly," the voice says. "Nice and easy."

The figure unbuckles, still shaking, and turns slowly toward the door, and suddenly I can see a face.

It's a woman.

For a split second, it throws me off. This entire time I had a mental image of the man who was stalking Ruby, the man who threatened to tie her up and rape her and keep her in a basement, the man who might be capable of overpowering her and taking her against her will.

But it's not. It's a woman, small and delicate and terrified, shaking and crying hysterically. Worst of all, she looks familiar.

I wonder if we got the wrong person, but then she steps out of the van and the spell's broken, instantly.

"Against the car!" someone shouts, and then the cops swarm her. They frisk her and cuff her while she sobs, her face red and her nose running, so utterly distraught that I almost feel bad for her.

I'm at a loss. I have no idea what to think or how to feel. I don't even know that we got Ruby's stalker, and if we did, I can't bring myself to think about punching this girl's face in.

A big, meaty hand claps my shoulder and I look down into a tanned, lined face.

"You good?" it asks.

It's Captain Dodson, the guy currently in charge.

"I'm good," I confirm.

"Great. You're gonna need to give a statement down at the station. Nice shooting, by the way."

Steven stays at the hotel while the Captain drives me to the police station in a daze.

All I can think is, *what if that's not him?*

"SHE DIDN'T DESERVE IT," the girl sobs, desperately. "The scriptures are very clear on that point. Matthew 19:6. 'Let no man tear asunder,' it says, and she tore their union right in half."

The officer in the room with her says something quietly, pushing a bottle of water toward her, but the girl doesn't take it. I'm on the other side of the one-way mirror, and though I'm not exactly supposed to be there, no one's raising any objection to my presence.

Her name is Lilah, and she looks familiar because she's the Senator's aide's fiancée, always around when we go to campaign events. I think she's also Lucas's sister, though that part is a little less clear since she won't say his name out loud.

She knew about the county fair because she was there

with us the entire time, and she stole her parents' car to drive to Atlanta late at night to mail the letters.

This whole time, we were barking up the wrong tree. She was *right here* and we were so, so wrong.

"And then Ruby got another chance," she hisses, her voice quiet but hateful. "You know where she should be? She should be in a ditch somewhere, her head shaved because that's what they used to do to shameful women—"

I turn around and walk out, pushing open the door and heading back into the main room of the Charleston Police Department, paper cup half-full of stone-cold coffee in my hand. This feels a thousand times worse than I thought it would, and I find a bench along a wall and just sit on it because I just need a minute amidst all the chaos to think.

Lilah's not well. That much was dead obvious almost immediately, and that was before she spent about an hour telling a police officer how she talks to angels in long, detailed conversations every night.

And how the angels tell her to do things. Specific things, and often things that aren't very nice, and furthermore, the angels have warned her that she can never, ever tell anyone about their conversations.

It took about thirty seconds for all my anger toward her to fade into awful, gut-wrenching pity, because it's dead clear that this girl needs a kind of help that she might never get.

On the bright side, even though she's told everyone about Ruby and me and our fornication, sinful in the eyes of God, no one believes her.

It's five-thirty in the morning. I'm supposed to be escorting Ruby to breakfast in an hour and a half, and though I'm sure that the schedule is non-existent now, I'm still hanging onto that. Because right now, that's what I want to think about: knocking on her door, her face when she opens it, the way she might sneak me a smile as we get on the elevator.

I don't want to think about her father quizzing me about whether Ruby and I have been fornicating. I don't want to think about whether I'll even be employed with them past today, or how it's going to be harder for Ruby to run away with me if I'm not.

All those things are coming, but I'm tired and the end to this story has been almost nauseatingly unsatisfying. Instead of a bad guy, there's just a girl deep in the throes of untreated mental illness. So I think about Ruby in the morning, her smile, the possibility that our fingers might touch when she passes the salt.

I'm still thinking about that when footsteps approach, and I look over to see Ray standing there, hands shoved deep in his pockets. His expression is almost aggressively unreadable, so perfectly blank that I know something is wrong instantly.

"What is it?" I ask.

His face doesn't change.

"Could you please come with me?"

"Is it Ruby?" I ask, heart seizing in my chest.

"Just come with me, son."

"Is she okay?"

Ray just starts walking away, giving me no real choice but to follow after him.

"Ray," I say, trying to keep my voice low even though I want to shout. "Ray, what's going on?"

He just walks out of the main room and into the reception area at the front, empty because it's too early for the receptionist.

"She's fine," he says, holding up one hand to stave me off. "But the Senator wants to talk to you."

I exhale.

"Of course," I say, rubbing my eyes. "I'm sorry, it's been a night, and with everything that happened—"

"Son, he wants to talk to you about Ruby's whereabouts last night," Ray interrupts.

I stop short, mid-sentence. I don't even shut my mouth, I just stare at Ray.

I'm not even surprised. It was too inevitable for me to be surprised, too many things that had to go exactly, perfectly right for me to be surprised.

But I know, in that instant, that the charade is over. I'm done seeing her every day and pretending that I'm not desperately in love with her. I'm done spending time with her family and acting like I'm not thinking about her lips on mine and her bare skin under my fingers.

He knows. I feel like I'm staring at a bridge that just got wrecked, and I have no clue which way I'll go now, but I know it's somewhere. I'm unmoored, in freefall, but I know exactly one goddamn thing and it's that somehow, I'm getting out of this with Ruby.

I toss my half-full coffee cup into a trash can, cold coffee splashing up the side.

"I know where she was," I tell him, my voice finding its lowest, most serious register. "She was with me."

Ray nods grimly.

And unto the Reubenites and unto the Gadites I gave from Gilead even unto the river Arnon half the valley, and the border even unto the river Jabbok, which is the border of the children of Ammon;

The plain also, and Jordan, and the coast thereof, from Chinnereth even unto the sea of the plain, even the salt sea, under Ashdothpisgah eastward.

I'M SO bored I'm reading Deuteronomy. The Bible is the only book I'm allowed to have right now, and if I don't do *something*, I might go out of my mind. And I know that virtually everything that's not Deuteronomy, which is mostly lists of who begat whom, is more applicable to my current situation.

But I'm in no mood to look to the Bible for help at the moment, given that my father's supposed obedience to its very letter is what got me where I am right now. So, in my boredom, I'm reading the least helpful part I can find, which is about which parts of Israel various tribes are supposed to own.

I flip the whisper-thin page and start a new section when there's a polite, hesitant knock on my door. That means it's not Pearl or Joy, whose room I've been moved into.

"Come in," I call, not looking up from the Bible.

The door opens about a foot and one of my new guards sticks his head in.

"Your father's asked to see you," he says, sounding a little nervous.

I've got three new guards, and I make them *all* nervous because they're *all* members of my father's church, and I don't think they like being around the harlot.

That's me, by the way. Obviously.

"What does he want?" I ask, not bothering to stand or be polite.

"He didn't say."

I smile, half-sweet and half-sarcastic.

"Any chance it seemed like he's going to let me go?" I ask, cocking my head to one side.

The poor guy looks simultaneously horrified and baffled, his mouth opening and then closing once without answering. It's okay, because I know the answer. The answer's no, but I guess my father wants to fight about it some more.

I scoot off my bed, my ugly skirt bunching around my knees as I do. I still hate the things, but it's not like I've got many other clothes.

The guard sees me down the hallway, up the stairs, and then opens the door to my father's office, letting me through. My heart's beating wildly, thumping through my veins so loud I'm afraid he can hear it, but I steel myself and walk through.

"Ruby," he says, still sitting behind his massive desk.

The door behind me shuts, and now we're alone. It's not

the first time that we've been alone in his office during the past few days, and if he thinks this meeting is going to go any differently than the others, he's sorely mistaken.

"Father," I say.

I don't move. I don't step forward, and I don't give any indication that he's in control here, even though we both know he is. After all, I learned all this from a consummate politician, even if he wasn't trying to teach me.

"I summoned you here to offer a truce," he says, clasping his hands in front of himself on the desk.

For just a second, my heart skips a beat, and I think that maybe, just maybe, my father's going to be reasonable.

"What are the terms?" I ask, keeping my voice steady and trying not to bely my excitement.

He stands, his leather chair groaning, and walks to the window, hands clasped behind his back. I can just feel a lecture coming on, and I know this stance is the one he does when he wants to seem official and important, like he's getting his presidential portrait painted.

"Ruby, do you remember making Easter cupcakes in Sunday school when you were five years old?"

Jesus, he's bringing this up again. I take a deep breath, forcing myself not to roll my eyes.

"Of course," I say.

You won't let me forget it.

"Your entire class baked cupcakes to celebrate the Resurrection," he goes on, the pace of his voice slow and steady, no matter how impatient I am. "When they were finished, there was to be one cupcake per child. Each of you selected your cupcake, and then waited your turns to adorn your cupcake with sprinkles."

They were blue sprinkles. My favorite color, at least at the time.

"And when it came your turn to adorn the cupcake, you wanted more sprinkles than Miss Nicole allotted you, because she needed to save enough sprinkles for the rest of the Sunday school class. She tried to take them away from you, but because you thought you didn't have enough sprinkles, you grabbed the container back from her and proceeded to pour every last sprinkle onto your own cupcake."

I almost tell him that I didn't mean to. I meant to get more sprinkles, but not *all* of them. I was five years old and clumsy. It was an accident.

"Your actions deprived the rest of the students of sprinkles," he goes on, now turning away from the window and toward me. "And I've thought of that story again and again over the past few years, each time that your selfishness has outweighed your loyalty and love for this family. In some ways, you're still that five-year-old, pouring sprinkles onto a cupcake."

I literally bite my tongue. I wonder if he brings this story up again and again because it's the only one he even remembers from my childhood. It's not like he took an active hand in raising me, preferring to be a distant figure while my mother did all the hard work.

"Here we are, once more, the metaphorical sprinkles all over the floor," he says, and I wonder if he realizes how dumb that sounds. "Your actions have called *my* reputation into question, as a father and as a politician. Your actions call into question whether I can effectively represent this great state of South Carolina when I can't even govern my own home. They call into question my abilities as a father, if I can't even teach my own daughter the difference between right and wrong."

There's a long pause, like he's expecting me to apologize, but I've got no intention of doing such a thing.

"What's the truce?" I finally ask.

He sighs and walks across the office, gazing up at the huge, ugly, backlit cross on one wall. I'm acutely aware that this is all theatrics, all for the sake of appearance, even if it's mostly wasted on me.

"Thankfully, not everyone is so focused on their own selfish pleasures to the exclusion of all else," he says. "Despite your insistence on sullying yourself, Kyle Pickett has offered yet again to marry you."

"No," I say, the word coming out of my mouth a knee-jerk reaction.

"I told him that you would consider carefully, over the course of several days," he goes on, like I didn't say anything.

"I'm not marrying him."

He can't force me to marry Kyle, that much I'm sure of. He can do a lot of things, but forcing me to say *I do* isn't one of them.

"Ruby, I'm not sure you'll have another chance," he says, his voice the epitome of patience.

"I don't want another chance to marry someone who frequents prostitutes and has never had a two-way conversation in his life," I say.

"You of all people should understand that someone can change and make amends," he says.

"I'm not marrying him," I say quietly, taking a deep breath. My heart's racing again, but I force myself to sound calm. "I'm not taking a truce. The only thing I'm interested in is walking out of this house, through that gate, and into the world."

We look at each other for a long, long time, neither one moving or budging. I've got a feeling that he's got a cupcake story, too, that a long time ago as a child he wanted something and took it through whatever means he could.

But instead of being someone's daughter, he was someone's son, and what he wanted mattered.

"Someday, you'll thank me," he says softly. That means *I'm not letting you go.*

"Are you sure?" I ask.

"It's my job to have your best interests at heart," he says, and smiles his politician's smile at me.

He thinks I have no options left, that after trying to escape unsuccessfully and after arguing with him, after a little while, I'll come around to his bidding.

But I've still got one thing left. I don't know whether he doesn't think I'm smart enough to think of it, or if he just thinks I won't dare, but he's wrong on both counts.

"Thank you, Father," I say steadily. "It's been a pleasure."

He just nods. I turn, open the heavy door, and walk back to my room, trailed by a slightly nervous guard. Inside, I sit on my bed and turn once more to the tedium of Deuteronomy, but I'm not paying any attention to the words.

Instead I'm mulling over the last, biggest thing I've got. It's going to take some doing. I don't even want to do it. I want him to call off my guards and let me walk away, but that's not going to happen.

I've run out of options.

It's time to go nuclear.

CHAPTER THIRTY-SIX

GABRIEL

I SIT IN MY CAR, outside Starbucks, and watch Ruby's brother Zeke walk into the store. He does it a little furtively, glancing around, and I smile to myself, because I'm sure coffee is the devil's liquid, or something.

I've been following him the past two days, and I'm pretty sure he doesn't know. I feel creepy as hell following a twenty-year-old kid around town, but as a male member of Ruby's family, he's got the most latitude by far. He's allowed to go places alone, with no guard. The kid's even got a job, something totally off-limits to Ruby and her sisters.

Plus, I think he'll help me. I've never exactly talked to him, but I know that Ruby likes him, and he's got something like that same spark that she does.

And he's here, at Starbucks, drinking Satan juice.

I get out of my car and wait for him, right where he'll see me when he comes out of the store, and sure enough, he does. He stops for a moment, then looks around. He takes a sip of his coffee, still holding the door open, like he's pretending to be casual.

And finally, he walks over to me.

"Gabriel," he says, nodding like everything is totally cool and we're just old friends.

"Hey, Zeke," I say. "Got a minute?"

He takes a deep breath, pushes his hand through his hair, and nods.

———

WE DRIVE to the Wal-Mart parking lot across the street, where I maneuver my car between the two biggest pickup trucks I can find. I'm pretty sure I'm being too paranoid, but then again, am I?

I don't know where Ruby is. Despite trying everything, I can't find out. I think she's still in that house, with even more security than before, but they could have already shipped her off to be re-educated. She could be in Georgia or Mississippi already.

The thought makes my blood turn to lead in my veins, like I'm fucking powerless, nothing I can do. Not that I know what to do, but at least finding out where she is seems like a good first step.

"She's still at home," Zeke confirms, staring through the windshield at another parked car. "They brought in three new guards, though, all from the church. They take eight hour shifts around the clock, sitting in a chair outside her room."

Jesus fucking Christ. I rub my temples, and Zeke takes another swig of his coffee.

"I think she's got a plan, though," he goes on.

I look over at him in disbelief, wondering what the fuck her plan can *be*. I've got no idea how to get her out of a place like that, full of twenty-four-seven security guards, none of whom will have any issues physically detaining her.

"She does?" I echo. "What is it?"

"She won't tell me," he says. "Probably so no one can get it out of me later. But I'm supposed to get her a phone, and I haven't been able to yet, because it's this whole *thing*, you have to figure out which phone to get, and then either get on a plan or get pre-paid and activate it, and —"

"I'll get her a phone," I say quickly. "Just meet me again tomorrow. I'll have a phone for her."

"Cool," Zeke says. "Sorry I don't know anything else."

Then he looks over at me, and even though he's got brown eyes, he's giving me the same cool, appraising look I know from Ruby.

"She'll be glad you stuck around," he says. "I think she's worried you're gone."

I frown, my hand on the keys in the ignition. That hadn't even occurred to me, even though it's technically true. I could just leave right now and forget this whole thing, but I don't think anything's ever appealed to me less.

"She is?" I ask, starting the car.

"It's hard to tell, since we can't really, you know, have actual conversations," he admits. "But she knows you could leave if you wanted."

I swallow hard, because the thought's almost physically painful. I got her into this. I'm here until the end.

"Tell her I'm still in town," I say quietly, both hands on the steering wheel. "And tell her I'm not leaving until I leave with her."

Zeke looks down at his coffee, and I think he's smiling.

"Got it," he says.

CHAPTER THIRTY-SEVEN

I WALK into the kitchen with a stack of dishes, and the moment I'm in the room, I take a deep breath. It's only for a few seconds, but it's the first time all day I've been alone in a room besides the bathroom. That, more than anything, is slowly driving me crazy.

Well, and I'm trapped. I don't know when, or if, I'll get out.

And I have no idea what's become of Gabriel. I don't know how to get in touch with him, whether he's still in South Carolina, or whether he wants anything to do with me anymore.

I think he does, and I want to trust him, but the reality is that I've got no clue. I don't know shit about shit, locked in my bedroom like the worst kind of princess.

I put the dishes in the sink and turn to go clear more off the table, but instead Zeke walks in, carrying a serving bowl and a gravy boat, and makes a face at me. I think it's supposed to be subtle, and it is *not*.

"Pantry," he mutters under his breath, eyes wide as he nods his head toward the pantry, just for good measure.

I head over, with him right behind me.

"I was just wondering if we were out of bread flour," he says, his voice a little too loud, and I roll my eyes.

"Just chill," I tell him, more than a little cranky.

"Sorry," he says, checking behind him one last time.

Then he pulls something from his pocket and shoves it into my hand: a phone and a charger, the cord wrapped around it. Instantly I lift my shirt and shove it into my pantyhose, both of us on high alert, adrenaline and relief both prickling through me all at once.

"Thank you," I whisper. I feel ridiculous, but tears are coming to my eyes, tears of gratitude and love for this kid, the one who's risking his own freedom by helping me.

"It was Gabriel," he whispers, raising both eyebrows urgently.

My heart leaps in my chest.

"The phone was?"

Zeke nods and suddenly, I'm grinning like an idiot.

"He found me and I told him you needed a—oh, he said he put his number in it," he says, just as someone else walks into the kitchen. "And he said he's not leaving town without you. YEAH, I THINK WE'RE OKAY FOR BREAD FLOUR, WE'VE GOT PLENTY."

I ignore my brother's terrible, obvious acting and stay in the pantry for another moment, staring up at shelves. The lump of the phone inside my pantyhose is slowly getting warm, and I just stand there and feel it against my skin.

It might work, I think, excitement and nervousness crackling through me. *This might really actually work.*

TWO HOURS LATER, I finally escape to the bathroom. There's a guard outside my door, but I reach deep into my pantyhose and pull out the incredibly uncomfortable phone, which has slid straight into my crotch since it's small and compact.

It's kind of hilariously appropriate, really.

I sit on the toilet lid, totally clothed, and turn it on. I'm not particularly good at using smart phones, since I've never been allowed to have my own—shocker, I know—but in a couple of seconds I've opened my contacts.

There's just one number, and just looking at those stupid ten digits makes me smile, my heart lighting up like a bonfire. I didn't really think he'd just leave, not after every-thing, but I didn't know for sure and now I do.

> **Me:** Thanks for the phone. And for staying around.
> **Me:** I'm sorry you got dragged into this awful mess.

Nothing happens. No answer, and I just stare at the phone for a long moment, practically *willing* it to text me back.

What if he gave me the wrong number by accident?

What if he changed his mind?

What if Zeke is secretly screwing me over and I'm actu-ally texting my father right now?

The last one doesn't make any sense, but it rattles my nerves anyway. I'm already a prisoner here, why the hell would my father need *more* evidence against me?

I click the screen off, shake my head, and plug the phone into the wall since I won't have a lot of chances to charge it. I'm sure Gabriel is in the shower, or has his phone off, or any one of a thousand other reasonable explanations that don't involve him changing his mind between yesterday and today.

I brush my teeth, wash my face, and use the bathroom as slowly as possible, deliberately dawdling so Gabriel can text me back.

Then, just as I'm about to give up and shove it back into my crotch:

Gabriel: I wouldn't have left for the world.

I make a fist with one hand and jam it to my mouth, because my eyes are filling with sudden tears. I feel like a dam just broke because of this one quick, sweet text, but I've never in my life been so glad to see tiny words on a little screen.

Gabriel: I'm at the Super 8 off of Towson Road, east of town, and I've got a car with a full tank of gas.

Gabriel: Zeke said you had a plan, but if it fails, I can probably ram my car through the front gate of your house to rescue you.

Me: Please don't!

Gabriel: I've always kind of wanted to.

I bite my lips together, trying not to laugh. I think it's the first time I've actually wanted to laugh in days, and I'm sitting on a closed toilet with a guard outside, staring at a phone.

Me: I have a plan, but I'm afraid they'll find this phone.

Gabriel: Gotcha.

Gabriel: Just tell me what I can do. Anything.

Gabriel: I mean that. Anything, Ruby.

Me: I will.

Outside the bathroom door, there's a shuffling sound as my guard moves around. I can virtually hear him hesitate nervously before he finally knocks, the sound hollow and timid.

"You okay in there?"

I roll my eyes.

"I'll just be one more minute!" I call.

He shuffles away.

Me: I gotta go.
Gabriel: Anything. I swear.

I don't know what to say to that, because it makes me feel warm and fuzzy and a little lost and adrift all at once, because if I've done something to deserve Gabriel, I don't know what it was.

Me: Thanks.

It doesn't feel like enough words, or like the right words, but I can hear my new guard shuffling his feet around outside the bathroom so I decide to find the right words later. I grab the charger and the phone, shove them both deep into my pantyhose, and step out of the bathroom.

"Sorry," I tell the guard, batting my eyelashes through my best fake-innocent smile. "You know how us *girls* are in the bathroom, always taking forever."

His face is half amused, half terrified, like I'm about to say the word *menstruation* and then he'd have to raise the alarm.

"No problem, just making sure you're safe," he says.

Safe. Sure.

"Perfectly fine," I say, and walk to my new bedroom, the guard two steps behind me.

———

AND THEN, I bide my time for a day. It's not so my father lets his guard down; the man has plenty of problems, but stupidity isn't one of them. It's for my new guards, and for Pearl, who's basically written *I told you so* on her forehead.

But finally, two days later, I'm lying awake in bed, staring up at the ceiling. Since for once I'm not wearing pantyhose, for the time being the phone is jammed into the side of my underwear, and I'm lying perfectly still, willing myself to get out of bed and finish this plan.

Pearl rolls over in her sleep, and Joy sighs, flopping one foot out from under her covers. There's a thin yellow line underneath the door, and I wonder whether my current guard is sitting there. Maybe he got up to pee, maybe he's taking a break because it's past midnight and he thinks we're all asleep.

Just try that way one more time, I think, still motionless in my bed. *Sneak out and call Gabriel, there's no reason to practically burn everything down, to alienate almost everyone you've ever loved...*

The plan's not *actually* arson, but it might be worse.

I don't move. I know I can't sneak out, because I tried. The first night *and* the second night that I was trapped here, I tried, and it didn't work either time. The guards all think they're here for my safety, and they are very diligent.

I take a deep breath. I sit up in my bed, long flannel nightgown rustling around me.

Pearl and Joy don't move, and slowly, I put my feet over

the side of the bed, seeking out the hardwood floor, standing as quietly as I can. They don't wake up.

I cross the room to our closet, open the door, get in, close the door. It's small and uncomfortable, but at least in here the light of the phone's screen won't wake my sisters up.

I turn it on, open the email program, take a deep breath, and start typing the email I've been planning for days. It's got a long and varied list of recipients, each of whom took me several bathroom trips each to find.

The Huffington Post. Politico. Time. Newsweek. The politics desk at the New York Times; a reporter at CNN my father is always complaining about; the Washington Post's Capitol Hill beat. Then, smaller markets: the Huntsburg local news, the Huntsburg Sentinel-Star, all the Charleston papers and TV reporters.

This is the nuclear option, because this email has everything. It's got my current predicament, being held prisoner by my father, a United States Senator who *just happens* to be currently running for re-election; it's got the cult-like police-state my family lives in; it's got my coerced marriage at nineteen; it's got Lucas's forced "heterosexualization."

In short, it's got everything that my father doesn't want the voters to see, all the ugly things he hides behind his facade of "old-fashioned American values" and "return to morality."

I include pictures. There's one of my father that I sneaked yesterday, reading the paper, just to prove I am who I say I am. There's one of my driver's license, one of the guard outside my room. If I were a reporter I'd still be skeptical, but with all this, I'd at least ask some questions.

Before I hit send, I text Gabriel again. I want to warn him but I don't even know how, because it's not like I know what the fallout from a nuclear bomb will be.

Me: You awake?

Gabriel: I am now.

I pause, suddenly unsure of how to tell him all this information.

Me: Are you still in?

Gabriel: Of course I am, stop asking that.

Me: I'm about to send a really long, detailed email to the press about my father, and I have no idea what's going to happen. I'm only pretty sure that he'll have no choice but to prove I'm not being held prisoner in my own home, and I'm also pretty sure he won't order anyone to tackle his own daughter in public.

Me: Voters hate that, you know. But I don't know what's going to happen, or when, or where, and I'm pretty sure this phone is going to get taken away.

Gabriel: Do what you have to.

Gabriel: I've got this.

Me: I wish I could tell you more.

Me: But I don't know what's going to happen.

Gabriel: I do.

Me: ?

Gabriel: I'm gonna rescue you and we'll ride off into the sunset together.

It's *so* cheesy, and I know it is, but tears spring to my eyes anyway. For all that I've told him time and time again I don't want to be rescued, right now I don't care. I've got someone on my side, and that's what matters.

Gabriel wants to drive me into the sunset? Fine with me.

Me: I hope your version happens.

Gabriel: It will.

Gabriel: There's always driving my car through the gates. Don't think I've forgotten that option.

Sitting in the closet, I grin like an idiot.

Me: I hope you don't have to.

Gabriel: I kinda hope I do.

Gabriel: Send the email. Get some sleep. And don't worry.

Me: Thanks. I'm trying.

I take a deep breath and go back to the email. Out in the bedroom, I can hear one of my sisters mutter in her sleep, and suddenly, I wonder if I'm doing the right thing.

If I do this to my father, what will it do to *them*?

CHAPTER THIRTY-EIGHT

GABRIEL

MY THUMB HOVERS over the SEND button on my phone, and I stare at the tiny, blueish screen, suddenly uncertain about the text I'm about to send.

It's dead quiet in the Super 8, the orange glow of the parking lot lights leaking around the edges of the blackout curtains. The only other light is my phone, this text I'm suddenly not sure I should send.

I want to send it. I haven't seen Ruby in days, haven't gotten to talk to her, to *be* with her through this hell, even though I'd do anything.

But as much as I really do want to drive my car through the front gates of the mansion, punch my way through a couple guards, rescue Ruby, and drive off with her, I know that's not what would happen. I'm outnumbered ten-to-one, for starters, and I don't think getting myself arrested for trespassing would do Ruby any favors.

If it would, I'd be in jail already. Lock me up.

Don't tell her now, like this. Tell her in person when you see her again.

Slowly, the urge passes, and I delete the words *I love you.*

———

SLEEP'S A JOKE. I try it for another hour, staring at the faded stains in the ceiling of this hotel room, but there's no way I'm going to fall asleep tonight so after a while I get up, turn on some lights, and sit at the desk in my boxers.

Politics and PR has never been my strong suit, but I lived in DC for a couple of years, and I got a pretty good first-hand view of it. The married congresswoman I slept with was a master of it, at least until she got caught with me.

I close my eyes, phone in my hands, and try to remember anything she told me, but it's not like we did a lot of talking. If we had, maybe I'd have gotten out of there earlier, though probably not.

Get out ahead of the story, I can almost hear her saying, into her phone. *Control the narrative.*

I rub my eyes and try to figure out how on earth the Senator is going to try to control the narrative. He'll probably have a press conference. That's politics 101.

And he'll probably try to find a way to keep Ruby from appearing, or at the very least from speaking. He can control lots of things, but he can't control what comes out of her mouth when there are cameras around.

I sigh.

Great, so he'll have a press conference and keep her locked away for a while.

God, I'm bad at this part.

I wind up spending an hour setting up alerts for every iteration of the Senator's and Ruby's names that I can think of. By now I'm just waiting for the news to hit, pacing back and forth in my hotel room, glancing at my phone every thirty seconds. The sun starts to come up outside, and the pale yellow light starts leaking through the curtains.

I get dressed, still waiting, and open the curtains. There's nothing on my phone, and my stomach is in knots, a heavy, horrible feeling in the pit.

No one believed her, I think, disbelief and astonishment heavy on my heart. *Everything she's been through, this fucking genius plan she figured out, and no one believed her.*

On the table, my car keys catch my eye. It's a ten-year-old Hyundai. The airbags are pretty good. I don't think I'd even break anything if I drove it through the gates.

I wouldn't get all the way to Ruby, obviously, but it *would* bring the news cameras out, and maybe I could convince some of them to look into the Senator a little more deeply…

Just as I'm about to grab my keys and go, my phone buzzes, and I snatch it off the table, pulse racing. There's an alert, thank God, there's an alert. It's from some trashy political gossip blog, but it's something.

Is Lunatic Senator Burgess Keeping His Own Daughter Captive?

"Yes!" I shout at my phone, and click to open it. It quotes her email almost in its entirety, picking out salacious key phrases to highlight in bold.

Then, before I can finish, there's another alert. And another, and another.

He Can't Control the Budget, Can He Control His Daughter?

His Re-Election is Nearly Locked Down—But Is His Daughter, As Well?

Now they're rolling in, so fast I can barely skim one article before I get another one. First is just blogs, but after a few minutes, the more serious news outlets get in on the game, too: Time, CNN, the BBC, the New York Times.

They're all skeptical—it does sound insane, after all—but he's going to have to respond, and he's going to have to prove that Ruby's there of her own free will. Which he can't, because she's not.

I can't stay here, doing nothing, even though I don't know what to do just yet, so I get into the car and drive into town, phone buzzing away. I don't go to the mansion, because I'm afraid that the temptation to drive through the gates will just be too strong, so I drive aimlessly.

I get gas station coffee and don't drink it. I drive by the Starbucks where I met Zeke, just for something to do.

And then, *finally*, the alert I'm waiting for comes through.

Senator Burgess to Address Allegations

He's giving a press conference at nine. From the front steps of his house, behind the gates, presumably surrounded by security. There's no mention of whether Ruby will be there or not, just him.

I've already got a bad feeling about this.

CHAPTER THIRTY-NINE

RUBY

THERE ARE seven grown men in this room on the second floor of my house. I recognize them all: my new guards, my father's lackeys, various church members. The Reverend himself isn't here, probably because he doesn't want to risk besmirching his reputation any more than has already been done.

I sit quietly in a straight-backed chair, watching the TV mounted on the wall. On it, my father's doing his full-on political act, somber-faced, looking as concerned as he can as he steps up to the microphone, sorrow etched into every line and pore of his face.

I've never hated him more.

Cameras snap away, and reporters start asking questions, but he puts one hand out, face still stony, and they all stop. He takes a deep breath, like what he's about to say pains him.

"First, I'd like to say that the email did, indeed, come from my daughter Ruby," he begins.

My eyebrows shoot up. I expected him to say that I'd been hacked or something, but this is a different approach.

The men guarding me in the room murmur to each other, not a single one of them looking directly at me. It's like somehow, I'm both the cause for all this fuss *and* completely invisible.

"I'm afraid that Ruby isn't well," my father continues, looking as sad and serious as he possibly can. "Her divorce and the ensuing spotlight have caused her mental health to deteriorate significantly, and in the past few weeks, she's begun having certain delusions."

Delusions.

My mouth drops open.

He's calling me crazy. My own father. He's telling everyone that I alleged all this because I'm a crazy person, that I'm imagining everything that's happened to me.

Instead of just letting me go—his *adult* daughter—he's telling the press that I'm literally insane.

I don't think I've ever felt worse, or more helpless. I thought that this was a slam-dunk, a surefire way to make him let me out of the house, out from under his thumb, but it's not.

Freedom is so close I can taste it—he's having to answer for his crimes, at least; people are suspicious, at least—but he's going to get away with it.

My chest tightens, and I feel like I can't breathe, like the room is closing in on me, because I don't know what else to do. I thought this was it, the thing that would burn every bridge I had with my family but that would at least get me out.

On the TV, he's still going on about what a sad tragedy it is, and I'm fucking sure he's tying it back to politics some-how. Reporters start shouting, asking questions, but he's an absolute professional.

Think, Ruby, I tell myself, but I can't think. I'm trapped, surrounded by the enemy, and right now I feel desperately alone and out of options.

I think of Gabriel, somewhere, waiting, trusting me that I'd get out and come to him. More than anything I wish I could, but there are two men in front of the door and five others just standing around, ready to tackle me if I so much as move.

So I sit there in stunned silence. I feel like all the blood has drained out of me, and I'm a dried, motionless, withered husk.

Then something happens. On the television. The camera swings around, the last shot of my father looking baffled. A female reporter says something hurriedly, and the picture is wobbling a little, like the cameraman is still adjusting.

And then, Gabriel's face.

Everyone in the room takes a step forward except for me. I don't move, but I lean in as the men I'm with murmur to each other in bafflement and confusion, because it's not like any of them is particularly bright.

"Ruby is in there," he says, looking dead into the camera. "Everything the Senator's saying is an outright lie."

"Now, you—" the camera wobbles and pans back a little, so we can see a female reporter, looking slightly out of breath like she's been running, sticking her microphone out. "—Until recently, you were part of the Senator's security team."

Gabriel looks *pissed,* and he crosses his arms in front of himself, glancing over his shoulder. As he does, I realize: he's right outside. The gate behind him is our gate, maybe a few hundred feet from where I'm sitting.

"That's right," he says, eyes flashing. "I was actually Ruby's personal bodyguard, and I can state unequivocally that she's not crazy, she's not delusional, and the Senator is holding her against her will."

The men in the room all move a little closer to the TV, enraptured, and I don't move a muscle. I'm thinking about what Gabriel said, the first time we went to an event together, before he found me drinking vodka backstage.

About distractions, and how dangerous they are.

"Now—" the woman says, looking around, like someone's talking to her. "Can you elaborate on the circumstances under which you left the Senator's employ? I'm getting conflicting reports—"

"I had an affair with Ruby," Gabriel cuts in. "Actually, that's inaccurate. I'm *having* an affair with Ruby."

The men in the room start talking louder to each other, still ignoring me, the person they're talking *about*. They bunch closer to the TV as they do, because they're a pack of stupid gossipmongers.

"So you have reason to be angry at the Senator," the woman says.

I stand, quietly, and look from man's back to man's back. I look at their doughy arms and their soft hands.

"Damn right I do," Gabriel says. "He's holding his adult daughter prisoner—"

I run.

In two steps, I'm at the door and I fling it open, burst into the hall, charge down the stairs. There's someone posted at the bottom, and he moves to intercept me, but I fake right and dart left.

All he gets is my hand, and I swing my arm in a circle, getting him off me.

Gabriel taught me that one.

I don't stop. I don't slow down, even though the ruckus brings people out of every room as I bolt for the front door. It sounds like a herd of elephants is right behind me, galloping along, and then I'm there, at the huge, ten-foot wooden doors, and I turn the knob, slamming my body against one.

It opens slowly, like a tomb, the sunlight and cool fall air rushing in.

At the front of the steps is my father, staring back at me, face astonished. Beyond him is a nest of cameras, black holes all staring my way. Beyond that, a driveway.

Beyond that a gate, a news truck, three people gathered around.

Gabriel turns toward me, right as someone grabs my shirt and yanks me backward so hard it pulls me off my feet and I fall hard onto the floor.

For a moment, nothing happens. Everyone is staring at me, arms and legs akimbo on the floor, mouths open. My father is staring through the half-open front door, and I stare back, stunned.

Slowly, I realize there's a sound. A dry, whispering sound, like leaves rustling, and I shake my head and take a deep breath and realize what it is: the sound of a dozen people clicking news cameras.

They just saw everything, and it takes me a moment to process what that means.

I get my feet under me, shakily. No one moves to stop me as I stand, brush myself off, push my hair off my face, cameras going constantly.

I step through the door, onto the front porch. I descend the steps, five feet from my father.

We lock eyes as I walk, but neither of us says a word.

I walk past him, onto the driveway even though I'm barefoot. The cameras turn en masse. Reporters start shouting questions, but I ignore them and keep going.

At the gate, iron bars in both hands, is Gabriel.

I force myself not to run, even though I want to run, skip, leap into his arms and cover his face with kisses. But that might look crazy, so I don't.

At the guard gate, I just look at the guy in the shack. The cameras have followed me, and even though he looks nervous and frightened, he doesn't fight me. He just hits the button and opens the gate without a word. On the other side, Gabriel's grinning like an idiot.

I'm about to cry, the tears threatening to spill over, but as the gate hums and whirs, I smile back at him.

Then it's open and I'm through and I'm in his arms, my head against his chest, and he's squeezing me so tightly I can barely breathe but we're rocking back and forth, together, cameras going off like crazy and people shouting questions at us.

I barely hear them, because I'm here, I'm safe, I'm barefoot on the sidewalk, and I just left behind everything I've ever known. We stand there for a long time, and I just breathe and cry and he holds me as tight as he can. Slowly, I start to relax, even though my pulse is still jumping.

We're totally surrounded by people, but Gabriel ignores them as he pulls back, just slightly, and looks down at me.

"Was that the plan?" he asks, a smile tugging at his lips.

I smile back, even though there are tears falling down my face and I'm half-sobbing.

"Kind of?" I say, and he leans down and kisses me gently on the lips, his hand on my chin, and then on my forehead. After a moment, he takes my hand in his, totally ignoring the press standing around, screaming questions, and laces his fingers through mine.

"Come on," he says. "I've got a white horse parked a few blocks away, only it looks a lot like a shitty old Hyundai."

I swallow hard, still crying, still shaking and shocked and

wondering a little if maybe I *am* having a delusion right now.

"You know sunset isn't for another nine hours, right?" I ask.

He just laughs, and we walk down the sidewalk together, hand-in-hand, away from my father's house.

CHAPTER FORTY

GABRIEL

ONCE WE'RE in my car, we just drive. For hours, we just *drive*, and even though I try to stop at Wal-Mart or something so I can buy Ruby shoes, pants, maybe a toothbrush, she won't let me.

So I take her hand and just keep going. I don't have a destination in mind, just take the interstate to a highway to a four-lane road to a two-lane road. We pass through quaint little Southern towns, we pass through fields and fields of soybeans and woods so thick it's like being in the jungle.

And I don't let go of her hand. I've never been here before, not physically *or* emotionally, and I have no idea what she needs from me but I know I'm not letting go, not if she doesn't want me to.

We drive into the mountains, where the trees are half-bare and half-covered in red and orange leaves. When the wind blows, they swirl around my shitty car, and it's actually kind of beautiful.

At last, Ruby takes a deep breath, then exhales. For the first time in hours she takes her hand out of mine and shifts in her seat, stretching, rubbing her face.

"Do you mind if we stop so I can use the bathroom?" she asks.

"Do you mind if we get you shoes first?" I ask.

Ruby looks down at her feet.

"Oh, God," she says, and starts half-laughing. "I don't even have shoes on. Jesus, Gabriel, this wasn't the plan."

We're coming up on a little town, and I turn off the main road and into the downtown area. At one end there's a drug store, and I stop there, go in, and manage to find her plastic flip-flops. After she uses the bathroom, she wants to get back into the car but I talk her into lunch at a barbecue place where I order at the counter and we eat at picnic tables out back.

"Where are we?" she finally asks, picking up a hush puppy and examining it. She sounds far away somehow, but I don't think I can blame her after the morning she's had.

"North Carolina, somewhere," I say. "We passed the state border but I haven't really been paying attention, I've just been driving. *Someone* didn't want me to stop."

She looks at me, looks at the hush puppy, and looks at me again.

"I was afraid I wouldn't start again," she says, her green eyes practically boring into me. "I was afraid if we stopped anywhere near Huntsburg I'd start thinking that I'd made a mistake and I'd want to go back."

I take her other hand in mine.

"And I don't want that," she says, her voice low and quiet and intense. "But it felt like I *could*, like when I walked out of there I might just go home again instead of moving on, and I was afraid that I'd have a moment of weakness or something and I'd go back because at least I know what to do when I'm there."

My heart feels sticky in my chest as she's speaking, like

it's hung up on something inside me. I think I get why she'd feel this way, like she might end up going back whether it's what she really wants or not, because it's what she knows.

But if she went back I'd be wrecked. Just fucking wrecked, the kind of broken I don't know if I'd ever get over.

"You didn't," I say softly. "And now we're in another state completely, and you're here, and I'm here, and it's gonna be fine."

I've got no way of knowing that. There's a few thousand dollars in my savings account, but that's it, and I very much do not have a job at the moment. I believe it, though, because I can tell that she needs me to.

Ruby looks at our entwined hands on the table, and for a second I don't know if she's going to laugh or cry.

Then she laughs, biting her lip a little like she's trying not to.

"I don't even have a toothbrush," she says. "I swear this wasn't the plan, Gabriel. The plan included a toothbrush."

"What about shoes?" I tease.

"*And* shoes and a change of underwear," she says, still smiling and looking down, laughing like she can't believe this. "I had them shoved in my purse. I thought he'd want to parade me in front of the cameras, somewhere in public, and I could just leave."

I raise our locked hands to my lips, my elbow propped on the table, and I kiss her hand. There are other people scattered around the barbecue shack's outdoor area, and they're probably staring, but I kiss her hand and couldn't care less.

"It doesn't matter," I say, and kiss her hand again. "The plan worked," —hand kiss— "You're gone," — kiss— "We're here," —kiss— "And your barbecue is getting cold."

She laughs again and it feels like sunrise, like nothing else could go wrong, at least today.

"Priorities," she teases me.

"I'm just saying, we can talk about what we do next while we're eating," I say.

We eat. We don't talk about what we're going to do next, because instead she tells me about the past four days, about how one of the new guards sometimes farted so loud outside her door that it woke her up, how another one seemed terrified of making eye contact with her.

"I think he thought I could take his soul or something," she says, reflectively. We've both finished eating, and now we're just sitting here, elbows on the rough wooden table, the occasional cloud passing over the sun.

"Can't you?" I ask.

"I didn't try," she admits. "Though I'm not sure why I'd want it. What do you do with souls, anyway?"

"Store them in translucent white rocks, and... give them to Satan?"

"You want to know something?"

"Yes."

"Twenty-six years of fighting a war against the devil, and I still don't know what he does with souls. I think he eats them?"

"I don't think I'd want my soul to get eaten," I offer. "Sounds unpleasant."

Ruby puts her chin in one hand, looking right at me. The sun hits her, lighting up her blonde hair, and right then she looks like a pleased cat in a sunbeam.

"You know, for the past six months I've done everything wrong," she says slowly. "I got divorced, I disrespected my parents, I lied, I drank, I fornicated—"

I grin, and Ruby rolls her eyes.

"—all these things that I always thought would put me on the miserable path straight to Hell, but I don't think I am. This doesn't really feel like the path to Hell."

I look around: sunshine, barbecue stand, quaint town, and best of all, Ruby sitting across from me and for once not looking over her shoulder to see who's listening.

Yeah, it doesn't feel like the path to Hell at all.

"I'm not gonna pretend to be a theologian," I say, "but Hell might be more for people who try to control their daughters' lives and lock them up when they can't."

"But at least he hasn't read *The Golden Compass*," she says, a wicked, ironic smile starting around her eyes. "Shit, I left that behind too."

"*That* we can fix," I say. "At least some problems have easy answers."

That gets another smile out of her. After a little while we leave the barbecue stand, and I talk her into taking a walk and finding somewhere to get ice cream.

We eat it sitting on a bench, in the park, talking about the size of the spiders in Afghanistan and the time that Ruby got poison ivy in her eye as a kid. She doesn't mention getting back in the car and driving further and neither do I.

For the rest of the day we do nothing but wander around the town, hand-in-hand, talking about nothing. After a few hours of that she leans against me as the sun dips low over the buildings, and I feel like the dragon-slayingest white knight of all time.

———

"Y'ALL ON YOUR HONEYMOON?" the woman behind the desk of the Conifer Motor Lodge asks when we check in, later that night.

"No, just passing through," I tell her.

She glances at my ring finger, and I swear her mouth tightens a little in disapproval.

I manage not to roll my eyes.

"We get lots of newlyweds heading on through to Gatlinburg or the Smokies," she says. "Gorgeous place to go for a honeymoon. Y'all thinking about getting married?"

Holy shit, this lady is nosy.

"We haven't been dating very long," Ruby volunteers, turning her sweetest smile on the woman.

"Well, the mountains around here are a great place to propose," the woman goes on, writing my name down carefully in a notebook. There's no computer behind the desk, just stacks of paper, receipts, and a credit card machine that might be older than me.

"I heard we missed the really good autumn colors by a few weeks," Ruby says, smoothly changing the subject. "Any idea where we should go to see the last of it?"

Just like that, she woman whips out a map and a pen and starts giving us obscure directions like *turn before where the Johnson's old outhouse used to be* or *if you go past a big graveyard, not a little one, a big one, turn around and look more closely for the turn 'cause you missed it.*

Ruby smiles and nods through the whole thing, and then we finally get to turn and leave, map and room key in hand.

"Was she for real?" I ask as soon as our room door is closed.

Ruby just laughs.

"You're just lucky she didn't start asking us what we wanted to name our kids," she says.

"That's not normal," I say.

"Well, I've got more than enough experience in avoiding conversations I don't want to have," she says, and stands on her tiptoes to give me a quick kiss. "You gotta control the narrative, Gabriel."

I just laugh, my hands drifting down her back.

"How about you control the narrative and I crash cars through gates?" I tease.

"Are we *still* on that?"

"I almost did it."

"Don't tell me that."

"I just figured that if I got arrested, which I would have, *then* you'd be barefoot on the sidewalk with no one to rescue you at all. Otherwise I might have."

Ruby rests her head against my chest, shoulders shaking with laughter.

"Thanks for your self-control," she says.

"No promises for next time," I answer.

After a little while, she takes a shower while I watch stupid television. I nearly ask if she wants company, but I have a feeling that after being watched for a week, she might also enjoy being left alone for once.

When she comes out, skin warm and hair wet, she crawls into the bed next to me. We're both half sitting up, her head nestled against my shoulder, and neither of us says a word as we watch some show about people who have to survive in the wild to win money.

I don't do anything. I'm halfway hard just looking at her, because of course I am, but I just keep my arm around her and sit there quietly, just being with her.

Because right now, I can feel the hours in front of us stretching into days, weeks, and months where she's next to me. Tomorrow morning I'm going to wake up and her head's going to be on that pillow right there, so right now we can just sit here, snuggling, knowing that there's gonna be more time.

Ruby's asleep before the first commercial break. She barely wakes up when I get up, take off my clothes, brush my teeth, and turn off the lights.

I curl myself around her, and she relaxes into me, murmuring something I can't understand. I fall asleep almost instantly.

CHAPTER FORTY-ONE

GABRIEL'S GONE when I wake up. I'm sprawled across the bed, sheets and blankets tangled around me, and for a moment I think I'm back at home, that I somehow just imagined everything, that I'm in a room with Joy and Pearl and a guard outside the door.

But then I blink and I'm in reality again: a double bed, the white walls with thin spidery cracks, the TV from 1995, the mismatched furniture. The pillow next to mine with an indentation in it.

I don't panic. Not exactly, but I sure as hell wonder where he went and whether something bad's happened. I sit up in the bed, still completely naked, and look around, half-dazed because I still feel like I'm in a strange dream, like I could really wake up at any second and this would all be over.

Then I see the note on the table and let out a breath I didn't realize I was holding. I crawl over, letting the sheets fall off me, and read it.

R—

Went to get you a toothbrush & underwear. You seemed like you needed the sleep. Back by 10 or 10:30.

Love,

G

I glance at the clock. 10:15.

I think I just slept for twelve hours, which might be longer than I've ever slept before, and now I just feel sort of pleasant and hazy, like I'm sleep-drunk.

I've got nothing to do right now, I think. *No one's here to disapprove or tell me that I should be productive. Besides, I don't even have clean underwear.*

I briefly consider hand-washing the pair I've got so I can re-wear it if I need to, but I don't. Instead I grab the TV remote, crawl back into bed, and start flipping through channels.

I've never laid in bed and flipped through channels before, not even in hotel rooms when we had to accompany my father to events. Turns out mid-morning weekday TV is kinda boring.

Ten minutes later, there's a key in the lock. I hurriedly pull the bed sheet up over myself as Gabriel comes in, plastic Wal-Mart bags in his hands.

"There you are," he says, setting them on the table next to his note. "You were *out* when I left."

"Thanks for running out to get that stuff," I say, sitting up in bed. The sheet falls down my body to my waist, and Gabriel's eyes follow it.

Something flutters in my stomach, and also lower. Even though we slept in the same bed all night for the first time last night, we didn't do anything after the day we had. I just fell asleep almost instantly in Gabriel's arms.

"I figured I couldn't get dressed with no underwear, so I

didn't bother," I say, tilting my head back against the headboard. "But I guess I can now."

"There's no rush," he says, grinning. "If you wanted to just hang out naked all day, that'd be fine."

"Are you sure you wouldn't mind?" I tease, tossing the remote to the other side of the bed. "You're not just being polite?"

Gabriel leans over and kisses me, getting his shoes off with one hand.

"Trust me," he says, in between kisses. "This has nothing to do with politeness."

He kicks his shoes off and then he's on the bed, between my legs, the sheet still half-separating us. Heat flares through me as I sit up straight, wrapping my arms around him, like we're magnetically drawn to each other. Gabriel opens his mouth against mine, flicks his tongue along my lip, and before I know it I've got one hand tight in his hair and the other under his shirt, feeling the muscles expand and contract as he breathes.

"I could get used to seeing you naked during the day," he says, running his lips along my jaw. "And I could get used to opening the door and finding you already in bed."

He finds a nipple with one hand and pinches it gently, rubbing his thumb along the pebbled surface. I suck in a breath, eyes closed, and Gabriel nips gently at my neck, laughing.

A crackle runs down my spine as his lips move lower, to the hollow of my throat and my collarbone, and *now* I'm awake. I know it hasn't even been a week since the table outside the bar, but I swear that right now feels like the very first time.

Except I'm not nervous as I pull his shirt off over his head, because we're not going to get caught. There's no one to catch us. For the first time, I feel like an actual adult.

And daytime is a great time to see Gabriel half-naked, though I only get half a second to appreciate him before he grabs me by the knees and pulls me down the bed.

I yelp, suddenly on my back, but my surprise turns into laughter of sheer delight as he tears the sheet off my body and plants his lips on my stomach.

"This is anything but funny," he teases, his lips brushing my skin.

"I'm not laughing *at* you," I say, winding my hands through his hair.

"Good," he says, a smile around his eyes as he kisses me again in the slight hollow above my belly button. "Because I've thought a lot about what I'm going to do to you right now, and it's no laughing matter."

He kisses the inside of one hip, his hands already stroking the insides of my thighs as he pushes them wider. I can't help but giggle.

"Seriously?" he asks, though I can tell he's laughing.

"That tickles," I say. I've already got the bedsheets balled in one hand, my whole body rigid in anticipation of what I know is about to happen.

Gabriel runs one finger, very lightly, along my thigh, and I squirm.

"That tickle?" he asks, his voice so low and wicked it makes my toes curl.

"Yes," I gasp.

His face is hovering right above my mound. I know I'm wetter than a waterfall right now, my body one huge, empty ache, and I know he can tell how wet I am. And he's teasing me.

He runs one finger along where my hip meets my pelvis,

an inch from my lower lips, and I squirm again, gasping for air.

"That?" he asks.

"Yes," I whisper.

Then I feel his tongue, teasing at my lips, just *barely* touching me, and I swallow a moan.

"That?" he asks, his lips brushing up against mine.

I try to say *yes* but the noise just comes out a half-gasp, half-moan. He does it again, slowly, his tongue sliding between my lips and past my entrance, making his way to my clit.

I swear I can feel Gabriel still smiling as he licks me in slow circles at first, teasing me, as I bite my lip and gasp. I've been sharing a room with my little sisters for the past several days, and besides that I haven't exactly been in the mood, so I haven't done anything since the night at the bar.

I'm wound tight as a spring, and Gabriel doesn't stop, never lets up, just licks me faster and faster while I clutch the bedsheets desperately and try not to make too much noise.

He's relentless and Jesus, he's good at this, his hands gripping my thighs, pulling me into his face like he needs this even more than I do. I'm right on the edge, back arched as I bite my lip and I force myself not to grab his hair in both fists, my breath coming in whimpering gasps.

"Gabriel," I half-whisper, half-whimper. "Oh my *God*."

He puts his mouth around my clit, sucking gently as he licks, and it pushes me right over. I gasp and moan as I come, still trying to stay quiet, even as his fingers dig into my flesh and Gabriel pushes against me mercilessly, his tongue traveling from my clit to my entrance with total control even as my whole body shakes.

When it ends, I realize I've got one hand over my mouth

and Gabriel's got his lips on my belly again, laughing, one nipple between his fingers.

"The hell is *this*," he teases, taking my wrist in his other hand and moving it from my mouth. Now he's in between my legs again before I've even had a chance to think, his hardness pressed up against me, rock-hard and thick.

"Force of habit?" I murmur, watching as he kisses the inside of my palm just inches from my face. He still smells like me, and even though it's still strange, it's still hot.

"Habits can be unlearned, right?" he asks, still grinning.

He laces his fingers through mine, then pushes ours hands into the mattress above my head, leaning his weight on it and pinning me. I swear his eyes flare in the dim sunlight that's coming through the covered window, like there's a fire burning inside him that's even more dangerous than I'd suspected.

"I think it takes practice," I say, curling my legs around him, tilting my hips forward. "Lots of practice."

"*That* I can do," he says, dropping his head down for a long, lingering, open-mouthed kiss.

I wrap one hand around his neck, the other still held tightly in his, and trail it down his back, and I shift my hips again. I need him, *now*, and I'm breathless and impatient.

"And I can promise that from now on, you can come as loud as you want," he murmurs. "I've got no clue what's going to happen next, but I know we've got each other and we're not going back."

He kisses me again, slow and deep, and as he does I grab the thick base of his erection and guide him through my wetness, between my lips, and then Gabriel groans into my mouth and I gasp as he slides deep into me with a single thrust.

"*Fuck*, Ruby," he murmurs, his lips still on mine, and I

just groan in response, clenching my legs around him even harder because having him inside me, skin-to-skin, doesn't just feel good, it feels right.

He clenches my hand in his and pushes against me even harder, like he's trying to get deeper even though he's already completely hilted, but as he shifts inside me I swear his cock hits every single sensitive spot I've got, and I moan.

"There it is," he whispers, and does it again. "Sometimes when we're like this your eyelids flutter and I swear it's the most beautiful fucking thing I've ever seen."

He moves again, not exactly thrusting, but this time I gasp and then roll my hips against him, savoring the moment and drawing it out because my *God* does it feel good. Slowly, we speed up, our mouths together as we both gasp and moan. I can feel myself starting to unspool, losing control over my own body as I get closer and closer.

Then, with no warning, Gabriel stops short. Before I can say anything he's already got one knee in his hand and he rolls me over.

"Oh!" I yelp, but he's already on his back, grinning as I straddle him, cock still buried inside me, and I keep moving my hips as he takes my hand and kisses my palm, his fingers already on my hip, his eyes moving down my body.

"You're sexy and I like watching you," he says, his eyes sparking, his hand moving up my body to cup one breast, pinch my nipple, and I lean forward slightly, anchoring both hands on his chest for balance. I'm almost self-conscious but this feels so good that I forget and just ride Gabriel slowly, electricity sizzling through my body.

"Good," I whisper, the only thing I can think to say.

His eyes are half-closed, and I force myself not to go too fast, to keep doing the same thing he just did to me, letting my body take over and letting my mind shut off. This feels incredible, having sex in the daylight while he watches me, and I forget completely about everything that's happening, I forget about being inexperienced and clueless and I let my eyes drift shut and let go.

And it's *good*. Gabriel takes my hand in his again, holding it to his lips as we move together slowly but surely, because my body knows what to do right now and it's my job to just follow along and let it happen. I'm gasping and moaning and I think I'm moaning his name, but everything is happening through a haze of pleasure and I can't even be sure, because it feels like my skin is crackling with electricity, like I might just explode if this feels any better.

Then he moves again, suddenly throwing his legs over the edge of the bed and sitting up, his arms around my back so I don't go over.

I gasp, clutching his shoulders but he just pulls me in tighter. We kiss and we keep going, my legs around his waist now, my face against his as I hold on tight.

"I like this way too," he whispers, his eyes and voice unfocused.

I've got one hand around the back of his head, and I can't do or say or think anything because the earthquake finally hits me and every cell in my body, every millimeter of me, starts shaking.

I press my face against his. I wrap my legs around him tight, and I can hear myself saying his name but I can't tell I'm doing it because I feel like the wind is being knocked out of me, it's so intense.

Gabriel tightens his arms around me as I come, pressing me against him, pressing me down like he needs to be further inside me. I can't tell where I end and he begins but it seems so totally right that I don't mind, I just whisper his name again.

As I do, I can suddenly feel him explode inside me as he growls into my neck, then moans my name. I'm still rocking, still shaking, and he holds onto me so tight I think he might break me in half.

Gradually, I stop shaking. Gabriel loosens his grip and kisses my neck, stroking my back gently as I lean down and kiss him on the lips, the kiss slow and lazy, like we've got all the time in the world.

And we do. It's morning, it's daylight, and no one knows or cares where we are. I get to do this whenever I want, and in that moment, I can't believe my luck.

CHAPTER FORTY-TWO

GABRIEL

AFTER A WHILE WE FLOP OVER, onto the bed, and lay there without moving. A pillow falls halfway onto my head, but we've got our arms and legs tangled together and I'm way, way too lazy to move it right now.

Ruby keeps dozing off, only to wake up, look at me, smile faintly, and doze off again. I think I could watch it for hours, because even though I've seen a lot of her already, I've never seen her like this, happy and carefree and safe and secure and naked.

"I've got a proposal," she says, somewhere around the fifth time she wakes up. Her eyes drift closed again.

"I hope it doesn't include doing anything useful," I say, my voice coming out slow and low.

"Of course not," she says, a smile tugging at her lips. "It's that today, we stay in bed and don't put clothes on. We can worry about everything tomorrow."

We're halfway holding hands, and I grab the fingers that I've got and raise them to my lips.

"We have to eat," I say.

She sighs.

"How about this," I say, brushing her hand with my lips as I speak. "We order pizza to the room, and I wrap a towel around myself to collect it. Just so I don't terrify the delivery guy. Or make him think this is some kind of porno situation."

Ruby opens her eyes and raises one eyebrow.

Right, I think.

"A lot of porn movies start with—"

"I know about porn and pizza delivery boys," she says, her voice slow and teasing. "My ex watched lots of gay porn, remember?"

"I can't say I'm familiar with gay porn conventions," I point out.

"I think they're the same," she says. "But I like your idea. No clothes, stay in bed all day."

We're both quiet for a moment, her eyes searching mine steadily, like there's something she wants to say but doesn't know what or how.

"Just us, in this bed, free to do whatever the hell we want," I say. "Everything else can wait until tomorrow."

I kiss her fingers again.

"Everything else is a lot," she points out, shifting slightly on the bed.

"I've already got some things figured out," I say.

"Don't tell me you were holding out on me," she teases. "If you already have a job and an apartment, tell me now."

"Ruby, I don't have shit," I say, teasing her back. "I just know that when we figure all this out, we'll be figuring it out together, and that's the part that really matters."

She glances down at our hands, slowly turning hers inside mine, knuckles against fingertips.

"You shouldn't feel obligated," she says, her voice

suddenly soft again. "I know that we have a *thing* and you helped me escape, but—"

"Are you fucking kidding me?" I ask, trying not to laugh.

She looks at me like I'm crazy, but I can't help myself. I'd do anything for her, and she's acting like finding jobs is going to be a big deal.

"No?" she says, raising one eyebrow.

"We don't have a *thing*," I say. "I fell in love with you, and I'm dead fucking serious about everything I said, because as long as you're willing, everything we have to do from now on we do together. Me and you. The two of us."

Ruby's smiling again, though her eyes are a little too bright, and she wraps my fingers around hers.

"I love you too," she says softly. "But I should warn you, I can't even—"

"I don't care."

"Seriously, Gabriel, I've never—"

"Don't care."

"—Had a *job*, or—"

"I don't *care*."

"—Written a check, I was technically on our checking account but Lucas always did that—"

"You'll learn in thirty seconds, I swear."

"—I don't even know how to apply for a library card."

She goes quiet. I've got her hand pressed to my lips, and I'm laughing at her quietly, because it's ridiculous that she *escaped a cult* and is worried about not knowing how to write a check.

"Are you done?" I ask.

Ruby bites her lip and starts laughing, too, her eyes dancing.

"Good," I say. "The library card reminds me, I got you something."

"Underpants with books on them," she guesses.

I give her a kiss, roll over, hoist myself off the bed, and paw through the plastic Wal-Mart bags until I find what I'm looking for.

"Close your eyes," I tell her, looking over my shoulder.

Ruby closes, her eyes, head propped on one fist as she lies on her side on the bed. Even *now* she's breathtaking: the way her waist and hip curve, her touchable, warm skin, the smile around her eyes because right now I think she's happier than I've ever seen her.

"Closed," she reports.

I pull it from the bag and set it on the bed right in front of her.

"Okay," I say.

Ruby opens her eyes, and she just starts *laughing* with delight.

While I was out, I picked up the entire *His Dark Materials* trilogy, since Ruby hasn't even finished the first book yet.

"You said you left yours behind, and I know you hadn't even read the last one," I say. "And it seemed like a good way to celebrate freedom."

She sits up and pulls one out of the box set, running her fingers over the cover as she reads the back, and I get back into the bed.

"Thank you," she says, and leans over me, her blonde hair whispering against my chest.

"You're welcome," I say, and she gives me a kiss.

True to our word, we spend the rest of the day in bed. We alternate between reading and fucking and ordering pizza, and even though there's a lot of heavy shit hanging over my head, I can't help but think it's one of the best days of my life.

———

TWO DAYS, still in Conifer, North Carolina, we've started trying to map out our lives. We've outlined all the things we need to do—find jobs, find a place to live, get bank accounts, get phones, everything—and it's exhausting, especially for Ruby. I've got a storage locker in D.C. that's got *some* stuff in it, but the truth is that I never owned all that much, and Ruby hasn't got anything.

That afternoon, we take a break and walk to a coffee shop. It's cute and quaint, little hand-lettered chalkboard signs adorning the walls, but as we order coffee, the middle-aged woman behind the counter keeps looking at Ruby strangely.

I'm about to say something, when instead, she taps her nails on the counter, sighs, and speaks up.

"Sweetheart," she says to Ruby. "This may be a real odd question, but have you got anything to do with that girl who's in the news for runnin' away from that Senator in South Carolina?"

I put one hand on Ruby's lower back, and Ruby clears her throat.

"I *am* that girl from South Carolina," she says, pushing her hair back behind her shoulders.

I can tell that every muscle in her body is tense, because this is what we've been waiting for. The Senator was a popular man for years and years, and there's a huge swath of the voting public who didn't really *know* him. All his platforms and promises, the whole *Return to Moral America*, sound fantastic until you realize what he really meant by it.

The woman gasps, one hand flying to her mouth.

"You poor thing," she says, then puts her hand to her chest.

Ruby tenses even more, and I step forward, ready to tell this woman off if I need to.

"I can't even imagine," the woman goes on. "My people are from South Carolina, and every time I see my mother all I hear about is *the Burgess bastard* this and *the Burgess bastard* that. Morality my fanny, he wants everyone barefoot and pregnant from the day they can breed 'til the day they die and I hope that S. O. B. gets what's coming to him."

Ruby's mouth is a perfect little O, and she's just staring at the woman.

"Lord, look at me," the woman says, shaking her head and looking down. "I'm sorry, hon, he's still your father, I don't know what I'm thinking going on like this, I just get so riled up sometimes—"

"He's absolutely a son of a bitch," Ruby says, her voice astonished.

Then she laughs, relaxing.

"I just don't usually hear other people admit it," she says. "*That's* new."

The woman smiles at us, leaning her elbows on the counter conspiratorially.

"If half of what that email you wrote says is true, I don't doubt it," she says. "And I think you're brave as hell, sweetheart. You staying around Conifer?"

We wind up chatting with the woman—her name's Margaret—for almost two hours over two cups of coffee and several pastries, which she won't let us pay for. Ruby slowly tells her the whole story and Margaret listens, wide-eyed, between customers.

"Did you see my sign?" she asks when Ruby's finished.

We both look around at the hand-lettered chalkboards adorning the walls, and I wonder which one she means.

Instant human, just add coffee?

Give me the coffee and no one gets hurt?

"The sign on the door," Margaret says. "It says 'Hiring, inquire within.' If you're in need of a job, I'd be happy to consider this an inquiry."

Ruby and I look at each other. We hadn't really planned on staying in Conifer, but we hadn't planned on *not* staying, either.

"You can think it over," Margaret offers. "Sounds like you've had a rough couple of days."

Ruby turns to me, eyebrows raised.

"Have we got a better plan?" she asks, keeping her voice low.

"I don't," I say. "Do you?"

"You *know* I don't," she says.

"Then go for it," I say, grinning. "Maybe later you explain how you have zero job experience but still got an offer before me."

She laughs and turns to Margaret.

"Can I fill out an application?" Ruby asks.

Margaret waves one hand.

"Don't worry about it," she says. "I haven't gotten any better applicants."

"Can I at least do it for practice?" Ruby asks.

Margaret just laughs.

"Sure, sweetheart," she says.

———

RUBY'S JOB isn't full-time, but Margaret seems to know everyone in Conifer, so in another week I'm doing odd jobs and landscaping around town with a brother of her cousin's friend. *He* knows someone who's looking to rent out a one-bedroom cabin a few miles outside town.

When Sarah-Joe—that's the cousin's friend's brother's buddy with the cabin for rent—finds out that Ruby is a cult escapee and I'm a veteran, she knocks fifty dollars off the rent and waives the security deposit.

"Listen," she tells us, standing in the tiny front room, a wood stove behind her. "Margaret likes you, and that old broad is a tough nut to crack. Besides, I know where you live."

We spend the rest of that day cleaning the place until it shines, and we move in the next day: a mattress on the floor, a kitchen table from the Salvation Army two towns over, pots and pans and silverware from the dollar store. One set of neighbors brings over chili and cornbread that'll last us a week, and the other set brings over apple pie and lasagna, just to come say hello.

That night, after I wash out the bowls and dry them with our only dish towel, Ruby's standing on the back porch, looking out at the dark forest, listening the creek below whisper. When I put my arms around her, she sniffles.

"What's wrong?" I ask.

She shakes her head.

"Nothing?" she says, her voice small and quiet in the dark. "I don't know?"

Ruby leans back against me, and I don't say anything. I don't know what to say, or if anything I'd say could even help.

"It's just that people are so *nice*," she finally goes on, her voice barely a whisper. "And I can't help but think that they want something in return, because that's how it works, and then I feel guilty for being suspicious of someone who's probably just being a good neighbor."

She sniffles again. I kiss the top of her head.

"Plus, I can't believe we're here, and we have a place to

stay and jobs and everything," she says. "It's... I don't know. I kind of always thought that if I left my family I'd be living on the street before long."

She swallows, and I hold her tighter.

"Thanks for sticking it out," she whispers, and I smile into her hair.

"You don't have to thank me," I tell her. "I'm here because you're here and I want to be with you."

"Thanks."

"Stop it," I tease her, and she laughs, then sniffles, then laughs again. "I love you, and a mattress on the floor makes less noise anyway."

"I love you too," Ruby says, turning her head to kiss me. "And our neighbors are half a mile away, so it's not like noise matters."

I grin, then reach down and squeeze her ass with one hand.

"Hey!" she says. "I'm *crying* here."

"No, now you're laughing and wondering how far sound carries in the woods," I say, and kiss her again as she turns and puts her arms around my neck.

"I don't think it's very far," she says.

"I know how to find out," I say, and before Ruby can retort, I scoop her up in my arms, step through the cabin door, and take her into the bedroom.

The neighbors never do complain.

EPILOGUE
RUBY

"DO I AT LEAST LOOK *NORMAL*?" I ask, looking down at myself.

Gabriel crosses his arms, furrowing his brow.

Then he shrugs.

"I've never been to a square dance," he says. "That looks like what people wear to square dances. I think."

I make a face and stick my tongue out at him, because he is *no* help when it comes to clothes or fashion, and even though it's been a little over a year since we moved to Conifer, it's the little things like this that still trip me up.

Because when you spend your life with really, really limited fashion options and then you can suddenly wear anything you want, sometimes you get it wrong. Like a month ago, when I wore a pencil skirt and heels to a party that turned out to be a casual barbecue in someone's back yard.

Or over the summer, when a friend's sister got baptized

in the creek and I wore denim shorts and flip-flops. Also the wrong choice of clothes.

"I can't have another Ellie's Baptism situation," I tell Gabriel.

"I don't think it's going to be a black tie square dance," he teases. "Listen, if we show up and everyone else is wearing ball gowns and tuxes, we'll just leave. How's that?"

I've got on the flat ankle boots I wear to my job at the coffee shop, jeans, and a plaid shirt rolled up to my elbows, because that seems like what you should wear to a square dance.

"I think we'd never hear the end of it if we just left," I laugh. "Tammy's been on me for months about coming. Though I think you're the one she really wants to see."

"If she keeps bringing me brownies I'll square dance with her all night," Gabriel says, laughing.

"Should I be jealous?"

"You should make more brownies."

He walks to the kitchen table and grabs his keys as I take our jackets off the coat rack and toss his to him. We've got furniture now—some from the Goodwill, but mostly they're hand-me-downs from the people we've met over the past year.

They're really nice, and I'm still not used to it. Even the people who agree with my father's politics and would have voted for him if they lived in South Carolina are really nice.

"You know, she bakes for all the men in the Sheriff's Academy," I point out, still teasing Gabriel. "It's not just you."

I shrug on my jacket, and he opens the door to the chilly autumn night.

"But I'm her favorite," Gabriel says, grinning. "She told me."

"She tells that to all of you," I say, and walk through the door as he holds it.

He grabs my ass, and I laugh. Tammy's the River County Sheriff's wife, they've got three hell-raising boys, and they still somehow find the time to invite us over for dinner once a week. If she wants to dance with Gabriel, it's fine with me, because she and Margaret have pretty much become my replacement moms.

I haven't heard from my real mom since I left. Every so often I hear from Zeke, who's still at home but trying to save up for an escape so he doesn't have to run away barefoot, or from Joy, who's still sneaking into college math classes.

But as far as everyone else is concerned, I'm dead to them. My father lost his re-election last year, and the huge scandal I caused is probably what did it. For months afterward, I practically couldn't answer my phone because news outlets wanted to talk to me about it.

I even got accosted walking around Conifer a few times by reporters, but thankfully it's died down. I don't want to be famous, or on the news, or anything.

I just want to be normal.

———

THE SQUARE DANCE is in Johnston's barn, and we park in a field outside. Gabriel holds my hand as we walk through the muddy grass, fiddle music already leaking out of the brightly-lit barn.

The moment we're inside, I relax about my outfit. This *is* what you wear square-dancing, because people wearing plaid, jeans, and boots are all do-si-do-ing and linking arms and spinning around and bumping into each other and laughing in the middle of the dance floor.

Johnston's Barn isn't really a barn, or at least, animals don't live here any more. It's owned by River County, so now it holds community events instead of horses.

People wave at us as we walk in. Gabriel and I wave back, and within a few moments, we're taking off our jackets and hugging people hello and talking about the crazy, late-in-the-season thunderstorm that hit a few days ago.

Gabriel keeps his hand on my back the whole time, a habit he's developed. I don't think he even realizes he's doing it, but I like it anyway. It's sweet and protective and it makes me feel safe without ever being overbearing or controlling, like he's got my back.

Which he does.

Minutes later, as we're still talking about this crazy storm, I see our friend Ashton walking toward us carefully, three full plastic cups in his hands. He hands one out to Gabriel, one to me, and keeps one for himself.

"My treat," he says, holding his hard cider up. "To three more weeks of Police Academy."

I grin and look over at Gabriel, holding up his cup.

"Is this a test?" he asks Ashton.

Ashton just laughs.

"Wouldn't you like to know?" he jokes. "This week's big challenge is getting the recruits blitzed at a square dance and then having you run five miles first thing in the morning."

"You would, you dirty bastard," Gabriel laughs.

"Knowing you, I'd wind up hungover as a motherfucker and you'd finish those five miles looking fresh as a goddamn daisy. Sorry for the language," he says, looking at me and nodding bashfully.

"I don't even know what those words mean," I deadpan, taking a sip, and Ashton laughs a little too loudly. It's probably not his first cider.

"Y'all see that huge old oak tree that got knocked across Old Lawyers Road during the storm the other night?" he asks, getting back to the topic on everyone's minds. "Old Man Emerson called it in but the county said they couldn't get to it 'til morning, too many power lines down and such, so once the storm ended me and Rob Junior went down there with some chainsaws and the winch on the back of his work truck...."

—————

AFTER THE CIDER, we get in the middle and dance. Since this event is specifically for beginners, the caller takes it slow and explains everything, so before long we're whirling and turning the wrong way and bumping into people right along with everyone else.

It's a blast. Half the town of Conifer is there—senior citizens, people our age, kids, the whole nine yards—and it's warm and friendly and downright *enjoyable.*

Forty-five minutes in, all the dancers and the caller take a break, so we head off to the side to sit on a hay bale. Instead, Margaret and her husband Tom are standing over on the side, and when they see us, they wave us over.

"Did you hear?" she asks, her voice hushed and quiet.

My heart sinks and clenches, like it's suddenly encased in iron bands.

"Hear what?" I whisper.

My mom's dead. My dad's dead. Something's happened to one of my siblings; they kicked Zeke or Joy out onto the street; Grace's husband left her...

"Lilah," she says, and takes my arm. "Come on."

Margaret leads me to a quiet corner of the barn, pulling

her phone out. My heart's hammering even though I'm relieved that my family is okay.

"Is it something with the trial?" I ask, walking behind Margaret.

Lilah's trial finally started about two weeks ago. I wasn't asked to testify, and didn't really want to, but Gabriel was.

I nearly had a panic attack at the thought of going back to Huntsburg, so I didn't go with him. I felt awful about it, but he's sworn up and down a million times that it's fine.

He also told me that the only member of Lilah's family to show up for her trial was Lucas, along with his partner, and I had no idea how to feel about *that*. Somewhere between *still angry* and *less angry* and *eventually forgiving but not just yet*, I think.

"Here," Margaret says, finally standing close to a wall where there are less people. She holds out her phone to me and I take it. She's got the Huntsburg Star-Ledger up on the tiny screen, and I swallow hard when I see the headline.

Stalker Receives Hefty Prison Sentence

HUNTSBURG, SC. — Despite the heartfelt pleas of some family members as well as her victim, Lilah Dawson, 24, was sentenced to seven years in prison, the maximum allowable sentence for aggravated stalking in South Carolina...

I close my eyes and tilt my head back against the wall of the barn, tears pricking at my eyeballs. Margaret takes her phone back, shoves it in her pocket, and Gabriel pulls me in close, Margaret's hand on my shoulder.

Seven years in prison. I can't even fathom it, and I can't help but imagine if *I* had to spend seven years in prison without having ever had a job.

It's heart-wrenching. I feel nauseous, and I feel powerless, and I feel unbelievably guilty.

"You tried," Margaret said.

"I should have gone down there instead of writing that letter," I say.

"You think that would have made a difference?" she says, rubbing my shoulder.

I pull back from Gabriel and wipe my eyes, trying to breathe deep and control myself.

"No," I admit.

"None of this is your fault," he says.

I sigh, still trying to get a hold of myself.

"She thought that cricket chirps were a secret form of Morse Code that would give her the key to unlocking ancient spells hidden in the Bible," I say. "She thought she could talk to angels. She shouldn't be in prison, she should be getting help."

"I know," Gabriel says, rubbing small circles on my back.

"Lilah never had a chance," I whisper. "Between my father and hers, she never had a fucking *chance*."

"And it's not your fault, sweetheart," Margaret says. "You did what you could."

"I could have done more."

"We talked about this," she says, using her mom-voice. "She threatened your life, and you still went out on a limb to help her."

I sigh. I'm not sure writing a letter to the sentencing judge was exactly *going out on a limb*, but deep down, I know Margaret is right.

It still sucks, though. I'm positive that my father had something to do with it, that after losing his election because of me he felt the need to control *something*, no matter what, and poor Lilah got to feel his wrath. He's golf buddies with practically every judge in the state.

We just stand there for a while, Gabriel rubbing my back on one side, Margaret with her hand on my shoulder. I'm incredibly lucky and I know it, because I'm here, with my boyfriend and my kinda-boss-kinda-mom in a town that I've come to absolutely love. I'm taking night classes at community college. I never, ever wear pantyhose.

But I know Lilah could have been *me*. If I'd had slightly different genetics, if I'd gotten unlucky in the mental health department, I could be going to prison and she could be here.

Out on the dance floor, the caller steps up to the microphone.

"All right, ladies and gents! Round two is set to start in just a few minutes here, so grab your partner and get on back to the dance floor..."

"Come on," Gabriel says.

I sigh dramatically, yet again.

"Don't make me quote Theo," he says, his voice gently teasing.

Theo's my therapist, a very nice sixty-something man who has reading glasses and accepts payments on a sliding scale. Sometimes Gabriel comes to our sessions, because he's ten thousand times more supportive of a partner than I think I deserve.

"'Release everything you cannot control,' or 'guilt is a vampiric emotion'?" I ask.

"I think both apply."

I make a face. He kisses the top of my head.

"I'll come dance, but I'm gonna feel bad about it," I say, taking his hand.

"I cannot control your feelings, and therefore I release them," he says, serenely, as we walk toward the dance floor.

———

I DOZE off in the car on the way back home, but I wake up when we stop.

And then I realize we're not at the cabin. We're in Conifer's tiny downtown, and since it's nearly midnight everything is completely dark and closed.

"Huh?" I ask.

"C'mon," he says, opening his door. "I want to show you something."

Groggy, I get out of the car. Gabriel takes my hand and we walk across the street to the grassy patio behind Bubba's Good BBQ, the picnic tables where we ate the very first day we were here.

He points to one, and we sit on the table, our feet on the seat, looking out at the park across the street and the stars above. The windows of the town glimmer darkly, and a breeze whispers around us. I'd be really nervous if he weren't here, but he is.

"You remember eating here, right?" he asks, my hand still in his.

I just nod.

"We had to buy you those horrible plastic flip flops from the drugstore because you left everything behind," he goes on, blue eyes the color of midnight as they bore into me. "And then you sat here and told me that you had been afraid that you'd go back, because you knew that you were embarking into a big, cold, terrible world."

"I wasn't," I say softly, and squeeze his hand. "It's actually not so bad."

Mostly because you're here, I think.

"I sat across from you and we ate ribs and I had no fucking clue what we were going to do," he goes on. "We'd known each other for a few weeks, I didn't even know your middle name, you'd never had a job and I was afraid that your father was going to track you down and take you back by force—"

"You never told me that," I interject.

"I decided to keep that particular fear to myself," he says dryly.

"That was probably a good idea."

"But even when everything was up in the air, I was totally, completely, a hundred percent fucking certain that I was supposed to be there, with you, even at this picnic table after you'd run away barefoot," he goes on. "That hasn't changed at all, and tonight, knowing what you've done for Lilah, just reminded me why you're my favorite person."

My throat's closing, my stomach clenching. I try to smile, but I think it might come out weird.

"Gabriel..." I start, but I don't know how to finish that sentence and just stare at him.

He pulls something out of his pocket.

It's a small box.

No, I think. *No, no, no, please no, please please no.*

I feel like I might puke, and when Gabriel looks at me again, horror flicks across his face.

"It's not an engagement ring," he blurts out.

I take a deep breath, and Gabriel starts laughing.

"Sorry, I didn't think the box through," he says, grinning.

Now I'm laughing with relief, one elbow on my knees, face in one hand.

"You have the *worst* reactions," he teases.

"I'm sorry," I say. "It's just—I mean, you know."

"Of course I know," he says, kissing me on the temple. "That's why it's not an engagement ring."

"It's not you," I tell him. "It's not. You know that."

It's that I've already been married once and that relationship was a hellscape. It's that every marriage I witnessed until I moved to Conifer had a strict hierarchy, and they were all practically prisons for the wives. It's that I was pretty much forced into it once, nearly forced into it again, and I just can't handle thinking about it right now.

Maybe someday. If I do get married again, it'll be to Gabriel, but I need time.

"I know that," Gabriel says softly. "And you know I don't give a shit whether we sign a piece of paper or not as long as you're mine."

"I am," I tell him, leaning my cheek against his shoulder.

"Good," he says. "Because I got you this promise ring to promise that I love you and I'll always be here for you, and I'll marry you if you ever want me to and I'll stay your life partner forever if you want me to."

Gabriel pops open the box. Inside is small silver ring with a thin band, one small green gemstone in the middle. It's not fancy and it definitely wasn't expensive, but it *is* beautiful.

"Getting you a ruby seemed too on-the-nose," he says.

I'm crying again, and I hold out my hand. Gabriel slides the ring onto my middle finger, then brings my hand to his lips and kisses it.

"I love you," I whisper. "There's nobody else I'd ever want to be my life partner."

"I'm glad," he says, grinning. "There's no one else I'd ever want to horrify with a proposal."

I laugh, and Gabriel kisses me, softly at first and then deeper. Still sitting on the picnic table, our mouths move against each other slowly, his hand creeping up my thigh. We pull apart, pause, kiss again, and this time I curl my tongue against his.

When we stop, I realize I've got one hand under his shirt. I pull it back as he nuzzles my ear.

"Let's go home before we wind up naked on this table," he says in the voice that still sends shivers down my spine. "People will talk."

"We can't have *that*," I tease, but he stands, takes my hand, pulls me off the picnic table and we head for the car.

Then we drive home, to the house that we share, the bed we share, the life we share, and I go to sleep with him curled around me and wake up to my hand in his.

And it's not perfect, but it's all I could ever want.

The End

ABOUT ROXIE

Roxie is a romance author by day, and also a romance author by night. She lives in Los Angeles with one husband, two cats, far too many books, and a truly alarming pile of used notebooks that she refuses to throw away.

Join her mailing list for release updates, free bonus scenes, and tons more!

roxienoir.com/newsletter
roxie@roxienoir.com

9 781957 049229